Plastic Emotions

Praise for Plastic Emotions

'An absorbing story of love and art set in a deftly evoked cosmopolitan mid-century era.'
— Romesh Gunesekera, Booker shortlisted author of *Reef*

'A luminous and intricate novel that vividly resurrects a neglected architectural pioneer.'
— Will Wiles, author of *The Way Inn* and *Plume*

'Pinto's writing is wise and evocative, unearthing a story so long shamefully neglected.'
— Olivia Sudjic, author of *Sympathy*

'An elegant, elegiac book; a devastating deconstruction of power, told by a fine writer with an admirably cool eye.'
— Preti Taneja, Desmond Elliot winning author of *We That Are Young*

'The most compelling feature of the novel is not only a focus on de Silva's work but also the insights it provokes. Pinto lets us see that architecture can serve a higher purpose than the merely functional. What do a nation's buildings say about its society?'
— *Asian Review of Books*

'*Plastic Emotions* is a love story that takes us into the beating heart of a bygone world through architecture and the lovers who brought that world, and each other, to life. It's a story we all need to hear.'
— *Mint*

Plastic Emotions

Shiromi Pinto

Influx Press
London

Published by Influx Press

49 Green Lanes, London, N16 9BU

www.influxpress.com / @InfluxPress

Printed and bound in Great Britain by Clays Ltd, Elcograf S.p.A.

Paperback ISBN: 978-1-910312-31-5

eBook ISBN: 978-1-910312-32-2

Editor: Kit Caless, Assistant Editor: Sanya Semakula

Proofreader: Momus Editorial, Cover art and design: Austin Burke *for L.*

'The Architect, by his arrangement of forms, realizes an order which is a pure creation of his spirit; by forms and shapes he affects our senses to an acute degree, and provokes plastic emotions.'

—Le Corbusier, *Towards a New Architecture*

'... the revolution which had aimed at the destruction of a formalized past resulted in the creation of sterile architecture, beautiful in its use of modern materials and construction but lacking the essential element of contact with the people and their regional life.'

—Minnette de Silva, 1998

attic flat, smoking and drinking and doing little else. So, we went. And Marcia and Werner came, too.

Paris was cold, but infinitely prettier. We ate pain au chocolat for breakfast and wandered the streets until lunch. There was no rubble to step over or bombed out houses to mourn. You were lucky. It was as if the city had gone on holiday during the war, only returning when it was over. The flat was in a typical old Haussmann-style block with a cage lift and wrought iron balconies. Do you remember it? You haven't been there for a while, have you? It is grand and elegant with enormous windows. It was also empty when we first arrived.

'Maman was a brave woman,' said Mimi. 'She was a member of the resistance, you know. Not one of those salaud traitors.' When she said 'salaud', she raised her voice, glaring accusingly at the walls. 'Ils étaient partout, ces salauds.' She shouted again.

I put a hand on her shoulder and told her I was sorry. Her eyes, which had been steely and angry, clouded over like two opals. 'This is my flat now,' she said. 'Welcome.'

I looked into those same eyes today, and saw my reflection. They are as clear and cold now as they were in the winter of '46, but that's the irony, isn't it? Because Mimi isn't cold. As I sat there, watching her smoke one of those long cigarettes, I marvelled at the struggle playing itself out on top of her head. It was hat against hair, Corbu. Her red ringlets were springing in all directions like frightened rabbits, so that her hat quivered like a jelly. You see, that's the real indicator of her character, that irrepressible mass of hair.

'Of course I'll take care of you,' she cried. 'I'll take you to Paris. You can hide at my flat. Claim immunity from your despotic father. You can spend some time with Basquin. He told me he'd like to paint you.'

Do you know Jean Basquin, Corbu? I met him that same winter. Mimi took me to his place one afternoon, shortly after Christmas.

Arriving at the door of a ramshackle looking building, I was not surprised to find a similarly dishevelled man in its entrance. Taking in his brambly hair, wrongly-buttoned shirt and frayed trousers, I was put in mind of the crooked man in his crooked house, and peered inside looking for a crooked dog. But Basquin was on his own.

His breath was bad, but his manners were very courteous. The house was cold and shambolic inside. He showed us to a greasy settee and we sat in it, Mimi dropping into it like an anchor, me perching on its edge.

'I would offer you tea,' he said, 'but the water in my pips is frozen. For sure, they will burst.' He turned away, his face looking momentarily pained, saying to no one in particular, 'Ah, the pips. The pips.' With that, he left the room. I was freezing. There was no heating or fire to speak of — everything had ceased to function since the war. How Basquin lived like that, I could not imagine. He was wearing an overcoat and muffler indoors, but his fingers were still purple.

Basquin returned bearing two saucers with little beige slabs on them.

I put up my hand to refuse, when Mimi pinched my leg. I stared at the saucer on my lap and the frozen square at the centre of it that had been, in a warmer life, cake.

'Mais vous êtes gentils, Basquin,' said Mimi, biting into her slice and chewing it with a grin. 'Merci.'

I followed Mimi's example, smiling and sinking my teeth into my own slab, but no amount of pressure would break it. Worse than that, my bottom lip stuck to the bottom of the icy block. I grated at the square with my teeth, letting the little filings fall and melt on my tongue. Basquin was not impressed by my efforts and cast me such a look of hurt when he took my plate that I immediately tried to take it back.

'Basquin wants to paint me, Mimi? Are you sure? Even after I was so rude last time?' Mimi looked at me blankly. 'The cake. Remember? I couldn't eat it.'

Mimi laughed. 'Oh, dear Minnette. What are you talking about? Of course he doesn't care about things like that. He thought you were charming. Timeless. That's what he said. "She is timeless."'

So, I am timeless. Just as well, Corbu, as I have a habit of being late to most things. And speaking of being late, I must dash. I'm meeting Mimi this evening for drinks. At the Fox and Hound, of course.

How I wish you were here, my love.

Ton oiseau
Minnette

1 June 1949
London

My dear Corbu, you should have seen me last night. I was
stunning. I wore my red silk sari and two roses in my hair.
When I walked through the Covent Garden piazza, everyone
turned to look. A young man smiled at me, another bowed. I
felt like a queen.

It was just like that time after the war, when Mimi and I went
to the reopening of the Royal Opera House. Everyone stared
then, too. Someone even presented me to the King and Queen!
I remember how Her Majesty smiled at me, admiring my silks.
She kept asking me about the colour and the drape and how one
managed to keep it secure. Since then, my saris have become a
privilege pass to all the parties at the Royal Opera House – all
the parties in Covent Garden, in fact.

Last night, I was beckoned to and passed around like a tray
of champagne. Mimi attracted a good deal of attention with her
auburn curls. Marcia and Werner were there, too. Each time I

reached for a glass of champagne, there was Marcia, wearing an expression of such horror, you'd think I'd been thrusting my hand into the jaws of hell. This is some new thing with my sister. Where has she gone, Corbu? In India, she was a virtual Bohemian. And in our younger days, we got into all sorts of trouble.

I remember us nearly causing a riot in Kandy once. We had been part of a pageant telling the story of how Buddhism came to Ceylon. Of course, I was Sangamitta, bearing the branch of the sacred Bo Tree. And during a break, I leaned over and took a puff of Marcia's cigarette. There was an uproar, and we had to be whisked away to safety. Marcia didn't even drop her cigarette. She puffed it through the corner of her mouth while leading me out of the throng of angry Buddhists. Now, my sister – the same woman who thought nothing of aiding and abetting scandal – thinks I'm an alcoholic. Just because I enjoy a glass or two of whiskey. She doesn't know that I've often shared the same with her dear husband. 'You vill not tell Mahcia,' he says, whenever we are out and she has disappeared to the toilet. He's very crafty, my brother-in-law – always lighting up a cigar afterward to mask the odour.

Marcia's caustic glares aside, the night was a success. I met a couple who enthused flatteringly about my architectural opinions. There was Tambimuttu, the wonderful Tamil poet, along with a number of other artists and photographers who were regulars at the Fox and Hound. And – best for last, Corbu – Ram Gopal! He looked splendid in a silk turban and shawl.

'Darling,' he said, embracing me, 'I haven't seen you for years, but you still look marvellous – marvellous.' You would love Ram, Corbu. He's a choreographic wizard. He's taken the dances of the Orient and translated them for a Western audience. His performances are spectacular. The last time he was in London, I had to lend him my flat. It was autumn 1947,

just a few weeks before Bridgwater. Ram rang me up in a fit because his manager had let him down. 'Minnette, darling,' he said. 'He's a waste – an absolute waste. A horror!' He rolled the r's to emphasise the injustice then, to ensure my sympathies really were with him, added: 'A beast!' The troupe was coming to London in two days, he said, and had nowhere to stay.

I offered temporary lodgings at mine and Marcia's. He accepted. Within two days, my Savile Row flat was transformed into a green room. Dancers pliéd in the sitting room and did the splits against my walls. There was make-up everywhere and amidst it all, Ram Gopal, gorgeous and shimmering like a sapphire on one of his many turbans. 'Look,' he said, spreading his arms wide as if to gather up his dancers, 'they are like my children – so obedient.'

As soon as Ram saw Mimi, he called out, 'Ah, the walking paradox rises amongst us.' This is Ram's nickname for Mimi: The Walking Paradox. 'She is so pale,' he said to me once, 'yet there is a vigor to her… like a radiant corpse.' We kept the corpse bit to ourselves.

Mimi, Ram and I spent the rest of the evening casting mischievous judgements on our fellow guests. Marcia was not amused, but she so rarely is these days.

So, Corbu, the night beckons, again. Tonight I stay in with a book, a cigarette and a small glass of whiskey – and no Marcia to tut-tut me for it.

Ton oiseau
Minnette

4 June 1949
London

I'm having tea from one of my finest china cups. This is not, in and of itself, worth writing about, but there is something about the colour of this tea that makes me think of Bridgwater.

The tea is not as bad as it was there, goodness, no. In fact, it's rather good. I like my tea the Ceylon way – plenty of milk and sugar with a shot of the best brewed BOP leaves to be found: those grown as high as possible in the hills.

I remember thinking this at Bridgwater. I was taking a break between talks, wondering whether I would ever get a chance to speak to you. I'll be honest, Corbu. I was desperate to speak with you. I wanted to impress you somehow. To make you notice me – the architecture student from the East. I wanted you to train those rounded specs on me – to look at me, to see me.

You were preoccupied. A fissure had opened up between the young and old architects. They were attacking you, Gropius and the Athens Charter with its absolute separation of functions within a city. Who could deny the unique and radical needs of post-war urbanism? Who could still believe that a site was a blank slate upon which a plan and its architecture could be imposed?

I have always wondered at the arrogance of supposing a place has no existence without a building installed according to a man-made plan. Sigiriya in Ceylon is exactly the opposite. It started with an enormous rock into which King Kasyapa carved himself and his entourage. It is the rock that stands out. The fortress – for indeed, that is what it became – is barely visible, hinted at only in contours from afar. Its monumentality is drawn from its natural state. Closer inspection finds intricate claws and a staircase disappearing into the suggestion of a creature's gaping jaws, but all of this is hidden until you're close enough to touch it. The fortress was an island unto itself. Buddhist monks had once used it as an escape from this material world. Kasyapa came to it to escape certain death at the hands of his brother for killing their father. The fortress, was always there, inherent in the rock. Much as Michelangelo would find his sculptures buried in marble.

People were milling about, sipping cups of tea and nibbling on hard biscuits. I was stirring two spoonfuls of sugar into my tea, absorbed by the vortex of liquid swilling about in my cup. I heard nothing but the ting of the spoon on bone china. Even that sounded so much like home that the air cooled around me. If I looked out, I thought, I would see green hills and a lake below, and creepers of carnelian flowers. And Amma would be behind me, talking to Jaya, our housemaid, about the intricacies of making love cake. Papa would be sitting on the verandah next to them, offering his opinion on the ratio of cadju to semolina. I turned around.

I felt you behind me, Corbu. I turned around to smile at you, to say, finally. No – I had much more to say than that.

Sigiriya – I was going to tell you about Sigiriya, Kasyapa, Michelangelo. About Marg – the magazine Otto, Marcia and I founded in Bombay. I was going to ask you about Poissy and La ville radieuse. And all the while, I would watch you watching me: my hair, my necklace, my sari. I was ready, holding all this on my tongue as I turned around.

There was no one there. The crowds had been winnowed to a scattered few, most engrossed in writing notes or brushing crumbs from their lapels. I turned back to my tea and drank. It was weak and cold. I considered the ratio of cadju to semolina alongside my imagined parents and Jaya, and somehow made light of my disappointment.

That's my confession, Corbu.

I long for your news.

Write soon.

Ton oiseau
Minnette

POST OFFICE TELEGRAM

11.17 Paris 16IEME
June 9, 1949

DESILVA 15 SAVILE ROW W1

FELICITATIONS ON ARIBA STOP IN LONDON IN
TWO DAYS STOP WE WILL EAT CAKE
LC

12 June 1949
London

You were here in this room, standing on this sloping floor, cursing it even as you smiled at me. Your shadow fills the room, throws its great darkness right over Berkeley Square. You were here. My bed is unmade. I am unmade. Cigarette ash makes a pyre at my feet.

I want to feel your heart again, know the sharp crease of it, feel it here, against my back.

I am leaving. This is the only command that governs me now and I must walk into the truth of it. With every step I shrink and duck. I can't, Corbu, how can I? Each step takes me back to Bridgwater, back to that moth's wing of a moment that swept fortune into my hungry mouth:

I have just finished a lunch of tough lamb. The lamb sits like a monk in my gut. The Bridgwater conference is over and we are invited to an evening concert to bring a formal end to the week. I forego dinner in favour of a nap, so that I will be fresh for the concert.

I take my seat next to a member of the MARS group. She is slim and pretty and one of my AA colleagues. It turns out it's not her seat. She shifts down and in her place sits you. We don't notice one another. I chat to the person to my right while you are engrossed in Miss MARS. At some point and without provocation, we both tilt our heads towards one another and smile. Someone introduces us then – Miss MARS, perhaps – and you say, 'Enchanté.' And then the concert begins: the lights dim, people reorient themselves towards the stage. I sit and listen, but I hear nothing and see nothing except your eyes, magnified within those unmistakeable frames, peering at me with the curiosity of someone who has made a rare discovery, and the only sound to fill my ears is the shhh-shhh of that one word: Enchanté.

We don't speak again that night except to wish each other a good sleep. It is that night that I inscribe your name in my diary three times, as if forging your signature in that intimate space will bring you closer to me. It is an incantation – a mantram – the repetition of which should draw you into my orbit, or me into yours. And it works, because the next morning you come to me at breakfast and do not leave my side for an hour at least. You ask me so many questions, replying each time, 'Ah, vous êtes sages.'

I say something about Benjamin Holloway and Robert Adams and you look at me with confusion. 'Vous-êtes architecte?' you ask, and are genuinely surprised when I say, yes. You ask me why, and at that moment, I can find no sensible reply. It is immaterial anyway, for you are captivated by the two roses in my hair. You tell me how much you admire my bearing and that elegance is somehow intrinsic to me. What flattery, but I accept it, eating it up whole, encouraging you further still to strew compliment upon compliment and smile a devilish smile that lights up those round glasses and convinces me that I have swallowed the sun.

I returned to London after that – to Marcia and Werner and dear, mad Mimi and before I knew it, was back to work. The Royal Academy was launching its Great Indian Exhibition and I was asked to measure every exhibit piece for the catalogue. It was a stroke of luck, giving me unlimited access to the Royal Academy – and the perfect excuse to invite you to London. When you came, I brought you to the museum early in the morning, when no one else was around, and showed you intricate bronzes of Hindu deities and Moghul paintings. How you examined them, listening intently as I described each item, admiring the voluptuousness of the figures with an academic eye, never once suggesting that they might be admired in any other way. (Later you would tell me otherwise, but that was later, when there was no possibility of offense, only laughter and indulgence.)

So it began: our meetings eventually with few words exchanged, as if we knew that words would return later, when we had time to savour them. You came to my flat, ascending these treacherous stairs without complaint, speaking of the crampedness of English spaces. I countered with something about the opportunities they gave for privacy and you laughed. But once inside, there were no more words to tell, only glances and sighs and my hands in yours. When Mimi and I visited Paris, timed assiduously for when Yvonne was away, you joined me at Mimi's flat. How we painted our days then, with the brilliant tones of muscle, bone and flesh. It did not matter that we could not see one another for more than a few days. It did not matter that those days were separated by months.

And now we are to be separated by an ocean, with months that will spin themselves into years. Banished to an alien land, purged of the reassurance of touch, what will we do?

Words, Corbu. Let us find consolation in them. Let our words make us whole.

How strange it will be to go back to Ceylon, that place that belonged to another as long as I have been alive. After centuries of European rule – by the Portuguese, the Dutch and finally the British – Ceylon owns itself again. It's been just over a year. Not much time, really, to recover from the shock of seeing one's reflection after so long, of finding oneself scored with age at the moment of birth.

This is where I am going, then. To a country I do not know any more. Indeed, a country that may no longer know itself. And in that country, exiled from my lover's touch, I shall be an island of remembering. I will look out upon my garden, with its pergola dripping red flowers and remember London, Paris and you. How you bent low to take my hand. How beguiled you were by the fall of silk on my shoulders. The lines, you said, were Grecian.

Ton oiseau
Minnette

II

December – June 1951

Stars, millions of them, beating like hearts. She sees them pulsing over the rim of her arrack glass. *The sky is an open book*, she thinks, *written in a language I don't understand*. She slides back into the planter's chair, tries to get comfortable, and fails.

'Baby Nona?'

She sighs, takes another sip from her glass. Jaya is standing behind her, looking at the almost empty tumbler. She will not offer her another one.

'Minnette, Miss? *Ivarada*, Miss?'

Minnette considers the contents of her glass. There is only just enough liquid left to wet the tip of a fingernail. One last sip. She feels the impulse before she recognises it. One last taste before she abandons herself to the community of sleep. That community, she realises, is up there, brilliant with dreaming. Millions of stars waiting for her.

She hands the unfinished glass to Jaya who tries, but fails, to conceal her disapproval. *Even if I gave it back to her full, she would not approve. Young ladies drink sweet wine, not spirits.* She smiles. *Am I still young?*

'Baby Nona?'

Minnette shakes her head. '*Hari, hari.* Thank you.' She waves Jaya away. *Baby Nona.* Even at thirty-two, Minnette knows she will only ever be the youngest, and so a child to Jaya.

Upstairs, in her room, Minnette collects her drawings. The Ariyapala Lodge is her first project. If not for her father, she might still be searching for work but fortunately, Ceylon – the new Ceylon – appears amenable to the ambitions of a woman architect freshly returned from England. It helps that the Ariyapalas are old family friends. Minnette's drawings are neat, precise. The Ariyapalas were impressed. The house is sited on a hill, overlooking Kandy Lake. Minnette has sketched the elevation of the building, considered its aspect. Her calculations are meticulous. The house will be Modern and yet intrinsically vernacular. Materials will be local, as will the decorative work. Exterior spaces, like the balcony, will be as important as the interior. The Ariyapalas agreed to the plans without fuss. But as the months go by, first one objection, then another, is raised.

The project was commissioned more than a year ago. The honeymoon period, in which Minnette's ideas were greeted with pleasant surprise and excited applause, has given way to suspicion, resentment, and occasional distress. '*Hanh,*' says Mrs Ariyapala, 'but why not paint the walls? Otherwise, it will look like an abandoned building, no?' This to Minnette's insistence that the interior walls remain unfinished. When Mrs Ariyapala realises that not only will the walls be unpainted, but they will also remain unrendered, she closes her mouth and does not open it again until she is alone with her husband, whom she then castigates for trusting an 'upstart woman architect'.

All of Minnette's energies are directed into the Ariyapala Lodge. She has set up her studio at Nell Cottage, hired local artisans to fire clay tiles, weave *dumbara* mats, carve and lacquer mouldings. The artisans are an extension of her studio, a community she, like her mother before her, hopes to nurture while engaging their considerable skill. She has forged friendships with weavers, learning techniques from them that she uses to create her own, exquisite saris. For Minnette, the Ariyapala Lodge is more than a house; it is the culmination of an architectural tradition that goes right back to Anuradhapura itself.

She examines her drawings as she arranges them into a pile. The foundations went down some months ago. Not easy, given her engineer had refused to work on them unless Ove Arup in London okayed the plans first. So, Minnette sent them to the famous structural engineer, whose first achievement had been the penguin enclosure at London Zoo. He approved them. The work continued. Still, Minnette has overheard the *baas* and his crew talking about that *pissu ganni*. They say she is crazy to site the house in an area vulnerable to earthslips. Minnette ignores them. Her task is to use every foot of land, sloped or otherwise, so that nothing is wasted. Anyway, it has been years since the last flood. She knows there is no risk.

She opens her notebook, makes two calculations based on measurements she took at the site earlier today. *Accept this little card as a promise of more to come,* he wrote. That was in June, just before she left London. *A kiss for every one of your fingertips. Believe me when I say, this is not the end.* And then, as a postscript: *Chère amie, do not be offended. I ask that you do not send letters to No. 24, but to my office at No. 35. I know you will understand.*

Minnette closes the notebook. She understood. She wrote back almost immediately: *Corbu, please forgive me. I don't know how it happened. Heartbreak, no doubt – a momentary madness. It wasn't intentional. I would never do anything to hurt Yvonne.*

In the quiet of her room, Minnette is suddenly, overwhelmingly, filled with need. *Why doesn't he write?* She has been waiting for months and she is tired of it. Moths circle her lamp, immolate themselves. She decides to forget Le Corbusier, to ignore his letter when it comes. Then she sits down at her desk, moves her drawings aside, and begins writing.

Joyeux noël, Corbu. I have not heard from you in so – She re-reads the words, crushes the sheet of paper, begins again. *Joyeux noël, Corbu! You must be busy* – She crushes this, too, lights a cigarette, starts again. *Joyeux noël, Corbu. This should arrive well after you have digested your goose or duck or whichever fowl Maman Le Corbusier is roasting this year. I'm sorry I haven't written for a while. Like you, I have been busy. The Ariyapala Lodge. Not without its challenges, Corbu. They are trapped in their parochialism. The Ariyapalas are short-sighted, lacking adventure. Sometimes I despair. I could really do with some of your advice, if not the certainty you bring to a room as soon as you enter it. The knowledge that I am what I am because of you.*

Minnette stops, considers throwing the letter in the bin, stubs out her half-smoked cigarette, and lights another. *Too late*, she thinks. She inhales and exhales a long puff of smoke, fanning it towards the window. Jaya would not approve of this either. Smoking is for prostitutes. As is arrack-drinking. Minnette applies the nib of her pen to the vellum sheet.

But what of the knowledge of who I am? That seems only to exist somewhere else, when we are together. I don't know if I can survive this separation, Corbu. So many months without a letter from you – without a word. All this waiting. It gnaws a hole in me. Minnette puts a hand to her stomach, is convinced she can feel it hollowing out. *This is what comes of being forgotten. Have you, Corbu? Have you forgotten me?* 'No,' Minnette says aloud, causing a moth to flinch before extinguishing itself in her lamp. *No, you cannot. Not yet.*

You wrote, all those months ago, not to give up on us, so I will not. I know you have a good reason for not writing – What am I saying? You are Le Corbusier. That in itself is a reason. Everyone wants something from you. So, in the spirit of Christmas, I am going to give you something, Corbu. Take as long as you need to write to me. This is my gift to you. Time.

Minnette signs off, folds the sheets, puts them in an envelope and seals it. She places the letter in the centre of her desk and stares at the address written in flowing blue cursive. No. 35, it says. Not 24. She can be sure of this.

———————

Two months later, a letter arrives at Nell Cottage. It is from him. Minnette turns it over and over, thumb over index finger. The script on the envelope is erratic, difficult to read. She commends the postman for deciphering the address, for ensuring that the letter arrived at its intended destination. *I will not open it,* she decides. She opens it.

There are few words on the page. She resists the urge to crumple the sheet, directing her gaze instead to the jittery lines of text. *Mais non, my little one,* it begins, *Corbu has not forgotten you. This can never happen!* Minnette shrugs. She is used to the hyperbole, tries to defend herself against it, and fails. *You are too generous, oiseau, sending me a credit note to claim against the months I have been absent. But you are right, too. Corbu is in demand!* She nods. Corbu is always in demand. He is a busy man, a genius. Minnette should know better than to expect more than what he chooses to give her. She glances at the rolls of drawings arranged on her desk. *It is nothing*, she thinks, *to build one house. My efforts are miniscule next to his.*

She reads on. *I have been asked to take on a project of immense scale in India.* She stands, begins pacing the room. *It is the dream of all architects, to build a whole city. For me, it will be Chandigarh. Nowicki's death, Mayer's resignation – these are the forces of Providence which state that Chandigarh will belong to Corbu. Like you, I will be working in a spirit of optimism – the optimism that comes with independence. Corbu will change lives – perhaps even a whole civilization. You and I, petit oiseau, will see one another once again, it seems!*

Minnette holds the letter to her chest, closes her eyes. For the rest of the day, she forgets about her drawings. She cancels her afternoon meeting with the Ariyapalas who would only be vetoing something else she has proposed. They cannot stop finding obstacles for Minnette to trip over. She decides that today, she will not be a spectacle for them.

Days peel away into weeks and months. Minnette's desk is piled with drawings, no longer neatly rolled or filed. She has been asked to design a new building for the Red Cross, and a day nursery extension, both of which she tackles with efficiency. Given a small budget, she opts for something simple for the Red Cross: a building with a large events hall, its roof raised above the adjacent walls. She insists on making a feature of the surrounding land, so that the building opens onto the garden, rather than sitting flatly in the middle. But ultimately, her design is rejected. Her plans for an extension to the day nursery also come to nothing. It seems few people are willing to pay for innovation. *They see it as a risk*, she sighs.

The Ariyapalas are not so different; they still oppose her choice of exposed stone and brickwork for the interiors. Mrs Ariyapala has continued her mute protest, darting glances of disapproval at her husband which he, in turn, translates into a diplomatic 'no'. Minnette does not know how to resolve this impasse. *I am weak*, she thinks. *What would Corbu think of me?* She has written one desperate letter to him, saying this much, confessing her shame. The great man replied: *Corbu can never be disappointed in his oiseau. Courage, mon enfant!* Minnette wishes she could summon the courage of a child – that blind wilfulness that compels children to climb to the top of a tree without a thought for how they will return.

She sits on her bed, smoking. Today's meeting with Mr Ariyapala went badly. When Minnette showed him her designs for the sitting room – floor-to-ceiling glass windows and doors – he shook his head. 'We never wanted such a grand design,' he said. He looked tired, like a man defeated by age or marriage. His head was bent, as if to study Minnette's drawings which were spread out on the table before him, but she could see that his eyes were closed. *So stubborn*, she thought. 'Well,' she said, 'perhaps we can talk about this again in the new year.' '*Hanh*,' he said, opening his eyes, but not looking up. She gathered her drawings and left.

Minnette flicks ash into her empty glass. She has

drunk half a thumb-length of arrack and is enjoying the numbness spinning a web at the back of her head. She stares out into the night sky and a million stars stare back. She pulls a small envelope from her sari blouse – a letter from Mimi – and opens it.

Inside: an invitation to join her in Paris for Christmas.

———————

I can breathe again. Minnette sips a glass of wine, shares a smile with a dark-browed Italian sitting two tables from her own. She is in Rome, her final stop. Before it, there was Venice, London, Paris. The heat of the evening reminds her of home. It has been more than six months since she fled Kandy for Europe, and now she must return. *So many returns*, she thinks. *So many exiles*. She observes the many couples, heads bent low over round tables, fingertips resting on cutlery. One man looks casually over the shoulder of his wife or girlfriend, and gazes at Minnette with deliberate and open intention. Minnette smiles, looks away. *Why do I always do that?* She looks at the man again, and this time he is the first to falter. She smiles to herself. Rome is grand and glorious and full of men with easy smiles. The 'eternal city'.

Minnette remembers she has not eaten and orders some bread and olives. She closes her eyes, sees Corbu's face, that amused expression he wears whenever he is about to take her to bed. *Paris*, she sighs. *He was not expecting me*. They had not had much time. She saw him, and her thoughts had come undone like a row of stitches. Yvonne was away. The flat was empty – No. 24! *How could we have? – the flat was empty. He told me about India, he called me his 'Inde'*. She shakes her head, cringes at her weakness. There was no time to speak. The snow fell silently outside the window, his easel blocking out the remaining daylight. They were standing, side by side in the front room, watching the snowflakes flatten and burst against the windowpane like moths on the windshield of a moving car. *What are words when flesh finds proximity after so many months apart. Words are unbearable then.* His palm against her back. His mouth against her ear. *How are you? Pas mal. Et vous? No. We used few words and so knew not – nor cared not – what the other had been doing between before and then.*

Christmas arrived and to Minnette, drunk from being with him, the whole city was briefly enchanted: duck and pheasant hanging upside-down in the market; the rue Mouffetard with its exquisite pastries. Mimi and Minnette bought a different pastry from each boulangerie they passed. The only sour moment – which sullied the rest of the day – came when Mimi leaned over a mille-feuille to tell Minnette that she had heard from W.E.B. DuBois, Picasso and Paul Éluard that Le Corbusier had refused to sign the Peace Manifesto.

'But Corbu would never ally himself with the fascists,' argued Minnette, who had years earlier gone to Poland to address the World Conference of Intellectuals for Peace. At first, she went there on a lark, reveling in the wonder and fluster caused by her saris, but she returned a committed activist.

'Picasso and Éluard are furious,' said Mimi, sending a gust of pastry flakes into the winter air. And she was right, because Éluard dropped by Mimi's later that evening for a drink, and he was fuming.

'Le Corbusier, that fascist. Thinks himself a genius but he's too self-important to put his name on a document that the world's greatest artists and intellectuals have signed. Our plea to the world for peace – our plea for disarmament. He thinks himself better than all of us. Genius? He is a fascist! A sympathiser. A traitor.'

Éluard spat burgundy all over Mimi's white carpet. His anger was not only palpable, but contagious. *Why*, thought Minnette as she watched Éluard's trembling cheeks, *why did Corbu refuse? Does he really think that we should be building stockades of more and more arms? The Americans in Korea* – 'Perhaps,' said Minnette, 'perhaps Corbu believes, like the Americans, that world peace is a Communist plot.'

Minnette shrinks now from the betrayal. At the time, Éluard had nodded and Minnette had felt vindicated in criticising Corbu. Now, sitting by herself at the edge of a Roman piazza, she is not so sure. *It is enough to think such things* – Minnette notices that her wine is finished; the bread and olives she ordered earlier remain untouched – *to speak them aloud is inexcusable.*

After Paris, Minnette went to London for the Festival of Britain, and watched the King open the new Royal Festival Hall. Models of tankers were moored in the Thames, while the V&A exhibited 'the only surviving model' of the Great Exhibition of 1851. The Festival Hall itself impressed her. A modern building for a modern age of entertainment, she had thought. She enjoyed the excellent acoustics in the auditorium itself, although the mass of the outer building troubled her, sitting like a hen on the ground.

Leaving London meant leaving her sister Marcia and brother-in-law Werner. Saying goodbye to Mimi was harder, but Minnette's friend crossed her heart and told her she would be sure to make it to Ceylon for a visit.

Minnette tries an olive. It is the first solid food she has eaten since breakfast. Her head is heavy with wine. She knows that if she stands up now, she will not manage the walk to her *pensione* with dignity. She orders more food, a carafe of water and no wine. She will remain here until the numbness at the back of her head thins. She starts on the bread. *Those winter months with Mimi were a godsend. If not for Paris, I would have been crushed by those Ariyapalas.* It is true. Minnette has received numerous telegrams from her clients, requesting her early return so that work on their house can continue under her direction.

She recalls the Ariyapalas' latest fearful demand – that she provide them some guarantee that their house would not 'succumb to an earthslip'. She shrugs at the thought, then imagines the relief she might feel at watching the house and everyone in it swept away by the rain.

The man with his wife/girlfriend is looking at Minnette again, open intent now replaced by hope. She sighs. After London, it was Venice – the Renaissance city, gilded, lustrous. An exercise in proportion. A marriage of water and stone. *Never mind that the city sinks, the romance of it is too great to ignore.* Islands of arches and campanelli, Palladio's Basilica, the Piazza San Marco – all of it fainting frame by frame into the Adriatic. *Even Rome, for all its claims to immortality, will lie in dust one day,* she thinks. *Ultimately all our work will find its match in the elements. Stone or concrete, brick or glass.*

She stares at her empty wine glass, remembers why she hasn't ordered any, then orders another. There has been no letter since Paris. When she arrived in Venice, she found herself drawn along the bridges and piazzas of the city, strolling beside handsome young men – all of whom claimed they had fallen in love with her. Mimi's painter friend, Francesco, was back in Venice and offered to take Minnette on a tour of the city's waterways last week. Sitting in a gondola with him, she felt the pull of the water beneath her like temptation. *It would not be difficult to believe everything any one of these young men says to me if only for a few days,* she thinks. His silence makes the option all the more attractive, yet every time she imagines herself reaching out, it is to Corbu and no one else.

Minnette feels that urge again, that churning, knotting need that seizes her when she is not with *him*. She has some wine and takes up her pen. *In the absence of your words, I allow myself to be charmed by others,* she writes. She describes her gondola ride with Francesco with enthusiasm. *Francesco is especially loquacious and beautiful in a godlike way,* she adds. *That is to say, beyond reach, as all divinity ultimately is. But to sit in a gondola and listen to him speak passionately of Venice's bridges, its rising waters and softening bones, is like drinking a smooth merlot. Which is to say, he is rather delicious in his own way.* She indulges in further detail – how Francesco painted her while she sat on silk pillows and listened to him talk. She omits mention of her clothing, preferring to let him think the worst –

Laughter. Minnette opens her eyes and wonders when she had closed them. The piazza is unchanged. The man and his girlfriend/wife remain two tables away. Minnette's food remains half-eaten. Her wine glass is empty. Her head is resting in the palm of her hand, but she is still in her chair. She pushes away the empty glass, drinks water and resolves to eat. Her letter to Corbu is open, unfinished.

She remembers their last conversation, his triumphant announcement as he lay next to her. They were on the floor of No. 24, staring at the snow thickening against the front window. *I will change the way people live,* he had said. *Of course he will,* she thinks. *He already has.* Minnette smoothes out the unfinished letter, scorns her erratic penmanship, wonders what Corbu will think of her, then decides she doesn't care. She resumes writing.

Here I am, Corbu, and you – you are crossing the ocean, finally, for a project that will change the way people live. That's what you whispered to me in Paris. Audacious words for any architect except that the architect is you. And why else would you cross the ocean, Corbu? Certainly not for me. I would not let you even if you offered.

She dips a piece of bread in oil, puts it in her mouth and enjoys the viscous feeling on her tongue. *So you are off to India. Shall I ask my father to put in a good word for you with Nehru? I know, I know. Nehru needs no such encouragement. He is always such a forward-thinking chap. When he visited us during those pre-Independence years, he was full of brilliant ideas about the 'new India' – a new industrial India.* Minnette was little more than a girl back then, but Nehru spoke to her without condescension. He was intelligent, charming and immaculately turned out. *Gandhi must have seemed a terrible throwback to him, clad in that white vettiya. But Gandhi was astute – mark my words – a brilliant tactician. He knew how to get everyone, whatever one's caste or religion, behind him. When he visited, he quizzed my parents on all aspects of the Ceylon National Congress' strategy for independence and their involvement in rallying the masses.* Though he did seem an awful husband, she thinks, recalling how he ignored Kasturba so that Amma felt compelled to take her for a drive. Amma had later told her that Kasturba wept in the car: no one had ever done such a thing for her before. *Nehru was exceedingly Oxbridge and exceedingly dashing and wasted no time in taking a young lady who was not his wife boating on Kandy Lake. In full view, I might add, of Kandy's evening strollers.*

Which is to say that Nehru is not so different from you, my dear friend. Except that you are discreet. I cannot say otherwise.

'So discreet,' whispers Minnette, 'that I have heard nothing from you for weeks.' Nothing, that is, apart from a brief telephone call two days earlier in which he apologised for being unable to meet Minnette again. *Do not despair, oiseau,* he had said, and Minnette had gripped the phone tighter to stop herself from hanging up. There was no need. Less than a minute later, the operator did it for her; a faulty line brought the call to an end with neither party having a chance to say goodbye.

We did not say goodbye, writes Minnette. *I like to think, Corbu, that there is no need for such banal exchanges between us. Not when we are within reach of one another. After all, there is plenty of time for words. They come later, on paper or card, across water and land, bearing longing and reflection. Inside me runs a torrent of words. 'Do not despair,' you said when we spoke the other day. I shall take that to heart, Corbu, as I wait for your next letter. Words are all we have now, so let us not shrink from the obligation – let us not despair of our mutual exiles.*

Minnette lays down her pen. She pours herself a glass of water and, glancing inside it as she takes a sip, sees a constellation of stars reflected on its surface.

III

February – July 1951

The sun bleeds out across the horizon in pink welts.

The architect leans over to get a better view out the window. His sketchbook is on the fold-out table. This is his first flight to India. It has taken four planes to get here.

Caught in this horizontal hurtle over land and sea, he knows that there is nothing but truth below. *Topography does not lie,* he thinks, *or pretend it is something else. It reveals itself in its nakedness, showing every contour, every ragged edge, every mass of water insinuating itself onto land and vice versa.* The plane rises and dips, and the passengers rise and dip in their seats, like jockeys on horseback. The architect imagines himself as he is, sitting in an upholstered armchair in a winged shuttle, floating. *Where does it leave us?* He wonders. *Hovering between sky and earth, undermining the vertical, rendering the right angle obsolete.*

The pilot makes an announcement. Passengers fumble for their seat belts. The plane begins its descent into Delhi. *When you have the airplane, where is man?* the architect asks himself. *What is the significance of the vertical – of man – between earth and sky? Man is mediator, interceding on behalf of one for the other, but now it seems man is taking sides.*

They are moving through clouds, or they must be, because he cannot see anything for a while. As they emerge from the fog, he finds the sky bruised purple, and then moments later, the sun, a hot coal flickering into nothing, replaced by a flat moon suspended in darkness. Below, a constellation of lights, winding around one another and hovering. *India is the centre of everything now,* he thinks, *a glittering mass that attracts us all like moths.* That constellation is matched by a pullulation of light above: stars, millions of them, beating like tiny hearts in the sky.

Two hundred years ago, Raja Jai Singh of Jaipur looked up and found the same little hearts beating in the darkness. To see into those hearts, he built monolithic astronomical tools – the Jantar Mantars – across India.

In Delhi, the architect walks within one of them, dwarfed by gigantic sundial counters and steep staircases. He sits on the stone spokes of the Rama yantra – a piece of masonry that measures altitude through shadows – and finds it difficult to reconcile this restrained work of architecture with, say, Borromini's fussy, baroque confections. One is spare and functional and points out a scientific truth: the sun stands at this or that angle to the earth. The other is contrived, overwhelming and has the shifty gaze of a liar. One looks to heaven, the other ultimately closes the vault on it. *It says, non, you must not question,* thinks the architect, *only admire the works of man, who is created by God.*

Muslim culture transcended this limitation through its mosques. Delhi's Kutub minaret, an evocation of the right angle, stands red against a sapphire sky. *They say it is the tallest brick minaret in the world,* he muses, as he climbs the 399 steps to the top, treading the same path used by hundreds of imams centuries before. A memory drifts up like dust caught in sunlight: the steps to her flat, awkward, inconsistent. *So many bumps to the head,* he laughs. *But what is that when there is a bird of paradise nesting at the top?*

The column of the minaret, a rod of pure iron dating from the fourth century, has not rusted for 1,500 years. The mosque itself is built of recycled material – the remains of Hindu and Jain temples (destroyed by their Muslim conquerors) brought together to create an ornate hymn to Allah. Lotus motifs abound while faceless figures ring the tops of pillars. Koranic verses emboss walls and windows. *Yes, it is a lot of baubles,* he thinks, *but the effect, somehow, is not distracting.*

In the following days, he continues his architectural tour arranged by Prime Minister Nehru himself. The architect has little choice in what he sees, but he considers this his good fortune. So far, there has only been one site unworthy of his time – Safdarjung's tomb, which he dismisses as tawdry. Humayun's tomb, on the other hand, is to him a perfect example of Mughal architecture: spare, clean, fine. Red sandstone walls, majestic avenues... a clearly defined geometric space interrupted only by lime-green parakeets dangling from facades. He watches the sun begin its descent, blowing gold light through *jali* screens. The tombs themselves are simple marble sarcophagi, as smooth and lonely as bone.

From Delhi, the architect travels to Chandigarh, a blank slate now amid arid plains. As the train pulls out of the capital, he sees a moving landscape of shanties and squatting poor. So many huddling along the rail banks, slowly metamorphosing into pigs snuffling through rubbish. *The people in India are poor*, he thinks. *So many surviving on nothing. The few that have wealth live like kings. But there is no jealousy. No hatred. Just a simple will to go on and to live with what one has because ultimately, all this richesse is meaningless. It is merely material.*

The architect opens his sketchbook and begins drawing, but thoughts of India's poor seize him. He writes:

Ultimately, all this richesse is merely material.

Contrast this with America and their equation: wealth=happiness. In India everyone walks – they WILL walk. In America the car dominates; it defines the plan of a city, the design of a home, the friends you keep. In America they stomp about, desperate to make the next deal, buy the next commodity, shaft their competitors so that they can clear the road to 'success'. In India people meander, their feet move like whispers on the road. And those who have nothing will give to those who have even less than them. America may have the car, but India has the cow – a source of food, fuel and travel. This is efficiency – so much better than the rasp of exhaust and the screech of four wheels.

The journey to Chandigarh is an endless belt of fields and half-built homes sprawling one after the other. The earth is dry. It is as if it has been waiting for the architect to bring it to life, to irrigate its land and shape its present. *Nehru asked me because he knows that India is ready to embrace modernism, that Chandigarh will be the symbol of this shift*, he thinks, and before he finishes the thought, another one occurs and he writes:

BUT – what is the nuclear expression in India? What is the smallest unit upon which all other units will be built? Reduced to its kernel – its core – it is the verandah. The verandah and the mattress beneath the sky – that sky full of tiny heartbeats just as Jai Singh saw it centuries ago. That will be Corbu's 1 in Chandigarh.

The significance of this 1 has been explained, at great length, by Seetaram, a member of the architect's team in Chandigarh. *Indispensible, this small, wise Hindoo*, thinks the architect. Seetaram explained to him the role that the 1 plays in Hindustani music, that it unlocks the meaning of a piece, that the musician plays with the rhythm, twisting around and around it, until finally landing on the 1.

Follow the beat and you understand the structure, thinks the architect. *Everything is relative to the 1. Formidable! So it is with the Modulor. Man is 1 and everything else relative to him.* The architect resumes writing:

Man is the essential measurement. Primitive man knew this instinctively so that the raw-hide tent placed within easy reach everything that he required for indoor living. Chandigarh will start with this principle – the bed and the verandah – but will move beyond it so that ancient and modern coexist. But externally, there is another juxtaposition of ancient and modern: ancient landscape vs. modern structures. This landscape? The Himalayas beyond. The Himalayas which project serenely, holding within them the implacable nature of geological time. At once ancient and beyond time, for their age is almost inconceivable. How does Chandigarh exist in relation to this gargantuan truth? Solution: Chandigarh will be an offering to those geological miracles. The Modulor is there, but the ratio between the city and those mountains must also be resolved.

Just as the architect smiles at the genius of the

Modulor – his own theory – he remembers his visit to the governor's house in Delhi. A palace of contentment full of galleries and drawing rooms. A palace fit for a king, but occupied by a viceroy and later the prime minister. Lutyens created it in 1931, shortly before India took independence – a British imposition of ancient Indian inspiration. Lutyens' geometry is pure and true. Every dome, column and arch is perfectly placed. India Gate stands at the opposite end, like a splendid Arc de Triomphe. The avenue leading to the palace is as wide as the Champs Elysées and is equally grand. The gardens are rationally laid out, like those of the Mughal era, made up of fountains, pools and greenery. While visiting the palace, the architect took out his tape, measuring here and there, anticipating an inevitable result that never materialised. He measured again and again, assuming that he had made a mistake. It seemed impossible – irrational even, but the ratios could not lie.

It is not the Modulor, he reminds himself now, and the shock of that first realisation returns to him in cold detail. The effect, however, is brief. The architect shrugs, as if sloughing off the thought, then picks up his pen and writes.

But the Modulor can also be stretched, for the ratio=man: room:house:neighbourhood:surroundings. And at each point, the interval between these objects can and will stretch. In Chandigarh, it is the Himalayas that compete with man, the one dwarfing the other, therefore distances between objects in the foreground will be exaggerated so that the whole makes sense when observed from afar. Perspective is food for the soul.

Where it is most important, the Modulor will prevail. Homes must be built to reflect the proportions of man, so that all operations within it, the art of living, are facilitated. Even the poorest citizen of Chandigarh should have a home equipped with all the accoutrements of modern living. *What is wrong with giving those who have nothing something to ease the burden of their daily lives*, he thinks. *A modern kitchen, a sanitary toilet, pourquoi pas?* In this way, those who have little are elevated through their living environment. The role of the architect is to bring progress to their lives, too. This is where it begins. At the most basic level. And before long, progress sweeps the city, lends harmony to its inner workings, keeps its heart beating and its citizens spiritually content.

In Bombay he saw children playing beneath shaded arches. In Delhi, they thronged beneath India Gate. Chandigarh, too, he decides, will have deep shaded arches full of circling air currents. Here, the public will congregate, even when the sun is at its height, strolling gently, unaffected by the heat. Others will sit in contemplation or lean against one another, deep in conversation. Open spaces thus become social spaces where members from all levels of society can mingle.

This is the architect's vision – to create a city that perpetuates democracy. As he sits in yet another plane, this time heading away from India, he knows that this vision will find solidity. In concrete and glass, brick and stone, the city will take shape and then, necessarily, shape the lives of those who live in it.

He looks out the window and feels tired. *I am not so young*, he thinks. He has left the calm of India and is filled with dread as the plane approaches the Alps. He hates them, stabbing upward like malformed teeth – a landscape of hideous molars. But on the other side of that mountain range lies his other great project: Ronchamps. That build is ostensibly for the spirit, the other for the mind, yet both, decides the architect, will speak to the soul: democracy+demagoguery.

When the architect arrives at his office at No. 35, he finds a letter from *her*. The envelope is small, marked in a precise hand. Someone passes it to him without remark, as if it were a glass of water. He knows they talk about these letters among themselves, that some of them have linked seeing her here at No. 35 with the sporadic arrival of these envelopes. He does not care. He is Le Corbusier, after all. It is expected. No one will tell Vonn. This is the most important thing: that his wife should remain ignorant of who, even if she knows there is someone. There has always been someone else.

He opens the letter a few days later while sitting in a cafe not far from No. 35. He slices through it with a knife, extracts the vellum sheets, lays them on the table, then lights a cigarette. She is upset. He knew she would be. She is often upset with him. It is not an endearing habit of hers. He excuses it because she is beautiful, and because it makes her more beautiful (the way her lips set themselves into an angry tulip bud, the way her back gathers itself into a straight line, taut with irritation). He has not seen such elegance before. His wife is a peasant next to her. *She* – she is aristocracy, a true bird of paradise. *Mon cher oiseau*, he thinks, smiling, reading the letter, shaking his head.

And then, unsmiling, he thinks, *I have been a shit*. He has brought a sheaf of papers with him, intent on setting things right. His pen is filled with ink – enough to last three pages, at least. He picks it up and writes: *Mon cher oiseau. Corbu has neglected his own little soul. You have been waiting, non? And I must make up for being a shit. Oui, c'est vrais. Je suis Corbu le salaud! Corbu la charogne! So let me restore myself. Are you sitting, Minnette? Good girl. Because Corbu is about to tell you a story – a long one – about l'Inde.*

———————

Weeks later he is in Hoddesdon for CIAM 8, the letter unfinished, the story untold. Architects from around the world – India, Japan, Israel – have come to talk about the city and its heart. But she is not there. Unexpectedly, the architect feels her absence like a weight in his chest. In her last letter, that letter he received like a glass of water, she wrote to him of heart and soul, and here, in Hoddesdon, this is all they talk of. CIAM 8 devotes itself to the new city, and the architects' plans for this new city will free people from the drudgery of their machine existence. They will be rescued by the architect and others like him and returned to their nature: to walk, to run, to interact as social beings rather than automata.

The heart of the new city is inseparable from its site. It draws its rhythm from its location: the angle of the sun, the steady gait of the hills, the incline of the plains. The new city does not protrude unnaturally, but assumes a position that, in retrospect, could only have been made for it. *Her point about that palace in Ceylon*, thinks the architect. *What was it called? Ah yes, Seegiriya.* The architect nods. A city imposed on a site is a city that is at odds with its surroundings. Thus dislocated, it cannot breathe, it loses its rhythm, its heart ceases to beat. Such a city is capable of spawning only robots, engaged in hollow enterprise, denied the possibility of an inner life.

The architect considers his own inner life, and is startled to find her folded within it, like a chrysalis tucked under a leaf. He re-reads her letter, which has been in his breast pocket since he received it, and feels the first prick of jealousy as he arrives at her description of the young Italians. He writes: *So you have been in Rome, oiseau, where there have been plenty of young men to interpose themselves between you and Corbu. You were captivated by this Francesco. Why not the other?*

The other is Francesco Borromini and his baroque churches. The architect was impressed by San Carlo alle Quattro Fontane, with its alternating convex and concave entrance. People flock to it for its engineering complexities. *Too bad these are worn on its skin – those guts hanging outside for all to balk at*, he thinks, then writes: *But given that you were taken by this Francesco and not that, perhaps it was Bernini who caught your eye instead: the quaking marble robes, St Theresa's ecstatic half-opened mouth (a mouth so familiar to us, is it not, petit oiseau?), the gold-tipped arrow, the shower of sparks shooting down behind them. Bernini's Capella Cornaro is the only thing worth seeing in that bordel Santa Maria della Vittoria. But Bernini saves himself by making real the voluptuousness of spiritual ecstasy. Did it take your breath with it, Minnette? Of course it did. Who can stand unaffected before it?*

The architect feels his own breath quickening. *We did not have enough time*, he thinks. *If I had known you were coming to see me*, he writes. *Never mind. We got to the point anyway. We were both greedy for it. This old man was too eager to hold youth in his arms again. And you did not complain, did you?* The architect closes his eyes, remembers her mouth opening like a flower. No. She did not complain.

He puts down his pen, strikes a match, lights another cigarette. Smoke curls up his throat, puffs out his nose. The hotel room is dark, unbearably English. He decides to finish his cigarette on the balcony. He stares out at the low line of rooftops almost disappearing into a blurring horizon. The sun is setting, spilling its yolk across the sky. The architect notes the colour, files it for later use – perhaps on canvas... perhaps for the house without a door.

The house without a door is yet another project. The architect has a client – a wealthy patron – in Ahmedabad. She has asked him to build her a villa, her only stipulation being that it be a home with no doors. The request is conceptual, capturing the notion of the door as an eternal entrance and exit. Not merely an unlocked door or door with no locks, but something that reaches into the very idea of the door: an opening that allows a continuous flow of light, air and individuals through space.

The door is yet another spiritual exercise, he thinks. In India, above all, it is charged with a certain mystical force. The door is the gateway into an inner sanctum and admission is gained through the performance of a simple ritual: the removal of one's shoes. *How to create this door that is at once closed and open?*

The architect drops his cigarette to the ground, watches it flare out before he grinds it underfoot. *It seems it is like this with human beings. Each of us has walked through the door of the other's thoughts. Once opened, we cannot push the door closed. It is, to those who have been allowed in, now a door without locks.*

He returns to his desk, puts pen to paper again.

They say the eyes are windows, but they are wrong, he writes. *Les yeux sont les portes qui portent l'homme vers l'âme. The doors were open for us before we met one another, petit oiseau. You, who looked on me with eyes of such natural wisdom. But where did Corbu's eyes first fall? Oh, my little bird, do not chastise me – the dog that I am – for it was your toes that captivated me first. Yes, those tiny digits peeping out from beneath panels of the purest silk. Such elegant feet in gracious slippers! You write that we shared our first smile without provocation, but this is a lie, oiseau. If not for those toes, perhaps I would not have felt compelled to look up at that moment. And perhaps, had you not felt the weight of this dog's curious gaze upon your feet, you would not have cast a glance (of pity, maybe?) at Corbu. Pity, too, must have moved you to speak to Corbu later.*

The architect sees the moment as if it were happening there, in front of him. *Ah*, he thinks, *this old servant, blind in one eye, how is it possible that he has captured the attentions of such a rare bird of paradise? Her feathers are of the finest texture – multi-hued, fragile, iridescent. Her bearing is stately, her movements refined. And then there is Corbu, the old crow, with black plumes and a scraping call. What a pair we make, with nothing to unite us except our genus.*

He stares out the open balcony doors at the sky, pink fading away into grey. He is weighted by an inevitable thought. In a few weeks, he will fly to his refuge at Cap Martin, to nest with his wife and listen to her sighs. This is not wholly unbearable. He reminds himself of her beauty – her well proportioned figure, her rural wit. But she is also too aloof – too unimpressed by his achievements. She complains that No. 24, the apartment that he had built for her in Paris, is 'killing her with light'. The cupboards in the kitchen, apparently, make standing and working at the countertops impossible. And the bidet by the bed – a sculpture in ceramic of the purest form – has been swaddled beneath a tea cosy.

In Cap Martin she will sit and drink, thinks the architect, *she likes her rouge.* And when she has had enough, she will sing lullabies, her voice smooth and oaky, wasted on infantile words: *do do, lolo*. Sometimes, she pulls his sleeve and pleads with him to sing to her. So he opens his mouth and crows ridiculous notes until the eyelids droop, the hand goes slack and the wine glass rolls.

With Vonn asleep he can sit in their cell: the wooden shack he built for her where he works throughout the day. There he paints. An image will sit on his shoulder: *la licorne*. She has orange wings and a tiny, delicate head with one fiery horn bursting from it. She is a phoenix with bare breasts, wide hips and the white legs of Venus. She first appeared on his flight back from India. *Born on the plains of Chandigarh, or dropped from the heavens? Her wings are not yet open, but once open, will they welcome or repel? She is multihued, the colour of fire. I draw her and it is as if she has come from somewhere else. Have I seen her perched on the crescent of a bull's horn, those bulls that are so ubiquitous in India?*

Through the one window in his cell, he will watch the sea sway, the sun lend its colours to a liquid landscape. Four walls, a roof, a window and a door. This is his 1.

The architect is writing again. *I dream of this 1, oiseau, from a hotel room in Hoddesdon. Because my cell is what I long for most: a place of pure reflection, discipline and application. Where else do I have the liberty to think and to do? (And most importantly, to paint!) Every home should include within it such a cave. Men must have an exclusive space free from material responsibilities – out of bounds to anyone else.* (Well, except Vonn, he reminds himself).

But this is not the case in India, thinks the architect. Among the poorest, homes consist of one room so that the whole family occupies the same space. Where then does the man find his respite? Or is it that the poorest are so occupied with the basic needs of survival, that they do not have the means or the need to indulge in such asceticism? Living a life in permanent want – what else is that if not a life of asceticism? Hence the wisdom of even the poorest man in India. It is an instinctive wisdom, born of involuntary self-denial.

He remembers the animals he saw in India's cities – balding, thin things. Delhi's roaming menagerie of creatures are at once participants in and spectators of the city. And then there are the slums by the railway station, where dwellings are little more than oily cloths and tarpaulins draped over sticks. A woman squats by a fire. Buffalo nestle between the rail line and the dirt slope that marks its outermost edge. Their grey-black backs curve smoothly over tucked-in legs so that they appear more like a family of mice piled up in a nest than tethered buffalo. Pigs pick through rubbish a short distance away. Agricultural animals herded and managed in an urban setting, in the epitome of the urban context: the slum.

So what does this amount to? He writes in his diary. *The ingenuity of man and animal to adapt to their surroundings. Therefore,*

1 room in India
=man's adaptation to his environment
=living within his means
=contentment.

Confronted with Chandigarh – with what is the greatest project of his life – the architect regrets that he has so little time in the city. Just one or two months per year. But his team, he knows, is excellent. There is the English couple and his right-hand man, Pierre. (*En fait, mon 'Sancho'.*)

There is Seetaram, and the possibility of Trivedi, whom the architect met here at Hoddesdon. Trivedi spoke so passionately and intriguingly of Ahmedabad's old city – a warren of richly carved dwellings no wider than the span of a man's outstretched arms – that the architect now feels compelled to accept his offer to work on the project team in Chandigarh. He thinks, *I will accept him on the strength of those pols.* There is also a squad of young Indians – enthusiastic architects eager to learn. *And leading them all, the knight himself,* thinks the architect. *Like that poor, deluded Don Quixote, Corbu battles windmills knowing they are giants. And Corbu believes passionately, unwaveringly in his quest. This alone makes it worthy and true.*

He re-reads the last sentence of the letter, which is now several sheaves long. He writes: *We architects must be idealists. We construct not just individual buildings, but whole cities. We plan cities, and in doing so, change lives. Chandigarh is an opportunity to do this – to improve lives. It is a radical experiment. A chance to take an inherently spiritual and instinctive way of living and fuse it with all the efficiency and rationality of modernity. We can take the best of both worlds and create a super city. And because India is the seat of so much wisdom, this blending of old and new, spiritual and material, will be a model for civilisations to come. And who must do this? Corbu. It is a great responsibility, but if not Corbu, then who?*

The architect weighs the question, considers the options. Pierre is a perfect doer. He takes the plans he is assigned and builds them to the expected standard. He does not deviate from instructions. The architect trusts him completely. The English couple are the same, though not quite as steadfast as Pierre. Elizabeth is the stronger of the pair. She is not bothered by her husband Richard's reputation or influence in England. If Elizabeth thinks her husband's interpretation of a plan is flawed, she tells him. *Balls cut, the cuckold does as he is told,* the architect laughs to himself. Elizabeth is sharp and irresistible, but her success is tied to Richard's. Still, he is Elizabeth's shadow. She eclipses him as soon as she walks into a room. Elizabeth was at Bridgwater. It was she who introduced the architect to *her.*

Even Nehru could not resist the charms of the thin English girl. *Elizabeth smiles and Nehru is beguiled,* thinks the architect. He is certain she has met Nehru privately for drinks. Richard seems not to notice, shrugging and leaning in closer to inspect his newspaper. While Elizabeth sits on a bicycle and roams the Chandigarh plain with young Indian men, Richard studies his drawing board and frowns.

This is the architect's team in Chandigarh. A better one cannot be found. But without the architect, they would be lost. He does not tell them this quite so explicitly. It is unnecessary; they know it themselves.

———

The church in Ronchamp is something else. The architect wonders why they asked him to build it. After all, he is not a Catholic. He has told the abbot this, but the abbot insists that they want an artist.

In the style of Michelangelo, I cannot, he thinks. *I cannot approach this with the fervency of the faithful.* The abbot has insisted that they want a building reflective of the modern age, and that only the architect can fulfil this brief. The architect cannot and does not refuse. This old mining town will have its modern icon – its cathedral of modernity on a green hill. Everyone will look up to it, this arm of progress, couched within the rubric of the Catholic church. Ronchamp will be a building of spiritual endeavours, stripped of the ornamentation that normally encrusts the interior of Catholic churches. It will be a space of pure contemplation. Of light and smooth surfaces. A place where symbols go beyond the right angles of the crucifix to more celestial archetypes. A cathedral of archetypes.

Such thinking will not make the agenda in Milan. The architect is speaking about Chandigarh, and possibly Ronchamp, at the Milan Triennale in September. He wants her to be there. *You must come*, he writes, then realises he hasn't written where. He scratches out the sentence, begins again, filling in the grey areas, tethering his thoughts to paper:

This work you are doing on the Ariyapala house, oiseau. It fits perfectly the theme of the exhibitions. Here you are using the decorative arts in a functional manner and in a context removed from Europe. It would be useful to shift focus a little from the western world, no? To look at modern architecture in the context of the Orient? Lessons of adaptation, integration with traditional methods so that new and old coexist – as you so eloquently put it.

This old Corbu would so like to see you, mon gentil oiseau. You have taught me much about l'Inde. Your precise descriptions of those extraordinary sculptures at the Royal Academy. The Indians knew how to translate the human figure in all its robust tumescence. And these are your gods and goddesses! Caught in fervent embraces, murderous blood-lettings or ecstatic dances. What then is left for mere mortals? Because we, too, must feed our appetites. To the Victorians, these figures were depraved. To us, they are aspirational. They show us what lies at the extreme ends of the possible.

And what is possible for us? We, too, are moving towards this extremity. Never are we more alive than when we caper on its tip. In your attic flat in London we discovered what it means to blunder onto this edge. You with tender fingers and eyes of fire, your wings beating against my heart. This old man does not deserve to find such vitality so late in life.

You served me tea. 'Corbu,' you said, 'you must at least stay for a cup. It is the finest BOP from Ceylon.' I did not ask you what BOP meant. I do not remember what the tea tasted like. The cups stayed in their saucers.

'I have measured every item,' you said. 'Every sculpture has a corresponding set of dimensions now. But these are meaningless to one who truly appreciates what he is seeing.'

I nodded. You wore green silk and like a parakeet you sat on your chair, a single white flower in your hair. Its petals peeped at me through black lustre.

'Large or small,' you continued, 'these are irrelevant when it comes to the overall impression such an object, in effect a religious object, leaves on your soul. This is unfathomable. No device can measure it.'

Still that green silk shifted – the only bright thing in the room. The windows were bare, the sun almost below the horizon. A faint band of light lay across our feet. Your face was in darkness. You looked around the room, preoccupied. You sighed. You crossed your arms over your chest and said it was cold. You bent to arrange your hem. The flower tumbled from your hair. Corbu swept down to retrieve it as you leant forward to do the same. Your fingers brushed a single petal. But the flower was already in my hand.

This old man was reborn in a curtainless, attic flat. My bird of heaven. You have split Corbu in two and now he is sentenced to a double-life. This crow is wily, it is true. His life exists on many levels, through many disciplines: painter, architect, urban planner, man of letters. But the heart is something else. How did you fall into it? I love my wife, Minnette. She is a goddess of this earth. But you are something else. Ethereal and sky-born. If she is water, then you are fire. Both are necessary.

You must come to Milan. Let Corbu chase any thoughts of godlike Romans from your mind or heart. What did that Francesco offer you, Minnette? He showed you art, then attempted to paint you on canvas. Impossible. It will be nothing but caricature. He has done you a disservice, and now gazes at his efforts with disappointment. I do not blame him. Nor do I blame you. I was silent, it is true. But see how much I send you now: words, words and more words. Words without touch. The pleasure is never as palpable, is it?

The architect lays down his pen, pours out a glass of water, calms his shaking hands. She is far away, perched on a jewel in the ocean, perhaps beyond the reach of this ream of thoughts. He has given her words because she asked for them. This was his objective, anyway, when he began this letter. But in the writing has come the realisation of something unexpected. Each time he flies to India, he is closer to her. *But would it be right for me to go there,* he asks himself? He lets the thought evaporate before he can write it. *There is safety in this exercise,* he thinks.

The architect wonders what it is like for her now. He has met her sister and brother-in-law – Marcia and Werner – and understands her ambivalence towards them. They love her; that is plain. Marcia is as beautiful as she is, but weighed down by Werner's Germanic sensibility. *All this Lutheranism,* he thinks. *It is bad for the soul.* He contrasts Marcia and Werner with Mimi, his *oiseau*'s dear friend. Marcia and Werner are like a gently warming stove. Mimi, on the other hand, is the blue in fire.

He met Mimi in Paris, the last time he saw Minnette. *Such an extraordinary whiteness. Mon dieu,* he thinks, and decides she must be anaemic. He thinks what a good friend Mimi is to Minnette, and smiles. She has told him too many times how lonely Minnette is. He hopes that Mimi has been a better correspondent than he.

He considers the work Minnette has done and what lies ahead. He feels the burden of his position weigh into him like some smelly man in one of these dingy English pubs. He knows that of the many things he is to her, he must fulfil the role of mentor right now. He writes:

You are a force in Ceylon now, Minnette. You are bringing modernism to that nation, and with it, progress. It is a fledgling country, ready, like India, to embrace something new. How different it must feel to be in a place that has, as you once put it, become itself again. What is it like, Minnette? The realms of possibility must be infinite. A new found confidence, the courage that comes of success. Imagine: here is a chance to start again, build anew, re-shape society and manners.

He pauses. This thirst for the new is a post-war phenomenon. The architect flies left and right across the globe, building new structures in Bogotá, India, New York, Ronchamp. At the conferences, architects talk about heart and soul, as if neither existed before. The Americans give the Marshall Plan to Europe, and money pours in for new buildings; it is a new era in reconstruction. England introduces a National Health Service, bringing free health care to the common man. *Everywhere, people are shedding the binds of war and demanding a better way of life,* he writes. *We can give this to them.*

We are pioneers, Minnette. You, even more so – Ceylon is ripe, ready to throw off the memory of colonisation (all those British buildings signifying British power). Why keep these relics when the country rejects what they stand for? Better to knock them down and begin afresh. Better to create a new building vocabulary as you are doing, rooted in pre-colonial tradition but firmly modern in its outlook. This is your mandate as an architect of the Modern age. Do not forget what you are.

Maintenant, écoute-moi, Minnette. Pay no attention to these Ariyapalas and their petty complaints. You must believe in your vision so completely that they bend to it. They will. We are the visionaries. Tell them this. Why else have they asked you to build their house? Because they do not know how to create as you do, that's why. So do not listen to them. Listen to me. Listen to Corbu. And to yourself.

Listen to me, too, when I say that Picasso and Éluard may attack Corbu just as children fling stones into the sea. War? Peace? Strike out one and embrace the other with a signature on a paper? Pah! The sea swells and rolls favouring neither left nor right. What does Nietzsche say? Man is nothing more than a polluted stream. 'One must be a sea to receive a polluted stream without becoming impure.' What is this sea? The Übermensch. 'In him can your great contempt be submerged.'

The sea will swell and roll, Minnette, and bring nourishment to those who recognise the potential within it.

To those who do not the sea remains impervious. Let them open their eyes. Let them come and look into the sea's depths and feed of its plenty.

The architect puts down his pen. The air around his ankles is cold, damp. Somewhere in this long and inchoate letter he has asked her to come to Milan, to the next conference. This is what she will expect – an invitation, a sign that he wants to see her again. The reality is more complicated. He wants to see her and he doesn't want to see her. She is a difficult woman. A beautiful, difficult woman. These two elements compete with one another, sometimes cancelling the other out, other times fusing together to make her all the more attractive or unattractive, depending on the architect's mood. Right now, he wants to take her to bed, to hold her fragile body in his old arms. This is what compels him to ask her to come to Milan.

He stares out through his open balcony doors into the night. The sky is a carpet strewn with miniscule fragments of glass – a million hearts beating, a million hearts sighing.

IV

August – October 1951

Crumbs of love cake are scattered across her plate. She skims its surface with moist fingertips, sweeping up the last of the buttery loaf. She has just finished reading his letter, the sweet weight of it now melding in her stomach with the cake. He has invited her to Milan. *I will go to Italy,* she decides. *I am going to Italy.* She leaves the empty plate at her desk, pulls out a suitcase and begins packing.

Weeks later, the case remains where she left it, leaning against the *almariya* in her room. The Ariyapala Lodge is nearing completion and cannot be abandoned again. So the suitcase must be unpacked. When she opens it, she finds her clothes still folded inside, like so many sparrows' wings. *It was like this when I arrived,* she thinks. *All my things – in trunks and suitcases – half-opened, reluctantly emptied.*

It has been three months since she returned to Sri Lanka from her Christmas visit to Mimi in Paris. The days are long, tedious, filled with meticulous work that stretches time. His absence, his silence, hollows out the hours, leaving her floundering in the loose skin of her days. When a letter finally arrives, the hours trip over one another, breathless. *So it is true, then,* she writes in reply. *The pleasure that arises from pain is sweeter than any other. At least, this is how we rationalise it, to save ourselves from despair.*

Her despair over her current project is checked only by the knowledge that he believes in her. Despite her brief escape to Europe and the threat of repeat abandonment, the Ariyapalas remain obstinate clients. 'Just where do you think we will get the money for that painting you are talking about?' Mr Ariyapala asked last week. Minnette had proposed they commission a mural for the living room. Her plans stipulate that the west-facing wall be modified to accommodate a mural set into it, creating the effect of a single floor-to-ceiling surface. The Ariyapalas finally agreed, although they continue to press for cheaper alternatives.

Mrs Ariyapala's only deviation from silence came at Minnette's first meeting with them following her return. 'How dare you leave us in the middle of this mess,' she seethed. Thinking about it now, Minnette knows her clients' anger is justified, but she will not admit that to them. *They huffed, I puffed, but the house is still standing.*

In fact, it will be finished in a matter of days. Some of the internal walls have been rendered, but her insistence on retaining the natural finish of the walls on the lower floor has been accepted with little complaint.

The lodge is a product of compromise, and Minnette comforts herself knowing that those compromises have been weighted in her favour. She understands that the balance of power between client and architect is fragile and that respect comes from a slightly uneven relationship where the architect leads and the client follows. Reverse the equation and the build is lost.

The architect is flanked by a new partner. Trivedi is his latest acquisition, another 'wise Hindoo' with secret knowledge of India's landscape. They are walking through the *pols* of old Ahmedabad, navigating narrow passages – *les couloirs,* he thinks – hopping from one *pol* to another. Old Ahmedabad is a riddle of its own. Secret roads bear them through temples and people's homes. They stop in open squares, admire blue doors floating against the bleached walls of crumbling buildings.

'The *pols*,' says Trivedi, 'are divided by religion.'

The architect notes that the Jain *pols* are full of bird feeders: carved stone towers rich with detail, they are multi-tiered gazebos. The architect marvels at their ubiquity. *Even the birds are cared for,* he thinks. The detail that goes into the bird feeders is no different from that applied to people's homes. The homes, in fact, are simpler. Entering one, he finds its width no greater than the span of his arms. Everything is within reach – *the Modulor by instinct rather than design,* he thinks.

In the evening, Trivedi takes the architect to a Jain temple. They watch men and women worship with mouths covered by masks, a practice, explains Trivedi, designed to prevent the accidental death of tiny insects that might otherwise be inhaled. But it is not all sacrifice and austerity. The architect stands for a long time, gazing at a heavily worked frieze clinging to the exterior of the building like a wasp's nest. In it, he observes dancing women with engorged breasts strumming guitar-like instruments while monkeys crouch and birds fly overhead.

Sacrifice, austerity, indulgence and, finally, charity. Everywhere the architect looks, he sees food: bird seed on the temple steps, plates of rice in the corners for stray dogs. *This old dog feels at home here,* he thinks, staring at his naked toes, *even if he is forced to take off his shoes.*

The architect has been in Ahmedabad for two weeks, working on the villa for his wealthy patron, ruminating on the riddle of the doors with no locks. He imagines these doors in a perpetual state of open welcome. But it is not a case of a door left open – or worse still – no door at all. *There must be a door*, he thinks, receding once again into contemplation.

He meditates on this question throughout his long and circuitous journey back to Chandigarh. The architect submits to the itinerary proposed by his companion, Trivedi. On the way to Udaipur, they stop at a step-well, a small version of a Roman bath. The architect cannot hide his astonishment. Five storeys of carved tiers and balconies, all in sandstone, incline upward from a 20km deep well. The heat outside is blistering, but within, it is cool and pleasant. Flights of narrow, stone steps project from all sides into the water. Taking those steps, the architect's head grazes a low-hanging lintel, leaving tiny pinpricks of blood on his scalp. Only at noon does the sun wander in, casting a brief eye into the well's liquid centre.

In Udaipur, they stay at a haveli. The architect is amused at the mass of the padlock bolting his door and the weight of its corresponding key. It is a key that feels important – that fills the pocket with its significance and slips into its carriage with confidence. Such a key is impossible to hide and even more impossible to steal, he thinks. It is cumbersome, but it is the right tool for the context. It is a key for a lock for a door that must be secured.

The architect is surprised that the doors need any lock at all, considering the men of this region. Unlike those in Chandigarh, they wear earrings and wide upturned moustaches. Their faces are sculptural, their bearing warrior-like. *This is a nation of fighters,* he thinks. Trivedi introduces the architect to Anop, who, though no longer wearing a moustache, continues to carry the impression of it on his face. Two notches in the skin above either end of his mouth suggest the extremities of a substantial broom handle. 'My father gave me permission to shave it,' Anop tells the architect. He also says that a man cannot twist his moustache upward until his father dies. Anop works in a mine and the dust, he says, makes it impossible to keep his moustache clean: 'It takes too long to keep it groomed. Now I can have extra sleep!'

From Udaipur, Trivedi takes the architect to Jaipur, outside of which lies the Amber palace. The architect can think of no superlatives to convey its grandness or its beauty. The decoration is profuse, with bouquets of flora painted into lierne vaults. These contrast with white interior ceilings inset with silver mirror. The floors are simple grey and white slabs of marble with intermittent, shallow gutters running through them. The gutters, decorated in a black and white herringbone pattern that suggests current and movement, allow water to flow through the room, acting as a natural cooling system.

Inset mirrors and stained glass – these are features that he finds especially provocative. The stained glass in Rajasthan is neither sepulchral nor narrative, he thinks. There are no sombre depictions of martyrs or sacrifice. White walls are punctuated by squares or circles of yellow or green glass – secret peepholes for royalty wishing to observe their subjects while remaining, themselves, unseen. The sun shining through them throws pleasing patterns across floors or walls. Function and decoration are wed.

Returning to Chandigarh, the architect is excited. He wonders how much more of the city has risen from the dust.

Not much, he discovers. Progress is slow. His focus is the government buildings – the vital core of the city. He looks from the unfinished city to the placid enormity of the Himalayas, and decides that the city will be both an offering and a challenge to it. Perspective is a powerful ally, he thinks. With one well-shaped dune at the end of town, he can shift the balance of power, throwing the Himalayas into temporary obscurity. For the architect, only one monument will capture the essence – the spirit of cooperation and generosity – of the city: the Open Hand.

When the architect introduced the concept of the Open Hand to his team member, Elizabeth, she joked that such gestures could be misinterpreted. How, he asked, could this symbol, both bird and hand, be anything but positive? 'This is a city in flight, away from the despair and corruption of the average capital, towards the hope and sincerity of the new,' he said. 'A bird in the hand,' quipped Elizabeth, pouring herself another glass of champagne.

The architect has since come to realise that a bird in the hand is no bad thing. It suggests thriftiness. So, he offers a government that is committed to saving money while ensuring that its citizens are looked after. Even on this mundane level, his symbol is a success.

———————

Minnette sits in her room smoking. The windows are open, the fan is on. Jaya is having an afternoon nap. In deference to her, Minnette smokes in private, winging the fumes out the window with the back of her hand. Whenever Jaya finds an unemptied ashtray in Minnette's room, she shakes her head and sighs, 'Baby Nona, don't. It will give you wrinkles. *So* ugly.'

Minnette agrees. She draws a little puff from her cigarette, simultaneously renouncing it for its filthiness. She would crush it out, but it is the only company she has, so it remains pinched between two fingers, spiralling smoke while slowly dissolving into ash.

In London, Mimi would tell her off for wasting cigarettes like this. Minnette had always been a reluctant smoker. She was more inclined to warm her breath with a short glass of brandy or, at Mimi's encouragement, whiskey. In the absence of such luxury, she drinks her father's arrack. Ceylon's rules of etiquette do not apply to her, she decides. *This is the privilege of the privileged,* she thinks, *to live outside the norms of society.* It is also the privilege of the artist, and for these purposes, she declares herself an artist, too.

But not a genius. Genius is beyond her. She is exhausted from her labyrinthine negotiations with the Ariyapalas. The shock of return, an absence of friends, the reality of being back home with her parents at age thirty-two. And Ceylon, newly wrought, vulnerable to the whims of idealogues. A new political party has emerged, courting Buddhist monks and nuns. Its entire premise, thinks Minnette, is unconvincing. She dismisses it as a fad. *How can it gain traction,* she thinks, *when we are a nation of so many others?*

The flag itself has been modified to reflect this reality. Earlier in the year, the golden lion, symbol of Kandyan monarchs, retreated a few steps to accommodate two coloured bands, one green and one orange, representing Ceylon's Muslim and Tamil citizens. Each band is exactly one-seventh the width of the whole flag and no more, to reinforce the ratio of majority to minority. This is where

Minnette feels comfortable – as a minority within the majority. She is Catholic and Sinhalese. She benefits on both levels.

Minnette blows a smoke ring out the window. It diffuses like a ghost in the gathering gloam. At her door: a knock, rustling silk, clinking bangles. Her mother waits, shakes her head, moves on. Minnette sighs and lights another cigarette. Earlier, she quietly refused her parents' invitation to join them for dinner at the Kandy Garden Club. It is a Party function, opening the United National Party conference this weekend. In two days, the Prime Minister will be addressing Kandy's citizens. But the thought of crowds of rich Sinhalese and Burghers sizing each other up at Kandy's oldest and most exclusive club does not appeal to Minnette today. Smallpox has been ravaging the district and she prefers to keep to herself. She knows, too, that the Ariyapalas are likely to be at the club this evening. Running into them, she decides, would be a fate worse than the pox. She is also aware that her parents are trying to introduce her to a young man: Densil or Dudley or something. Again, Minnette demurs. She does not want to meet someone she will never love. *What is the point in pretending*, she thinks. *It will only disappoint us both.*

Minnette grinds her cigarette into the bowl. She scans her desk, sees his letter, and is overcome by that familiar urge. Something hollows out inside her, sucks away her breath. She picks up her pen.

If only the Ariyapalas would respect my competence, she writes. *If I were a man, there wouldn't be all the questions, criticisms and second guessings. They would take what I said at face value and thank me for it. Instead I am told I am mad, irresponsible, even arrogant.*

Minnette pauses to consider her latest victory. The Ariyapalas have agreed to the wall mural in the living room and the artist, her friend Siri Sinharaja, has agreed to paint it for a lower fee in return for some free publicity. The Ariyapalas are lucky. Siri is not yet well known, but among the critics he is considered a raw talent. His style is a combination of Hindu-Buddhist fresco painting, Fauvism and Cubism. His paintings are exhuberant, colourful celebrations of the body – often, the female body. This is ironic, given his tight-lipped, asexual nature. A quiet, serious man, he is more suited to the monastery, thinks Minnette, than the artist's studio.

It was her mother who had introduced them. She had invited him to Nell Cottage and Minnette had sat and looked at his sketchbook in the garden. His drawings touched her, and his quiet demeanour made her feel safe. That was some years ago. Minnette and Siri grew into a comfortable friendship, one that thrived despite Minnette's time studying in London. They rarely wrote, but whenever she went back home to visit, he would turn up, sometimes painting a work in the cottage garden while Minnette sat reading or writing notes. They would discuss art and the philosophy of Ananda Coomeraswamy. Even now, she can picture Siri's small bald head floating on top of that long, sturdy body. The thought of it makes her smile.

The moon rises over Nell Cottage. Minnette leans back in a planter's chair on the verandah. Mosquitoes crowd around her ankles. Jaya appears without being asked and lights some incense. Minnette wants Jaya to sit next to her and chat, but says nothing. She knows it would only embarrass her. A shadow crosses the garden, spills onto the verandah. It is Siri. In three steps, he is sitting beside her, staring wordlessly at the sky.

Jaya brings him a glass of arrack which he accepts without looking up. He gazes at it, then leans back in the planter's chair and slings his legs over the extendable arm rests. Minnette does the same, staring into the velvet dark. Millions of stars tremble above them – *one for every heart beating on earth,* she thinks.

She casts a glance at Siri. His eyes are bloodshot, his face ashen. His friend Eric, a photographer and former protégé of the late Lionel Wendt, is not with him. In the last year, Siri and Eric had become close. Each man seemed to share the other's shadow. They had talked of collaborating on a photo-art project, and had even generated some early visuals which no one had actually seen. Like Siri, Eric often went off on his own to work. Eight days ago, he headed north to the jungles around Polonnaruwa. There, as he tried to take a photograph of an elephant, it charged him. He was killed instantly.

The elephant is lucky to have committed its crime in an independent Ceylon. Under the British, it would have been hunted down and dismembered, its tusks fitted with silver and stapled to the walls of the governor's residence. The Ceylonese, by contrast, dress elephants in silks and sequins, entrusting them with the greatest of religious relics, the Buddha's tooth. The government even made a gift of three elephants to London Zoo, shipping them to England where they walked from the docks right up to Euston station.

Minnette thinks of all this while watching Siri watch the sky. Her eyelids droop. Siri opens his mouth. A million stars vanish.

'We are a nation of lions in thrall to the elephant,' he says. Then silence. Minnette's eyelids open and the stars reappear. When she wakes, Siri is gone. His glass sits untouched on one armrest. She drains it and goes to bed.

She dreams of elephants, concrete and calculations. In the morning, she waits for the monkeys who roam rooftops in packs, planning kitchen raids. They arrive while she eats breakfast. They stare at her as she finishes a plantain. She does not take her eyes off them, and eventually they move on. Minnette pushes her plate aside and turns to the unfinished letter she has brought to the table.

I tossed a great deal before waking today, she writes. *The mornings here are cool, but that soon gets eaten up by a slow and steamy heat. And before the heat come the monkeys. What a nuisance they are! They have raided our pantry several times before and the mess they leave is awful. I wouldn't mind so much if they were tidy thieves. As it is, they behave like small-town thugs, ripping apart bags, smashing jars and strewing rubbish everywhere. Jaya has now locked everything into the cupboards. And woe betide the monkey that dares enter her pantry.*

Minnette recalls a recent altercation between Jaya and one of these miscreants. Jaya threw a pot of cold water at the creature, then knocked it on the head with a broom. It never returned, although Minnette suspects it was among this morning's unruly gang. She decides to keep a closer watch on them tomorrow, in case they are plotting something terrible.

She returns to the letter, describing Siri's recent visit. *'We are a nation of lions in thrall to the elephant,'* she writes, quoting him, then stops to consider what he meant. It is something Siri says frequently, without introduction or explanation. She shrugs. Siri is an artist prone to speaking in riddles. *Perhaps it means nothing,* she writes. *But artists are not known to waste their words. Isn't that right, Corbu?* He hasn't wasted many words on her, anyway, she admits. His letters are sporadic at best. And yet they have the power to transport her – to carry her into the front room of his apartment at No. 24 or back to her attic flat in Savile Row. *Write to me*, she wants to say, but she drops the pen before she can betray herself. *Why won't he write to me?* The question deserves an answer, and she has one ready. He is busy. 'He is aways busy,' she tells her empty plate.

She bends down to retrieve the pen. *I am sorry I couldn't come to Milan. I wanted to. I even packed a case. But I wanted to see the Ariyapala Lodge completed. It's almost finished – my first build. Also, I couldn't abandon them again. Mrs Ariyapala would have had a stroke!* She imagines old Mrs Ariyapala's face turning the colour of boiled beetroot. Minnette smiles then swats the thought down. *Poor Mrs Ariyapala*, she writes. *She can't help herself.*

Minnette describes the Ariyapala Lodge to him in detail, promising to send him photographs once the house is complete. She closes the letter with a wish for his continued good health, then signs herself his *oiseau* and lays the pen down.

Two monkeys sit across from her, one grooming the other. Minnette knows that she must check and re-check her drawings, tick off what has been done, note down what remains to do. Soon it will all be over. She sighs. Today has only begun, but once she has finished with her drawings, there will be nothing more to do but watch and wait for the morning to return.

———————

He is at his desk. Not his desk, but a rented desk, a desk common to these old colonial era hotels. Not just any desk, of course, but a desk fit for a viceroy or a visiting dignitary or a prime minister, like himself. A desk of mahogany, of ivory inlay and secret openings. He opens one to see if he can and closes it again. He scans the leaves of paper before him. The words must be perfect. The pitch must be perfect. He imagines the faces – all those sweating, dark faces – watching him, some waiting for him to say the wrong thing, others the right. The monks will be there, too, bald heads tilted slightly, ears cocked towards him, ready to attack with pious grapeshot. Dangerous, those monks.

He puts his smooth, dry palms on the desk, this beautiful desk, and levers himself to his feet. He paces in front of it, still thinking of the monks, their saffron robes, their polished heads – as shiny and hard as this desk. And he thinks.

The other party has the monks in its pocket. The other party has seduced the nuns, too – the bikkhunis, who rarely make public declarations, whose piety is unquestioned. Language and religion are the emotive issues. The majority are ruled by these concerns, and though his party has the majority right now despite these concerns – has in fact tamed these concerns – the majority are fickle. They must be reminded of what will make this country great. They must be reminded of the power of secularism. *These monks would have us scurry back to some mythical past,* he thinks. *They want to make heroes out of us Sinhalese and villains out of everyone else on this island.*

He leaves the weight and magnetism of the desk for the balcony. Looking up he can see the night sky awash with a foam of stars. *Millions of points of light,* he thinks, *one for every heart beating on earth.* One for every zealot and every saint. One for every atheist, secularist, monarchist and anarchist. One for every man, woman and child – a fraction of whom are here, in Ceylon, waiting for him to speak tomorrow. Waiting for him to tell them what is right for this country, what this island fought for to rid itself of the English, to finally smash the chain of imperialism.

It is not too much to say that he is the architect of that victory. It was that victory that sealed his subsequent victories. Now he stands under a sky that is as deep and righteous as the ocean and is ready for the deluge of stars that threatens to shower down on him. He needs it. He will need this special kind of light to reach out to the masses and make them listen. *First they must see me*, he thinks. *Then they will hear what I have to say.*

What will he say? He leans against the balcony railing and sees two bats jerking away from each other. He sees the spine of the moon reflected in Kandy Lake. He considers the relevance of location, the reverence with which people flock to this town to worship the last known relic of the Buddha. A tooth that no one has seen, much less touched. Dental remains with a questionable provenance, routinely paraded on the back of an elephant. Tomorrow, he will stand within earshot of the temple and declare Buddhism outside the bounds of politics. He shudders. *The monks will be enraged.*

They are an army with a power that needs no other weapon than precedent. He thinks of his own journey, from devout Buddhist to Anglican and back again. Now, less devout, more pragmatic. He has switched beliefs to suit his path: Christianity guaranteed him privilege at school; Buddhism granted him access to politics. In his advanced age, he believes in neither. He goes to temple to make a point with his constituents, not because he wants to perform the austerities required of *sil*.

The *sangha*, too, is grossly pragmatic. He has come to this realisation late in life. Perhaps this is the enlightenment he was seeking in his younger years. Perhaps this is the complete awareness he was striving for. He knows all too well the material weaknesses of the order. *So many fat monks, stuffing themselves on the charity of others.*

The other party has been buttering up the monks with gifts, food, money. Their supporters scorn Ceylon's path to independence for being too peaceful. They condemn Ceylon's membership in the Commonwealth as a sycophantic allegiance to her colonisers. *What would they have us do? Declare ourselves a republic like India?* He recalls the bloodshed and violence that accompanied that country's independence and grows weary. Sectarian killings, displacement, war. *It was supposed to be the greatest day in India's history. Instead, it is remembered for its barbaric carnage. What we achieved was independence by diplomacy. It was a battle fought and won at the very highest levels. What is the shame in that?*

It is true that Ceylon's independence followed India's. India led the way and Ceylon followed. But it is also true that independence came to Ceylon when she was ready to seize it. There is no shame in that. He knows it, and so do the thousands who support his party. After all, Ceylon is now a beacon to her neighbouring countries. Its standard of living, education, employment – all of these things make it a great country. He nods. He is right to be proud of what he has achieved. There is still the question of introducing the vernaculars, to satisfy the demand of the lower classes who wish to carry out their jobs in their mother tongue and not English. They have a point, of course. He himself has come from the lower classes, although many people, including him, forget this.

But for now, the pressing need is to find a way to quell the Buddhist element. This will be his final act, he decides. His weariness earths him. What he wants right now is to be back in Colombo, riding his horse along Galle Face Green, the ocean sighing in the half-light, his spine loosening gently with the sway of the horse's gait. He considers his two sons – Dudley and Robert – and wonders which is the worthy successor. Dudley is the next in line, but too soft, he muses. *He was always too sensitive, always staring at the sky and getting shat on by crows.* He clasps the balcony railing, anchoring himself as laughter threads through his muscles like a chord of music. *Poor Dudley,* he thinks, then giggles like a schoolboy.

Fireflies flash by his temples. He sobers, returns to the case at hand. How to get rid of the monks? What did the Americans do? Separate the church from the state. So too must Ceylon, he thinks, then reminds himself that this is what he has already done. So, what do you do when the majority wants religionists in power? Remind the religionists of their duty. He nods, returns to his desk, and picks up his pen. He thinks for a while, then writes: *There is no need to reduce such a sublime creed to a state activity.*

He smiles and lays down his pen.

———————

'There is no need to reduce such a sublime creed to a state activity.' The words pinch another smile from her. With these words, declaimed in front of the Temple of the Tooth, the Prime Minister raked the monks back into their rightful patch. Minnette wanted to shout out her assent. Instead she offered the dry applause expected of a woman of her class. Her admiration for Ceylon's leader is tempered only by her reservations about language. *What is the point of knowing Sinhala or Tamil outside of Ceylon?*

We didn't become a great country with them. We did it with English. She shakes her head. Not for her the sentimental parochialism of the nationalist. She knows the architect wouldn't approve of this perspective, but what does he know of Ceylon? He calls her his *Inde*. That alone tells her how much he cares to know.

After the rally, Minnette's parents introduced her to Desmond. Cambridge educated, a lawyer – hand-picked by Minnette's sister Marcia and her husband sidekick Werner. Minnette could see the eager look in her parents' eyes, and so immediately took against Desmond. She was surprised to find him pleasantly likeable. She had dinner with him and his sister, at their invitation. She took Siri along to distract him from Eric's loss – and to save her from boredom should things go badly.

Desmond and his sister, Lakmini, proved diverting hosts. They smiled when, on Minnette's insistence, Siri told them he had painted a large mural for the Ariyapala Lodge. 'Sha!' said Desmond, while Lakmini shook her head and looked impressed. Talk soon turned to the Prime Minister's speech and Lakmini, reminded of the monks' shock, extemporised sacrilegious recitations of Buddhist verses. Desmond broke into an impersonation of the leader of the opposition. The pair were like a cabaret act, and Minnette laughed, forgetting to put a hand over her mouth. No one seemed to notice Siri slowly turning to stone. Nudging him eventually, Minnette found he was as silent and impenetrable as Sigiriya itself.

'Come on, Siri,' she said, 'please don't be like that,' but Siri would not be moved. He neither ate nor drank and when it was finally time to go, it took two generous prods from Minnette to oust him from his chair and eventually the room. Minnette walked Siri to a taxi, all

the while apologising for dragging him out that evening.
'Such good news, Siri. Your painting – going up at the
Ariyapalas' house. It is stunning, absolutely stunning.'
This seemed to reach something deep inside him and
a smile softened his eyes before dissipating. He looked
at Minnette without seeing her, his gaze slicing through
her to the trees behind. Minnette watched his face open
like a rose, full of terror and sorrow. She wanted to put
her arms around him, to put her hands over his eyes and
stop whatever was tormenting him at that moment, but
there was something in his manner, something cold. She
backed away from him.

———————

Minnette arrives at the Ariyapala Lodge in one of her best
saris. As she ascends the central staircase of this house
– with its finely painted black balusters – she imagines
what she will say to the man she is about to meet. And
then she is upstairs, and he is holding his hand out to her
as she mouths the words she was just practising.

The Prime Minister greets Minnette with wide eyes.
'So, you were at the AA?' he says, sounding impressed. 'I
believe we have heard of your progress here in Ceylon.'
He studies the interior closely, taking in the peculiarly
Kandyan artwork – the doors inset with palm leaf, the
detailed design work on the staircase. When he enters
the living area, his eye goes immediately to Siri's ecstatic
wall mural alive with the cacophony of a market crowd.
The Prime Minister stops and considers the painting for a
long while before asking Minnette who the artist is.

She takes him to the balcony, pointing out the views of
the town and the opportunity the building's aspect offers

for observing sunrises and sunsets. 'The glass doors,' she explains, 'allow in continous daylight.'

The Ariyapalas, who have been following behind, nod vigorously. 'We see ourselves as pioneers,' says Mrs Ariyapala. 'We gave Miss de Silva her first opportunity to design and build a house here in Ceylon.' She looks at Minnette without meeting her gaze. 'It has been a… an interesting process. And the house is truly beyond anything we could have imagined. It has given us an entirely new way of living.'

Minnette sees how uncomfortable the Ariyapalas are and feels sorry for them. She is grateful that they can see the house for what it is. She is also pleased that Siri's work has caught the eye of the Prime Minister.

'Today is a day that looks to the future,' says the Prime Minister, 'one that heralds the construction of a new Ceylon. Good work, Miss de Silva.' With that he is gone – to lay the foundation stone of the new wing of the Temple of the Tooth.

Minnette is surprised and flattered that the Prime Minister took time out of his schedule to inspect her work. She takes it as vindication of months of argument and negotiation. Her joy is short-lived. When she re-enters the kitchen, she realises with a drop of the stomach that her calculations of the kitchen measurements were incorrect. She sees the Ariyapalas' cook and servant girl, Dilini, standing on stools to work at the counters. She has miscalculated the ratios, adapting them to the larger frame of the western woman. She berates herself for failing to apply the Modulor, then corrects herself. The Modulor is irrelevant here, based as it is on the proportions of a tall man.

When she apologises to Dilini, she looks confused. '*Nona*, this is very beautiful,' she says, 'the blue tiles are like the sea.' The Ariyapalas are no less enthusiastic, telling Minnette that the house provides them daily pleasures: exhilarating views of Kandy Lake, dramatic sunrises and sunsets, seclusion.

Minnette returns home triumphant. She shuts herself in her room, pulls out her writing paper and begins a letter to him.

Corbu, I am vindicated, she writes, telling him of the last few days, skipping gently over the details of her outings with Desmond. She regrets the omission, however, and inserts several paragraphs on their first meeting and subsequent dinner. She spares no detail, dwelling on his immaculate grooming and quick wit.

Lovely, and such a gentleman. Marcia and Werner have taste! Lakmini is divine, Corbu, you would love her. Such a kind face with clever green eyes. Minnette smiles, thinking of Lakmini's sharp observations the previous night. *I am among the living again. It is such a relief to finally find someone I can talk to. Siri is such hard work these days. Even in the old days, before his friend passed, he didn't say very much. Conversation with Siri is haphazard. Throw a word out into the darkness and he may catch it or match it with another word or two. How can I converse with a man who speaks in riddles?*

Minnette shrinks, remembering her friend's stony silence the night she took him to meet Desmond and Lakmini. She wonders whether they offended him with their sarcasm, but brushes the thought away. Siri may look like a monk, but he is not religious. He is an artist, after all.

Mimi is so far away, but you, my dear friend, you who are so close to my heart, you are the furthest of all. She re-reads the sentence and is surprised by the emotion in it. She had thought her acquaintance with Desmond was enough to dampen the spell.

How I wish I could have come to Italy to see you once again. A reunion in Milan. How wonderful that would have been. But my work has kept me here – I'm sure you understand. So, my suitcase, like me, remains propped up in a corner of my room. Today I removed two blouses and one shawl from the bag and returned them to their appropriate drawers. I should be finished unpacking by mid-October. Or, perhaps you are coming to India shortly? Perhaps I don't need to empty my bag at all? When do you return, Corbu? After all, India is not so difficult for me to get to. If you tell me now, a trip can be arranged. Or you could come here. I could arrange some talks, maybe even a commission. There are many opportunities here as well.

I realise that you're busy, but that is only because your genius demands this of you. You thrive on the possible in the impossible. Just look at Chandigarh. It is a work of such magnitude and you have embraced it. Your team are among the finest. Elizabeth and Richard: of course I remember them! Elizabeth, I see, has caught your eye. But your description of Richard is unfair, Corbu. His features may not be memorable, but his skill – we were all, at the AA, so impressed by him. Elizabeth I only knew to say hi to. But I don't for a minute believe that she would do anything to undermine her husband. You are being naughty, Corbu. Elizabeth is morally upright. I feel sure of it.

By contrast, lovely Mimi slants rather, like that marvel of engineering, the Pisa Tower. Still, I love her for it. And so do many others, sincerely or otherwise. She has been thinking of coming to Ceylon to visit me to escape the drudgery of the Big Smoke. I know her life is far from boring and that she is more likely to be running from scandal than anything else, but she is always welcome whatever her reasons. Perhaps she will bring one or both of her Italian friends with her!

Francesco has not written to me, but he did send me a sketch shortly after I returned to Ceylon. It was a replica of the painting I'd sat for before I left – quite a good likeness, I think. He signed it with a kiss. So affectionate, the Italians. I wonder whether Mimi will bring him with her when she comes?

Minnette puts the pen down and lights a cigarette. A chill has crept into the air now that the sun has flared out. She brushes stray ash from the pages of her letter, wondering whether he knows. Whether her longing is obvious. She remembers them lying on the floor at No. 24 and shrugs. The snow falling against the window – this is what she focuses on – those fat, goose-feather flakes, shutting them in and everything else out. Here, in Ceylon, she is an involuntary shut-in. There are no galleries, no fine operas, no pubs.

This island is lost, like a jewel from a precious heirloom. I have been spending too much time with Siri, I am writing in riddles. What I mean is, it is just so different here. Cultural life is limited to the tastes of a few and those tastes often tend to the provincial. Which is why a painter like Siri is still not well known. Lionel managed to slip past and make a reputation for himself abroad. If not for that, he would have languished here. Most people are embarrassed by the audacity of his photographs. 'Nothing but naked men,' they say. They don't see the beauty in the execution, the honest portrayal of human beings labouring, whether as fishermen or toddy tappers. These people would rather paint a vision of Ceylon that is stripped of its bucolic truth. To them, Lionel's photographs are a betrayal.

So, this is what it is to be in Ceylon, Corbu. Away from you, away from my friends, away from an informed, critical eye. You asked me, didn't you? But I should not be so negative. After all, enclosed here is a clipping from the Times of Ceylon. She irons the newspaper article flat with her palm. *They ran a special feature on the Ariyapala Lodge. Now, everyone is talking about 'that spectacular house on the hill'! Tell me what you think. I am sending photographs through Mimi, who will be back in Paris in December.*

And, before I forget, happy birthday, dearest.

Minnette blows smoke into the night. She wants to cross out that word – *dearest* – and leave it impaled on the page.

V

December 1951 – January 1952

Back in Paris, the architect finds several letters from her. They have been waiting on his desk since October, while he has been flying across India. On top of them is an envelope of photographs. He studies these with a smile. Her house – its balcony with detailed balustrade, the glass 'walled' salon, the views. *C'est formidable*, he thinks, *she is learning.* He sits at his desk and begins the work of opening her many letters. Inside he finds a matter-of-fact tone, and talk of another man. This new man puzzles him. He smiles and again the thought comes to him: *She is learning.* He reads her description of this 'D' – this Cambridge interloper – and feels envious. He reaches for his pen, ready to defend himself, but stops. This is what she wants. And he is Le Corbusier, not some pimply teenager. He knocks the pen off the table and leaves it on the ground. *She can wait a little longer*, he decides.

But as he reads further, he remembers her hair, pulled into a lustrous knot and pinned with roses. Those moist petals against the metallic sheen of her braid. Flowers he plucked with two fingers from their inky nest.

Cher oiseau, he writes. *I am just now back from India and what do I find but a pile of letters from my little bird. I looked for you in Milan, oiseau, but you did not come. And only now I find the reason why. Bravo on completing the Ariyapala Lodge, Minnette! The house looks marvellous.*

The photos of the house arrived with Minnette's 'pale friend', Mimi. When his workers at No. 35 handed him this envelope, they seemed to smirk. It was not the envelope but its bearer who prompted the response. The architect shrugs. *Ils sont comme ça.*

I like very much the detailing you introduced on the balcony, the purity of the circle which appears at regular intervals along the parapet/balustrade. Before I even opened your letter, I found these pictures – thank you for sending them to me.

He empties another envelope and pauses to read the newspaper clipping which contains a lengthy article by her. In it, she writes of synthesising regional tradition, both geographical and cultural, with the needs of contemporary living – what she calls, *modern regionalism.*

Instead of the cosmetic application of modernism, she writes, *that shallow copycatting that is ubiquitous in Ceylon, we must look at and understand our own traditions. It is only in understanding them that we can determine which concepts are still valid for contemporary living. It is these that we must integrate with Modern techniques, not forgetting the vast skill of our traditional craftspeople and artists. Indeed, a building should be a combination of all these disciplines: the architect's, the craftsperson's and the artist's.*

The architect considers the photograph of that grand mural, painted by her mute friend, and nods. He reads on: *Our extended families are large, and our homes must expand to accommodate them when entertaining.* To this end, she has introduced sliding doors and panels so that rooms can be partitioned off or opened out where necessary. (The architect smiles, recalling his own use of partitioned rooms for his first build – his parents' home.) She satisfies her concerns about heat and glare by introducing deep eaves and coopting outdoor spaces, adding the flexibility of shutters or other devices.

The verandah, she writes, *was the most enjoyable place in our homes, but today, land is too expensive to accommodate these wide galleries that were a staple of traditional dwellings. Covered balconies, louvred transom windows and central, open courtyards – the 'meda midula' – are effective ways of creating cross-ventilation, allowing the steady flow of air in our warm and, at times, oppressive climate. The master-builders of our ancient city of Anuradhapura used columns to achieve this sort of airflow as far back as the third century BC. We can use columned spaces similarly, but with an entirely Modern approach.*

The architect considers the photographs again: the sun-filled living room that opens onto that impressive balcony, the split-level rooms, the doors inset with bespoke textiles. Her manifesto – for this is how it reads to him – promises something new and exceptional, even if it doesn't observe his own principles. There is nothing of the Ville Radieuse in there, but what of it?

Merci pour ton essai excellent, he writes, unable to express himself in English. *Tu as bien expliqué tes idées. Je crois que tu es en train de bouleverser l'architecture en Ceylan. Vas y! Ils vont te suivre jusqu'au bout.* He writes to her of Ahmedabad, Udaipur and the Amber palace. She is clever, his *oiseau,* her essay is another proof of this. She can follow the thread of his thoughts, his theories. She is not like Vonn. Vonn is interested in wine and food and sex and children. At least, she was. Now she is only interested in wine and children. It disgusts him to see his wife like that. Sometimes, her company is unbearable, but he sits with her anyway, because it is expected – because he has flown back to Paris for no one but her.

He stares out the window. The white stuff is falling again. Another Christmas arrives. He recalls that evening with her, watching the snow fall, the apartment noiseless and waiting.

He looks down the corridor towards the bedroom, then looks away. Vonn is waiting for a gift he will never give. She is too old, anyway. He has bought her a little dog instead. *She can carry it around and dress it if she likes. Corbu need not be too involved.*

He stands up with the envelope and decides to post it immediately. He longs to be out in the air, under the snow, and within moments, he is.

Minnette re-reads his letter, searching. Sweat pricks her brow even in the morning cool. At first she thinks she has misunderstood something, but it is clear on second reading that she hasn't. He has been to India and back without mentioning it before. He invites her to Italy, and remains silent on India, knowing that one is impossible for her, while the other –

Yes. The other. It would have been easy: a trip to India. Anger beads on her forehead, tightens her back. She watches the words collide against one another as her palm swallows them up. She throws the balled-up letter into the bin.

Standing by the window, she stares out across the hills, down towards Kandy Lake. Birds chatter in the trees; a gecko flashes up her bedroom wall.

I like very much the detailing. His words, indisputable now. His critique of the Ariyapala Lodge is full of pride. *He claims it for himself,* she thinks, but this is not true. The architect is genuinely impressed with her work and her thinking. He does not waste words. She turns and plucks the crushed papers from the bin. Flattening them out on her desk, she reads their contents for a third time. This time she forgets herself, clinging to his praise. She has done well.

In fact, there has been nothing but praise for the Ariyapala Lodge since its completion. The Ariyapalas have had a steady flow of guests, all of whom, she knows, have come away from the place in awe. Minnette has received several contracts – a house in Piachaud Gardens nearby, another in Colombo – and Siri has won numerous commissions. Even the Prime Minister heralded the lodge as a beacon of modernity. Yet it is *his* words that matter most to her. She pores over them again and again, forgetting her anger now, drinking them in as she would a bottle of wine.

When she goes downstairs, she finds Dr Sivathamby standing in the hallway. She dislikes Dr Sivathamby and his worn-out checked hankies, but greets him with a smile and offers him tea. He shakes his head and Minnette is relieved. She wonders what she would do if he drank tea from a saucer again, as he did the first time she met him. She was just a girl then, and had laughed out loud before being sent outside.

'How is Amma?' she asks. He mops his cheeks and forehead with a handkerchief and sighs. Before he can say anything, Papa appears.

'Ah, Siva,' Papa says, and escorts him into the garden. Minnette watches them wander through the pergola, their backs to her. She goes through to the dining room where a breakfast of fruit awaits her. She eats mango and imagines what Dr Sivathamby might have said had he had a chance to speak. *Ah, Minnette. Your mother. Ah…*

Dr Sivathamby reserves his considerable expository skills for her father. For Minnette, there is only hesitation – a kind of futile diplomacy. Upstairs, Minnette's mother lies in bed, sweating and listless. She eats nothing. Nothing will agree with her.

Minnette looks at the hollowed out mango skin and feels guilty. She has eaten half a mango and is poised to eat the other. She has already had a plantain and some buttered bread. The guilt does not stop her from eating one slice of pineapple and then another, before demolishing the rest of the mango.

She remembers her mother slicing through mangoes with a paring knife, scoring the flesh, and laying out one half each for Minnette and Marcia when they were girls. Minnette always traded her half for the seed. While Marcia and Amma spooned ochre diamonds into their mouths, Minnette would suck the slippery seed until it was bare.

Minnette returns to the main hall via the verandah. She spots her father and the doctor sitting on Amma's bench beneath the jasmine creepers. Some years back, Minnette's mother had the bench placed there especially, so that she could sit and read, enveloped in the flowers' fragrance. Seeing the doctor and her father sitting quietly on Amma's bench – Papa looking at the flowers, the doctor at his own feet – Minnette smiles. The two men look like a couple on an awkward first night out. She thinks this might be the first time her father has actually sat on that bench for any length of time. Papa does his ruminating upstairs, in his study; Amma reads her books and newspapers on the bench. Sometimes, she would sit for hours and Minnette would wander by to pick the jasmine off her hair and sari, tossing the small white flowers into the grass.

The doctor brushes flowers from his lap and shoulders, pulling out his hankie more and more frequently to dab at his nose. Papa is oblivious. Flowers land on his head, his lapels, his knees, and remain there until the wind blows them away.

Upstairs, Minnette listens to her mother's breathing from the bedroom doorway. Amma is asleep. Her skin is the colour of putty. Her eyelids are like shells – smooth and glossy. Minnette watches the gentle floating of the bedcovers, their reassuring rise and fall. Minutes later, she is back in her room, searching for a distraction. She reaches for the letter, but before she can open it, Marcia walks in.

Minnette is startled to see her sister standing in the middle of her room, dressed in a grey blazer and skirt, and a blouse buttoned right up to the neck. Her cheeks are pink and her hair is clotted at the temples. 'Marcia!' cries Minnette. 'You're here already?'

'This heat is frightful,' says Marcia, as she grasps Minnette's shoulders and kisses the air next to her cheeks. 'It's been a terrible journey. Werner is asleep... how's Amma?'

Minnette shakes her head. 'You'd better ask Papa.'

'I will. He's with Sivathamby right now. Perhaps he'll have something coherent to say now that the doctor's been to see her.'

Minnette sighs. She suggests a bath and a rest to Marcia. 'Papa and the doctor won't be done for a while,

I don't think,' she explains. 'And do try wearing a sari, you might find it more comfortable. You can borrow one of mine if you don't have any.'

Marcia cringes.

'Then perhaps unbutton your collar and forget about the blazer?'

Marcia looks conflicted. It has been too long since she wore a sari – too long since she indulged in low-cut necklines and backless dresses. Back then she was single and charming, tempting a young, wealthy and unattached Werner Reinhardt with her subtle cleavage.

Minnette has always found them an unlikely pair. When Minnette had been practising architecture in Bombay, Marcia had fled India without warning, leaving behind *Marg* and the Bombay Intellectual. Somewhere along that journey, she lost a little of her flamboyance as well. She had been working as a journalist when she first met Werner. She'd been assigned to interview him for the *Times*. They had only exchanged a greeting when he tripped over his shoelace and fell at her feet, taking a teacup and saucer with him. They were together barely a year when Minnette moved to London, and married shortly after in Cambridge, Marcia wearing a simple gown in cotton lace. ('Nothing showy,' she had told Minnette earlier, it being her second marriage.) At the reception, a humble affair at one of the colleges, she laughed throatily at Werner's dancing. And when he got drunk and fell off a punt, Marcia dove in to rescue him, dress and all.

Within a year of getting married, Werner turned into a responsible, cautious man, while Marcia's collars grew higher and tighter in direct proportion to a bizarre new interest in the Temperance Movement.

Nostalgic for the Marcia of old, Minnette presses her once more. 'I promise you, leave a couple of those buttons undone and you'll feel much better.' She smiles, gently undoing one of her sister's collar buttons.

Marcia's initial affront is followed by growing relief. She takes Minnette's hands and squeezes them. 'Right, I must see what that layabout Werner is up to,' she says and leaves the room.

With Marcia and Werner's arrival, Nell Cottage soon acquires a festive spirit. Marcia and Minnette decorate the house with velvet bows, Jaya parcels out Amma's Christmas cake for the many visitors who will drop in during the season, and Werner and Papa make sure the liquor cabinet is well stocked.

Amma remains confined to her bed, although her condition has improved. Minnette offers her something special every day – mango, plantain, a slice of Jaya's love cake – and each day, Amma gently shakes her head. Marcia tries to convince her to taste the food, while Minnette nods and takes it away, determined to try again the next day. Dr Sivathamby returns several times at Papa's request to check on her and speak at length with Papa. To Minnette and Marcia he says very little, apart from assuring them that she is getting better. Christmas comes and goes.

One morning, Minnette walks in with a plate of mango and love cake, and Amma sits up and says, 'Here, let me have some.' Minnette watches her mother as she picks through the fruit and cake with the delicacy and thoroughness of a bird. By the next day, Amma's cheeks are warm with colour, and within a few days, she is sitting on her bench under the jasmine, reading the newspaper and surveying the garden.

As she watches her mother from her bedroom window, Minnette is unknotted by relief. She puts a hand out to steady herself as her body loosens with unexpected force. In two days, they will leave the hills and travel down to the coast. There is a New Year's Eve party at the Mount Lavinia hotel. Desmond has invited Minnette and her family to join him and his sister there. Minnette sees her suitcase, which she had taken so long to unpack, still propped against the almariya. She opens it and finds there are still three saris inside – clothes carefully chosen to wear in Milan for Corbu. She shrugs – there is no need to unpack now – and lays some dresses alongside them.

———————

When they arrive at Aunty Sheila and Uncle Reggie's – old friends of the family in Mount Lavinia – it is late afternoon, and everyone is weary from the drive. Minnette's legs have gone numb and Marcia, who has resumed wearing the blazer/blouse combination, cants to one side with exhaustion. Her face is bright pink and covered in a fine mist of sweat. Aunty Sheila, who is English and from Tonbridge Wells, takes one look at her and barks, 'What *men*? Someone tell this child she is in Ceylon. She might get away with that nonsense in Kandy, but down here, she'll have a stroke. *Ayyo!*' With this, Aunty Sheila hurries upstairs in her leather slippers, sari wafting behind her.

Marcia finally relents and wears a summer dress to dinner. It is Aunty Sheila's idea. It is also Aunty Sheila's dress: a shell-printed cotton frock from the 1940s. Marcia looks ten years younger and Werner seems so astonished to see his wife's collarbone in the open that he looks at nothing else for the rest of the evening. Everyone dines on crab curry and fried rice, and after a few glasses of wine (Marcia excepted), the party moves off to the verandah where a convivial lethargy descends on them. Marcia and Werner curl into a planter's chair. Reggie and Papa share a Scotch, with Reggie egging Minnette's father on: '*Machang*, drink. You're on holiday, *men*.' Amma and Sheila play a game of cards, and Minnette sits off to the side. From where she is, she can see the ocean, which seems closer tonight than usual. She wonders whether it is creeping further inland, as everyone has been predicting, ready to storm the ramparts erected some years back. The ocean had once threatened Mount Lavinia train station. It is only a matter of time before it erodes the entire coastline, swallowing up the railway tracks with it.

Minnette leaves the verandah for the beach. She is drawn to the rush and push of the water. Black waves hiss in the darkness, sucking sand with each retreat. Looking back at the house, she can see her family: Amma, Papa, Sheila, Reggie, Werner, Marcia – lit up by lamps on the verandah. They seem fragile in the winking light. *One lap of the sea's tongue and the light would go out,* she thinks, *taking everyone with it.*

She wakes with the sea's lips poised at her ear. 'Shhh,' it keeps saying and Minnette immediately remembers her first meeting with the architect – the *shhhh* of his *enchanté*. She wants arrack, a cigarette. She wants him with her, a crow and his *oiseau du paradis*, wings drawn up around their weary heads. From her bed, she can see the ocean surf up to the shore, its manner casual, its intent unreadable.

She returns to her desk, finds his last letter and re-reads it. She imagines Christmas in Paris. The snow, Vonn in red velvet, and him at the head of the table carving a goose. Add two apple-cheeked children and the painting would be complete. For a moment she permits herself the possibility of a different painting, where a child sits on either side of Minnette and Corbu. A weight slips from her throat to her chest.

She wonders at her sister's slow transformation – the magic that a loosened neckline can bring. *He* would approve, she thinks. She knows he would. He has never appreciated a woman who makes an effort to cover her charms. 'It is not natural,' *he* would say. Minnette feels herself growing defensive of Marcia's dress sense. *It is her choice. Even if ill-judged in this weather.*

She smiles, thinking of Marcia's chaotic appearance in her room the day she arrived, her own surprise and bemusement. She tries to reconcile that wild-eyed figure with the one she saw nestling with Werner in a planter's chair last night, the two of them as snug as two ferrets. What a difference a few days make, she thinks. Again she recalls her sister's union with Werner – their accidental meeting. If she hadn't been assigned to interview Werner, the German-born Englishman and rubber importer, Marcia would never have met him. From the letters Marcia sent her at the time, Minnette knows that her sister had started seeing a young film-maker shortly after she left India. He was someone she knew from her film days in the 1930s. Back then she had found him intriguing, until the English poet, whom Minnette adored, came along and ruined his chances. Marcia found her way back to the film-maker once again, only to be distracted by bumbling Werner. She would always say that Werner's devotion to her was plain from the moment he fell at her feet. 'Oh, he *says* he tripped over his shoelace,' she would intone with a nod, 'but really, he was just looking for an excuse to touch my ankle.'

The film-maker had melted from the picture after that. He went off to work with Powell and Pressburger, which pricked Marcia. She still saw him once or twice while in London, although he had found a new object to pursue by then. 'He was not constant,' Marcia would say, damning him for having the temerity to continue with his life after her.

A bit of old Marcia is back, writes Minnette. *You would like her, Corbu.*

———————

At breakfast, Minnette watches her sister stir her tea, and spoon marmalade onto a slice of toast. Werner is so engrossed with his newspaper that he feels obliged to share it with everyone, reading out passages, and lacing each with commentary. Papa and Amma are still upstairs. Reggie has gone for a jog, and Sheila is doing calisthenics on the verandah.

Minnette tucks into an egg hopper and onion sambol.

Marcia grimaces at her, peeling a plantain to go with a thickly buttered slice of bread. Butter has been a scarcity, with rations being doled out erratically. Marcia spreads what looks like a tablespoon of it onto her bread. Minnette stares at the plate.

As if reading her thoughts, Marcia takes a large bite and smiles. 'At least I won't stink of fish and onions tonight. Desmond is coming, you know.'

Two weeks have elapsed since Minnette last saw Desmond. He dropped in at Nell Cottage to ask after Amma. Minnette showed him some of her drawings and took him round the garden so he could see the blooms studding the pergola. It was nothing more than she would have done for any friend, but Marcia invested the gesture with something more intimate.

Marcia stops chewing her butter and bread and looks at Minnette as if trying to count each line on her face.

'So they've finally done it,' bursts in Werner, his eyes trained on the newspaper.

Marcia turns.

'They've banned the British national anthem.'

'Yes,' says Marcia, adopting Papa's tone. 'It's the prerogative of an independent nation.'

'Well, not banned as such,' Werner continues. 'It will be permitted during royal visits. So they will have at least one more opportunity to hear it ringing out across this jewelled isle.'

'February,' says Marcia, referring to Princess Elizabeth's impending visit.

'February,' Werner replies, and lapses into silent contemplation of the *Times of Ceylon*.

Minnette slips back to her room, unnoticed.

———

When Minnette goes downstairs again, it is to join a crowd of well-heeled men and women – at least 150 of them, she thinks. The women are dressed in their finest, most colourful saris or chic dresses. Necklines are low, the better to display several strands of pearls or plain gold. The men are suited, though as the whiskey flows more liberally, collars loosen and ties are stuffed into pockets.

Minnette catches sight of Desmond. Without realising, she smiles at the lock of hair dangling over his forehead.

When they are finally within earshot, she speaks mockingly of her sister's assumptions about her relationship with him. 'After all, we're just friends, aren't we?' she says, taking his hand. Desmond nods slowly and disengages from her grasp. 'How about a drink?' he asks, and disappears.

While Desmond searches out a drink, Minnette settles in next to her mother and Sheila Aunty. Amma is telling her about the bougainvillea which are currently swooning all over the periphery of Nell Cottage.

'But that reminds me of Sissinghurst, Agnes,' exclaims Sheila, jerking her wrist and sending wine splashing across the front of her georgette sari. Whenever Sheila gets drunk, Sissinghurst Castle looms into view. A single visit has convinced her that the gardens there are better than any in Ceylon, including Peradeniya. *She is wrong*, thinks Minnette. *They can't compete.* Sheila's face is flushed and whole bundles of hair make a wild dash for freedom from the chignon at the back of her head. 'The gardens at Sissinghurst are marvellous, *men*. Think of the Rose Garden – and the White Garden. Who could have imagined such a variety of flowers – all in white!' More shakes of the arm and the wine seeps through to her skin. 'Breath-taking. Minnette, you must have gone when you were in England, no? Marvellous, isn't it?'

Minnette nods while her mother leans towards her friend. 'Sheila, darling, perhaps you would like a drink of soda?' Without waiting for a reply, Amma signals to Minnette who excuses herself and heads to the bar.

Minnette finds Desmond again while scouting for the soda. The service has completely degenerated, with many of the servants abandoning their posts as soon as Reggie and Sheila abandoned sobriety. Those operating the bar, however, are more disciplined. Minnette catches sight of Desmond, who is grinning and chatting with a slim, pretty young woman. Minnette has not seen her before. She is young and flirtatious, and when she laughs, it is like the sound of running water. She wears a deep blue, halter-neck dress that sweeps right to the floor. Minnette cannot stop staring at her, thinking how much *he* would admire her, too.

Standing there, watching Desmond and the halter-neck woman, Minnette becomes gradually aware of the soda bottle in her hand. She exchanges a glance with the bar man, who seems to be waiting for her to say something. She orders a shot of whiskey, which she marries with the soda and some lime juice. Before she knows it, a cigarette is on her lips, the measured burn of smoke chasing the fire that is already halfway down her throat.

Desmond does not notice her. Minnette asks the barman to pour her another whiskey into a separate glass which she takes to the edge of the verandah where the most drunken of the guests have beached themselves. The sea rasps against the sand, and Minnette thinks of all the miles that divide her from the architect, whole countries of people standing between the two of them. As she watches the night, the moon melts into the water casting mercury onto the shore. Palm trees lean further and further in, poised as if waiting to dive. And Minnette's head sways in rhythm to the gentle loll of palm fronds blowing in the breeze.

She doesn't know how long her eyes have been closed. She doesn't remember closing them. But when she opens them again, Siri is sitting next to her.

'The moon does strange things when caught out over the water,' he says. He is doing what he always does –

speaking to no one in particular, directing his speech at whatever happens to be in front of him: in this case, an empty plot of sand and the distant sea. 'It indulges in a night-long repartée with the ocean, jumping from sky to water to sky again, trading places with its reflection with such frequency that come morning, it has forgotten where it is and simply fades away with the coming sun.'

Minnette kisses her teeth. She wants to pinch Siri but offers him the Scotch left in her glass instead. Rebuffed, she tips it out onto the beach to foil temptation. 'Have you seen my sister anywhere?'

Silence. Mundane questions are not Siri's forté.

Minnette tries to get up, but her sari is in such disarray, she stays put. She leans against Siri, who takes no notice of her weight or her presence, and surveys the area around them. Couples lie in little heaps here and there, wound around one another in drunken slumber. A portly man is stretched out in full abundance on the verandah, snoring beside an empty bottle of champagne. Two young ladies have fallen asleep holding hands in a planter's chair. And in the chair next to them, a man and woman cling to one another like frightened children.

'She's there.'

Minnette flinches, startled. Siri has not followed her gaze, but somehow seems to know what has caught her attention.

'On the verandah.'

She ignores him, beguiled by the embracing couple. Not one limb is out of place – no secretly numbing arms or laboured necks. Their union is seamless, with all the solid tranquility of a marble sculpture. She can see neither's expression: both are turned towards one another, the man's face obscured by the woman's head. She imagines them with still lips and pulsing eyelids, both caught up in the same, fervent dream. In the gathering light, she can make out swells of red silk rippling to the ground. A sari so luxuriant, so unlike her sister. And yet it is; the couple are Marcia and Werner. She had not thought them capable of such easy passion. Not any more.

The air turns cool and Minnette leans in closer to Siri. He remains still, contemplating the slowly dissolving moon. 'The dance is almost over,' he whispers.

Minnette wonders where Desmond and the beautiful woman have gone. They are not among the couples scattered around them. She wonders about his sister, Lakmini, whom she hasn't seen all evening. She wonders whether Amma and Sheila are still waiting for their soda water. She wonders herself to sleep, right there, against Siri's shoulder. But when she wakes in the morning, he is gone, she is lying in a planter's chair, and a column of ants is marching around the chair leg.

Sunlight fills the house like a giant spotlight, detailing the mess engulfing Reggie and Sheila's. Bottles litter the verandah, wine pools in corners, bits of food are smeared all over the floor. Ants feast left and right, scurrying from one stain to another. *Thank God for the servants,* she thinks. They sweep the ants away and tend to the floor on hands and knees, all without complaint. Minnette thinks of Jaya and checks herself. If ever there was a party at Nell Cottage, Jaya would spend the next day casting admonishing looks at the household. Drinking and carousing were signs of weak moral fibre in her eyes. Even Papa took to drinking his arrack in his study, away from her withering gaze.

Minnette clears a few bottles from the tables, relieved that Jaya is down south with her family. Sheila calmly gives orders while polishing the woodwork. Marcia is right behind her, buffing the silver and glassware. Reggie is upstairs in bed, as are Amma and Papa. Minnette creeps upstairs, too, ducking the chaos.

In her room, the sun is louder than the crows outside. She can see Siri in the distance, lying like a dead man under a tree, with an arm over his face. Downstairs, the servants and Sheila and Marcia are sweeping, washing, polishing. Minnette's head throbs, her mouth is dry. *Some tea would do me good,* she thinks, as she lies down and falls into a thick, relentless sleep.

When she wakes again, it is after three. She chastises herself for sleeping the morning and half the afternoon away, like some dissolute aesthete. Still, it is fitting, given that the afternoon will be devoted to one of Sheila's informal salon days. Anyone could drop in. Whoever they may be, Sheila will greet them with an 'Ah, hallo. Come, come. Come and sit down, *men*.' Sheila has embraced Ceylon's artists, counting among her regular visitors Lionel Wendt (before he died), George Keyt, Ivan Peries and other members of the illustrious '43 Group. She tolerates their hangers-on as well, always wary of turning away a potential new star. She may doubt the splendours of Ceylon's flora, but her appreciation for Ceylonese art is absolute. As for the artists, they are flattered by this English woman's interest in their work, and relieved to have found such a non-judgemental patron.

Siri is the first to attend Sheila's post-party salon. He sets up camp on the verandah, sleeping on a *padura*, a reed mat, wearing nothing but a sarong. His earlier nap on the beach has done little to revive him. He is followed by a poet with the slight build and darting gestures of a gecko. The poet stretches out on Sheila's chaise longue in the sitting room, smoking a blend of tobacco and marijuana that fills the house with an intoxicating kind of incense. Minnette sits by him, drinking in the sweet smoke that ribbons from his lips and across the room. Sheila joins them with a cup of tea. She glances at the figure occupying her verandah.

'Anyone would mistake him for a servant, no?' She laughs. The gecko smirks, drawing another puff. Sheila sips her tea and examines her nails, running a thumbnail under the others to lift out the dirt. She pauses. 'Here, Minnette, why is that boy so quiet?' She gestures to the verandah with an upturned palm.

Minnette shrugs. She doesn't want to bring up Eric's death and Siri's subsequent grief, in front of the gecko. 'Siri's been busy,' she says, deflecting the question. 'Several of his paintings are going into the Colombo Exhibition.'

Minnette wishes she hadn't mentioned the exhibition. She thinks of the frenzy taking over not just the park that is hosting it, but the whole of the island. New roads are being built, building facades are being scrubbed. All in anticipation of the English princess and her husband, who will soon be in Ceylon to open the great festival that includes the Colombo Exhibition. Minnette shivers at the thought of a royal visit, not because they are coming to her island, but because they will also visit her first build: the Ariyapala Lodge.

In fact, architecture is a key component of the event. Pavilions will display models of planned buildings. Asia, Europe, Australia, North America and Great Britain will all be represented. The dominant force, however, will be Asia, with commercial projects taking a central position.

'So Siri will be exibiting?' Sheila smiles. 'Wonderful. I understand David Paynter and George Keyt will be showing work there, too. Smashing!'

In with the new, out with the old, Minnette thinks. The government is planning to clear Colombo's slums. She wonders what will happen to the city's poor once they have lost their homes, and decides they will find a way as they always do, fashioning new accommodation somewhere out of sight.

'And what about you, Minnette? Are you exhibiting anything?'

Minnette sits up in her chair, conscious of the poet nodding off on his chaise longue. 'The Ariyapala Lodge has been co-opted into the Exhibition, as I said.'

Sheila nods, urging her to continue, but Minnette has nothing further to add. She has not been asked to contribute anything to the exhibition, aside from the lodge. When Minnette first heard about it, she had thought that this, finally, would be the opportunity she had been looking for in Ceylon – a chance to share her ideas about public housing which she assumed would be a priority for a nation building itself anew. But no one approached her. She'd had individual expressions of interest – private clients wanting a block of flats built or a new house done. But nothing to allow her the inroad she craves – the chance to play a role in shaping Ceylon's future architecture, to work on structures designed for common use. *He would understand*, she thinks. *Le Corbusier – builder of new cities, architect of new ways of living. It is the dream of all architects. But I suppose I am not brilliant enough to steer a project like that.*

Still, the prospect of her next house excites her. Sited in Alfred House Gardens, a quiet, tree-lined road in central Colombo, the house has taken shape in her head and on paper. It is not like the Ariyapala Lodge; it has a central open courtyard – a 'meda midula' – and will be raised on pilotis like the old Buddhist image houses still found in villages. Those pillars will be fixed into a flat reinforced concrete slab, which she has already had designed by her friend at Ove Arup. It will be the first house with a slab in Ceylon. She has sketched the boundary walls, to be made of limestone and punched with triangular peepholes. The bedrooms will all be verandah rooms, and rather than have a long, wasteful driveway, she opts for a carport, so that parking, *loggia* and courtyard garden are all in one columned open space. It is a public space, designed for entertaining and family gatherings. Private spaces, like the kitchen and bedrooms, are all located up a dramatically curved and balustered staircase. The house is for an old family friend who asked her to build it for him while also claiming he had no money. It is a familiar request, and one she takes seriously. Her builds must always be cost effective. And for this old friend – always friends! – who took her out for ice creams when she was a child, she will not command a high fee, despite having very little money herself.

'I expect they will be most interested in my use of modern and traditional materials,' says Minnette, recalling Aunty Sheila's question.

The poet stirs, drops some ash on the recently scrubbed floor. Sheila frowns. 'Yes, I saw lovely pictures of the house.' She beckons to one of the servants and points at the fallen ash. 'Really, I must come and see it next time I'm in Kandy.'

As the day goes on, more artists drop in: a failed playright, an alcoholic potter, an unfeasibly fat acrobat. They all congregate around the gecko, smoking his sweet-smelling cigarettes and drifting off in turns. Siri is still on the verandah, eyes open now, body inert. He puts on a shirt, making it less awkward for Minnette to sit by him. She knows the architect would laugh at her prudishness, he who is so at ease in his own skin – painting canvases in the nude. *There is no shame in seeing your lover unclothed*, she admits. *But a friend? Not advisable in Ceylon.* She can hear him admonishing her already – for conforming to outdated social norms. Yet, he thinks nothing of his own efforts to conform, or rather, of the efforts he forces on her to preserve the fallacy of his marriage. She addresses her letters to his office as directed. She dares not ring him at home for fear of having him drop the phone with that terse: *Connais pas.* He sees no contradiction in these things. He is Le Corbusier. That is the only truth she is permitted.

'What time is it?' Siri looks at Minnette with bloodshot eyes.

The air has stopped moving; the sun is at its peak. It is too hot to think of lunch. 'I'm not sure. Late. Past lunch time, maybe.'

Siri shifts onto his back. 'Lunch time,' he sighs.

'They're smoking some nice cigarettes in the living room,' she says. 'Sheila's salon. It's like an opium den in there. Shall we go inside? There's a fan, at least.'

Siri sits up. Minnette smiles, imagining them joining the motley gang, but he shows no sign of actually standing. 'It aches,' he says, running a hand along his ribs.

'Well, if you must sleep on the ground, Siri. What can you expect?'

He shakes his head, looking miserable. 'Come on,' Minnette says, drawn by the intimacy of a companiable smoke. 'It will be good for us.'

Siri is not convinced. They sit in silence, waiting for something – anything – to stir the air.

VI

March 1952

She can think only of the heat. Minnette is sitting next to her, smiling, and she wants to put her arms around her, but she has still not recovered from their first hug. She wonders how little she can get away with wearing here, on this tropical island, where everyone is so much smaller and darker than she. She is wearing a modestly cut dress, which covers her shoulders and is higher around the neck than she is used to. She had judged it a prudent choice, one that would not offend Minnette's parents, but right now, she regrets putting it on.

She holds Minnette's hand – even that proves too sweaty for her – and looks out the window. The car chugs past roadside stalls that seem to evaporate into the ubiquitous palm trees as they journey onwards. Up and further up they go, along a tightly winding road that takes them to the very edge of jagged precipices. If the car slips, they will die in a web of wet leaves.

Minnette is quiet, probably asleep behind her sunglasses. The driver hunches over the wheel, glancing from time to time at the rear-view mirror to nod at her.

He seems unimpressed by her whiteness. She searches his face in the mirror from behind her own dark glasses, and finds nothing but concentration there. She is relieved he is driving with such caution, given the undulating path. *Like driving in the Lake District,* she thinks, recalling a particularly steep and narrow road somewhere east of Ullswater. She had gone out there with one of her Italians, but she wanted to walk and he wanted to drive. They returned to London separately.

As they travel further into the hills, the heat fades and she finds herself watching the passing scenery with more interest. They drive through vast tea estates, where groups of women in fine colours punctuate an otherwise green landscape. The women carry baskets on their backs as they edge their way through the plants, swiftly plucking leaves and moving on.

White waterfalls crash down boulders in their haste to reunite with the river below. A kingfisher sails up like a kite into the sky, its body a brilliant blue. Mimi cannot believe that she is here in this place that seems to have risen from the jungle, still half-formed and wild. She decides it is the right place for her, being herself wary of too much order. Here, there are no fans and, best of all, no old beaux to pursue her. Francesco is probably in Italy by now, sore from their third and last separation. Hyde Park was not enough to keep the hordes away, so she is here, with her dear friend, in this newborn country that still seems to be kicking and waving its soft limbs about.

She looks over at Minnette, whose face is turned towards the other passenger window, and squeezes her hand. Mimi has missed her – her elegance, her readiness to abscond, the subtlety with which she has pursued and won one of this century's greatest minds. She smiles in admiration of Minnette's quiet persistence, and soon the smile turns to laughter. The driver looks up, puzzled, and Mimi shakes her head. She covers her mouth and goes back to staring out the window.

Nell Cottage sits snugly in the dense grip of steaming foliage. Bougainvillea leap over walls like purple ferrets. The driver takes her luggage in while Mimi stands, mouth ajar, adjusting to the voluptuous scene. There is the scent of something sweet and hypnotic perfuming the air. A green bird with white-rimmed eyes keeps watch from the top of a palm tree. Small white flowers seem to be raining from the sky. She has travelled thousands of miles, over sea and land, to come here, to this place where nature asserts itself with seductive precision. Mimi thinks how perfect it would be to remove all her clothes and bathe right here, in the middle of this garden, under the gaze of that little green bird.

Inside, she finds the house as quiet as a mausoleum. Minnette has said little since they arrived, disappearing after showing Mimi to a simple but beautiful room. An ornately worked bed and cupboard are its central features. From this room, Mimi can see the front lawn – the road snaking up to the house, groves of palm trees, and the hills below. She makes her way to the bathroom where she sinks into a tub of warm water and doesn't emerge again for another hour.

She finds Minnette on the verandah in the late evening. 'What a marvellous chair,' she says, taking the planter's chair opposite and resting her feet on the extendable armrests.

'They are, aren't they?' says Minnette, eyes closed, feet similarly elevated, right hand clasping a glass of yellow liquor.

Mimi helps herself to a glass of the same. 'Do you have a cigarette, darling?'

'No.'

Mimi smiles, not caring. She feels like she is on the edge of heaven here. *It is better than Venice or Rome. It is still. And it is not still.*

When she opens her eyes, the sky is like an open book. Stars teem in the darkness like strings of jasmine. That was the perfume she had smelled on arriving at Nell Cottage – jasmine, floating on the breeze, blowing to the ground, and now, it seems, sewn into the sky. 'I don't miss London,' she says.

'Not yet.'

'Not yet, no.'

Minnette sips from her glass. 'I do.'

'I know.' Mimi feels something prick her ankle and slaps it.

'Mosquitoes,' says Minnette. 'I'll get some citronella.' But before she even stands up, Jaya brings a bottle. She lays it by their feet, looks pointedly at their drinks, and goes inside.

Mimi glances at Minnette, who shakes her head and smiles. 'Take no notice,' she says. '*I* do, of course. But I have to share a home with her. You're a guest. You can do as you please – within reason.'

'This, ' Mimi points to her glass, 'is within reason?'

Minnette nods.

———————

Jaya wads some coir and scrubs the two glasses. She can still smell arrack on them. She rubs in more Sunlight and scours them again. *Hmmhh*, she snorts. *That dirty arrack,* and she leans towards the window in front of her, taking in the untainted breeze.

Darkness wanders in like an elephant, swallowing shadows. Tiny pricks of light hop in the trees: fireflies that make her smile. The rains are starting. Soon it will be impossible to wash the clothes properly. Nothing dries at this time of year.

She sniffs the glasses a second time, detects only wax and lemons, and puts them in the cupboard. Jaya has known Nona and Mahattaya (as she calls Agnes and George) for decades. *And all that time I've had to keep quiet about their nadagan*, she thinks. In truth, it's really Mahattaya who is the problem. Nona only drinks sweet wine from time to time. Jaya puts this down to her sickliness. *But Mahattaya. Ayyo. Always in his office with his arrack bottle. Chi!* When she found Baby Nona taking drinks from the Mahattaya's bottle years ago, she had not been surprised. *Like father, like daughter. Chikay! But this is the way with the rich. What to do?*

She considers the floor. No matter how many times she sweeps, there is always *something*. Rice and ants. Jaya remembers how her own mother always said the kitchen floor must be spotless. Jaya agrees. She sweeps away the last of the crumbs, only to expose a column of ants, each as long as her big toe. She pushes them back with the sharp ends of her broom. The swish and scrape of it on the cement floor comforts her. The patterns it makes in the dirt are soothing. So many paths that then flow into one as she gathers everything up and empties it into a corner of the garden. She will burn the rubbish later.

A cry rises in the valley below, then another and another. The *koha* is calling. This time of year is full of *koha* calls. The sound makes her teeth chatter. If there were a man around, she would leave the room. It is not a good sound. Whenever Jaya hears it, she remembers her small self trying to sleep. She would watch the flowers on the cloth that hung between her parents' bed and hers. Orange flowers on a brown background. *And that dirty koha sound coming from Amma and Thatha's bed. Thank God I didn't know what they were doing then. But now? Chi! I can't stand to think of it.*

Jaya feels her face getting warm as the birds' cries intensify. *Thank God my quarters are behind the kitchen. I am far away from everyone, so I don't have to hear their sneezes or padas or koha cries. Shi!*

A tiny light pops in the darkness, joined by another. So many little fireflies. A bat veers in and out of the kitchen. Jaya's neck hurts. She tilts her head back, then plants her broom at her side and slides her shoulder blades together. *The body must stretch like an uncooked roti*, she thinks, and feels the tension release in her spine.

It is quiet again. The *koha* has stopped its moaning, replaced now by something else – a long peel in the night that makes the hairs in her nostrils tingle.

The *ulama*, the devil bird, is somewhere out there. People say it calls when death is coming. She kisses her teeth, dismissing such nonsense, then freezes. *What was that? Shrieking ulama. Why do you crack the darkness with your screams?* She suspects it is the white nona. Jaya has smelled the evil on her – this woman with hair like fire and skin so white – whiter even than Baby Nona's. When the white nona had arrived, Jaya wondered who she was, walking into the house on legs glistening like snake eggs. Those crooked red lips. That blue-white flesh. Jaya immediately distrusted her.

She runs her palms over her own brittle skin. *My arms are like wood, hard and dark. See how everything knots when I squeeze the broom. That is my body and my strength. I cannot afford to be delicate. I don't want to be.*

———————

Mimi wakes to a deep hooting sound in the distance. She sits up in bed and studies the treetops. It is not a bird – at least, no bird she has heard before. She opens the window wider to let the noise in, and disturbs an enormous beetle with iridescent blue wings. The creature whirs off, its plump body weighing it down so that it blunders through the air. She watches its erratic progress with a mix of pity and amusement.

Forgetting why she opened the window, she returns to bed. Her body still seems to be adjusting to land. The gentle and ubiquitous rocking of the ship had become familiar to her. She finds this stillness underfoot disturbing. Curling up on her side, like an ammonite, she imagines the *shhhh* of the ocean. When she untucks herself again, the sun has risen higher into the sky and steam rises from the trees.

Minnette had warned her it might be raining when she came, but Mimi had been sanguine about the possibility of a monsoon, and was disappointed to find the sun shining so unequivocally when she arrived. She imagines the rains in Ceylon to be operatic. She does not have to imagine for long, because as she lies there watching the sky from her window, the sun disappears and the heavens open up like a wound. She closes the window just in time. Seconds later, the rain strikes the pane and blots out the world.

Mimi hears nothing but rain roaring against the roof. She thinks of the jasmine outside, helpless against the downpour. She imagines the soil strafed by fat, relentless drops, bougainvillea hammered into the earth.

No one else seems to be awake in the house. It is not early. Mimi opens her bedroom door and peers down the hall. Everything is dark, and the doors remain closed. She pads downstairs and finds the ground floor deserted. The house is as quiet as a tomb. Mimi wonders whether it is because of Minnette's mother, Agnes, whom she met on arrival but has not seen since. Last night, she saw Minnette emerge from Agnes' room looking pale and solemn. That was after they had shared their drink on the verandah.

She knows that whatever Agnes has, it is serious. Only something that grave would remain so persistently unsaid. Mimi also knows it will remain unsaid, and that there is no value in raising it with Minnette. She remembers her own mother wasting away in a secret room during the war. She remembers the whispered confessions: that she had unwittingly shoplifted a lipstick from the local boutique when she was seven; that she had thought Mimi had been born with a defect the first time she saw her hair; and that although she would never stop loving her late husband, Mimi's father, she realised – too late – that she preferred women to men.

Mimi imagines her mother sitting happily in old age with one of her closest friends. When her mother died, it was this friend who washed her body and chose her burial dress. In a different world, Mimi thinks, her mother and her friend might have made a home together, instead of sitting across from one another talking about the war. Perhaps such a thing could only be possible in a place like this – this island cast off another shore, drifting towards the end of the world.

Mimi feels herself drifting with it. She opens the front door and watches the rain needling down. Before she can think about it she is outside, walking barefoot, the rain sewing itself into her skin.

Jaya tenses in bed. Someone – or something – has entered the house. Grabbing her broom, she hurries down the corridor, imagining a *rilawa* – a macaque – has broken in. *I will knock its head with my broom*, she vows. *Can't be discussing with them. Just give a good paara so they never come back.*

When she gets to the living room, there is nothing there, not even a gecko. She assumes it was the rain, then notices the front door is open. She frowns.

There is someone outside: a lady in shiny pyjamas – the white nona. Jaya can see her back: her fire hair hanging wet and heavy, turning the back of her pyjama top transparent. Jaya snorts. *These white women have no shame.*

The white nona's white soles are smudged black. She is tall – much taller than most of the people Jaya knows. She is like no other white nona Jaya has seen before, and she has seen quite a few. Agnes Nona had friends who would come from outside, as did Baby Nona and Podi Nona. There were more white mahattayas than nonas, like Podi Nona's first husband who was always kind to Jaya.

Yes, I've seen my share of suddhas. This one, though, is pissu. She is walking so slowly and getting very wet. Jaya accepts that the rain can be calming. She listens to the *pit-pat* that sounds so much like applause in the middle of the jungle. She had heard her Nona telling the Mahattaya that the white nona is an actor in plays. *Maybe she likes the rain because it reminds her of all that clapping?*

The white nona has stepped off the verandah now. Her white feet are in the grass. Jaya thinks she should not be out there with her soft feet. *She is not used to it. Not like my odd-shaped toes and dry heels. I don't need slippers, really. My feet are tough like an elephant's.* Jaya can't bring herself to interrupt her. The white nona is smiling in the rain. Jaya understands. She likes the rain, too. She remembers she has not yet bathed and wonders if she should get her Lux soap and *reddha. I can do it now,* she tells herself, *just like malli and I did when we were about half the size of this broom.* She remembers how her brother and she rubbed the soap into their thin bodies until it foamed all over so they were as white as the white nona.

The white nona wanders towards the jungle. Her red curls stretch downward. Water runs from beneath her pyjama shirt. *Mad English.* Jaya's mother always called them this when she worked for Nona's mother. *Suddhas – never dressing properly. Always in suits, sweating and getting mad.* Jaya has never worked for any of them. She has heard from others who have – and of the constant demand of polishing shoes or silver. Jaya has only ever worked for Nona, who is kind and gives her extra money when her mother or father needs help. In a few weeks, she will need to visit them in the village down south, to take her father to the doctor. Jaya does not like going to the village. She doesn't want to see the toddy tapper staring out from someone's verandah.

She had married him when she was sixteen. He was thirty. Like many toddy tappers, he soon grew more interested in the sap he was harvesting. Often, she would find him under a tree, reeking of alcohol, sweat or another woman. She left him, following her mother and a job to Kandy. Her father disapproved, but her mother understood.

At Nell Cottage, she doesn't have to worry about the toddy tapper and his oily breath and creeping hands. She never liked how he climbed on top of her. How he spoke to her while he did it, whispering words that embarrassed and made her mad. She never liked anything about him and now she doesn't have to. She is free.

She wonders if the white nona is free. She must be to be wandering around in the rain like this, practically naked. The white nona pauses by a tree, staring at something. Jaya opens the door a little wider and sees it: a small lizard with a long, sickle-like tail, clinging to a tree trunk. The lizard's red mouth is open in deep thought. The white nona first shrinks back, then leans in to examine it. She stares at the dragon lizard; it stares at her. And then something catches its attention and it darts up the tree, its tail whipping left and right.

The white nona turns and walks back across the lawn. She hasn't seen Jaya. *If I joined a circus, this would be my special skill. They'd call me the incredible, see-through woman. I am expert in not being.* The white nona's face is smooth and relaxed. Barefoot, with her hair like a rag on her head, she is not the bleached, dangerous thing Jaya had imagined. She goes gently without direction or speed. And then she stops. Her brows squeeze together. Her face splinters with alarm and disgust. She starts shaking one foot and then the other, opening her mouth like the dragon lizard of a few moments ago.

Black shapes glisten fatly on her feet. The white nona flails like something out of a *jataka* story and Jaya doesn't want to miss what happens next. She keeps shaking her legs and stamping her feet. Jaya runs back to the kitchen with her broom and returns with some salt. She goes to her, telling her to keep still. Somehow, the white nona understands her, and Jaya applies salt to the leeches. She doesn't like hurting them – *they're just innocent creatures after all*. But watching them seize up and drop off the white nona's skin, she can't help feeling revolted and a little satisfied, too.

The white nona puts her hand out for the salt and continues what Jaya has begun. They work together in silence. Then, the white nona looks up at Jaya with her grey, dead eyes. She says something, nodding her head. She looks thankful, so Jaya stays with her, making sure to get all the leeches off. Then she walks the white nona back to the verandah and shows her the mat where she must wipe her feet before going in, because Jaya doesn't want to be polishing up after her mud.

The white nona puts her hand on Jaya's arm. Jaya looks at her hand, both pink and blue, and tells herself to accept it. If she doesn't, she will think her nothing but a rude village woman. So, Jaya nods and pulls her lips into a smile like hers. They look at each other for a while and to Jaya, the white nona really seems to see her, even though another part of her knows she can't. Someone approaches and they both turn towards them. It's Baby Nona.

The white nona's eyes crinkle as her face splits into a smile. Her hand falls from Jaya's arm and the servant draws away, relieved, unseen.

———

Minnette hands Mimi a rag. 'You can wipe your feet with this. Don't walk around in bare feet, Mimi. Not here, and certainly not in the rain. You're lucky you didn't get bitten by a viper.'

Mimi looks at Minnette with genuine surprise. She hadn't thought of snakes and admonishes herself for being so stupid.

'We'd better go in,' says Minnette. 'I should check whether there are any others on you. They don't just attack from the ground, dear.'

In the bedroom, Mimi lets Minnette inspect her. She closes her eyes and tries to think of something else.

'How many more did you find?'

'About eight,' says Minnette casually. 'You can open your eyes now. They're all gone.'

Chastened, Mimi curls up on the bed. 'It was a stupid thing to do.'

Minnette gently rubs Mimi's back. 'Mmm-hmmm.'

'Thank God for your maid.'

Minnette laughs and stands up to leave. 'It will scab over and look unpleasant for a few days. But you'll be okay.'

Mimi rolls over and chastises herself for being such a coward. She can still see the leeches feeding on her flesh – their shining, bloated bodies. *Like goose shit*, she thinks, shuddering. No more walking barefoot in the wet, she decides. Strictly for the natives.

Later, as she steps onto the verandah, Mimi declares, 'I despise leeches.' Insect wings catch the lamplight as they flicker past. The darkness seems full of life – buzzing, chirping, whining.

'Quite,' says Minnette. 'Unpleasant things.' She has her glasses on and is studying a drawing.

'What's that?'

Minnette points to a cross-hatched rectangle. 'See this. I'm trying something new.'

Mimi leans over to take a better look. She can see the outline of a house which seems to sit on an incline. Beneath it is a sketch of the ground floor, with a staircase at its centre, and a rectangle next to it. The rectangle, explains Minnette, is the loggia and 'carport'. When the car isn't parked there, it will double as a space for the children to play or could be used as an extra bedroom. The house is nearby, in a street named after a French man. 'I've created a similar loggia in the Colombo house,' she says.

Mimi isn't sure about the carport being used as a bedroom, but she likes the versatility of Minnette's design. 'I'd *love* to see your Colombo house,' she says, hoping to see more than just the building site.

Minnette smiles. 'I'll arrange it.' For a moment, Mimi feels guilty about her overenthusiasm. The building doesn't interest her as much as the prospect of seeing the capital. 'Lovely,' she says, and a shadow falls across the pair.

Mimi looks up in alarm to see a tall, bald man wearing a white shirt, and a piece of cloth instead of trousers. Minnette raises a hand and smiles. 'Siri,' she says, 'come, sit, sit. Come and meet my dear friend, Mimi.' Siri takes up an empty chair next to them so that all three stare out into the night. 'Mimi, this is Siri, also my dear friend. He's a fantastic artist.'

'I feel I already know you,' says Mimi.

Siri says nothing.

'Don't be rude,' whispers Minnette to him, half in jest.

There is a long silence before Siri opens his mouth. 'Moths search for the moon but find the oil lamp instead.'

Mimi looks at Minnette who shakes her head. She decides there is no point in pursuing conversation with

Minnette's friend. *Far better to study his paintings*, she decides.

When Mimi next meets Siri, it is over lunch at the Queen's Hotel. This time he is wearing a suit which is so at odds with his physique that he looks like Babar the Elephant. The thought makes her smile and Minnette, misinterpreting it, smiles back. Siri focuses on the act of eating, while Minnette concentrates on the hotel's interior.

'Dear girl,' says Mimi, following Minnette's gaze, 'since *when* have you ignored a good meal to admire the view?'

Minnette looks blank. 'I'm not admiring it, really. I mean, it's a piece of Ceylon's history, of course,' she gestures upwards. 'But sometimes I find it so gloomy and oppressive.' Mimi looks at the white ceilings and polished wood floors and can find nothing to criticise. 'I rather like its... colonial charm,' she says. Minnette and Siri exchange a look. Mimi shrugs it off. She likes the ceiling fans, the service and the lake views.

As Mimi contemplates this, Minnette drops her fork. Before she can retrieve it, a waiter materialises beside her and grabs it. He offers her a new one. Minnette thanks him without looking at him. She is occupied with something else at the other end of the dining room. 'What is it?' asks Mimi. Then she sees him. A tall man with curly hair, a lock of which hangs over his forehead. 'Who is he?' she says, in a hopeful voice. Minnette says nothing.

'Desmond,' says Siri.

Mimi, who has so far been unable to shift her gaze from the stranger, turns abruptly towards Siri. 'Who?'

'Desmond,' he says, tonelessly.

'Yes, but who *is* he?' she asks, then notices a young

woman following him to a table. She slumps with disappointment.

Minnette recognises her friend's predatory gaze and half smiles. 'Oh,' she says, looking absently at the new fork and then at Mimi. Mimi knows it is her impatience that causes Minnette to pause. 'He's… a friend,' she says, finally.

Mimi steals a look at the man again. 'Ask him to come over here.'

Minnette shakes her head. 'I can't. I mean, he's *with* someone.' She looks doubtful.

Mimi is puzzled. She turns to Siri for help but finds him staring out the window, consumed, it seems, by the act of chewing his food. She considers his smooth face and hairless scalp and thinks how different he is from the *fakir* she saw in the park. The Hindu holy man of Hyde Park, with his thin legs, gaunt face and wild thicket of hair. And yet, there is a stillness about the two men that draws them together, almost into one person, in her mind.

Minnette, on the other hand, is now wearing that mischeivous expression Mimi remembers so well. 'My dear,' she says, 'perhaps I will call him over, after all.'

And this is how Mimi ends up dancing with Desmond at the end of the evening, and in bed with him later that night. Technically, of course, they are not in a bed. They are in the back seat of his car, in an unlit lane, rearranging their clothes. Mimi opens a door and lights a cigarette, not caring about the mosquitoes. Desmond smiles at her. She is disappointed to find he is like any other Oxbridge boy – competent and efficient.

Still, he *is* beautiful. And, mercifully, he said very little throughout. He had driven Minnette and Mimi back to Nell Cottage, but once Mimi had seen Minnette to bed, she returned to the car. She told Desmond that Minnette wanted an early night, and put out a hand to shake his and tell him how delightful it had been to meet him. He smiled and opened the passenger door. 'Let me show you Kandy Lake by night,' he said. Mimi got in and they drove up, high into the hills, deeper and deeper into the darkness. Neither said a word. Mimi leaned back in her seat and stared at the night sky. Stars – millions of them – looked back at her, willing them forward. Mimi thought about Desmond's smile, as open as this sky, and as discreet as the stars sewn into it. She smiled.

They seemed to drive for hours, the road threatening to disappear every three feet. Mimi thought she might die here, in these hills. She knew little about Desmond, aside from his name and that he was or was not Minnette's friend. 'This is not the way to Kandy Lake,' she said to him at some point during their drive, and he had smiled again. It was a smile she could trust, she thought, a smile she had seen so many times before, even used herself. They were not going to Kandy Lake.

When he finally stopped the car and got out, they were high above the town. 'If you look from here,' he said, 'you can see the lake.'

Mimi looked down and saw only darkness. 'I'll have to trust you,' she said.

Then they were in the back seat of the car, Mimi sitting astride Desmond, looking out into the starlit jungle, thinking how lovely he smelled and how his hair was almost identical to hers, apart from the colour. She kept her face turned away, as she often did on these occasions, focusing on the silver tops of leaves outside. A thin breeze entered the car, cooled their sweating skin. Somewhere, a cricket called and was answered by another before the night went quiet.

Mimi draws deeply on her cigarette. Standing between the open door and the car, she leans against the chassis and looks up. So many stars, she thinks. She makes a wish and sends it up to one of the many millions above, where it will remain. *Until the end of everything*, she thinks.

VII

April 1952

Mimi gazes at the valley, the mountains rising around them. She has just finished shaking the architect's hand and is watching, now, as Minnette disappears into his embrace. The great man plants two sizable kisses on each of Minnette's cheeks and smiles at her through his round frames. The glasses magnify his eyes comically, and Mimi finds herself biting back a smile.

Later, as she sits in the room she is sharing with Minnette, she contemplates the plunging views of Simla. This is where the architect and his team are based when they are not camping in Chandigarh. Lighting a cigarette, she slings her legs over an armrest and leans back, blowing rings as tightly coiled as her hair. She is on her seventh perfect 'o' when Minnette walks in, face flushed. She looks at Mimi but does not see her.

'You're a lucky woman,' says Mimi, holding her cigarette out to Minnette.

'How so?' she asks, refusing the offer.

'Your friendship with Corbu, darling.' Mimi rotates her foot, slowly stretching it at the ankle. Her shins shine white in the light. 'Just think. No need to commit. He has a wife who does that for him!'

Minnette casts her a look that says, *only you would consider a wife an advantage to a relationship with a man.* Mimi's grey eyes twitch. 'You think too much, darling,' she says, thinking for a brief moment of the back of Desmond's car. 'Just let go. Have some fun. You don't want to end up like something out of *Brief Encounter.*'

She watches Minnette dress. It is an intriguing ritual – the pinning of the underskirt, the fastening of the sari jacket. *A glorified bra*, she thinks, studying Minnette's smooth midriff. The jacket is almost entirely backless, and Minnette's spine ripples like a braid of flowing water. The jacket is silk, printed with tiny red and gold birds. On the bed lies a length of red and gold silk which Minnette begins winding around her body. The cloth is so fine that it clings to her, draping naturally over her hips, and then over her shoulder. She fastens a spray of white flowers in her hair and smiles at Mimi.

'He's taking me to see Chandigarh. It's a long drive but I *must* see it. Will you come, too?' she asks.

Mimi frowns. 'No, darling. Too tired. Maybe tomorrow. I'll see you at the English couple's for afters?'

They hug and Minnette is gone. Mimi wonders whether they will make it to Chandigarh, whether the architect will seduce her slowly or throw himself on her like a bull in heat. She knows it could go either way. She has heard stories about him and his appetite. Some women have attested to his charm and prowess, others to a brusque selfishness.

The architect is dynamic, funny. He is a great man, and Mimi, like Minnette, finds him charming. But for Mimi, there is no attraction. She does not understand Minnette's obsession with him. *So old*, she shudders, thinking of his wrinkled hand on her smooth skin. Mimi has had little interaction with him, anyway. A drink while they were all in Paris together and later, delivering a letter or package for Minnette. She is intrigued by his work, has admired his buildings (the exquisite villa at Poissy), his paintings. She has had two conversations with him, both of which he is unlikely to remember. *Too busy staring at my legs*, she thinks, although she had been wearing trousers at the time. She replays the scene once again, and recalls that she was indeed wearing trousers – herringbone patterned – and Minnette had been standing behind her. *Minnette*. The realisation makes her blush.

———————

Seetaram watches them from the rear-view mirror. He has work to do on site, so when the architect asked if he and his Ceylonese guest could drive to Chandigarh with him, he agreed.

The woman is like a small queen in the back of the car. The architect sits beside her, a smile on his lips. They are quiet as they plunge down the mountain roads. Seetaram is hungry but dares not reach for the bag of spiced chickpeas he brought for the drive. The air is heavy as it is. They have said nothing to upset him – have been faultlessly polite – yet he feels like an intruder in his own car.

The architect clears his throat then falls silent.

'Would you like me to go round, Monsieur Le Corbusier?' offers Seetaram. 'To show Miss Minnette?'

The architect nods. As they approach the Capitol Complex, Miss Minnette sits up in her seat. Seetaram has diverted their route so they can approach sector 1 from the south. The road is a dirt track, pitted and rough so that they lurch from time to time against each other.

'Look at the Himalayas – the view is stunning,' she gasps. In the small rectangular mirror, Seetaram sees the architect's eyes turn towards her, shining. He looks away.

'Bravo, Seetaram,' exclaims the architect. 'You have found the perfect approach for Mademoiselle and me,' then bending towards her he murmurs: '*Oiseau*, I am taking you to see the site of another exquisite bird.'

Oiseau. Seetaram arches a brow at this term of endearment directed at the queenly Miss Minnette. He has not witnessed tenderness in the architect – not even with the English Mrs Elizabeth. He directs his attention to the road in front of him.

'The Open Hand,' he hears the architect announce. The Open Hand has not yet been built, but it will be here, where Seetaram has stopped the car. Since his arrival in Chandigarh, the architect has been obsessing over it, talking at great length with Seetaram about the ball bearing required to allow it to pivot.

'You see?' continues the architect. He leans closer to Miss Minnette and lifts his left arm up to point outside her window. 'The *Palais de Justice* is being built right here.'

Seetaram's eyes flick again to the mirror as Miss Minnette turns to admire the beginnings of the High Court building. He watches the architect whose head is now almost touching Miss Minnette's.

'And across from it, the *Palais de l'Assemblée*?'

'*Oui*,' says the architect. 'With a reflective pool in front of it. It will be a plane of water, like pure glass.' The Assembly Hall and reflective pool are on the other side of the car, directly opposite the High Court building and therefore out of view.

The pair haven't moved. They look out the same window, wordlessly, while Seetaram looks on.

The darkness beyond the verandah seems foreboding from her vantage point at the piano. Mimi sits with her back to the door, knowing that Minnette and the architect have walked in. She can hear them exchanging pleasantries – Elizabeth pressing them with questions about dinner, saying what a shame it was that they couldn't have dined here. Mimi twists round on the bench and leans against the piano. She holds her glass aloft towards Minnette in greeting. Minnette offers a gentle nod. Her hair is faultless, the flowers still pinned firmly in place. Her sari is immaculate. *She is perfect*, thinks Mimi. *As demure as a virgin.*

She turns back to the piano and begins playing. After a few false starts, *Clair de lune* takes shape on the keyboard, Mimi's fingers splaying nimbly to accommodate the chords. Richard hums the melody to himself as he makes his way towards the architect. Mimi remembers playing this piece once for Francesco who smiled until it was over, then called it trite. She had mentioned Verlaine, but he remained unimpressed. *Cretin*, she sighs, and scolds herself for thinking of him again.

She glances at the architect and Richard, both of whom are engrossed in conversation. The architect is smoking a cigar and smirking at something that Richard has just said. Mimi carries on with the piece, her fingers moving effortlessly, spooling out notes in melodic waves. She closes her eyes, severing the last tie between consciousness and the unconscious motion of her hands, surrendering to the physical memory of the piece. Notes flow like light on water as she moves from *andante* to *rubato,* quickening then slowing the pace.

She thinks again of Francesco, imagines herself standing in a kitchen, hair wrapped up, a red-faced, red-haired child in her arms. This fragile thing is hers to mould as she sees fit. It is a responsibility she does not want, thrust on her by a man she had never intended to keep. Mimi's fingers work up the keyboard in waves, bringing the piece to a close. Her eyes remain closed – her mind open to the sight of her loose belly and tired face. As she plays the last note, she opens her eyes to her life as it is and is relieved.

'Bravo!' shouts the architect and Mimi turns to see him looking at her as if for the first time. Everyone is looking at her. Minnette and Richard are smiling, Elizabeth is mildly amused and the architect is applauding, his gaze unmoving. Mimi stands and bows.

Minnette approaches, sits at the piano bench, forcing Mimi to sit back down. They light a cigarette each, and begin a simple duet to obscure the sound of their voices.

'You're glowing,' says Mimi out of the corner of her mouth, cigarette bouncing on her lips. Minnette says nothing, tapping out a simple melody with her right hand while holding her cigarette with her left.

'That Elizabeth and Richard,' says Mimi. 'Yawn.'

'Stop,' says Minnette, sounding like she has heard this kind of talk before. 'They're lovely, really.'

'I must have missed something, then,' Mimi replies. 'Richard was leaning so closely towards me, I could have eaten his hair.'

'Now, Mimi. You must leave poor Richard alone.'

'I did,' Mimi replies.

Minnette is puzzled. 'You did?'

'Correct. I did.'

Minnette stops playing to take a sip from Mimi's drink, which is still where Richard left it, on top of the piano. 'This must be a first for you,' she says, grinning.

Mimi is unexpectedly transported back to Desmond's car. She thinks that she missed the more apt opportunity for restraint before Richard came along. 'Yes, a first.' She picks up her glass and toasts Minnette, not looking at her. 'To firsts,' she says, taking a sip and handing it to her.

'To firsts.'

Mimi can feel the architect approaching before she sees him. Neither she nor Minnette turns, even when he is directly behind them, humming tunelessly. Mimi can see him reflected in a mirror-worked vase sitting on the piano. His face is broken into little squares and stretched clownishly across its bulbous stomach.

'Ah yes, to firsts,' he says, raising his cigar.

Minnette concentrates harder on the keyboard. Mimi puffs expertly on her cigarette while continuing to play. She can see the architect's gaze is directed at Minnette. His expression is open, warm, almost gentle. Elizabeth appears behind him like a shadow.

'Ah, Corb, what were you saying?'

The architect turns to smile at Elizabeth. Mimi notes a slight hardening of his features. 'We were toasting to firsts, my dear,' he says. 'And of course, you know, my protégé here –' he points to Minnette '– has collected many.'

'Has she, now.' Elizabeth's thin greyhound's face angles towards Minnette.

'*Bien sur*,' cries the architect. 'Her first build is *formidable*! It has attracted the attention of the Prime Minister.'

'Churchill?'

Minnette stops playing and turns around. 'No, no. The Prime Minister of Ceylon, he means. The late D.S. Senanayake.'

'Ah,' says Elizabeth, 'yes, of course.'

'And the English princess,' adds the architect triumphantly.

Minnette looks at her lap and shakes her head. 'No, I'm afraid that didn't happen. She was due to visit the house for the Festival of Ceylon, but of course, the King died so…'

'*C'est vrai?*' asks the architect, looking concerned.

Elizabeth, now joined by Richard, laughs while Minnette and Mimi look at one another uncertainly. 'Corb, you must have known,' says Richard amiably.

The architect shrugs and puffs out his cheeks. 'I am too much with my work,' he says.

Mimi wonders whether this is true or whether the architect is affecting ignorance for the sake of making a statement. She thinks that at least in this case, it is an admirable quality. Minnette, too, is smiling to herself, which Mimi takes as agreement.

'*Écoute,*' says the architect. 'Your King is dead, okay. But she –' he points again at Minnette '– she is setting records in Ceylon. She will go far.'

Minnette shakes her head, embarrassed.

'Actually,' says Richard, 'I read about a new project in Ceylon. Is it in Galle?'

'You must mean Gal Oya,' says Minnette. 'It's a rehousing and settlement scheme.'

Richard leans forward, interested.

'A quarter of a million people will be housed on a quarter of a million acres of jungle. They say they will harness the Gal Oya river – up in the hills, so nowhere near Galle – to irrigate the surrounding area.'

'And what is it all for?' asks Elizabeth, nose twitching.

Mimi glances at Minnette and notes the subtle stiffness around the mouth. She sips some sherry, crosses her legs, and waits for Minnette to speak.

Minnette looks at Elizabeth. 'Well,' she begins, 'it was conceived as an initiative for the masses. For the peasantry. In the end, there will be a house and land and a livelihood for all these people, on previously uninhabitable land. It's an ambitious project driven by hope.'

Elizabeth nods slowly, mouthing the word 'hope', while Richard frowns with concentration. 'After all,' says Elizabeth, 'it isn't so different from what we are doing here. All these post-partition refugees will get a modern home. Such a horrible mess, partition.' Everyone goes quiet until Richard turns to Minnette.

'So, who is managing this Gal Oya?' he asks.

'A company of American engineers –'

'*Pah!*' exclaims the architect. '*Toujours les americains!*'

Minnette smiles at him. 'Actually, they're doing good work, Corbu. They've been there for three years and have accomplished quite a lot in that time. And they're working closely with our own people.'

The architect waves an irritated hand. When it comes to Americans, his judgement is impaired. Mimi knows this well, having witnessed some of his more colourful outbursts. And Minnette has told her one or two stories, too.

This distaste does not extend to American women, of course. Mimi knows about the American. She does not speak of her with Minnette, and Minnette has never mentioned her, though she, too, knows. It is the nature of the architect that his affairs are commonly known but never alluded to. And it is the nature of his women to carry on as if oblivious, all the while carrying around the knowledge of his adultery like a used tissue.

Several nights later, Mimi is back on the verandah, smoking a long cigar. Richard had given it to her earlier that day when she dropped by for a visit. Elizabeth had been out on one of her ubiquitous bicycle rides ('With one of the chaps from the site,' Richard explained), and Mimi thought it was just the diversion she needed for the afternoon. She returned with nothing more than the cigar, which Richard promised would be 'very relaxing'.

Puffing on the smelly thing, Mimi is not relaxed. She screws up her face and pulps the end of the cigar into a bowl. As she reflects on how glad she is to be returning to Ceylon tomorrow, Minnette walks in. Her appearance is impeccable. Mimi is impressed, considering where she has been. Minnette has confided to her that their meeting places are not always indoors, that there have been tents and picnic blankets, and that the architect has developed a knack for tying a sari.

Mimi beckons to Minnette to join her, and when she doesn't, goes to embrace her. 'My dear Minnette,' she says. Minnette says nothing. She is tiny in Mimi's arms, her bones as delicate as a bird's. Mimi is surprised she has not broken beneath the force of the architect's hunger. She knows that he is voracious – she can see how he looks at Minnette during the day, even while they were touring Chandigarh the other day, observing building sites, shooing away cows.

'You look shell-shocked,' she says, seating Minnette down and pouring her a drink. 'I know… tomorrow –'

'– is already here,' says Minnette. She says this quietly, without emotion.

'Chin up, old girl,' says Mimi. 'You had a marvellous time here, didn't you?'

Minnette is quiet for a moment. 'He will forget me,' she whispers.

'Of course he won't,' exclaims Mimi, knowing that he will while he is with the American, his wife or another woman. 'He's very fond of you, you know. His eyes go wide whenever you're around. He can't stop looking at you.' This is true. When the architect is with Minnette, no one else exists for him. *Except that night, at the piano,* thinks Mimi, before hiding the memory away. 'Yes, he really should be more discreet. Elizabeth was really sniffing about that evening, staring at you both like there was a story to tell.'

Minnette sighs. 'Well, I have no say in how he behaves. I can only control my own behaviour, right?'

Mimi strikes a match, lights a cigarette. She takes an ashtray to the verandah. 'Of course, darling,' she says. 'I didn't mean anything by it. I was just saying. Of course you can't control him.' She snorts at the idea of it: a woman controlling the great architect.

'The only woman who has any influence over him is his mother,' says Minnette. 'He's terrified of her.'

Mimi laughs. 'How old is she now?'

Minnette shakes her head. 'I don't know – one hundred?'

Mimi looks up at the star-filled sky. In it, she thinks she can see her mother's face. She holds her arms up towards the night, as if to embrace it. 'To mothers,' she whispers, raising her cigarette in lieu of a glass.

Minnette lifts her own tumbler. 'To mothers.'

When Minnette and Mimi return to Ceylon, Minnette insists they go to Colombo. She takes Mimi to the site at Alfred House Gardens, where she inspects the slab that has just been put in. Mimi watches as Minnette climbs the scaffolding in her leather slippers, hoisting up her sari to gain a better foothold. She is a stranger to the woman in India, who looked to the architect for affirmation, and sat with soft eyes as he spoke to her of himself.

Mimi notices that she isn't the only person watching Minnette. In a corner, stands a teenage boy, whom she later learns is the client's son. He giggles as Minnette climbs the ladder, but soon grows quiet, his eyes drawn to her calves and exposed back. Minnette is wearing a backless sari jacket, held together at the neck by silk rope, its tied ends following the lay of her spine. The boy's lips part with wonder. Mimi's smile signals to the boy that he has been noticed, and he turns his gaze upward, feigning interest in the slab Minnette is inspecting. Mimi can see the edges of his ears reddening, and smiles again.

Back on the ground, Minnette peers at a worker over the lenses of her glasses. She shows him the papers she has in her hands, and points upward and into a corner, then back to her papers. The worker looks at the documents and then at Minnette. He calls his men over and seems to repeat what she has just told him, gesticulating much as she did a minute earlier. Some of the men kiss their teeth and giggle, but the head worker – the one Minnette spoke to – shouts at them and they get on with the work. Minnette's face grows serious as she looks at the men, then she nods at the head worker, who wobbles his head apologetically and smiles.

Minnette continues her progress around the site,

followed by the boy, his sister and their parents. Mimi does not follow. She watches the party, Minnette at its centre, walking and speaking at ease, stopping to examine corners and walls as if they were a particularly arresting book. The boy lags behind, and seems to follow the rope dangling from Minnette's neck. It is as if he, too, is tied to it, and cannot look away. Mimi understands the boy, and remains where she is, watching him watching her, until she can see neither.

———————

Minnette and Mimi arrive in the eastern town of Batticaloa a day later than planned. Minnette's father had insisted they stay at least one day to celebrate Ceylonese New Year with the family. That gave Minnette enough time to contact old family friends and arrange to use their bungalow in a bay north of the town. Minnette and Mimi took a steam train, pulling into Batticaloa under the fierce gaze of the sun. Siri arrived with a friend, Laki, in a borrowed Morris Minor, and drove them all up the coast.

Emerging from the bungalow, Mimi pulls the rim of her hat down to shade her eyes from the glare of the beach. The heat is oppressive. She joins Minnette, Siri and Laki, as they meander up and down the coast.

'Girls, look at that!' exclaims Laki in his clipped English. 'The blue sky, the purple bay. The sun takes a brief siesta behind a cloud, then at once puts it to a side. The sun wants to see us, no? To hold us in his hot eye.'

Back at the bungalow, Minnette had whispered to Mimi that Laki had 'a touch of the village about him', although she maintained that he was 'nice enough'. To Mimi, he is quite agreeable, his dramatic descriptions endearing. She follows his gaze, holding a cigarette to her lips. They are standing on the shore, staring out into the Bay of Bengal. 'Darling,' she says, 'the sky and the water are blue, the sun is hot, shouldn't we be jumping in, instead of spectating from up here?'

The ocean receives them calmly like intimate friends. Mimi, in a white bathing suit with black edging, is an Art Deco sculpture come to life. Water pearls on her skin, catching the light so that she shimmers like a saint in a medieval illumination. Laki dives in after her, his body sliding through the water like a long, dark fish. They swim deeper into the sun as Siri and Minnette lay on their backs, floating like two otters in the arms of a temperate sea.

Mimi kicks forward beneath a small wave, Laki following swiftly behind. He hangs back, letting her gain the advantage. The water is warm against her skin. She can feel her limbs stretching and sighing with satisfaction. After days of indolence, her muscles are engaged, powering her through the ocean.

On she swims, with Laki now at her side. Soon he is in front of her, his long lithe body slipping effortlessly forward until Mimi loses steam and can only watch him disappearing into the sun. She flips onto her back and fins softly under a gently pinking sky. Once she has regained her breath, she swims back towards Minnette and Siri.

The pair are still lying on their backs, with their eyes half closed. Siri's toes poke above the water like dried out corks. Neither he nor Minnette notices that Mimi is there.

'What do you think of my dear friend?' asks Minnette.

'Who? Mimi?' asks Siri sleepily. 'She's very beautiful. Like a Klimt… *The Nuda Veritas*.'

Minnette nods. 'The same red hair.'

'The same uppishness. She is dangerous, that one.' His

lips twist momentarily. 'Laki likes her.'

Minnette laughs. 'It is a profound Biblical truth. When man meets Mimi, man falls upon his knees and worships her.'

'Not all men,' says Siri.

'Oh, don't worry,' says Minnette, 'you'll get your chance. Everyone does. She's generous like that.'

Mimi turns away, stares out to the horizon. She sees a speck moving against a half-submerged sun and kicks silently towards it. The speck grows as it bobs closer and closer to her. When Laki comes face to face with Mimi, he grins. 'Your hair is like a piece of the setting sun,' he says. He tugs at one of her ringlets then lets go so that it springs back against her head. 'So strange. I have never seen this kind of hair before.' His large, long-lashed eyes are rapt.

Mimi smiles. She considers his broad shoulders and tightly muscled frame, and smiles deeper. 'Let's go,' she says, turning towards the shore. The sun continues its descent into the ocean behind them. When they get to the beach, there is no one in sight. Mimi peels off her bathing suit and jumps back into the ocean, laughing. Without a word, Laki does the same. They dive into waves, whooping like children.

The sun has almost disappeared into the water, leaving a crest of orange fading in its wake. In the twilight, Mimi sees Minnette and Siri approaching. She assumes Siri is coming to shout at her for carrying on with Laki, but is surprised to see him stretch out a hand to them instead. Minnette follows just behind. They, too, have left their bathing suits on the beach.

Mimi blinks at Minnette's nakedness, and forgets about Siri. She has seen Minnette in passing once or twice (when they shared a room and found themselves dressing or

167

undressing in front of each other), but nothing like this. The fragility that Mimi has always imagined, that she has always detected beneath layers of silk, is nowhere in sight. Minnette is small, but strong. Her shoulders and hips are broad, her belly slightly rounded. She walks with purpose, without embarrassment.

'Minnette!' cries Mimi.

'What?' she replies. 'These things aren't just for the French, you know!'

Mimi laughs. She smells alcohol on Minnette's breath, although she doesn't seem especially drunk.

'Anyway,' continues Minnette, 'it wouldn't be fair for us to keep our suits on when you and Laki are without.' She reaches out a hand.

Mimi grasps it and clears first one wave and then another. She imagines what their friendship might look like if it overlapped into intimacy, and finds the picture acceptable, even desirable – if only briefly.

The moon is a silver lozenge on an inky tongue. Waves roll in beneath Mimi and Minnette, Laki and Siri. The four of them stand, hand in hand, jumping rhythmically with each swell of the ocean. Holding Minnette's hand, Mimi is caught off guard by the sense of elation thrilling through her.

Minnette and Siri have retreated to their campfire further up the beach. Mimi finds Laki a willing companion. In the moonlight, his wiry frame looks almost feminine. Laki's shoulders are broad, like Minnette's. This alone (there is no other resemblance) is enough to fuel Mimi's earlier reverie. A boat lies face-down on the sand, the paint on its sides peeling like skin. In the shadow of the boat hull, Mimi and Laki begin something inexplicable. There is no kiss, no smile exchanged. Holding one another, they look past each other and into the eye of their imaginations. Waves spit themselves onto the shore as the pair twist and struggle in the dark. And when it is over, they lie motionless, wound around one another like two geckos, still nesting in that faraway place. As Mimi drifts into sleep, she is dimly aware of Siri watching them, his hand darting in the darkness over a sketchpad.

'How did it turn out?' Minnette asks Siri the next day. The four of them are sitting in the shade outside the bungalow, eating string hoppers and sprat curry for breakfast. They have lingered over their food for the past two hours. It is almost afternoon. 'The painting. Did they like it?' Minnette pinches a photograph from Siri's sketchpad and shows it to Mimi. 'His latest commission,' she says.

Mimi pores over the picture: fishermen hunched on tall, thin stilts, cast their lines into the sea. The water is clear, the sand like cut glass. Two yellow dogs stare out towards the waves, ears stiff and alert. Their stance is echoed by two boys sitting on a boulder along the shore, backs straining upward to give them a better view of the fishermen. Further inland, a man in a string vest and sarong walks his bicycle towards the scene, a small girl in tow.

'The painting is called *Malu* – "fish",' explains Minnette, returning the photo to the sketchbook. She turns back to Siri. 'So?'

'They gave me a good price for it.' Siri digs into a string-hopper with his fingers and pushes it around some gravy.

'He means they liked it,' says Laki, scraping together the last of his hopper noodles.

'Good,' says Minnette, laying down her cutlery and

reaching for a glass of water.

Mimi glances round the table. Everyone has gone several shades darker after the previous day's excursion; all, that is, except her. She looks at her forearms which are as pink as a cooked prawn. 'That was delish,' she says, putting her fork down slowly. Her gestures, normally fluid, are now comically stiff. She grimaces as she reaches for her teacup. 'I'm like burnt ham hock.'

Laki laughs. 'Ham? No. No! Your skin is the whitest of butters, cool and bending, fragile, a…'

Minnette frowns.

'Darling,' says Mimi. 'My skin is neither cool nor bending. Right now it's as hot as an overcooked sausage and as brittle as a rusty boat hull.' Mimi blanches as soon as the words leave her mouth. Everyone, including Minnette, falls silent. They all stare at the floral pattern on the tablecloth. Mimi thinks she can hear someone's nose whistling.

'So hot,' Laki says, eventually.

They all murmur their agreement, issuing slight variations on the obvious.

'Baking,' says one. 'Like a bloody oven,' says another. No one repeats mention of the boat hull.

Mimi and Laki remain aloof from one another, a habit they have been practising since the previous night. When everyone piles into the Morris Minor and heads back to Batticaloa town, Laki sits up front, while Mimi and Minnette lean against each other in the back. As the day wears on, Mimi finds it harder and harder to believe that anything had happened at all. *In truth*, she thinks, *nothing has happened* – not between them. She is relieved that Laki appears to feel the same way. Right now, he is preoccupied with an empty crab shell he had found on the beach. And Mimi is concentrating on the walk to the lagoon.

Siri sighs, his sketchbook tucked beneath his arm. Everyone, except Laki, walks under the shade of a parasol. With his bald head and austere manner, Siri looks every bit the monk. Mimi and Minnette sport broad-brimmed hats, taking no chances in the beating sun. Laki is wearing the hollow crab shell on his head. 'I will sketch it later,' he says.

They borrow two old canoes and paddle into the middle of the lagoon. Minnette pairs up with Laki, leaving Siri and Mimi together. They manoeuvre their boats to their chosen spot and tie the boats together. Minnette pulls out a bottle of champagne as if from nowhere and hands it round the group.

'I shall be charred like a spit-roasted pig,' says Mimi, taking a sip and passing the bottle on.

They huddle beneath their parasols, waiting for the sun to drift further down the horizon. Even Laki takes cover, leaving the crab shell to bleach in the light. He has a set of charcoals with him and begins a meticulous anatomical study of the creature on paper. Siri dozes and Mimi perches by his head, careful to shade them both beneath her parasol. Siri's sketchbook pokes from beneath his arm. Mimi considers pinching it. She is moved by a curiosity – a need – to see what he had drawn by the boat hull the night before.

Siri opens his eyes. He puts a hand in Mimi's hand. She shudders and he lets go. 'As the sun withdraws, the soul returns, exposing the pink heart that beats inside a translucent fish.'

A hum, almost identical to the harmonics bowed on a cello, rises from the water. Mimi looks around and sees that everything, including the washed out crabshell, has taken on a richer tint.

'The fish are singing,' says Minnette as she folds her parasol.

Mimi scans the water for signs of life. The surface is as smooth and still as an infant's cheek, but beneath it, waves of white tissue – small jellyfish stretching and contracting in the current.

Minnette leans over the stern of her boat and whispers into Mimi's ear so that Laki and Siri can't hear. 'This is the mystery of the lagoon,' she says. 'People come from all over the country to hear its eerie symphony.'

'But they aren't *really* singing, are they?' whispers Mimi.

Minnette shakes her head. 'No one knows. They say the lagoon's fish are the only ones in the world that can make this sound. Amma once told me it's just the sound of water flowing through the fluted bodies of some kind of shellfish.'

'This lagoon is haunted,' says Laki, peering over the edge of the boat. His head is cocked towards the surface of the water.

'Careful,' says Minnette, 'the lagoon witch will reach out and gobble you up.'

'A sacrifice,' says Siri, looking at Mimi.

Hearing Siri's words, Laki flinches backwards, rocking the boat.

No one else moves.

The hum continues its ascent, riding the air currents. Like a needle on a record player, it draws them deeper into a groove, binding them together in its infinite, harmonic ring. It hangs in the air like a fine mist. Mimi holds her breath and listens. *It is the rush of heartbeats that fill your ears while rocking in the arms of a lover*, she thinks.

The madness that freezes the brain in the moments when grief is absolute.

Siri leans towards Mimi. She is intrigued, unable to look away. Gradually, their heads draw nearer. He puts a hand on her cheek, his fingers searching forward to the nape of her neck. She closes her eyes. She can feel him looking at her – at her serious mouth and impertinent chin. And then she feels something unexpected – the warmth of his breath against her face, followed by his fingers closing around her neck. Mimi wants to open her eyes to see what everyone else must be thinking, to witness everyone else's shock, even as she reins in her own. The fish sing louder. Her breath balloons in her throat, then flows free. And Mimi opens her eyes again just in time to see Siri stepping across the stern of the boat and diving, fully clothed, into the lagoon.

Laki appears not to notice. Mimi and Minnette watch Siri swim away, his white shirt and trousers like an aura around him. No one speaks.

Mimi glances over at Minnette who shakes her head and shrugs. Both of them eye Siri's sketchbook. Mimi looks at Siri, who is now floating like a lagoon jellyfish, face-down, several yards away. She takes the sketchbook. Minnette leans across to look over her shoulder.

The sketchbook's cover has vertical red and brown stripes, like a child's exercise book, and is stainless. The spine, bound in cloth, is well worn. Mimi lifts a corner of the cover and hears Laki sigh. Both women look up, frozen, but Laki is facing away from them. He brings his arms up, then reaches behind and pulls off his shirt. The muscles in his back shift and ripple the surface of his skin like geckos caught under tightly tucked bedsheets. Stripping to his underwear, he slides into the water and swims towards Siri.

Mimi opens the sketchbook. There are hairline pencil drawings of all of them: Laki, Mimi, Minnette. There is a study of a *paraya* dog, its haunches sunken and covered in sores. The lines are thin but steady, shadows detailed with the flat of the nib. Next to it is a drawing of Laki, his face turned away, but his identity clear from the compactness of his body – the tightness of the muscles between his shoulder blades captured in a mix of light- and full-weight strokes. Several minute studies of Mimi follow: one of her unmistakeable silhouette – tall, slim, long-necked; one of her eyes, capturing a gaze as cold and deliberate as a cat's; two viewed from above, of her upper lip to her upper chest – with the lips fluted and swollen in contrast to the smooth plateau of her ballerina's chest. Two drawings are of Minnette, her face set in relief against a horizon of smudged grey waves, her gaze directed at something just outside the frame of the picture. Between each of these naturalistic portraits are a series of deconstructions, in which the preceding images are separated into their constituent parts and reassembled from conflicting perspectives.

Eventually Mimi finds the sketch, but unlike the others, there is no preceding portrait. The only truly recognisable thing in the picture is the boat hull, which sleeps like a beached whale on the sand. Next to it is a mass of muscular etchings, a frenzy of cuts and thrusts of the pencil which leave a blur of movement in its wake. In the centre of it all are two mouths, at once locked in a brutal embrace yet gaping in ecstasy and horror.

Mimi closes the book, embarrassed. Minnette had already pulled away as soon as she saw the boat sketch. Mimi wonders what Minnette saw in the picture. She can find nothing of her exchange with Laki in that fury of cross-hatching. She finds nothing of her brief wish for something more with Minnette – a friendship embroidered with intimacy. There is only a primitive writhing – a scene barren of intellect or the tenderness of restraint.

'He rips open the secret heart of all of us,' whispers Minnette, her voice shaking.

Mimi, who has taken cover beneath a pair of sunglasses, affects calm. 'Curiouser and curiouser grows this wondrous place,' she says, reclining at the bow end of the canoe, her head propped up on a bag. Locks of hair stream over the deck. She reaches out and takes Minnette's hand.

'Your hair,' says Minnette.

'Shhhh.'

Minnette pauses. Water laps against the side of their boats. 'What?'

'The fish,' says Mimi. 'They've stopped singing.' She lifts a foot up to the sky, then lowers it into the water. A heron flies overhead, its figure amorphous in the fading light, like a handkerchief dabbing at the sky. Mimi squeezes Minnette's hand.

'Are you ok?' asks Minnette. 'Do you need something?'

Mimi lets go. 'No, no. Sorry, darling.' She is glad she is wearing sunglasses. She does not want Minnette to see her conflicted expression, her confusion at feeling so strangely drawn to her friend. There would be no way to explain it without lying, and Mimi is tired of lying to Minnette. She considers telling her about Desmond, but dismisses the thought almost as soon as it arises. 'That was strange, wasn't it?'

'What was?'

'Siri.'

'Oh, that. Don't take any notice.'

Mimi looks over at Minnette. 'How do you mean?'

Minnette puts a finger through one of Mimi's ringlets trailing over the prow of the boat. 'Siri has his, you know, oddities. He likes to play with people… Like you.'

From her reclined position, Mimi can see Laki and Siri floating together on their backs. In her quest for something more, she has divided these two men, introducing suspicion where none existed before. She sighs, knowing she will be returning to London in a few days, and then Paris. 'Do you want me to take a message?' she asks, not wanting to. 'When I go to Paris?'

Minnette says nothing. Since their return from India, she has not spoken about the architect. Mimi has grown to appreciate this reticence. As the days have worn on in Ceylon, even a cryptic reference to him steeps Mimi in confusion. She finds it easier if she brings him up, so she isn't surprised or disappointed. 'I can take him a letter, if you like.' Mimi wonders whether she might throw it into the sea – whether this will turn out to be yet another betrayal. Minnette waves away the suggestion and Mimi is relieved.

She leans back on her elbows, her foot still trailing in the lagoon, the skirt of her black and white polka-dot dress splayed across the seat of the canoe. Her chest, framed by the halter neck, is red. 'I'll be peeling all the way back to England,' she says. 'So many days in the sun and I look like a skinned watermelon.'

Minnette smiles. 'You look lovely, Mimi. What will I do after you've gone?'

'Be wonderful, as always,' says Mimi. 'Your work here is magnificent.' Minnette looks down. Mimi lights a cigarette, blows rings into the dimming sky. 'You should see more of Des. He's here. He likes you.'

'He has a girlfriend.'

'And *he* has a wife. Does it matter? I don't think it's that serious, anyway.'

Minnette looks out towards Siri and Laki. They are sitting on a boulder, their backs to the boats, their shoulders almost touching. 'They look happy, don't they?'

Mimi follows Minnette's gaze. She thinks it must be more complicated than that, but for the moment, whatever ill will flared between them earlier has burnt out, leaving this exhausted truce. She drops her cigarette into the water, hears it spit as it goes out. She closes her eyes and feels, for the first time, the gentle shift of the current beneath her.

VIII

November 1952 – December 1953

He dreams. The two of them lying at opposite ends of a bed. His legs crossed in blue shadow. She, at his feet, bird eyes fluttering, mouth open, blue wings spread. His foot in the foreground of her breast. He dreams.

He returned from Cairo to Paris in October to find a single letter from her – a letter so incendiary, he could hardly hold it. *I know you will not see this for months, but I need to go back to that place we have just left,* she wrote, and immediately, he was back there with her. *Forgive me for wanting to live in the past. I know this is something we Modernists should scorn. It's a Baroque pursuit, isn't it? All this wallowing. So this is me, walking San Carlo alle Quattro Fontane, with the guts of my memory hanging out everywhere.* Later she asked him to forgive her the *balm of repetition,* before methodically revisiting their reunion in Chandigarh.

He re-reads the letter now, sitting at his desk in north India. He cannot escape the geography of this place, now imbued with new meaning after her visit. Each site is transformed: Elizabeth and Richard's piano and the guest house where Minnette and Mimi stayed in Simla, Chandigarh's rough plains and river banks – now a landscape in which so many symbols play hide and seek. He navigates all this with reserve, conscious of being caught in a reverie by the ever alert Elizabeth.

The architect does not crave a confidante. He is accustomed to this sort of thing – the 'under the table' intimacy best not talked about. It is a fragile, precious story that loses its value in the telling. So he remains silent in the face of Elizabeth's cross-examinations.

Last night, she sat across from him, her shrewd eyes digging into his lapels. She interrogated like a spymaster, circling around the issue, digressing, returning again to the same question, always through a different door. It has been going on for days – nonchalant comments dropped at breakfast, on site, after dinner: 'How did you meet her?'; 'If she is as good as you say, perhaps we should bring her into the project?'; 'We need talent like hers!'; and then the most under-handed, 'She is striking. Did you notice Trivedi couldn't stop looking at her?'

Each time she posed her questions, her back would be turned to him. Richard would be there, too, his beak stuck in a newspaper. They were a spy film cliché, a comedy double-act – unexpected entertainment for the architect.

The architect, in turn, repeats the same story. That Minnette is his pupil whose interest in and commitment to Modern architecture deserves more than the attention he has given her. Her visit in April was arranged, in part, to remedy this imbalance. The couple appear to have accepted this explanation, but the questions keep coming.

This is why the architect is sitting alone in his study. No one, not even Trivedi, is allowed to disturb him right now. He sits alone, thinking of her. He did not expect to feel this way. It is a feeling he remembers from his early days with the American. But just thinking of the American here, in Chandigarh, in a city that has become so wholly his and hers, he feels uncomfortable, disloyal, even. This is unexpected for the architect who, until now, has assumed joy as his right. The only person who deserves his loyalty is his wife, by virtue of the vows they made years ago. And by virtue of the love he still feels for her, regardless of who she is now.

There is the love he holds for his wife, but there is also this feeling he has for *her*. She is everywhere in this place. He can see her here, against his desk, or there, fluttering across a yellow landscape like a rare bird. And he can see her on that beach, as she described it in her letter, standing next to her three friends, all of them as naked and content as infants. He laughs at the thought. There, on that beach, order and chaos were subverted.

It is the spirit of the times, he thinks. When the architect flew west to Cairo, the Egyptian King proclaimed his sovereignty over the Sudan. The architect smiles. *And now the English are sweating themselves pink.* The French, too, are being told to pull out, in this case from Tunisia. The question of Tunisia has gone before the United Nations, which promptly looked the other way, declaring that they believed the French would eventually set Tunisia free.

The UN has no balls, thinks the architect. *The UN is an American puppet, with its headquarters sucking up money in New York. What a failure that building is. Obstinate fools. They spit on Corbu? Corbu spits on them!*

He opens his journal and begins calculating, comparing expenditure on Chandigarh versus the United Nations headquarters.

- ◦ *Cost of the UNHQ=US$65m.*
- ◦ *Cost of Chandigarh (Capital + schools + police + hospitals + social services enough for 150,000 inhabitants) = US$32m.*
- ◦ *Cost of Chandigarh capital complex alone=US$2m.*

America is a waste, muses the architect. *A failure of the machine age. The only symbol that prevails in that country is the All Mighty Dollar. Commodity is valued over community. It is a nation of automatons full of women who mask themselves beneath chemicals, painting their faces and nails, obscuring their natural scent, removing any sign of hair on their bodies so that their skin shines like plastic. Empty eyes and fat wallets. Welcome to America. Happy shopping!*

He retreats to the substance of Chandigarh, which he intends as a modern day Acropolis. The sacred capital is the pinnacle of this human city; it will be the head which steers everything else. Seetaram has described to the architect how the Hindus order themselves according to the Sacred Man: the *purusha*. 'The hierarchy of Hindu society is born from the sacrifice of the purusha,' explained Seetaram. 'From his mouth came the Hindu priests; from his arms, the warriors; from his thighs, the farmers; and from his feet the shudras, who do lower but essential types of work'. *In other words*, thinks the architect, *they shovel up our shit.*

The capital complex will be the realm of the priestly – the governing class. The architect plans to make it a vast temple. And Chandigarh as a whole will be a body in eternal sacrifice. And with that sacrifice will come its corollary: perpetual regeneration powered by the female principle. The architect recalls Seetaram's words: that the female principle is what revived the dismembered body of the purusha and made him whole again. 'You may assume that this mystical birth implies a hierarchical order in which the top tier is to be superior to the one below it,' he had said. 'The truth is subtler. Without the feet, the head can only imagine what it would be like to run.'

The architect thus imagines: the Legislative Assembly topped with the pure forms of the pyramid and cube – the pyramid being that great index pointing to the sky: the right angle in triple dimension. At its apex: the sun. He imagines this, too: the assembly hall arranged within the walls of a tower that, at its peak, admits a powerful shaft of light. The tower is an observatory to the cosmos. Sun and man unite. *So then, the eye of Apollo/Helios/Surya meets the eye of man. Neither blinks!*

When the architect arrived in Chandigarh, he found that his drawings – the drawings he had made of the great plan for the city on his last three visits – were so dessicated by the sun that when they were unrolled, they crumbled like an old man's memory. These were the blueprints for the first new capital city in India in two hundred years. *Those fools*, he thinks. *They should have wrapped them in linen; instead they left them in a corner to turn to dust*. It was Seetaram's ingenuity that saved them. He drew a copy of the city's plans on the ground – in the dirt – which became the legitimate contract for Chandigarh.

Thus does the architect realise how *she* and he have been threaded into the fabric of this sacred theatre. A drawing lifted from the earth. Their imprint left in that earth now grafted into the foundations of the city.

And then there is the Open Hand – a cognate to the

Acropolis' Athena. Why a bird? – this is always the question asked of the architect. This bird that fell from his dreams into the palm of his hand – the winged siren with wide hips and fanning wings – the siren is the body's lost soul. In the Open Hand, the soul is united with the body; the city with its spirit.

Elizabeth remains unimpressed. She continues to question the architect on what she has dubbed the 'weathervane motif'.

'Why should fickleness dominate the city?' she asks the next day after dinner, her thin lips drawing up into a hairline smile.

'*Mais non!*' replies the architect, affronted. 'Not fickleness, *chère amie*, but adaptation. To survive, a city must adapt – it must take a barometric reading of the political, social and cultural climate and decide accordingly. You see, it is not that it will be vulnerable to the slightest pressure – no! It will be aware. Aware of the next trend, developments on the horizon, obstacles, opportunities. It looks left and right, always considering every direction before proceeding upon this or that path.'

What the architect does not say – because he thinks it obvious – is that the Open Hand is the mystery of the right angle made real in Chandigarh. For some, the ultimate truth of the right angle is expressed by the crucifix, embedded with Christian code. But for the architect, this is an impoverished interpretation. The right angle is a symbol of regeneration – the union of opposites. The x-axis meets the y-axis, uniting all possibility. So, the right angle = man + woman. And ecstasy lies at their intersection.

The architect has almost finished his great poem of the

right angle. He wants to send it to *her*, as soon as it is finished. In it she will find the symbol of Chandigarh. She will find the siren and the *taureau*, which has haunted him since he first stepped foot in India. In Cap Martin it spread itself across his canvas in red and blue and grey. And on his shoulder, perched the siren, a chimera of unknown constituents.

While he painted, Yvonne lay ailing. She could hardly move. If she asked for wine, the architect gave it to her. If she asked him to sing, he sang. In September, when they were in Cap Martin, the architect showed her images of herself in the poem – depictions wedded to the soil: every curve a reminder of the abundance of the earth. Sometimes she smiled, but often she was upset. 'Must I always be without clothes?' she asked. She did not understand her part in the poem – that he cast her as the symbol of fertility and growth. *Add to this the winged siren and the picture is complete*, thinks the architect. *One cannot exist without the other.*

———————

The architect's client, Prime Minister Nehru, meets him in Delhi at Lutyens' palace. Walking through those magnificent doors again he feels a twinge of regret, a pang of envy for the genius that had composed this hymn. Nehru greets the architect with an outstretched hand, wearing a suit of brown silk overlaid with tiny rosebuds.

The architect speaks to Nehru of the UN headquarters, of America's vast wealth and cultural poverty, of the ridiculous calculations that create such a mass of waste. 'Contrast this with our new capital,' he says. 'There is no comparison. The machine age failed with America.'

'It may yet succeed with India,' says Nehru.

Perhaps, thinks the architect. *But is that what India wants? The car to eclipse the cow? Tyres to replace sandals?* This is not how he sees Chandigarh. 'People walk in India,' he says. 'And in Chandigarh, people will walk. They will not be choked by the fumes of vehicles, or disturbed by their roar. One will be separated fully from the other.'

'You spoke of America's cultural poverty,' says Nehru. 'It is true that the spirit of acquisitiveness leads to moral erosion. The Indian frowns upon such motives, even if, at the same time, he secretly wishes he could have more. Ultimately, individual wants are less desirable than working for the good of the many.'

The architect speaks admiringly of the work ethic of Indians – how they toil from 10.00 to 17.00, always reserving several hours of the morning and evening (the best hours, in fact) for leisurely activities. 'That is living!' he exclaims. 'In America there are no people, only machines. They do not know how to divide their day for real living. What lies at the heart of this difference? The absence of ego. In India you do not work for advantage or personal gain. You work from a sense of duty. You are led by a noble thought and that nobility is distilled into your everyday actions.' The reward, therefore, as Seetaram and Trivedi have told him, is in the doing.

Nehru nods again. *His eyes*, observes the architect, *mirror the beatific gaze of a Hindu bronze*. 'Industry shall drive India. And science.' Nehru smiles. 'My friend, what we are striving for, you and I, is a synthesis of old and new, of past and present, of philosophy and science. So it is that we have carved out new symbols, used logic to order the activities of Chandigarh's citizens. We are creating an international city that will speak to people of all nations. Its citizens, too, will share this multinational outlook.'

'Truly,' says the architect, 'it is a city with a noble soul. It is logic and science, yes, but ordered according to certain cosmic truths. Always, there is a simultaneous glance back and a gaze forward.'

Nehru and the architect nod to one another, at once uniting India and France in their common understanding of progress. 'This is a city of the future,' concludes Nehru. 'Let the world look to Chandigarh – to India – to see what progress is.'

Some weeks later, the architect is in Ahmedabad, resolving his patron's request for a door without a lock for her villa. It is the symbol of Chandigarh that provides the missing clue. *It has always been there in the Open Hand*, he thinks. *The Open Hand that looks east and west – why didn't I see it before?* The architect's solution is a swinging door, a door that encompasses two possibilities at once – the eternal *bonjour/adieu* as he puts it. Once ajar, it allows permanent flow. The impression it leaves is of a pure circle: an eternity of movement whose centre is found in the pivoting axis – the fulcrum – of the swinging door.

The house is almost complete, but other projects take the architect into and out of Ahmedabad. Each time he arrives, he finds another intriguing mystery in the *pols* of the old city. Still, he remains an intruder in a private world.

Walking through the city's narrow, maze-like roads, the architect finds himself face to face with the Minotaur himself – in the guise of an angry dog. It curls its lips at him, but the architect looks away too late. Minoto sees red and, accompanied by his thuggish help-mates, chases him through the alley with sharp barks. The architect runs on his old legs until he picks up some stones and flings them at his assailants. With a howl, Minoto melts away replaced by three shivering dogs. A pitiful sight. The architect does little more than raise his hand and they run off, yelping.

But Minoto will not leave the architect. He lumbers onto his canvases and switches sex. Sometimes gruff and haughty, other times, soft and complacent, the creature grows its horns in oils and watercolours.

The architect shows one of these paintings to Mimi. She is in Paris for Christmas. She drops by No. 35, where one of the Minoto canvases hangs, with news of Minnette. It is the first time the architect has seen her since Chandigarh.

He watches her now scrutinising the painting from the end of her impudent nose.

'How did you find India. And *Ceylan*,' he asks.

She smiles at him, her eyes flitting from grey to blue and back again. In her many letters to him, Minnette has always described Mimi's eyes as feline, but looking at her now, he disagrees. To him, they are more like a lizard's: the tilting lenses, the hollow intensity.

'Generous,' she says. She tells him about their trip to Batticaloa, but does not mention Siri or Laki. The architect does not mention Minnette's letter.

Mimi peers at the painting, her eyes reflecting the red of the canvas. She smiles again and sums up Ceylon as 'a jewel of a place' where 'all is possible'. She tells him how charming she found the ladies and most of the men. She describes the clubs and dinner dances, the 'enormous and elegant claws' of the Lion Rock Minnette wrote to him of so long ago. And she mentions Minnette's 'D', who was missing from her last letter.

'Desmond is frightfully handsome,' she says, lizard

eyes now mirroring grey. 'Not the best dancer, but enough wit to make up for it.'

He shows Mimi around No. 35, watching how the young men follow her about the room with furtive eyes.

'How are your painter friends?' he asks.

'Very well, Corbu,' she says flatly. 'I'm sure I will be going to Italy with one of them soon.'

The architect takes Mimi out for lunch. She is uncharacteristically quiet, nibbling her beans and staring out the window. Once the wine arrives, she relaxes.

'Basquin still has no heating,' she says. 'The winter is coming and that man will bundle himself in rags, regardless of his blue hands. He hasn't bathed for months. The smell is awful!'

The architect recalls one of Minnette's letters from years ago, in which she ate ice to avoid hurting the painter's feelings. He knows Basquin from his exhibitions, but has never met him in person. He is grateful for this small mercy, having heard many tales of the artist's poor hygiene.

'He insists on living like a beggar even though his paintings are fetching thousands.' Mimi shakes her head. 'Such a pity. I cannot go inside that house any more. It stinks! My poor uncle.'

'I did not know you were related,' he says, momentarily baffled.

'*Mais oui*,' Mimi is matter of fact. She looks out the window at an old man walking by with his dog. '*Mignon, Corbu! Regardes.*' She points at the dog. The architect obliges with a nod. 'He's my mother's cousin,' she says. 'So, I suppose, not quite my direct uncle, but close enough.' She pours herself another glass of wine. 'He will get pneumonia and die this winter. I know it.'

'Let us go and meet him, then.' The architect surprises

himself with the suggestion. He can't explain why he has made it. The thought of cramped quarters and an unwashed body have already killed his appetite.

'Oh no. I've taken too much of your time already, Corbu.'

Ah-ha! Generous Mimi gives me the chance to excuse myself, thinks the architect, before saying, 'Of course we must see how your uncle is doing, Mimi. It is no burden.'

The scene swiftly changes. Bistro is swapped for paralytic house. Assymetry rules here. The architect recalls Minnette's long-ago description of the painter's 'crooked house', though it is now so bent and twisted, it is genuflecting to its neighbours.

The architect ascends the crumbling steps, handkerchief at the ready. Mimi tiptoes behind him, telling him it is not too late to turn back. He ignores her. The bell is struck but there is no sound. It does not work. Mimi reaches from behind and pulls on the knocker. This time there is such a loud thump that both the architect and Mimi step back, expecting the house to tumble to the ground like a man who has been shot in the head. The house does not fall, but the door opens. The architect's handkerchief is already upon his nose. Uncle Basquin peeps out, wrapped from head to toe in an old blanket. His face is spattered with blue and green paint.

'*Petit Mimi*. And who is this? Another of your friends?'

Mimi steps from behind Corbu and kisses her uncle on both cheeks, holding her breath. 'Basquin,' (she does not call him 'Uncle'), 'why – you must know M. Le Corbusier?'

The architect bows, restores handkerchief to pocket, smiles as he comes level again.

Uncle Basquin's eyes are like Mimi's, but without her

intense gaze. His is milky and confused. 'Le Corbusier,' he whispers. 'The architect?'

'At your service, monsieur.'

Uncle Basquin peers at him, as if at an apparition. 'But you are not dead, monsieur?'

'Not yet.'

And so the conversation continues on the doorstep, Uncle Basquin shrouded like Lazarus in dirty blankets, the architect, still alive, speaking while trying to hold his breath, Mimi looking past the old man through to the gloom inside. Neither Mimi nor the architect are invited in. They are not disappointed.

'There must be mice!' says Mimi, as they leave Basquin's house.

'Mimi,' says the architect, 'you will have to get your painter friends and stage a temporary eviction. He cannot live like that in the winter or any other season. The odour is *insupportable*.'

Mimi nods. One week later, he receives a message from her: *Eviction accomplished. Uncle in bath.*

Rain pounds the windows. France is plunged under water. The architect is at his desk, listening to Stravinsky's *Firebird*. Its soaring dissonance reminds him of *her*, provides the impetus for him to put pen to paper.

What a year it has been, he writes. *The Unité – that great ark upon the Mediterranean – is finally complete. Marseille's construction workers will have a home to live in now. Still, they reject it! And yet it is a complete organism – a vertical city. You must see it, if you can, dear friend.*

You will see something of Rajasthan in it: the concept of those colourful peepholes which I have interpreted as cube-shaped portholes cut into the walls and painted in primary colours. I have created fifteen different types of apartments within the

Unité, each of which can be personalised by its inhabitants. Light sweeps through rooms, apartments are double-storeyed, and access is variable, sometimes on the ground floor, sometimes on the upper. There is an indoor market, walkways through this 'vertical village', and a roof garden. Everything is contained within. Form and function are thus married, and convenience, or ease of living, is prioritised.

The architect is pleased with the result, and believes that the construction workers will change their minds and move in. If not, there will be others to take their place. *I invited Picasso to visit the completed building and he came. The good man looked at it with a frown. Fifteen minutes and he was gone. Fifteen minutes, oiseau! What can one see in fifteen minutes? Corbu takes more time to buy his carrots! Picasso stands in front of the building – does not enter it. Pah! He is still smarting, I think, from that Manifesto. A signature on a piece of paper whose worth is debatable. And here is Corbu with a building that signifies peace: community spirit, harmonious living, homes for those made homeless by the war (but who made homes for others; it was they who re-built the port of Marseilles after it had been bulldozed by the war). Picasso was oblivious.*

The great artist stood in front of my building, pursing his upper lip like a rhinoceros. 'The trees are very green,' he said, finally. It was my turn to be silent. The trees are green, it is true. The Unité is surrounded by greenery and these are the lungs of this self-contained city. All true. All obvious. I did not know that Picasso was capable of such banalité!

Stravinsky's symphony rises at a steep angle in the room, a beguiling and fearsome presence. Harp and clarinet compete with the rain beating outside; mythology and geometry collide.

My pen scratches with the insistence of bow on violin, he

writes. *Ivan is chasing the Firebird; feathers are flying! Once captured, strings weep, wings flutter, the Firebird pleads for its freedom, a deal is struck.*

What is this Firebird? Is it the siren that haunts me at every turn?

Oiseau, I can see you on that beach, hand in hand with friends, standing in the shadow of a wave. Your little toes press into the sand, push your feet up, propel the rest of you over that great tongue of water. Your friends do the same, in perfect time. It is a simple ballet performed by moonlight. In one choreographed leap, everything becomes possible. Reality does a somersault. Strangers become lovers. Friends become voyeurs. Identity surrenders to the power of symbol. The landscape is consumed in an infernal dance.

Night has fallen outside. Yvonn waits for me. Christmas again. What gift will I send you, oiseau? What gift will I give her that will heal her sickly body? She continues to coddle the little dog. In her eyes, it has lost its canine properties. It lies in her lap and is fed by her indulgent hand. It makes her happy – happier than this old dog can. In Kandy, you sip a glass of whiskey. It is warm and comforting, an abiding friend. It makes you happy. On both shores, Corbu is a failure.

So then, to my buildings. Here, too, the clouds threaten to piss. The Unité is rejected. The UN building is derided. They deny they want a monument while pursuing a monumental vision. Even in Chandigarh, Corbu's team bicker. Elizabeth with her minor rebukes. Trivedi and Seetaram trying to keep the peace. A fault-line is drawn between sector 1 (the capital complex) and everything else. The body is decapitated.

But no. It is not so bad. For India has at its core the comfort of peace. Nobility, purity of heart and mind, an absence of real rancour. Yes, Trivedi and Seetaram renounce ego to ensure that the vision for Chandigarh remains true. Why? Because, as Nehru told Corbu, 'individual wants are less desirable than the good of the many'. It is this principle – this truth – that will propel Chandigarh forward and make it a success.

And each time I return from India, this truth: the power of selflessness, fills my eyes. I cross the ocean with clearer vision. I see Paris through a lens that has taken in the cows and buffalo and lilting rhythm of India, the women in flowing silks, the civilization that is and will always be Chandigarh.

The architect hears his wife moaning in the other room. She is calling for him. He does not go.

It sets me free, oiseau.

Corbu flies from continent to continent, full of the grace that is India. And beating always in his heart are the wings of his petit oiseau.

A very happy new year to you, ma chère. A kiss upon your forehead.

He sits back in his chair and kisses his fingertips. He looks out through the rain battered panes at Paris, now dissolving into a watery dream.

———————

A failure, Corbu? Never. You have not failed me yet. Don't ask me to enumerate all the ways in which you keep me floating above the earth, while moored to your soul. And as for Vonn, how can you say you have failed her? She has her little dog, after all.

Minnette thinks of Vonn and the dog and smiles. When he first told her about it, she had thought him callous. But reflecting on it now, she finds it an acceptable substitute for a child. It is better than growing a garden or a baby, she thinks. At least it gives back, unconditionally, and with little effort.

She herself is not much of a daughter. She thinks of

her mother, how she – Minnette – has been absent for so many years. Even during Mimi's visit, she chose to leave her, knowing she was ill, because she couldn't cope with being back in Ceylon away from *him*. Right now, she is deciding between two dresses for tonight's New Year's Eve party while her mother lies ailing in the next room. Minnette will welcome another year with a room of strangers at Colombo's oldest hotel.

Amma has been ill since last week. Minnette and her family had just arrived at Aunty Sheila and Uncle Reggie's in Mount Lavinia. The following morning, Agnes couldn't get out of bed. Minnette's father is now a sentinel at her side, sitting and staring at her, saying nothing.

'For goodness' sake, George,' scolds Amma, 'am I Sodom and Gomorrah that you have turned into a pillar of salt?'

Minnette tells herself that there is no value in taking up position next to her father. The time for this has passed. There is little Minnette can do to alleviate Amma's pain. She can only listen to her when she talks about the past, her days as a suffragette demanding the right of all women, whatever their background, to vote.

'Can you believe, it was your father who helped us get the women's vote,' says Amma, gesturing towards the empty chair where Papa had just been stationed.

'Papa? Really?' says Minnette, recalling his initial refusal to support her architectural studies.

Amma nods. 'When the Donoughmore people came to talk about constitutional reform, your father was one of only two men who supported our demand for women's franchise. That's how we got it discussed at all.'

Minnette leans forward, passes Amma a glass of water,

who takes a sip and continues: 'I remember we put up anonymous notices inviting people to debate women's franchise. You know, in those days, we women couldn't call a meeting ourselves. Not done, you see.' Minnette frowns. 'But it worked out very well for us. People came out of curiosity. They wanted to know who posted the notices. They were moved by intrigue.' Amma smiles, tucks a loose hair behind her ear. 'I was strong then. I could go from one place to another, talking to big crowds. I had a fire inside. But now…' She closes her eyes with a sigh.

Before she leaves for the evening, Minnette sits by her mother and holds her hand. They both look out the darkening window. Minnette can feel her father's gaze on her. She does not look at him. Instead, she kisses Agnes on the forehead and wishes her a happy new year.

Outside, Marcia is waiting in the car with Werner. Minnette has noticed a coolness between her sister and Werner since they arrived at Mount Lavinia last week. As Minnette gets in the car, Marcia hands her a glass of champagne.

'Marcia?' Minnette says, looking at the glass with surprise. 'What's this? What happened to all that Temperance stuff?'

'Oh *that*,' says Marcia, rolling her eyes. 'It was a bit much, don't you think?'

Minnette looks at Werner, confused, but he is staring out the car window, his expression blank. Minnette shrugs and accepts Marcia's offer. The two sisters finish most of the bottle on the way to the Galle Face Hotel, while Werner remains withdrawn. By the time they arrive, Marcia and Minnette are both light-headed and unsure of their feet. Minnette can feel the weight slipping from her body, senses herself floating up like a child's thought.

The room spins. The band is playing a foxtrot and someone puts an arm around her. His mouth is against her ear.

'That dress! Beadwork glittering like so many diamonds, cinched waist,' he purrs. 'You are a thousand candles lighting up this room, dear Minnette. A comedy of divinity.'

She leans back to get a proper look at her dance partner. Laki grins at her, his dark face shining with sweat. 'Rascal,' she says, hugging him. 'You mean, divine comedy, no?'

'Yes, yes. As you wish,' he chirps, and dips her.

Minnette lays her head on his shoulder, relaxing into his embrace. 'Did Siri invite you?' she asks.

'I invited Siri.'

She looks over Laki's shoulder into Siri's eyes. He is nodding to Werner and Marcia, saying nothing, watching her. She smiles. At that moment, Marcia turns around, catches Minnette's glance and smiles back.

Minnette studies the physical distance between her sister and Werner. They stand parallel to one another, like two stakes in the earth. She wonders what has happened, why Werner is so aloof. Perhaps because of Amma's illness, no one seemed to notice the couple's marked estrangement. Even Aunty Sheila, not one to refrain from awkward observations, had said nothing. Marcia's voice rises now as she chats to Siri. Her gestures are animated, her grin making a caricature of her face. In the full glare of this society party, Minnette sees for the first time that something is very wrong. She feels the stares and raised eyebrows aimed at her sister, and closes her eyes.

Minnette's foot falls at the wrong beat and Laki turns her the other way. Couples step lithely, some of the men in full tuxedos, most of the women in ball gowns. Necks, wrists and fingers refract light like so many tiny chandeliers. Trays of champagne snake through the room like a caravan of gold camels. Lulled by the spectacle, Minnette finds herself falling asleep on Laki's shoulder.

He pinches her awake. 'Come. Sit, sit.'

As soon as she does, Marcia joins her and Laki drifts off. 'Where is – ?'

Marcia glances at the crowd without interest. 'Not here. Must have wandered off to the beach. Or to get a drink.'

'A whiskey,' says Minnette with a smile. 'Lovely, dependable Werner.' Marcia shrugs. Minnette doesn't say what she really wants to. A memory comes to her in startling detail: Marcia fleeing India years ago, leaving the Bombay Intellectual tight-mouthed and sullen. Minnette hadn't asked then, either. 'Well, he seems…'

'Drunk,' blurts Marcia, smoothing out her dress. Minnette is confused. Werner had refused the champagne in the car and had only now gone in search of a drink. Marcia, noticing the silence, winks at Minnette. 'Me, silly. I'm a wee bit drunk.'

'You *and* me,' says Minnette, relieved by the change of subject. 'What else can we do when Amma is like this? And Papa –'

'The human pillar of salt.'

They both laugh, and Minnette takes Marcia's hand. 'Amma's jokes.' She lays her head on her sister's shoulder. 'Too bad Papa can't laugh.'

'No sense of humour,' says Marcia. 'What to do?'

The sisters sigh. The band plays a waltz, and all of Colombo's finest pace out squares on the ballroom floor.

Siri and Laki appear and disappear like shards of light.

'Now don't go thinking I'm always drinking like this, Minnette,' Marcia says after a long pause. For a moment, she sounds like Temperance Marcia. 'I still believe it can be terrible for you. But, you know, moderation makes most sense, no?'

Minnette looks up and finds herself on a slow merry-go-round, watching the crowd pan by. Marcia's shoulder, bony as it is, is a longed-for pillow on this absurd carousel. Minnette considers the gulf between Marcia and Werner, finds it somehow difficult to accept. She cannot find an explanation for it. After all, they had seemed so happy last year. 'But you and Werner,' she says without meaning to.

Marcia smooths the hair around Minnette's temple and strokes her chin. 'He's fine. We're just… you know. Old marrieds. Sometimes we have problems. I –' Marcia's face flushes '– I did something, Minnette. I don't know why. Boredom, I suppose. And it hurt him. He's still – we're still –' Marcia clenches her fist, hiding her thumb in its knot. 'And *someone* found out. Somehow, someone *here* knows.'

Minnette says nothing. She is still on the merry-go-round, watching the tuxedos blur by. She thinks, although she cannot be certain, that a number of the women and men have been peering at her and her sister.

'Sometimes, I can't stand it here,' Marcia whispers. 'Everyone always staring. Always attacking me when I write my articles, or have an opinion, or wear the "wrong" dress… For a while, I lost myself.'

Minnette thinks back to that period of high collars and dudgeon, and squeezes her sister's hand. For a time, that had been the anomaly – until Minnette grew to accept it. That is, until the last visit, when Minnette compelled Marcia to loosen her collars and hips. Was Minnette to blame, then, for Werner's fate?

'Sometimes, I wish I could just be. Like when we were in Bombay, remember?' Minnette nods. 'It was just us, working on *Marg*, surrounded by all our friends – Otto, Homi, Minoo and all the others.' Marcia's eyes shine.

'Little Zubin with his violin,' adds Minnette, while also noting the ommission of the Bombay Intellectual from Marcia's list. She does not mention him either.

'Sometimes, I still long for Bombay.'

Minnette remembers Bombay, that rush of being away from the demands of Ceylon society. Setting up with Otto Koenigsberger, her architectural mentor at the time. Engaging in extended disputations with Homi Bhabha, the nuclear physicist. The shambolic beginnings, when they all fanned out into the streets to collect those first precious subscriptions that would allow them to produce *Marg*. It was the same desire for freedom that sped her towards London. She understands her sister's restlessness, yet feels a pang for Werner. She misses the camaraderie they shared – the sneaky whiskeys and casual ribbing. They were happy, after all, Werner ecstatic at the 'return' of Marcia last year. But Minnette will not voice her confusion to her sister. Marcia has always been secretive about her affairs, essential given the gossip that has followed her like midges. She spots Werner loping towards them and leaves Marcia where she is.

She moves through the room, acknowledging familiar faces with a smile. A *baila* band has taken the stage and men gather around them, belting out crude lyrics. Couples shuffle and wheel on the floor, retracing old Portuguese dance-steps. She skirts round them, making her way to the great verandah, and walks straight into a man.

'Sorry!' she says, then notices who it is and smiles. 'Ah, Des,' she clasps his hands, 'thank goodness.'

Desmond grasps her hands. 'Minnette!' His cheeriness turns to concern as he notices her reddening cheeks. 'Are you alright?'

The music roars in Minnette's ears, and the crowds press closer. Her breath seems to bubble in her chest. 'I'm sorry,' she gasps. 'I need to – this – it's too much. Will you take me home?' A frown pleats Desmond's forehead and he lets go of her hands. He looks around as if for someone. 'Oh,' says Minnette, 'of course – you must be here with your – with someone.'

'No, no,' says Desmond. 'Rita's not well this evening. Come,' he offers his elbow, 'let's go.'

In the car, Minnette rests her head against the open window. She can hear the ocean engaged in an eternal, rhythmic prevarication. Salt tingles in her nostrils.

'Feeling better?' asks Desmond as he starts the car and drowns out the ocean.

Minnette takes a long, slow breath. She is still dizzy from the champagne, but nods. A *paraya* dog lies curled on the beach, its snout buried beneath its tail. She is glad it is too dark for her to see the sores and bald patches. 'Poor little thing,' she says.

Desmond doesn't hear. They pull away onto the road and drive in silence. It is a dark night, and Minnette concentrates on the various objects that appear like ghosts in the car's headlights: more *paraya* dogs, a man on a bicycle, winged insects.

Minutes later they have left the Galle Face Hotel behind and are driving along the ocean road. 'So, how are you, Minnette?' Desmond asks again.

Minnette glances at him. His eyes are on the road but

he is alert, waiting for her reply. She can think of only a bland summation of her feelings. She is fine. No more, no less. Amma is ill. This is just the reality of things now, a weight she hefts into each new day. And yet her contract in Alfred House Gardens buoys her, challenges her to find new ways to integrate outdoor and indoor living.

'You know, I'm building a new house in Alfred House Gardens.'

'Ah, really!' Desmond's face lights up.

'This one is different, Des. I'm taking all the outside space – everything that can be considered a garden – and enveloping it into the house.'

The possibilities for cross-winds, for a whole new way of living – accommodating and responding to the elements – inspire her. No one else has done this. Her clients, family friends who saw her in school whites, gave her free rein. 'My clients are thrilled. They love the concept and the idea of having a tree within their home.'

Desmond snaps a surprised glance at Minnette. '*My!*' he says.

'They find the overlap with the temple aesthetic comforting – even though they're Christians and not Buddhists.' Minnette has instructed an artisan to shape a *bo* tree motif into the iron gates which, in her clients' eyes, magnifies the effect of the home as sacred space.

'The aspect is vastly different from the Ariyapala Lodge and the other Kandy house – you know, the Piachaud one. There are no views of hills or lakes. Instead, I've planned viewpoints into the house. You see, while it looks out onto leafy surroundings, the eye is also drawn within: along corridors, through glass windows that look from kitchen to sitting room or from balcony to hallway.' The materials she has used – terra cotta, limestone – evoke a sense of the location's broader habitat.

The house is near completion, a fact Minnette finds mildly deflating. She is loath to let it go, and yet impatient to see it finished. She thinks she will even miss the children calling her Aunty Minnette, adding fifteen years to her still youthful frame.

'It's like nothing I've built before,' she says.

Desmond nods. 'Sha! You must show me it when it's done.' They trade glances, run a hand over their hair,, each mirroring the other before they notice what they're doing and stop. 'So, what's next?'

Minnette gazes at the passing trees. 'I'm doing some research on low-cost housing. And starting a house in Edward Lane.'

'Ah!' says Desmond, drumming the steering wheel with cheerful fingers. 'Very busy, Minnette.'

'I'm considering decamping back there –' she waves a hand backward, towards the Galle Face Hotel ' – from Mount Lavinia.' In truth, the idea had only just struck her. Laki and Siri have set up in Mount Lavinia, sloping about the house while Siri, she suspects, works on a new painting. 'I love that old place.'

'Yes,' says Desmond. 'Pure Imperial charm.'

Minnette slaps his arm. 'That is not why I love it, although,' she grins, 'well... maybe it is. All that pannelling, all those chandeliers. And the wonderful staff –'

Minnette sits up in her seat. 'Here – what time is it?' She looks at her watch. '*My*, almost midnight!'

Desmond turns the car up the drive to Aunty Sheila and Uncle Reggie's house. 'And here we are,' he says.

'Quick,' says Minnette, already halfway out of the car. She runs up the path, Desmond behind her. They slip into the house and hurry to the verandah where they find Minnette's parents with Sheila and Reggie. A tray of fluted glasses glitters on the table next to them. They turn to look at Minnette and Desmond, surprise followed by cheers. Sheila is holding up a glass, and although she smiles, doesn't stop her countdown: 'Six – five –'

Minnette swoops towards Amma, whose frail body seems to be held together by her voluminous sari. She is tiny on the grand chair. Minnette puts her arms around her and feels the weight of the day recede. 'Happy new year,' she whispers, and buries herself in her mother's embrace.

Yes, she thinks now, waking up to the new year at Aunty Sheila and Uncle Reggie's. She is relieved she was with Amma at midnight, but she can't help this absence overwhelming her. *Another year gone – another one spent away from him.* She is surprised by the thought. In five months, he will be in India. She wants him to come to Ceylon, too. He could come to Kandy, to Nell Cottage, and finally see her studio. He could lecture on architecture, consider building something on the island. *Why not?* she thinks. *Why should that privilege rest only with India?*

She thinks of him lunching with Mimi and feels envy. She can picture them across from each other, eating little cakes and drinking wine. His rush to help Mimi – to visit Basquin with her – rankles. The fact that Mimi has seen his Taureau painting before she has, fills her with bitterness. *But I cannot begrudge her when I am here and she is there*, she thinks.

She reaches for some paper and writes: *Corbu, I am so*

pleased that you took Mimi out. I admit to feeling a bit dessous that she has already seen your Taureau painting when I have not. I have so looked forward to seeing it. But, I cannot begrudge her when I am here and she is there, can I? She is there... and I am here. And that is how it is.

Minnette stops. She re-reads the passage, to be sure she has kept the tone genial, not self-obsessed and certainly not jealous. She knows this is what he expects of her – another haranguing letter. A letter like that will give him the excuse not to reply. This time, she thinks, he will be surprised. Not only has she remained calm, but she has told him something she knows he wants to hear. In admitting his proximity to Mimi, she offers her permission. She gives permission yet she knows it isn't needed, after all, he takes what he wants when he wants.

She looks out the window and onto Mount Lavinia beach. The sea rolls up to the shore, and fans itself beneath the feet of a salt-stained boy.

———

One month later, a card arrives. *Happy birthday, petit oiseau. I hope this little card reaches you in time for February.* In fact, it is a full two weeks early; Minnette has not even thought of her birthday until now. *Corbu is hard at work, in perpetual motion across this globe. Ronchamp is gathering pace. The foundations are down and the tower goes up. It is like a giant ear to the sky. A perfect companion to the funnel/ telescope at the Assembly Hall in Chandigarh. These are not separate structures, you see. Through Corbu, a visual and spiritual harmony spreads itself from India to France.*

Do not despair, mon enfant. That spirit also includes you.

In a matter of months, Corbu will be back in India, and, who knows? Perhaps he will have time to visit his dear friend, too. If not, there is always Aix in July. You will come, oiseau? Another CIAM conference is scheduled and your input is much needed. We must look beyond the Occident, n'est-ce pas?

Yes, the Occident is too concerned with itself. And without the Orient, it will perish.

There is no mention of Mimi, and Minnette puts the card down with satisfaction. But her relief soon gives way to dread. *It is in the unsaid that meaning really takes root.* She turns this over in her mind as she draws on a cigarette, exhaling and watching the smoke ghost up and gently tear itself into nothingness. In this way, she rationalises that as long as this thing remains unsaid, it is not real.

Minnette turns the little card over between her fingers. She studies the sketch on the front – a mini taureau – and thinks, *it is not enough*. It can never be enough until she, too, is standing in his studio. She puts the miniature into a box containing his other letters and packs it into her trunk. She has gathered everything she thinks she will need for the coming months to complete the build at Alfred House Gardens. Even if she forgets something, it is no great loss. She can drive up to Mount Lavinia any time from Havelock Town.

Minnette moves into the flat Siri and Laki are sharing in Colombo, just south of where her new build is sited. The flat, a roomy place surrounded by tall trees in Havelock Town, belongs to one of their friends, Thomas Brohier, an artist and keen traveller. Minnette thinks the move will do her some good. She hasn't been on her own, away from family, since her time in London. When she steps into the Brohier flat, it feels like she is back on Savile Row again. Berkeley Square finds its sister in Havelock Grounds, stretching out verdantly before her. The evening fog is replaced by slow-motion bats stirring into dusk. And the pitched roof of her erstwhile attic flat widens its arms in its eastern incarnation.

Minnette has never met Thomas Brohier, but standing in his home, she finds it easy to deduce who he is. His book shelves are filled with volumes on Japanese inks and the art of calligraphy. There are tomes on the history of typefaces and a whole series of *Punch* magazines bound in leather. Rich batiks hang alongside contemporary artworks, including Siri's. There is nothing hysterical in the way the flat is decorated. Art objects are placed carefully throughout rooms, with plenty of white space around them, giving them the attention they deserve.

Minnette has the upstairs room while Laki and Siri occupy the rooms downstairs at the back of the flat. They have set up their easels in Thomas' studio space, where he normally draws his cartoons. In this room, Siri paints while Laki watches, observing the great man's technique, for Siri is, by now, a 'great' painter. He is in demand: all the Colombo 7 types want a Siri Sinharaja to hang on their walls. But Siri will not paint for everyone. These days he is working on a series of vertical tableaux. At the moment, they are simple rectangles of rich colour with no other discernible shapes. He has yet to draw the detail out from beneath thick layers of paint.

In her room, light pelts Minnette like rain as she labours over her plans. A commission for an open air theatre has arrived without warning. The repeated demands of clients to minimise costs has led her to indigenous building methods which provide unexpected inspiration. Then there is the house in Edward Lane, a modest build that, nonetheless, requires much thought. She has no assistants, no office – unlike the other practices in Ceylon. She must manage the process herself, from concept right through to the final build. These are obstacles that would deter other architects, but Minnette is used to working under straitened circumstances – and falls on her tasks with quick determination. Away from the coast, from the rush and push of the water, she finds her mind at rest. It is not Nell Cottage – it is almost better. No family to distract her, no excessive reflecting on the architect. Siri and Laki are busy with their own work so that an overall feeling of industry permeates the flat.

Minnette recalls Aunty Sheila's cautionary words before she moved out. 'Minnette, you know how people will talk, you shacking up with two boys and all.' Minnette frowned. Even as Aunty Sheila spoke, she recognised the absurdity of the assertion. Tongues may have been snapping here and there, but most people knew that Laki and Siri posed no threat to Minnette's virtue.

She chuckles at the thought, knowing her virtue has long since departed. She is neither young nor naive. There is little she has not seen. She imagines Amma in Kandy and shivers at the thought of her discovering the truth. It is nothing to Minnette to have lived these things, but to be confronted by Amma's interpretation of them fills her with shame. She buries the thought. Amma would never have cause to find any of this out. To her, Minnette remains her brilliant daughter, with all the decency she attaches to the title. Or, perhaps Amma knows it is not true; she sees Minnette drinking and smoking, after all.

Amma is no *naïf*; she, too, has seen life, and has imparted a thirst for it in both her daughters. But Minnette – and Marcia – have stepped beyond even that. Maybe it is easier for Amma – and her – to maintain the artifice.

Minnette looks over her research into early wattle and daub construction. How straightforward and unpretentious those houses were. There is no ostentation in the design. She thinks that rammed earth walls are a more feasible option for homeowners and considers how she might incorporate this technology into her own designs. She writes a letter to an engineer contact to find out how effective these walls might be as load-bearers. She has more – much more – work to do, but her father and mother have insisted she break for the Sinhala-Tamil New Year.

So Siri, Laki and Minnette close up the Brohier flat and make their way to Kandy in April, where Jaya's sticky *cavum* and fried *kokkis* await their arrival. Minnette doesn't know why Siri and Laki seem to prefer her family to their own. She has heard that they both come from down south – somewhere beyond Tangalle. But neither has ever confirmed this with her, let alone referred to a family member in her presence.

Minnette is puzzled. Siri is well known now. She can't understand why his people haven't come up to Colombo to find him, if only to claim some of his financial success. She thinks he may be an orphan or from a difficult home. Siri gives nothing away. As for Laki, Minnette knows only slightly more. She has heard from someone, she can't recall whom, that his mother had been a temple dancer and that his father had disappeared when Laki was still a baby.

Minnette studies Laki through the corner of her eye.

He has the lithe qualities of a dancer – muscular limbs and an elegant spine. Perhaps it is the fact of his physical beauty that lends itself to such speculation. Or perhaps the rumour is true and he has inherited a natural athleticism. Whatever the reason, Laki and Siri continue to spend the holidays with the de Silvas. Minnette's parents have no opinion on the nature of the men's relationship. The two keep to themselves, dipping in and out of conversation as necessary. No one obliges them to speak or take part. They are simply part of the fabric. Sitting by the two, Minnette's whole person floods with warmth. She reaches out and squeezes Laki's hand. Affection and relief envelop her in equal parts. Affection, because she is so fond of the pair; relief, because they are her buffer against the loneliness that shadows her daily.

When Minnette, Siri and Laki arrive at Nell Cottage, they find Minnette's father pleading with her mother to eat one more *cavum*. 'George, I can't stand the stuff,' says Amma, but Papa keeps smiling, pushing plates of the oily cakes towards her. Minnette swallows her laughter because the look in Papa's eyes frightens her. He flaps about Amma, plumping her pillows and pressing her hands and feet. Minnette doesn't want to consider why he has reduced himself to this. Instead she, too, takes up the lobby, entreating her mother to eat *kokkis*.

'Not you as well,' she says, as Minnette holds one of the crunchy wheels of fried batter to her lips. She wrinkles her nose, but accepts the offer. She can't resist Jaya's *kokkis*.

Two days later, even Amma is well enough for the drive up to Nuwara Eliya. Laki announces that the new year's fruitfulness will begin at the races. He and Papa put money down on a horse called Blaggard's Knave.

'George,' says Amma, raising a caustic finger. 'You both will lose. You watch. It will be a waste.'

Minnette, too, secretly put money down on the horse, so that she cheers alongside Papa and Laki when it wins. Siri and Amma say nothing; Siri, because it is his wont, Amma, because she has been proved wrong. She sits with rouched lips, but the lines around her eyes tell a different story. They are lines Minnette knows well – lines that steal the smile from Amma's mouth and set it gently in her glance. Without these lines, Minnette thinks she would never have known what Amma really thought of her, all those years ago, when she ran barefoot through cow dung, or asked a lunch guest whether they intended to stay for dinner as well.

Later, as they stroll between mock Tudor houses and strawberry bushes, their pockets heavy with their takings, Papa sighs. 'They say the Korean war is finally ending.'

'Peace at last,' says Amma.

Papa nods. 'Yes. Good for Korea and the Europeans and the Americans. But for Ceylon?'

'Look at those roses,' says Minnette, pointing to a rambling bush, wet with pink flowers. Everyone stops for a moment to admire it. Minnette turns to her father. 'How do you mean?' she asks.

'The fat times are ending,' he replies. 'The subsidies are being cut. Farmers will be competing without an advantage. The war boom is ending.'

Minnette nods. The papers have been reporting the threat of subsidy cuts for weeks – months even, as if the government were trying to prepare everyone for the inevitable. At the same time, the countryside is being transformed. No longer does the peasant farmer rely on a buffalo to plough his fields when the tractor can do this in less time and at less cost. Minnette weighs up the cost of feeding a buffalo against buying a tractor.

When the Prime Minister died last year, he was replaced by his son. Dudley, however, seems less concerned with keeping religion out of politics than his father was. Across the country, people are grumbling that the Ceylonese have misplaced their identity – that they lack nationalistic zeal.

'They complain about the use of English, too,' says Papa, as if reading Minnette's thoughts.

'Who is this *they*?' Like a lizard that has thawed its muscles in the sun, Siri snaps into life.

'These people,' says Amma, 'who cry endlessly for Sinhala only.'

'But we are the majority,' says Siri simply.

Everyone turns to look at him, Laki more sharply than the rest. 'We? Who is this *we*?'

Siri shrugs, says nothing.

'Bloody rubbish,' says Minnette. 'We will all be out of a job if they pass a law advocating either language.' Nobody laughs.

'All?' asks Siri. 'Or just the upper classes?'

Minnette finds Siri's sudden loquaciousness irritating. For as long as she has known him, he has been as silent as a library, the little that left his lips doing so in opaque riddles. Where once she found it irksome, she grew to love this enigmatic nature of his. But now, most unexpectedly, he is speaking plainly, revealing not some marvellous pearl of wisdom, but a simple-minded chauvinism. Only the other day, a school headmaster condemned the government for conducting its business in the language of its former oppressors. Condemned it for its lack of nationalistic sentiment.

'English may be a foreign language,' says Minnette, 'but it has opened us up to a larger reality. It will give us the world instead of the dirt in our navels.'

'As long as the farmer keeps to his land, tilling the soil with his buffalo, keeping out of government because he doesn't understand the language, Ceylon will remain that gem in the Indian ocean. A frozen paradise for the world to ogle.' Siri says this in a monotone, much like that night long ago, when he was grieving the loss of Eric, the photographer. Then, he spoke of lions and elephants and Minnette had not understood his meaning. But as they walk through this little piece of England, exported to Ceylon's hills, as they wander between white houses with their chocolate brown beams, she begins to understand what Siri has been saying all along. *We are a nation of lions in thrall to the elephant.* It is time we rise up, he was saying, to fulfill the destiny of our forbears.

The three return to Thomas Brohier's flat. An iron silence descends between Laki and Siri. Laki spends less and less time watching Siri and more of it tending to his own canvases. Minnette remains upstairs, toiling in her temporary studio while contemplating the cricketers on Havelock Grounds. On a whim, she searches through her trunk for the little box of letters and pulls out the architect's latest card to her. The taureau is still there, eyes round, nostrils flaring, forehead stubborn with lines. She considers his invitation to her to go to the next CIAM, but there is no way she can leave now, not with her work, not with Amma's health so fragile.

I am not sure what I can bring to CIAM, Corbu, she writes. *What can I bring from this patch of the Orient to set against the Occidental hegemony you describe?* Minnette can think of many things she can bring, so many ideas, but there is no value in describing these when it is impossible for her to go. CIAM will have to do without her insights on rammed earth technology and low-cost builds. *At any rate, I am stuck here with this contract. And I can't afford to make the journey either, despite winning money on Blaggard's Knave. So you must come here, instead, my friend. Venez me voir. I will organise some work for you.*

She must tempt him with more than just herself. There must be the promise of professional challenges, of a chance at glory. But her own agenda slips through, invades the page. *It is only a short trip from Bombay to Colombo. I can meet you here, take you to Kandy, to the beach, to crumbling forts. Please, you must come, Corbu. I have been too long without you.*

Minnette seals the pages swiftly into an envelope without re-reading them. She knows she has broken her own rule, exposing her need unnecessarily. She decides to post the letter immediately, before she changes her mind and tears it into a hundred pieces.

The architect does not write. He does not come to Ceylon.

Tea estates fall away from her as the train creeps up into the Kandy hills. The air is heavy with moisture, but Minnette is happy to be away from Colombo and the stultifying atmosphere of the Brohier flat. Laki and Siri have said little to one another since April. Siri's newly articulated nationalism has opened a fault line that has been thickening with each passing week. Minnette has tried to remain neutral, but Siri's opinions shock and repel her, so much so that she finds herself questioning her friendship with him. She wonders whether it was ever really genuine when so much of what he believed remained hidden from her for so long. She asks herself whether this is the same Siri she has known and respected for the past several years. Then she remembers his solid presence that night at Reggie and Sheila's, when Minnette had been drunk and inexplicably upset about Desmond. Siri had sat there, while she leaned against his shoulder, and he had spoken to her in that whispering rhythmic way, spinning out a riddle that made her forget her hurt.

Minnette thinks of her mother. Fear butterflies up her throat. Amma is ill again, worse than before. Minnette has left her sketches of the arts centre on her desk in Colombo. She has had to leave the Edward Lane build as it is. She thinks with irritation of the last time she was called out to Kandy, how angry she had felt when it had appeared that Amma was perfectly healthy. She hopes that it will be the same case this time. It would be a relief to see her sitting upright with colour in her cheeks. But Minnette knows this is not the case. Her mother has cancer. She will not recover.

Minnette stays at Nell Cottage for three weeks. Each afternoon, she sits by her mother, watching the monsoon fall thickly outside. A clamminess hangs in the air, intrudes into the most secret recesses of their bones. Papa brings them tea. He arrives and departs as silently as a nun. His expression is always cheerful, even if there are no accompanying words. Amma often watches him with a bemused frown. She looks at Minnette and shakes her head.

Minnette is irritated by her father's silence. She finds his gormless smile unsettling, and his insistence on waiting on Amma trying. 'Why can't he just leave these things to Jaya?' she asks her mother one day, after he has served the customary tea and biscuits. Amma holds up her palm abruptly. 'Don't,' she says, and the two of them return to the scene outside the house: the steady shower, falling with sibilant force against the trees, the roof, the lawn.

———————

When Laki's letter arrives, Minnette is already longing to return to Colombo. In it, he begs her to come back for the Roberts Cup in August. *This is **the** show, Minnette,* he writes, telling her it's her chance to be seen in her best frock on the Havelock Racecourse. *You'll be the talk of the papers!* Minnette smiles. She would rather her work be the talk of the papers, but with her builds not yet ready to show, she thinks a nice dress might be the next best thing.

It would provide a welcome distraction from the impending 'financial bankruptcy' that Ceylon's policitians have been warning of. The government has been threatening to abolish food subsidies, and the price of rice is expected to triple in the coming months. Each time Jaya returns from the market, it is with another story of rice selling out because people are afraid they soon won't be able to afford it. Minnette knows they are probably right. The price of rice is going up across South East Asia.

The threatened rises have struck political discord, with the Communist Party particulary vitriolic. According to them, the Ceylon government is going out of its way to cow-tow to the Americans while downplaying China's support. Everywhere there is talk of a strike.

So I shall be doing more than simply parading across the racecourse next month, she writes. *I shall have to put some money down as well. Let's hope there will be another Blaggard's Knave to carry the shortfall threatening all our pockets.*

She tells the architect she is sorry she can't come to Aix for the next CIAM. *I had hoped that members of the Marg contingent would be there to counteract, or at least set in relief, any Occidental bias there. But it seems they were relying on me.* Minnette has, in fact, written several times to the *Marg* group, urging them to organise themselves, create some guiding principles for them as an entity. She has had no reply. She sent a selection of photographs of the

Ariyapala Lodge, sketches of Alfred House Gardens, and an essay to Bombay for discussion in Aix, which she now also shares with the architect. *Can you find a way to present this?* she writes, knowing he won't. Still, she imagines, with satisfaction, the architect's reaction to these submissions, the pride with which he is certain to look upon her work again, this time in the context of the work of others.

She thinks how much she still misses him, how deep the old need has burrowed, like a worm, into the hardest part of her. She is impressed by its tenacity these past six years – much as she despairs of it, and succumbs.

Days later, she is back in Colombo, drinking tea while sitting on the balcony with Laki. They are both surprised by the sudden price rises – rice has nearly tripled in cost, tram fares have doubled, postal rates are up, too.

'Fortunately, I posted my letter to him just before the price of stamps went up,' says Minnette.

'I think it's high time we shifted ourselves to the races, darling,' says Laki, smiling. 'I have a tip on a horse called Bedouin Fire.'

Minnette wears a balcony dress, strapless and covered in swooping geometric patterns. She preens alongside the well-groomed ladies of Cinnamon Gardens, all displaying the latest in frock fashion. 'I could sing a *baila* about those shoulders,' croons Laki. Siri remains behind at the Brohier flat.

Bedouin Fire runs the third race at 8-1. 'Are you sure about this?' Minnette asks, but her doubts are soon laid flat. Their horse, an Arabian with a lustrous coat, comes first, winning them a substantial sum. Laki unrolls the wad of bills in his hand and whistles in disbelief. 'Champagne?'

Sharing a bottle between them, they lay bets on two more horses picked solely for the musicality of their names: Jeddah Express and Farouk bin Farouk. Both prove hopeless. 'Never mind,' shrugs Minnette. She buys another bottle of champagne with their reduced takings and they totter home.

Navigating the steps up to the Brohier flat proves especially difficult for Laki, who stumbles on each riser. The genteel floridity of his usual speech also stumbles. *'Malu malu malu!'* he sings, quoting the *baila* classic in which a man brings his wife fish, as one might bring flowers. *'Dhang genapu malu.'* He trips up a step, falls forward onto his palms. They laugh. 'Shhh,' says Minnette, filling the stairwell with a hiss. This, too, is hilarious. Minnette lapses into Burgher English, Aunty Sheila's preferred accent. 'Anh, what men? Bringing fish for Siri? Your Surangani?'

'Surangani! Surangani! Surangani-ta malu genava. Malu, malu ma—'

She shushes him again, sending them both into hysterics. Minnette sits on the stair next to him. He is still on all fours, body jerking with laughter. *'Illai, illai,'* he cries, reverting to Tamil. *No. No.* (It is the only Tamil word Minnette knows.)

'That bastard,' he says, wiping his eyes.

'Who?' asks Minnette.

Laki twists round, sinks onto a step. 'Siri. Who else?' He is still smiling, contradicting the rancour in his voice. 'He's angry at me. Because of Batticaloa.'

'Batticaloa?'

'And now all this nonsense about *swabasha*. He wanted to teach me Sinhala. I said no. That, too, put him into a black mood. He goes to temple, sits with those mad monks, then comes here and paints the Mahavamsa. Have you seen the latest? Dutugemunu's victory over Elara. This is it, Minnette, the triptych that he has been fiddling with for months. The painting that brought him here, to Colombo, this 'great work', what does it amount to? Death. The smashing of the South Indian ruler – even the Mahavamsa called him 'just'. At the front, march an army of monks. Where is the *ahimsa* – the non-violence – in that? These monks are meddling in things that are not their business. What is the use of fasting and begging with one hand, when they are throwing grenades into Parliament with the other?'

Minnette nods. The monks have been complaining since Independence, claiming that Ceylon's unique Buddhist culture is in danger of disappearing. Minnette cannot understand how that can be possible. Buddhists are a majority in Ceylon. They say that a lack of respect for Buddhism undermines the nation. In other words, Buddhism *is* the nation. And Sinhala is the language of nationalism. The leader of the opposition party claims that only ten per cent of Ceylonese speak English, yet Ceylon's leaders speak nothing but. He points to this as if it were something to be ashamed of but, reflects Minnette, *what use is Sinhala in the realm of international relations? Is promoting Sinhala and only Sinhala really the best way forward for Ceylon?*

'He's a hypocrite,' Laki hunches forward, elbows on knees. 'The darling is happy to keep company with the '43 group, keeping his mouth shut while his reputation goes up. He'll nicely stay at Thomas' flat or Aunty Sheila's. And then he comes back and paints this… this hatred onto canvas. You should see it, Minnette, how Elara is pulled into pieces. That is where the painting starts. With something that is not even in the Mahavamsa.'

'It's a painting. It could mean anything – the very opposite, in fact, of what you suspect. It is not necessarily a reflection of what is in his heart.'

Laki shakes his head. 'He is not the man I knew.' This last sentence comes sighing under his breath, like an invitation slipped beneath a door. Minnette sips from her bottle of champagne, offers some to Laki. He refuses, staring at his lap – white trousers wrinkled and smudged with clay-coloured stains. He smoothes down the creases with a distracted palm. 'Dutugemunu united the island for the first time. But only after killing Ceylon's wisest ruler.'

Laki shrinks on the step while Minnette slumps against the railings. Their earlier elation, fuelled by their win and subsequent champagne celebration, has dissolved. An ache wraps itself around Minnette's forehead. Laki is still ironing his thigh with a palm. Minnette finds the hiss unsettling. She stills his hand with her own. The door behind them closes abruptly. They look at one another. Minnette hadn't heard it open. She wonders how long Siri must have been standing there, listening to them. 'Who cares,' Laki says morosely. He reaches for the bottle of champagne and drinks from it without stopping.

They slink into the flat on tiptoe. A dim light glows at the back of the apartment, throwing bleak shadows into the corridor. Minnette nods to Laki, bidding him goodnight, but he takes her hand. 'Please. I want to come with you.'

Minnette offers him the small room beside hers. As the days go by, he slowly moves his belongings upstairs. 'Why not just ask Siri to leave?' she whispers one afternoon, then feels a traitor for saying it. 'I suppose,' she says, regretting her earlier question. 'I suppose Siri's politics are his business,' and reminds herself that politics should not interfere with her friendship with him. Yet he, too, has lost sight of his friends – has put ideology before everything but his ambition.

Not surprisingly, Laki says no. He checks his coals, arranging them in order of density. 'He's my friend, no? Or he was.' It is the reply that Minnette expects, the answer she would have given too, had the question been put to her a few weeks ago. 'All this started in Batticaloa,' he says. 'Because he is obsessed and I don't care.'

Minnette stands by the only window in her room and looks out. There is a tree just below, and below that, sprays of bougainvillea lurch like drunk men over the parapet wall. 'I don't understand.' She pictures them all standing on the beach, reaches back to that afternoon spent floating in the ocean with Siri, staring at his crumpled toes, the two of them scorching under the sun. Laki and Mimi rising naked from the water. Laki and Mimi tangled like fish in a net. Siri with his hands around Mimi's neck. 'Was he jealous of Mimi?'

Laki shifts the coals around in his box. 'He must think I'm sleeping with you now.'

She laughs. 'But that's ridiculous,' she says, then stops when she sees Laki's expression. 'Isn't it?' For a moment, he doesn't answer.

He smiles. 'Yes, yes, ridiculous. We're friends, you and I. Nothing more.' His tone is apologetic. 'You understand, no?'

Minnette understands nothing, but nods anyway. 'Yes, of course. I hope I haven't given a different impression?'

'No, no, not at all.'

'Perhaps we should be clear with Siri, then.'

Laki shrugs. 'No point. Siri thinks what he wants.'

'But,' the room presses closer against them. 'Do we know what he's thinking?'

'I know.'

'Do please share it with me, then.' A blind falls over Laki's eyes, scrambling his expression like code. Minnette tries a different approach. 'Why did he do that to Mimi that day? I thought he was just being, I don't know... eccentric.'

Laki smiles and shakes his head. 'I told Siri she had a neck as smooth as bamboo. I don't know why I said it.' Minnette can tell from the flippancy of his remark that he is lying. 'Bamboo?' she says, stretching the lie. 'No, more like... marble. She is a living piece of sculpture.'

Laki slides shut his box of coals and sits on the bed. He darts glances around the room, like a sparrow scanning for danger. 'Marble, yes,' he sighs loudly. Then quietly, in a whisper, adds, 'What if he can hear us?'

Minnette glances at the doorway. It is empty, as is the corridor beyond. The only audible sound is the creaking of the long case clock downstairs. 'He must be out,' she mouths, shutting the door. They sit beside one another in silence. Minnette is loath to speak, not wanting to scare Laki away or discourage him from saying what he seems too frightened to say. Minutes go by, measured out wheezily by the clock downstairs. She crosses her legs, jigs her foot. Laki does the same. Fifteen minutes go by, then twenty. A bicycle bell pings outside the window. Someone sneezes. 'We saw you,' Minnette says. Laki freezes, alert. 'That night, by the boat, you and Mimi. We saw you. Siri didn't know I was there. He was sketching you both.' Laki covers his face with his hands.

Minnette tells him about the drawing, how she and Mimi had found it in Siri's sketchbook. How Laki and

Mimi had been reduced to two howling mouths scratched into the page. 'I'm sorry,' she says. Laki, bent almost in two, remains still. Eventually, he unfolds himself and smiles. When he speaks, his voice is calm. 'But why did you watch us?' It is the inevitable question.

'It was an accident, of course,' she says to Laki. 'I was having a stroll. How was I to expect that you and Mimi would be *in flagrante* in the open like that?' Laki flinches. 'You can't blame me. As for "watching", I wasn't really. I left as soon as I realised what I was seeing, but not before I saw Siri.'

'Never mind, Minnette,' says Laki. 'Mimi is lucky. She has no one to remind her of what happened. I doubt she would remember, anyway... It has already lost colour for me.'

Not me, Corbu, she writes later to the architect. *The moon had been bright that evening, and Mimi's skin glowed like marble. Laki's black limbs wound around her pale flesh like a serpent sliding through milk. They had been sleeping when I found them, still clinging to one another, bodies unclothed, daubed with wet sand. All this the moon showed me, but only as I sat beside Laki did my mind's eye open to this lost footage. In Batticaloa I saw us, Corbu – a crow and his oiseau, wings parted, feathers tesselating against one another. Yet the moon had shown me otherwise. I remember it now, that sensual canvas. And though it looked so much like us – so much so that I was fooled – it was someone else's pleasure, someone else's truth and, later, someone else's forgetting, too.*

The market heaves with people, each armed with carefully remembered lists of goods they want to buy. But as the days wear, frustration rises. Men and women haggle at one stall and then another, with little success. Rice is almost beyond their reach now. Other staple foods follow suit. Everywhere, a call to strike – led by the Communists – takes hold. Rate rises and the 'relentless expansion of the American hegemony' are quoted as grievances.

The fragile alliance between the Communists, Bolshevik-Leninists and Trotskyites is motivated by a common desire to crush the ruling party. The day before the *hartal*, or strike, questioning in Parliament turns to the value of tear gas imports into the island. The following day, people march across the city like a column of ants, and tear gas reserves, whatever their provenance, are duly called upon.

Seven thousand harbour workers in Colombo strike off work; boats are left unloaded, cargo remain in their holds. Bus, rail and tram networks are in disarray with gangs stoning them at every opportunity. Rail tracks are torn up, signal lines cut. A coconut processing factory in Pettah goes up in flames, and as the police and fire brigade try to put it out, crowds pelt them with rocks and bottles.

Curfew is declared from 6.30 p.m. to dawn. The city tenses its shoulders, roils with a dyspeptic silence. A State of Emergency stretches like a spider's web over it. The web extends across the island, muffling fury beneath its sticky grasp.

Arrack and toddy taverns are ordered closed. Drunks stay in, imbibe their poison and beat their wives with extra vigour. Mothers watch suppers grow cold at the table and worry when their children fail to come home to eat. Marriages gradually repair themselves while lovers, deprived of an opportunity for late night trysts, lose hope.

Bren machine-gun posts appear in various locations, including the middle of Colombo's Pettah market. Kandy, however, is virtually untouched. Some parts of the island remain oblivious to the chaos. Ceylon's ladies (only the well-heeled need apply) compete to become the next Miss Lanka. Next to news reports of petrol bombs and looted shops are exclamatory announcements on the latest selection of ladies to make the Miss Lanka shortlist, most of whom are middle-aged and rich.

Throughout the Emergency, Minnette and Laki keep watch from their balcony. They use their takings from the Havelock races and buy everything – Australian ham, English whiskey, off-ration rice. They eat, with newspapers spread before them, reading about the strikes, and disparaging the Communists.

As the unrest continues to plague the island, the government comes down hard on its detractors, with Dudley, the reluctant Prime Minister, looking more and more worn out.

By the time the Emergency ends in September, 21 people have been killed, 175 are seriously injured and nearly 400 arrested. The Prime Minister resigns, and is replaced by a pompous and clueless knight. The Tamils are dismayed.

At some point, early in the Emergency, Minnette and Laki realised Siri had left. His absence was palpable: air flowed unchecked through the flat, clearing it of the August heat. They searched the ground floor, stepping almost jauntily from room to room. His things were still there, arranged neatly on shelves. And in the centre of the studio was the triptych of Dutugemunu's victory, casting a rectangular shadow on the floor. Elara's death filled the centre panel with all its horror. Dutugemunu's expression was calm, cold-blooded; Elara's, a mouth gaping in the full ecstasy of annihilation. It was like nothing Siri had painted before.

Laki and Minnette stare mutely at the painting. It is the first time, since they found it in the summer, that they have stood before it again. Weals of red pigment penetrate yellow pools leaving spidery veins along its surface. Rage and despair hurl themselves at one another, causing an anguished wailing. Directing it all is the steady gaze of Dutugemunu, righteous and unmoved. Laki and Minnette leave the room.

Sat on the balcony, they scan the road, half-expecting to see Siri wandering across it. No one appears. They do not go looking for him. They do not report his absence to the police for fear of implicating him as a *hartal* hooligan. And although they try, they fail to get through to anyone who might have known his whereabouts. In the end, Laki and Minnette decide he must be at a temple somewhere. His sympathies certainly don't lie with the Reds. His stance against the Communists' campaign to give plantation Indians voting rights made his political intentions clear enough. His heart lies with the opposition party – with that man Bandaranaike and his (as Minnette put it) Sinhalese Buddhist bias and pseudo-antielitism. 'Everyone knows that Bandaranaike will happily send his children to English boarding schools abroad while insisting that Ceylonese children be taught their own language (meaning Sinhala) at home,' she had once said to Siri. *It is a party for hypocrites*, she thinks now, *so Siri is in good company*.

Again she asks herself when all of this began. She wonders whether it has anything to do with Eric, the photographer, and his untimely death by elephant. She knows how grief can void a person's heart. Or, worse still, perhaps he has always harboured such unpleasant thoughts.

Minnette wonders whether he was caught up in the fires consuming the island. He has been missing for months. This realisation disturbs her. She does not understand how she has forgotten him so effortlessly. She wonders whether she has abandoned him because his politics no longer suit hers. She returns to this riddle again and again, and finds that the truth is more complicated: their disappointment, and therefore abandonment, is mutual.

As for Laki and Siri, their friendship seems to be over. Minnette does not think she has ever really understood it – the two of them, bound together by a strange kind of passion. It is not the details of their intimacy that disturb her, but the pair's curious mismatch, and their temporary contentment despite the odds. As the relationship crumbled, so did Siri's hold over Laki, and Laki's work is now blossoming into something distinct and beautiful. Minnette recalls some of Laki's recent sketches – works of divine abstraction, of fleeting light and shadow, of creeping insects shimmering in the glare of the sun.

Whatever it is, Minnette does not miss Siri. She is relieved that he isn't around, casting his gloom across the flat. She is more concerned about her missing letters – letters she was expecting from the architect. She has not heard from him since her birthday in February. It is October now, his birthday, and she is obliged to put aside her misgivings and mark the occasion with a letter.

Happy birthday, Corbu, she writes. *Is it only when we are so far apart and out of touch that we think of birthdays? Such a convenient expedient, providing us the justification we need to initiate contact when all indications suggest we do otherwise.* She re-reads the words and sighs. He is likely to think her harsh, but this is nothing new. He expects her anger, even invites it. She decides she will not give him that satisfaction.

I suppose that bloody Emergency is to blame. Your letters to me must have burned before they ever had a chance to be delivered.

———————

Laki and Minnette gradually spread out to the bottom floor of the Brohier flat. He works in the studio, though he dares not touch the triptych which beats like a rotten heart in the centre of that room. Instead he chooses to work along the periphery, staring out the window at the tall trees, the rambling bougainvillea and the road beyond.

Minnette remains attached to the upper floor, particularly her balcony. She sits there, musing on the house in Edward Lane, her thoughts often returning to the architect. *So long without a letter from you and I don't understand why,* she writes, knowing she sounds pathetic. *I know you're busy and as I said before in my birthday note, my frustrations are directed rather at fate, for your replies to my letters must surely have been claimed by the fires of this, our first Emergency since Independence.*

We have a new Prime Minister now, but I suspect that things will never really return to what they were. The rice ration, however, fell just before your birthday, Corbu, from 70 to 50 cents a measure. So now we only have to pay twice what we paid before.

The rains are coming.

The rains are not coming. They're here. How much better would it have been had they come a little earlier to put out the fires that were swallowing the island in August. Never mind.

Minnette looks down from the balcony and sees a thin rain darkening the red dust below. She thinks that the architect will return to India soon. Her longing for him is tempered by the demands of her own practice. The house at Edward Lane is a simple structure, built for the realities of an increasingly densely populated capital. *It's a simple cube, split into three levels,* she explains to the architect. *I have continued to explore the potential of split-level floors to increase airflow. This cube-house is based on that theory. It has a small footprint, and the central staircase acts as a courtyard, chanelling air vertically and horizontally. Each level will have a balcony to drive air into the house as well.* Like her other builds, Edward Lane also has a carport and loggia – everything tucked into or under the house to maximise use of what horizontal space there is. *I long to hear of your discoveries and triumphs as I toil here on my humble projects,* she concludes, then thinks: *How small I feel next to his greatness.*

4 December 1953
Paris

My dear heart. My apologies for not writing earlier, but Corbu is like an albatross, great wings spanning the circumference of the globe. I have been busy with Ronchamp, Aix – so many things. But first, felicitations, my dear friend. I can hear the wheels of your keen mind turning even on this page. Your cube house and that one in Alfred House Gardens – each one takes you to a new understanding. I wait for the photos! Embrace the new life it gives you, in the face of this nightmare of politics you describe.

He taps the pen against the page. There is no such new life in his, only absences. Vonn grows feebler every day and she depends more and more on him. An ache spawns in his knees without warning. *I am no better,* he thinks, *than the small dog she carries around with her all day.* He knows that Vonn is disappointed in him, that he is too absent from her, from Minnette and from all the others.

You do me the favour of thinking the best of me, he writes, *but this is my first letter to you since – when was it? Your birthday? – yes, February. You must understand, Corbu is very busy.* Even as he writes this, he knows it is a poor excuse. Still, it is the only excuse she appears to understand. She herself uses it to free him from accountability. There is no harm in deploying it again.

He had wanted her to come to Aix. She had wanted him to come to Ceylon. Instead, he had sat in India, where time is elastic, and refused digression. He sat in India while Ronchamp continued to rise up on its haunches.

The architect spent weeks sweating in the June heat, speaking with Seetaram and Trivedi about the possibility of establishing a Fondation Le Corbusier in India. *Why not?* he thought. After all, India is where he finds stillness of heart and mind. It is the logical, the intuitive place in which to store his life's work. He did not speak to Elizabeth or her husband about his thoughts. They have been too occupied with their own agendas. On each return to Chandigarh, the architect finds his plan slightly modified and it is always too late for anything to be done about it.

Despite these small transgressions, he must put his faith in his team and keep his grip on the capital complex, the head of Chandigarh. And as he builds the head of this fine city – a city which he mapped out in its entirety – he is grateful for having found his heart in this place, this great peninsula reclining beneath Europe. Why not build his foundation in India – in Chandigarh – at the foot of the Himalayas, in a place where an ancient civilization was spawned and continues to thrive unspoilt by the ravages of material culture?

It is a land bursting with archetypes. The architect does not consider himself a high priest exposing truths or coining symbols. He is innocent, a *naïf* who sees only what is obvious to everyone. Though obvious, not everyone can articulate it. This is what he does: he articulates.

He recalls looking up to the sky while he was in India, and finding two eyes looking back at him. These eyes, round and frightened, looked out from the moon, and below them were a nose and a round mouth. It spoke in a language he cannot remember though he understood it at the time. Never before had he seen a face – any face – in the moon. But there it was, opening its mouth as if to speak, no words falling and yet words entering the architect's ear. The architect sketched this face and now it has been placed in the south window of the church at

Ronchamp. Is it the face of God? The face of a demon? Or is it some cosmic being projecting itself upon the surface of the moon? Just as our eyes are a complex mechanism of mirrors projecting images onto surfaces which flip and are finally seen by us, the moon is suddenly another eye for the architect. And now this celestial projection projects itself into his cathedral in round surprise.

The architect returns to his letter. *A state of emergency, oiseau*, he writes. *I am relieved that you have emerged safely from it, and have eaten well of foreign hams and other delicacies nonetheless!* He reads her description of Siri and Laki's dying relationship and thinks how unfortunate it is to have to watch a bond like that dissolve. He knows that he himself is not immune to such events either, and describes his old friend, Ozenfant. *Remember Ozenfant*, he writes, *my old comrade. Old friend, partner, enfant terrible. But ultimately a traitor. I carry around the symbol of his cheapness in my breast pocket every day. A cheque for $5. His meanness must never be forgotten!*

So it must be with her two friends, he continues. Their separation is political, philosophical, too. They are divided from one another by a difference that one cannot ignore of the other. *It is not surprising that pale Mimi is mixed up in there, too*, he adds playfully. *She is thoughtless, that one.*

Later that day, Mimi visits the architect at his office. She sweeps into No. 35 wearing a fox fur coat, white face made whiter by a soufflé of red curls. The architect drops his pen. It is like seeing that face in the moon again. This Mimi, as pale as a faraway planet, is his window from Ronchamp come alive. When she pauses to kiss his cheeks, her skin is like glass.

'*Chère Mimi*,' cries the architect, hiding his discomfort.

Mimi throws her cold furs around him, smothering him in another chilly embrace.

'Corbu,' she purrs. 'Always such a pleasure. I am in time for lunch, *non*?'

The architect cannot decline the offer. He takes her to a cafe nearby where Mimi sits like a plaster cast, resplendent in her fur coat. She strikes a match and blows it out. 'I've quit smoking,' she says, lighting another one. She eyes the flame. Outside the snow falls, silent as a thief. The windows steam.

'How is Vonn?'

The architect is not interested in discussing his marriage. 'She is very well. How is your new play?'

A smile on Mimi's face. 'Splendid. Just splendid. It has closed for now, but resumes in the new year. I am grateful for the break, but… you know how it is.'

Yes, thinks the architect, he knows this state well. The relief at having some free time, the mental agitation when there is nothing on the plate to attend to. But with him, there is always something. If not a building, then a book, a painting, a plan, an exhibition. His mind is always full, his hands always occupied.

He puts a hand on Mimi's cuff. 'This is a fine fur, Mimi. *C'est magnifique.*'

'A gift, *cher ami*, what else? From one of my Italians.'

The architect marvels at Mimi's agility – how nimbly she steps between so many interests. Even he has had his moment with her. He frowns, thinking about it – how cold her skin had been beneath him. It lasted two weeks. Neither he nor Mimi minded when it ended. He has no regrets. He enjoys her company.

After lunch, he returns home to No. 24. He can hear Vonn moaning. He has left her alone for too long. Today, it is his turn to look after her. He does not always watch over her – there are friends and others who take on this task happily. They must do it with more commitment than him, he thinks. They never complain.

The sight of Vonn lying in bed, her face as grey as an English sky, is almost unbearable. She is listless, slurs her words and does not have the strength to pour herself a glass of wine. He does it for her.

'*Tu me manques,*' she says. Her eyes are closed, and the architect is relieved to have been saved the sight of her flat expression, the deadness in her eyes. He takes her hand, strokes her forehead. She does not react. Even her eyelids are smooth and undisturbed. *When did my Vonn become this zombie?* he thinks. *When did all the life leak out of her?*

'*Chère Vonn,*' he sighs. Once she laughed and told rude jokes. A tall, beautiful peasant girl. Now, long legs that have forgotten how to move. Broad mouth that cannot tell a joke. *My rustic wife has deserted me. She has deserted herself.*

He sits, holding her hand and stroking her head. He tells her about his epic *Poem of the Right Angle* and about its origin. 'It is you,' he says, 'you are the origin of this poem. You are the joy that lies at the intersection of these perpendicular lines.'

Vonn does not open her eyes. She half-smiles. '*Une femme sauvage,*' she whispers.

He shakes his head. Vonn has always complained that his drawings of her are crude. She has never understood. *This is not pornography*, he says. But to her, that is all it is: a rude caricature of some imagining of her. 'How can this be me?' she once asked. 'There is no resemblance. No resemblance at all!'

He clutches her fingers. 'No, *chérie*, it is not like that. It is primordial, not wild. You are the first woman. That is how I have shown you. As the first woman.'

She is not listening. She has fallen asleep, snoring softly, face turned to one side.

The architect wonders whether it will be like this at Christmas. Her days are not always as lethargic as today. *Perhaps it will be Christmas with Vonn in her wheelchair,* he thinks. He imagines rolling her through the park, pointing out a snow bank that once might have provided them fuel for a snow fight. Or taking her to Rue des Gobelins to peer into patisserie windows and decide what to buy before stepping inside. Or remaining at No. 24, lighting white candles and sharing a dinner of goose and purple wine. He might sing to Vonn, Vonn might sing to him and the two might exchange *des cadeaux mignons*: tiny gifts worth nothing but the smile with which they are received.

He scorns this portrait of perfect domesticity, this Norman Rockwell painting in Walt Disney colours. It does not belong in France or anywhere else across the Atlantic or below Texas. Even in England, he thinks, the colours are not so bright, though the fire roars and the tree glitters with baubles. In his mind, this imagined Rockwell is a Francisised version, with Modernist colours and European bathos.

And what about you, oiseau? he writes, returning to his desk and to Minnette. *No doubt your maman is, if not preparing, overseeing the preparation of, her infamous Christmas cake? And your papa? What does he do? Ah yes, of course, he assists. He is her able-bodied assistant alongside your trusty Jaya. Quelle belle image! Rockwell in Ceylan, then, but with tropical colours and long, airy verandahs. Imagine that, Minnette. In a Rockwell! I wish you a Christmas of happy smiles and full bellies, of rekindled friendships and tall cocktails. That is the life, dear child. Among family and friends. The conversation surges like the hearts of lovers. Glasses clink. The night is close. Snakes disappear into bushes. Guests snap off into little groups like squares from a chocolate bar. And best of all, everyone laughs. Everyone is happy – so very happy – including you.*

For Vonn and Corbu there will be family, too. Maman Jeanneret will see that a fierce, gastronomical feast is prepared. Perhaps there will be laughter, if Corbu is in the mood to make jokes. For Vonn, it would be better if it were summer and we could indulge ourselves at Cap Martin. Still, the snow has its uses... a mask of forgetting cast onto the streets of Paris and beyond. A marvellous invention. A vindication for the Modernists, this clean white pate, as far as the eye will look.

The architect shifts in his chair. Vonn is crying. He folds the sheets of paper so that all that is visible is the blank whiteness of the reverse of the pages. He lays his pen across them and goes to her.

IX

October 1954 – July 1955

Minnette and Laki hadn't seen Siri since the riots. During the following months, they grew accustomed to his absence, and hosted salons, inviting Aunty Sheila and her coterie of artists. Discussions were random, fuelled by cannabis and arrack. Obscure, brilliant points rose and immediately sank into a miasma of alcohol and tobacco fumes. The flat rang with the sound of talking, shouting, laughing.

Siri turned up after one of these salons, which had lasted into the following afternoon. The guests had all finally departed, Minnette and Laki were on the balcony, watching the sun set over their gin and tonics. The sound of a click at the door shocked the pair. Fearing a thief had entered the flat, they crept down the stairs holding brass lamps in their shaking hands. They gripped these objects with the intention of giving the intruder a good thumping. The sight of Siri standing wide-eyed in the corridor brought shock and relief. Laki clutched the brass lamp to his chest, as if it might lash out at Siri on its own. Minnette set hers safely down on the floor.

'Hi,' she said.

Siri stared. There was no look of recognition, no smile. His eyes were blank, his face, now thinner, seemed to have set solidly against bone. An aura of dust and sweat rose from him. He looked like he had walked the full length of the Galle Road from Hikkaduwa to Colombo.

'You're back,' said Minnette, surprising herself with her own glibness.

Siri turned around and walked down the corridor towards his studio. Even his steps were quiet.

'Maybe he's joined the *sangha*, after all,' whispered Laki, conjuring the rumour that had been floated at the salon earlier that day. 'Maybe he's taken a vow of silence.' This made them both buckle with laughter, although the sound of it choked and died on their lips.

Before long, they had returned to that familiar inertia, the persistent silence, the gooey slap and scratch of paint on canvas filtering down the corridor. Minnette and Laki slipped into a gradual paralysis, their thoughts, even breaths, oppressed by the gloom. Siri sucked the air from their lungs, flinging it onto his triptych. He brooded and sulked. He refused to speak to them for the whole of October.

In November, Laki roused himself and declared he was leaving. 'You cannot,' Minnette said, breathlessly. Speech had become exhausting.

'Why not? You can leave, too.'

Minnette considered this option, wondering why she hadn't thought of it first. That someone's silent will should strangle such a basic notion disturbed her. And yet, how was it possible that she had got up and continued to work? That she had visited the site of her project every other day, without fail?

'Minnette, there is no need to stay. Siri can take care of the place until Thomas returns at Christmas. We would have had to leave then, anyway.'

'Christmas?'

Laki hadn't mentioned this before. Minnette glanced around the room, at scrolls of her drawings, piles of papers, sketchbooks. Packing all this away would take an effort she could not make. Not at that moment in the drudgery of incessant rain. The rains had started a week before and would persist until mould dotted her books and soured her clothes. She sighed.

'It's up to you,' said Laki. 'But I'm not staying.'

'Where will you go?' asked Minnette, knowing he had nowhere. It was an idle threat which depended on her for its successful execution. There was nowhere else *to* go but Aunty Sheila's.

Laki stayed, but only for a few more weeks. It was not Siri's stoniness that drove them out in the end, but Minnette's mother's illness. By the end of November, both Laki *and* Minnette were back in Kandy. Her houses in Edward Lane and Alfred House Gardens had been completed before the rains started. The Arts Council building had come to nothing in the end. But there were more commissions – several more houses, a block of flats. She would have to work on them in Kandy.

When they arrived at Nell Cottage, Minnette was surprised to find her mother in the garden, pruning a small rose bush. Her father, nowhere in sight. Minnette was annoyed, watching Amma nimbly at her work. She wondered whether Papa had misread the situation, before concluding otherwise. Here he was, exercising his will again, she thought, forcing her back home when she was thriving away from it, much like he had done when she had been studying in London. She embraced Amma before marching into the house, bent on confrontation.

Minnette paced from room to room looking for her father. She found him upstairs in his study, standing by the window. His back was to her and he was humming. From the doorway, she could see that he was watching Amma working outside. His hands, clasped behind his back, military style, unknotted themselves periodically to scratch a cheek or an eye. Eventually he stopped humming and began kneading, his hands still behind his back. His shoulders shuddered. Minnette withdrew quietly to her room to unpack and reconsider. She told herself it was time she had a break anyway, given she'd just finished two contracts. It would be a welcome retreat from Siri. It wouldn't hurt to spend some time with Amma either.

Then came Christmas and the New Year, which crept in gently, with popped corks, but no drunken outbursts or indiscretions. January eventually evaporated into the rising heat, and on an especially sunny, perfumed morning, Amma died.

It was Papa who found her. He woke up and she was still curled like a leaf against the place where his back had been, her skin cool to the touch. This is how Minnette imagines it because her father never told her. They had been sitting down to breakfast when he had appeared, washed and shaved and smelling of cologne. 'Your mother's gone,' he had said, as if offering her a piece of bread. Then he turned away, went upstairs and shut himself in his study. Minnette rushed to the bedroom. Jaya was already there, kneeling by Amma, shedding tears into a handkerchief. Amma was on her side, eyes closed, hair more silver than black against the white cotton pillow. 'She's not gone,' Minnette said. 'She's just sleeping.' She put a hand on her shoulder, brushed her cheek. It was as cool and smooth as a seashell. She kissed her and her lips turned to ice.

The funeral was sombre – no wailing or other dramatic displays of despair. Marcia remembers little of the music or speeches, only that Amma's coffin slipped softly into the earth on a windless afternoon, the sun casting its soporific spell on everyone.

Later that evening the mourners gathered at Nell Cottage. Along with them came a disparate group of homeless people, picked from various corners of Kandy by Jaya and Sheila for the *daana*. Marcia and Minnette had the task of feeding them. A space had been set up on the verandah especially for them, with plates, cups and cushions. Marcia showed them through. Minnette, she observed, smiled at each one, careful not to breathe too deeply. Still, the odour of their unwashed bodies – the sweaty skin, the matted hair, the torn and blackened fingernails – nearly winded them both. Two of the strangers, a woman and a man, were blind, their eye sockets seemingly filled with white wax. Another five beggars trailed yellowing bandages from oddly abridged limbs. There were three children among the group, unattached, it seemed, to any of the adults. Dust covered their withered legs and their collective expression was empty and hopeless.

Marcia doled out rice, Minnette followed with pumpkin curry and Jaya offered a fresh salad of *gotukola*. Marcia watched how her sister served each person, keeping her movements as economical as possible so that she might move quicker down the line of hungry mouths. At the end of the row sat an old man, shrivelled like a prune and veiled in the sticky odour of excrement. Marcia held her breath as she spooned out some rice. When Minnette reached him, she went pale. She served him, put the ladle back into the pot, handed it all to Jaya and went into the house.

She did not return until the *daana* was over.

At the *daana* Minnette felt no remorse. She had done her best but could not hide her distaste. Much as she pitied those people, she could not help but feel repulsed by the slow putrefaction on display right there on their doorstep.

She went up to her father's empty study and found half a bottle of arrack on his desk. She poured herself an inch and sat by the window. The rose bush, which her mother had so carefully tended to before she died, was in plain sight, a new flower blooming from its middle. The sun had all but gone and the last of the light was drawing away. Gradually, everything was consumed by obscurity, the tiny rose bush outside disappearing like a shadow in twilight.

A steady murmur of voices carried up the stairs, punctuated now and then by drunken laughter. Having eaten their fill, the mourners had moved on to the alcohol with equal intent. Papa was among them, slurring his consonants louder than anyone else. 'Marr my worz,' he kept saying, though which words were lost to Minnette and probably everyone else. This was the most she had heard from her father since Amma died. He had not said anything at Amma's funeral; Marcia had filled that role instead. Now he was lording it over the wake, filling it with talk of politics. Minnette turned around, ready to go down and face him – rescue him, if she could. Siri stood in the doorway. She shrank back.

'I was thinking it was time I went down,' she had said, 'to see how Papa is doing. I think he needs some rest?' It had come out more a question than a statement. Siri had looked perplexed.

'I think Laki is seeing to that,' he said. 'He has taken your father to the verandah for some air.' Minnette thought of the beggars and grimaced. 'They're gone,' he said, and she felt guilty.

'I came to offer my sympathies, Minnette,' Siri's tone was flat, but his face looked pained. 'Your mother was…' he searched for the right words but none came. He looked past her, out the window. 'Why didn't you tell me she was ill when you left?'

'Why…?' she blinked at Siri. She was still holding her empty glass. Her fingers tightened around it. If she loosened her grip she knew the glass would find its way to Siri's forehead. She moved towards the desk, filled the cup with ice and poured herself another measure of arrack. Siri stepped into the room and they exchanged places, he now standing by the window, Minnette sitting behind the desk adjacent to the doorway. She sipped the arrack, letting the ice loll against her upper lip. Cool vapours rose from its surface.

'Siri, this is the first time you've spoken to me in months.'

Siri turned to face the window, sighing. He kept his back to her. She could see his face reflected in the darkening window. 'Not here,' he whispered. 'I came to say goodbye to your mother.'

'And to us, too, I suppose? Why are you really here?' She pressed him with questions about his time away, why he'd come back, whether it was true that he'd been working on a new painting. His reply, if one came, was always the same: 'Not here.'

She stared at the meaty plane of his back, the short neck, the jutting shoulder blades, the growing bulges of fat above his hips. Siri had lost weight from his face, but the jowls about his waist, which had been held in check for so long, were springing from his sides like two fleshy fins. As she sat there, breathing in the icy air from her glass, she decided it was absurd to conduct a conversation with his back. And yet, facing her or turned away, his responses would be the same, his expression as inscrutable as that of a goldfish.

'What were you doing that night, Siri, in Batti?' she whispered. 'Why did you stand and watch them like that – Laki and Mimi? I saw you. I was – walking by. And then I saw you there, with your pencil, *sketching*.'

She could tell from the rapid rise and fall of his shoulders that he had heard her. She could almost hear his quickening pulse. But she couldn't tell yet whether he was angry or afraid. 'Surely, Siri,' she continued, 'surely these things – men and women – don't *really* interest you?' Siri was still breathing fast. 'Were you jealous of Mimi? Or was it Laki who disappointed? Ah, but what can you expect from a *demala*, no? We all know what you think of them. It's right there in your painting – the triptych – your great masterpiece that no one else has seen.'

As Siri turned around to face Minnette, she felt triumphant. She almost smirked. But her elation died away in seconds. Siri's face was slack, uninterested; his eyes were vacant. As he opened his mouth, Laki walked into the room.

'What are you two whispering about?' he asked, pretending not to be surprised by the sight of them together.

Siri looked at Minnette, then at Laki. 'Minnette has had too much to drink,' he said, and left the room.

Laki waited until Siri had gone downstairs before speaking again. He kept looking to the doorway, ears alert to Siri's fading footsteps. Finally, he sat on the desk and helped himself to half an inch of arrack. 'Chin-chin,' he said, clinking Minnette's glass. 'What was all that?'

She examined the carpet through the bottom of her empty glass as if through a microscope, searching for something to say. But nothing was in focus. Siri had been right about her. She was drunk.

'How is Papa?'

Laki crossed his arms. 'He's fine. Werner and I took him up to his room. He's asleep now. He'd had a bit too much to drink.'

'Like father like daughter.' Minnette ran her fingertips along the desk. 'You didn't put him in the old room, did you? Their room?' Laki shook his head. 'Jaya made up the spare room for Uncle. He won't sleep in the other room now. He can't.'

Laki and Minnette both looked out the window. There was nothing to see but their own reflections staring back at them. The moon might have been out, but it was obscured by the light in the study shining yellow and artificial on the pane.

Laki shifted a leg, scratched underneath it. 'What did he say? Did he tell you where he's been? Why he came?'

Minnette told Laki.

'So that was it? He came for Aunty.'

She nodded.

'I suppose it isn't so odd. He's an old friend of the family, no?'

Again she nodded.

They didn't say anything more for a while. The guests were still downstairs, chatting and laughing as if it were a party. Minnette could hear Aunty Sheila regaling someone about Sissinghurst Castle. Werner's growl carried up the stairs, too, and she imagined him inadvertently spraying his listeners with the force of his Germanic gutturals. As long as Marcia and Werner remained downstairs, there was no need for Minnette to be there.

Laki slipped off the desk and stretched. He shook out his legs, rubbing behind his thighs. He began pacing the room. Minnette followed him with her eyes.

'Didn't he say anything to you?'

Laki paused, looked at her.

'He was downstairs for a while. You were there, too. Did he speak to you? Did you speak to him?'

Laki shrugged. 'He said nothing to me. I said hello and he nodded. That was all. He did shake hands with Uncle… and Marcia and Werner. Sheila Aunty and Reggie Uncle, too. He kept saying how sorry he was. Then he went out onto the verandah. He must have come up here after that. To look for you.'

Minnette looked away. 'I don't know. I don't think he was looking for anybody, certainly not me. I don't really know why he came up here.' She swilled the contents of her glass, noticed it was empty. The bottle of arrack, too, was almost empty. Minnette thought of her father lying in the guest room and felt tired. Amma was gone, Siri was gone, she was gone – her mind curling up like a sick dog. She put her head in her hands and closed her eyes.

'Don't stay here too long,' said Laki. His trouser legs chafed loudly against one another as he perched on the edge of the desk. 'It's bad for you here.'

'And what about my father?'

'Marcia and Werner will look after him.'

'And when they're gone?'

'Sheila Aunty and Reggie Uncle.'

Minnette contemplated this. Sheila and Reggie were a good option. 'Are you saying we go back to the Brohier flat?' She knew Laki was shaking his head even without looking at him. Laki had no answer. Perhaps he was thinking of himself. He really didn't have anywhere to go. Back to his village was out of the question, so was the flat. Staying at Nell Cottage had lost its appeal now that it was a house in mourning. So where could he go without Minnette?

After all, thought Minnette, as much as she loves Laki, she knows he is one of those friends who 'hang on'. They are found latched like a limpet to a man or woman or, indeed, a house. They appear at parties or dinners and somehow infiltrate a person's life, and before you know it, they have attached themselves to you and made you responsible for them.

Minnette felt no guilt in thinking this. One is acquired by such friends only because one permits it, she decided. It is not a parasitic relationship, rather one with comforts and rewards. If Laki needs her, she also needs him. This makes Siri's attitude towards Laki, his careless dismissal of him, all the more galling.

She poured Laki the last of the arrack and pushed it towards him. He accepted it, leaving it untouched. He was half smiling.

'You know it's not for me that I'm saying all this, no?' he said.

Minnette believed it when he said it. He looked so earnest, holding the arrack glass like it was her hand, directing his words at the golden liquid. She soon realised that he was really talking to himself. An exercise in building conviction. First, address the thought to oneself, then to the real subject. Rehearsal and performance. The end. And then she saw it. Regardless of what she decided, where she went, she would arrange for Laki to stay with Sheila and Reggie. She would take care of him.

'I know,' she smiled. 'You mustn't worry, Laki. It will all work out in the end. I'll make sure of it.'

Minnette didn't leave Nell Cottage right away. After Marcia and Werner left, she followed her father about the house, checking that he was eating properly and taking care of himself. He quickly grew irritated. 'Please, child,' he said one day, 'stop all this spying. Your old *pater* is quite capable of looking after himself.' With that, he locked himself in his study.

Minnette thought he did look like he was doing well. He shaved every day, ate three wholesome meals and spent hours working in his study. Not once did she see him cry or turn to the bottle after the funeral. But she didn't really believe that he was okay – was convinced, in fact, that he did nothing in his study once the door was closed but brood and think of Amma. She was finally persuaded otherwise when he began holding meetings there with Party members, talking for hours about immigration policy or the state of Ceylon's export market.

That was the day that Minnette went up to her room, lay down, and didn't get up again. She was relieved. Days' worth of exhaustion slackened her limbs. She was too tired to think about her new contracts. The thought of speaking to strangers, of talking enthusiastically about aspects and media, seemed ludicrous. Why bother when she had a wonderful room overlooking the greenest of Kandy's hills and a comfortable bed from which to study them? Jaya brought her meals, most of which she didn't eat since eating, too, seemed an odd thing to do when all she managed in a day was to roll onto one or the other side or perhaps sit up in bed. She smoked cigarettes and admired Kandy's verdant hills until they assumed the role of stalwart friends.

Eventually, her father came to speak to her. He sat by her window and surveyed the room, focusing particularly on the spent matches, the crushed cigarettes. He avoided her gaze. 'Minnette,' he said, 'if you don't have much work coming up, perhaps it would be good for you to spend some time with your sister. London might do you some good, no?' He looked out the window to the gradually pinking sky. 'I'm sure you miss Clara, too.'

It has been six months since she arrived at Marcia's flat.

Kensington, with its leafy roads and proximity to the museums, was judged the best remedy for Minnette's condition. In those early days and weeks, Minnette had sat right here, saying nothing, subsisting on Marcia's bread, butter and jam sandwiches. There was no need for paper or pen or table. She sat and stared at her feet or the floor. Eventually, she noticed her niece Clara who, it seemed, had cooed and kicked her way nearly into her first year. Minnette took in the meaty fists and impish grin, both inherited from Werner, and hoped she would grow into them quickly. This vain hope was the beginning of Minnette's recovery, led almost entirely by Clara's daily triumphs and despairs. *I think it is she, more than anyone else, who has brought me back to myself,* she writes later to the architect. But right now she does not feel like she is back anywhere, only dangling, like a half-amputed limb.

She glances over what she has written so far, checks the date of the architect's last letter to her. She re-reads his description of a Rockwell Christmas in Ceylon and smiles. If she is truthful, she will say that hers was less than ideal, that Amma had had to provide instructions for her infamous Christmas cake from bed because she was too weak to get up. But time has cast its nostalgic glow on her memory, conjuring a portrait of a family celebration, complete with Marcia, round with the fullness of pregnancy, and Werner – yes, Werner happily by her side again. Reggie, Sheila and Laki are there, too.

They had decided not to go to Mount Lavinia for the New Year. Instead, they remained in Kandy, watching the fireworks like dandelions exploding over the lake. They had cocktails on the verandah. Amma sat amongst them, reclining on a padded planter's chair. Papa flitted about, offering her cutlets and patties, which she accepted with one hand and gave to Minnette with the other. She did it discreetly, so that Papa wouldn't see, because to him refusal was tantamount to giving in to the illness. He would not accept that she was physically unable to eat – that swallowing was too painful. So, for the sake of her husband, Agnes would deflect his offerings with a joke. 'You always wanted a fat bride,' she would say, smiling at Papa. 'Always wanting a handful of something!'

Minnette remembers the look on her father's face – of affront and relief – and laughs quietly to herself. That night she had wanted to hug him, but mocked him instead, saying, 'Papa, really! What a *kukula* you are! *Chi!*' This accusation – that he was a rooster among hens

– shocked him so, that he abandoned canapé-offering altogether.

Minnette's laughter, which in spite of herself is now audible, attracts Clara's attention. The child totters towards her and puts her head in Minnette's lap. Minnette takes her into her arms and kisses her nut-brown hair before setting her free again. Immediately, Clara drops to her bottom and shuffles towards a well-chewed elephant, dragging the small rug she is sitting on with her. Minnette smooths her lap and turns her gaze to the window where once again her thoughts collide.

———————

Marcia stands just outside the doorway and watches. Minnette is hunched by the fireplace, staring out the window into her climbing roses and beyond that, the road with its frequent dog walkers. Clara sits at her feet, babbling to a stuffed elephant and chewing its trunk.

It is a picture of domesticity, something Marcia wears now like a veneer. Her daughter is a miniature acrobat, pulling herself up on the furniture with strong arms. Marcia is always surprised to see her, this homunculus who arrived in her home in February, demanding her love. Dropping the elephant, Clara stuffs a fist into her mouth, covering it with spit.

Marcia looks at her sister again. The sun pries its way over her shoulder onto the notepad on her lap. The fire is lit, despite the mild air. Minnette is always cold these days, the chill eating into her bones like a famished grub. Clara is now tugging on the hem of Minnette's dressing gown. Minnette does not respond. Marcia does not call her away. She knows her sister needs Clara, needs to be dragged from her stupor into this world.

Marcia, too, has had to draw herself back into reality. She considers her flat in leafy Kensington, its wood floors and handwoven rugs. She had not expected to get pregnant. *One never really does*, she thinks, remembering the horror of that first time with the Bombay Intellectual. She had found a doctor – a Parsee – who helped her get rid of it before she sailed to London without ever telling her partner.

This time, there would be no Parsee doctor. With each passing month, Marcia learned to accept her growing belly. Werner's delight at the strange movements soon turned into her own. Despite the doctor's advice, Marcia travelled to Ceylon with Werner in December. The picture of her last Christmas with Amma hangs brightly in her mind. Within weeks of their return to London, Clara arrived. And then they were back in Ceylon.

Marcia closes her eyes and listens to Clara cooing. She is holding her stuffed elephant, poking its eye with a spit-soaked finger. There is nothing in the house that hasn't acquired the sheen of Clara's spit. Werner does not care, but Marcia finds it distasteful, although she says nothing. She had not anticipated the degree to which babies emit fluid. She is constantly changing Clara's bib, or her own blouses. Marcia wonders when she can return to her research. She had been planning to write a book, when Clara came screaming into the silence. She does not resent her daughter. But she is weary of the constant vigilance, the measuring out of the day according to the whims of an infant.

Minnette is an easier charge. When Papa asked her to take her after Amma's passing, Marcia accepted, relieved that her father hadn't demanded she care for her in

Ceylon. Marcia missed having her sister around, missed her sharp and serious manner. Minnette was neither of these things when she arrived. Withdrawn and silent, her eyes were damp, expressionless. Not much has improved since she came a few weeks ago, but Marcia will persist, always grateful that she is not in Ceylon.

Clara is sitting under Minnette's chair now. Her face is turning red. Marcia thinks she is either filling her *paddi* or getting too hot, or both. In a few moments, Marcia will put out the fire and drape a shawl over Minnette's shoulders, while thinking of some other distraction to occupy her child.

———————

Standing in her cheerful, yellow kitchen, Marcia presses the cold edge of a glass to her lips. The water tastes like it has come from an artesian well – she thinks she can detect the mineral edge of stone. She decides she has never had a more delicious glass of water, and wonders if her life has become such a desert that water should arouse such passion.

A restlessness grows within her. Her thoughts cycle back to the very early days: her first marriage to the Irish poet – a marriage that would not have lasted even if he had survived the war. For Marcia, the poet had been a way to properly escape Ceylon, but he had loved it there, and brought her back to that claustrophobic island. When he shipped out to war, the whole family were aghast, Minnette especially. But Marcia went to London and was immediately absorbed into the film world. She was writing a script for Zoltan Korda when she discovered the poet had been killed.

Laughter trickles down the corridor. It is not Clara's. Marcia pauses her thoughts. She approaches on tentative feet, stopping halfway towards the sitting room. She hears it again, soft as a breath. It's Minnette. Marcia hugs herself, overwhelmed by relief. She has not heard Minnette laugh since she arrived. Not since Amma's death, in fact. How difficult that had been, returning to Ceylon with a month-old Clara in tow. The mosquitoes and unclean water. So many ways to kill an English baby. Marcia shakes her head. She had been on high alert, ready to despatch any insect that dared land on her daughter's gossamer skin. But Marcia was needed elsewhere and had to hand over care of precious Clara to Minnette.

Although unable to deal with Amma's affairs, Minnette was a surprisingly good nanny. While she saw to Clara, Marcia and Werner arranged the funeral. Papa remained in his study, replying to letters from Party constituents. Jaya made preparations for the *daana*. Minnette's friend, Laki, hovered in the background, ready to assist wherever necessary. It was he who broke the news to Aunty Sheila and Uncle Reggie, both of whom immediately drove up to Nell Cottage.

Back in her yellow kitchen, Marcia takes another sip of delicious water. *I am no judge*, she thinks. What had she done, after all, when her first husband died? London had no longer felt tenable, so Marcia went to India, stopping at an ashram in Bangalore for a few weeks' recovery before decamping to Bombay where she edited *Marg* with Minnette and the Intellectual. It was through him that Marcia all but erased the Poet, who had made little impression on her anyway. Marcia and the Intellectual were equals, arguing over whom to profile next in the magazine, creating scandal by choosing to live together.

Those Bombay days had been filled with debate, writing and learning, all undone by a pregnancy that precipitated a period of self-denial and forced righteousness that she believed would absolve her of her earlier turpitude. When Minnette moved to London and found this new version of Marcia, she was shocked. Even Werner had been disappointed, although he loved her too much to complain.

Now Marcia is here in London, leading this uncomplicated life, her plans stalled by the unexpected demands of motherhood. She does not feel the need to mortify herself with abstinence. She is reconciled with her restless self, and plumbs its depths for memories that power her through another day of nappy-changing and housekeeping. Marcia examines the condensation on her now empty glass and finds a constellation of memories clouding the surface. She wipes it with a finger and leaves it in the sink. She will do the dishes later.

———————

Minnette glances at Clara, who is busy putting the ends of the rug into her mouth, strand by strand. Despite being back in London, Minnette is unmoved by her former nostalgia for the city. Marcia's home is a haven; Minnette need not affect contentment for her sister. Marcia knows Minnette: she demands nothing of her.

Mimi's impromptu arrival yesterday did little to revive Minnette. Mimi took her to Hampstead Heath, telling her along the way how sorry she was about Minnette's mother and how much she understood what Minnette was going through. 'Poor mite,' she kept saying. As they walked upon the Heath, Mimi pointed out the ponds and suggested they go bathing some day soon.

'In this cold?' Minnette asked and Mimi laughed.

'Do you remember the lake with the singing fish?' said Mimi. 'How hot it was! I shed an entire layer of skin – like a snake!'

Minnette smiled. 'Yes, you were quite pink. It was the first time I'd seen any kind of colour on you.'

'But I didn't go brown. Underneath, it was just the same old white. As bland as a potato.'

Minnette knew it was all pretence. No one, certainly not Mimi, would ever believe her bland. They had left the ponds behind and were rambling beneath a thicket of trees – an eerie glade reminiscent of a William Blake. Once through it, they headed for the Spaniards Inn. The chill had set into their backs and Minnette was determined to set things straight with a hot toddy. The pair blew smoke rings at one another, smiling with the memory of those early days when the city had frozen and their friendship had caught alight. That was the first time that nostalgia crept in, warming Minnette like a long draught of Scotch. Her thoughts inexplicably turned to the architect, as had Mimi's.

'Corb has been a great friend. He has been so helpful with my Uncle Basquin.' Mimi rolled a cigarette between her fingers. 'I'm afraid I must have become something of a burden to him. Even so, he never shows it. The perfect gentleman. The perfect knight.' She struck a match, held it to the cigarette's end and puffed it into life. 'And he always takes me out for lunch, no matter how busy he is. I suppose he, too, is intent on putting colour on my cheeks.'

Minnette thinks back to the architect's last few letters, and puzzles over the omission of these lunches. She does not know when she will next see Mimi, who is busy with a new play which opens in a few days. Although Mimi invited her to the opening party, Minnette declined. She finds she has no stomach for public events. She glances at Clara and laughs as her niece puts the entirety of the toy elephant's ear into her mouth. She thinks how much easier it is to make conversation with Clara, how effortless their bond.

She wonders at the architect's refusal to allow his wife – or himself – this comfort. *Denying her a child was a cruel limitation on her life. And the gift of the small dog, crueller still.* She wishes things had been different for her and the architect, while not daring to imagine what that difference might have been.

She pens a letter to him and encloses a card with one thumbprint, courtesy of Clara and a jam sandwich. *Do not attempt to taste it,* she writes, before signing off.

The architect watches his colleague Trivedi's son chase a bicycle wheel along the verandah. The boy keeps it upright with a stick and several warning squeals. His bare feet slap red cement. His laughter is contagious.

No one wants to see the wheel fall, least of all the architect. He imagines the drama if it does – the injustice of it. And just as he thinks the unthinkable, the wheel clatters to its side. Tears drop from the boy's eyes. No one is surprised or disturbed. Everyone smiles at his frustration and tells him to try again.

A servant appears with some lemonade. The boy stops crying long enough to drain the glass. He resumes only when he thinks his father is watching. But it is not his father. It is a shadow or, more likely, the boy's own reflection in the mirror at the end of the corridor. The boy sniffles, but his eyes are dry. Within seconds the wheel is rolling again and he is darting after it. This simple Sisyphean game enthrals the architect. It is all the more fascinating for the enthusiasm with which the boy pursues it, heedless to the futility of the enterprise.

The architect sees himself in the boy. He considers the wheel and finds he is chasing one of his own. Currently, he is preoccupied with creating the tapestries that will hang in the Secretariat. Enormous, embroidered with new symbols that will speak across time. Elizabeth has suggested he create these symbols, showing him examples of work that she and Richard have done in Ghana. But the tapestries must be accepted by those who will work there, which the architect knows will not be easy. Beyond this, he is consumed by the pursuit of payment. After all, he must eat, too. Having been wooed to take on this project of the New Era – of the century, even – he is forced to beg for for his pitiful wage. Why should he have to beg? His demands are legitimate, his work is sound, indeed, he is a member of the pantheon of twentieth century greats. It is unthinkable that he should be treated in this way. He decides he will write to Nehru.

But India is the land of slave labour. And the advantages of this policy are profound. Cheap labour yields flexibility of design. If the architect makes an error judging the rise of a wall, it is no problem – they can build it again. Not so in the West, where labour is dear and designs must be far more methodical and include all manner of contingencies. *So here*, thinks the architect, *you put up with the goats nibbling grass in the middle of your site. You accept the children crouching on the periphery. You pay little attention to the cows that wander in and out of rubbled courtyards, leaving behind their shit. Why? Because if it isn't right the first time, you can try again and again until it is correct – without worrying about cost.*

This is the freedom of India for the architect, this concept of live design. Here the architect can truly be an artist. Right now, 200 hands are polishing stone. Those same hands are ready to take down or put up walls or windows and anything else on the architect's instruction. The results are organic – unpredictable. He envies Minnette for having all this at her disposal, and is grateful for the brief experience he has of it in India.

The architect opens her last letter to him and re-reads it, shuddering. He imagines finding his own mother lying dead and feels panic. He knows that right now, she is sitting primly at home, probably at the piano, her mouth drawn into a severe pout as she concentrates on her playing. *She still breathes this earthly air*, he consoles himself, and in that moment feels Minnette's loss.

He wants to embrace her, help her touch life again, but he cannot do this in a letter. Instead, he tells her of the year gone by and is soon carried away by the weight of his own achievement.

It has been a busy year. The architect completed the building for the millowners of Ahmedabad, and two villas. All three buildings share similarities, like siblings in a family of eccentrics. There are ramped entrances and sliding exits, windows with sun-breakers, and airy roof terraces from which life below, whether slicing through a pool or sailing along the river, can be observed. The architect's client – the one who had challenged him to create a door with no locks – clutched her fat dachshund and shed small tears of joy when the architect showed her his solution: a swinging door. He applied the same principle to the millowners' meeting room. These were the architect's small triumphs in Ahmedabad – morsels of hope, stored like fat in a camel's hump.

Against these he places the colossus Chandigarh. The architect had wanted to create a sumptuous palace for the governor of the state. If Lutyens could have Delhi, he reasoned, then he would have Chandigarh. But Nehru refused. 'India is a democracy,' he said.

The architect did not argue. Instead, he presented an alternative: a museum of knowledge, open to everyone, containing past and present, with the power and obligation to enrich all those who enter it.

The architect snorts. He, too, has been placed in a museum. *Paris Match* has declared him one of the greatest figures of the twentieth century alongside Stravinsky, Einstein and Picasso. *Le chambre Le Corbusier* has been installed at the Musée National d'Art Moderne. Gradually, the architect feels himself atrophying into an item on a shelf, fixed in time, irrelevant to the present or the future.

He wonders what can reverse this process. The architect has been fascinated by the relationship between Trivedi and his son. He has watched the boy investigate his surroundings and use deductive reasoning to overcome limitations of size to get what he wants. He judges the boy sharp for a three-year-old, for the boy observes him with shrewd eyes and asks questions that he knows the answers to. *It is as if he is testing me, checking to see whether this old man still has all his marbles.*

As his thoughts turn to the possibilities of fatherhood, he remembers his bedridden wife and feels the prick of frustration and guilt. Frustration, because Vonn's illness demands all his time, like a small child. Guilt, because he has cheated his wife in the worst way, maybe even himself.

Oiseau, you are right, he writes later to Minnette. *I have done the unforgiveable in denying Vonn her greatest desire.* He thinks of his wife and realises what he has always known – that she is a better person than he. During all the months that he was away on projects, she could have entertained someone else, even had a child by another man. *She was certainly beautiful and clever enough to attract any man,* he writes. *But she did not. Is Corbu so steadfast? You know the answer to that, oiseau. As do so many others. Does Vonn regret it? Who knows what she thinks, lying in her bed weeping the afternoons away. The tiny dog licks her tears. Corbu watches and waits.*

The architect wonders what he will do if his wife should depart before his own time is up. *What will I have left?* he asks himself. *Some buildings?* It is at this moment that he is struck by the true value of children – as living mementos of their parents. *Bad luck if they don't resemble them!* he laughs.

Sitting back in his chair, the architect surveys the landscape beyond Trivedi's home. He admires the white-haired peaks of the Himalayas, and runs a palm over his own scalp, smooth and hairless. He remembers Minnette's only trip to Chandigarh and feels a twinge in his chest. She is in England now, while he is in India. It is forever thus, he thinks and writes: *We are frustrated by this turning world. Like two sheep we trudge its surface, one behind the other, following at the same pace, always too far apart to make conversation possible. But I am back at the end of the month. The church awaits. If you come to Paris in December, then we shall defy the movement of the earth and stand in the same place for a change.*

He smiles at this turn of phrase, congratulates himself on the passion he conjures, at least on paper, then realises the date and castigates himself. He has left it too long. She will not have time to make her plans.

This is what angers you, no, little bird? he writes. *Corbu's habit of speaking at the last minute. Forgive him. Forgive me. Corbu is a dog, it is true. Old, bad-mannered and unworthy.*

Unthinking, too, he tells himself, before continuing.

I return to France in just over a week, oiseau. Maybe I can make a trip to London? Or, you will come – won't you? – to Paris. Mimi is always there. It will be good for you to spend some time in the bosom of someone else's family for a change. Mimi and her smelly-but-kind uncle make an admirable foster family for the time being. And then there is Grand-père Corbu. Yes, he is old now and vaguely doddering as Elizabeth likes to tell him, but he is a worthy friend. Do not forget him.

Elizabeth, chuckles the architect. Still up to her old tricks, still attracting the curious noses of a certain type of Indian male: handsome, well-to-do, playboyish – all of which leaves Richard reaching for the nearest newspaper. The architect knows now that Elizabeth's interests are not innocent. So does her husband. *The pair work side by side, but do not speak,* he writes, hoping to lift Minnette's spirits with gossip. *Elizabeth spends more time with ancient Corbu than with her husband. There are plenty of beautiful women around, but Richard is too English to notice them. He likes his women straight and narrow, thin-lipped and deathly pale. In this he is completely without adventure.*

Corbu is puzzled by Elizabeth's popularity with the men here. She is plain compared to the local women. It can only be Elizabeth's facility with a bicycle – her defiance of convention – that fascinates them. After all, she is no Mimi. There is nothing ethereal about Elizabeth (I have not met a woman more of this earth than Elizabeth – her feet cling to it with conviction). She is pretty enough, but lacks Mimi's porcelain fragility. Mimi, as we both know, is capable of great strength, but she does not wear it on her anatomy. It runs through her like a thread of silk – imperceptible until it is needed. When men lost their heads over Mimi here, none of us was surprised. But Elizabeth? I have admitted a small weakness for her quick-witted tongue, but this wears thin over time. Corbu shrugs. It is not his business. Let Richard pine after his errant wife. Corbu has other things to occupy him.

Alors, mon enfant, we shall see each other in Paris. Corbu will bring a smile to the beak of his little bird of paradise. Two old friends will meet again, I will not take 'no' for an answer. To make sure, I will write to Mimi, too, to ask her to bring you with her to Paris. À bientôt.

The architect breathes in the sweet evening air and folds the completed letter into his breast pocket. He will see her again in Paris. Of this he is certain. He takes another slow breath, to calm the thrill rising in his chest, and turns in time to avoid colliding with the bicycle wheel being driven towards him by Trivedi's son.

———

Waves break against the shore at Cap Martin. The July heat is a relief to the architect, who watches the sea from his cabin. The shore is his canvas today, the window the frame. And through that frame flows the tide, gentle as a child's snore.

Watching this tranquil scene, the architect finds it difficult to reconcile it with the storm in February, when a wave gouged out the stone beneath a row of carob trees, flattening a tiny pine along this very shore. The cabin was untouched, though the winds howled, sweeping the sand into sticky dunes.

Today, there is no sign of this drama. The sun rakes its triumphant gaze over the sand. The sea glitters. Vonn lies on a blanket in the shade of a giant parasol. Her toes point towards the water, her chin to the sky. Her eyes are always closed.

Cap Martin is the architect's last refuge. In March, a model of the Open Hand was erected. Nehru inaugurated the Palace of Justice and Chandigarh captured the attention of the world. But at every turn, the architect has found himself sparring. The engineers do not trust him, fearing the 'abomination' of unfinished concrete. The architect sees what they cannot: the integrity and athleticism of the medium, the beauty of its simplicity. They, on the other hand, prefer the devious costume of marble. *All that dressing*, thinks the architect. *So superfluous. There is courage in concrete; it is a declaration. It says: I am here. But they cannot see it.*

With the church in Ronchamp, there are no such issues. The priests instinctively understood the honesty of unfinished concrete, and its relevance to spiritual enterprise. The church was dedicated in June, and those who entered were awed by the naked truth of it.

In Chandigarh, writes the architect, for he is in the habit of writing to Minnette from his 'cell', *minds are petty and concerned with superficial expressions of majesty.* This does not extend to Nehru, who is far away and has delegated much of the overseeing functions to lesser bureaucrats. *Just look at how they insult Corbu!* he continues. *In America, the architect's fees would be 10%. For Delhi, Lutyens received 12%. And what do they offer me? 2–3%. At the same time the work demands two to three times the amount of research! Not only must Corbu beg for his dues, but he must do so with a smile. Not only must he smile as he politely demands his right, but he must convince these fools of the wisdom of his choice – and vision. They are blind, so blind that they deploy obstacles of ignorance. This is your battle with the Ariyapalas writ large, oiseau, with so much more at stake. Imagine – this is not just a house but an institution. Corbu raises his fist to the sky in exasperation, and sighs.*

Anger is futile in India. Nothing can be resolved with it there.

The architect pauses to consider this axiom. His mind floats on this word, *futile*, calling to mind Minnette as she looked that December day. He had been surprised to see her on Mimi's arm. Minnette had not rung him beforehand. He thought she had decided to remain in London with her family. Instead, she was sauntering along the pavement, shaking snowflakes from her black hair. He was not the only man to notice. One after the other, they turned to look at her, prompting the architect to cry out: '*Oiseau! Quelle belle surprise!*' thus claiming the apparition for himself.

They had lunch – Minnette, the architect and Mimi. They broke bread at a round table, sharing a carafe of red wine, Mimi, as always, the most animated amongst them. Minnette smiled and remained quiet. And the architect? *Always with a few breadcrumbs at the corners of his mouth, n'est-ce pas?* he snorts to himself. He and Mimi did their best to cheer up Minnette: two jokers flanking a princess. The architect is certain she laughed. A reluctant sound at first which later bloomed into something more sincere as she dipped deeper into the carafe. Later, after Mimi had left them for the more sober company of her uncle, her mood fell. *I am sorry if I spoke too much about my wife's health,* he writes. *I did not mean to ignore your grief. I was trying to console you. Corbu is guilty of poor timing. On this occasion, at least, the chivalrous powers of that Quixotic knight failed him. It appears that Corbu's charm withers with his aging body. Ah, to look at you, still so young – to think that I once had the guts to touch that skin, to lay my cheek against that breast. The reality of it dims, is occluded by the dullness of your gaze. Those downturned lips.*

After a little more wine, the architect and Minnette had found themselves at Mimi's empty apartment. Minnette's lips were cold, her skin tepid. The wind had frozen everything. They fell into the old habit, but without the laughter or the urgency. Minnette kept turning her face to the window, 'to watch the snow fall', she said. And the architect, too, eventually faced the other way, staring at their shadows blurring against the flaking wall. They smoked a cigarette and then the architect left her to sleep. He told her he had to get back to his office at No. 35, but he went home to check on Vonn.

Alors, we did not meet again for some days. I was busy, and, I think, you were with Mimi and her uncle. Maybe Oncle Basquin had more frozen cakes to offer or maybe Mimi took you all out to a patisserie so that neither of you would be forced to risk a tooth. When I saw you for the last time, your smile came a little easier even if your gaze was less certain. I was relieved to see my little bird less tormented by the ghost of her mother. You never mentioned her, of course, but I know how deeply you feel her loss. What a fragile thing you are, mon oiseau du paradis. You have flown into the darkest well and have yet to find the sun. Down you whirl, like a leaf torn from a branch. Even when I had you in my arms, I could feel you falling.

The architect encloses something to uplift Minnette

– something to help her come to terms with life's great cycle – that eternal journey from earth to aether and back. He hopes it will elicit a reply, for he has heard nothing from her since their last meeting in Paris.

This is my Poème de l'angle droit. A meditation on the germination of life. At the heart of it is the right angle: the union of male and female, sky and soil, body and spirit. My dear Vonn can be found at its centre, yes, but so can that mysterious firebird, the winged siren who haunted my paintings when I first came to Chandigarh. Take it, my dear friend, and study it carefully. I believe it will bring you some consolation.

X

August 1955 – August 1956

Minnette leafs through his book – *The Poem of the Right Angle* – and is drawn by the breathless illustrations. His depictions of Vonn (for it can only be Vonn) are reverential. She wonders how much she saw, lying on her sick bed – whether she recognised herself in these swooning, fleshy figures. Minnette ogles the drawings, because she does not understand the poetry. She can read the text well enough, but all nuance, and therefore meaning, is lost on her.

She has been back in Ceylon, back at Mount Lavinia, since May. It is nearly September now. She thinks she should write to him, to at least acknowledge receipt of the book, but she cannot find the words. He has sent her two letters now, and his office has sent an urgent note asking her whether the book arrived. The note is folded into the book, covering one of Vonn's breasts.

Beside the book is a letter from Mimi, in which she raves about Ronchamp. The architect completed the cathedral and invited Mimi to view it at the beginning of August. Minnette imagines Mimi gliding through the church's stark interior like a candle. *The silence was of a tomb,* wrote Mimi, *fractured by exquisite beams of colour.*

Minnette nods her head. She has not seen Ronchamp – the architect did not invite her to see it in its half-finished state – but she knows that it is Jaipur's Amber Fort, transported to France. The architect had once told her this would be the case. *Anyway, fort, church – how different can they really be?* she thinks. Both palaces, both statements of grandeur.

But Mimi calls Ronchamp 'subtle'. *Not the typical visual carnival associated with Catholics.* Minnette pauses at these words which sound so like his. The church is restrained then. She decides she will see it for herself one day and send him her own observations.

She tries to remember whether he had invited her to see the church while she was in France. Her memory of this last trip is bandaged in gauze. She tells herself she was not in the right frame of mind to see it anyway, and that the architect would have understood this. On the other hand, it could have been what she had needed at the time – something to seal her grief. She shakes her head. There is no point in thinking about it. She did not see it. At least she saw him, subdued though their reunion was. *As restrained as his church*, she thinks.

You saw me at the beginning, she writes, not sure she will even send this letter. *By the end, I fancy I was back to my old self. Almost, for we can never really be what we were. That would suppose a certain atrophying of the individual – an unwillingness to be shaped by experience.* She puts her pen down and thinks back to the previous months – the socialising, the plays, the dinners. She'd watched Mimi on stage several times, took Clara to the park almost every day, went to the galleries, spent evenings with Marcia at the opera. She did not drink or smoke, aside from the cigarette and wine she shared with the architect in Paris on that ill-judged afternoon. She had stopped smoking and drinking because she no longer felt like it. As her outlook improved, she spent more time with Clara to give Marcia time to continue her research.

By April, she'd had enough of Europe and wanted to get back to her studio in Kandy. She had three houses to finish and four blocks of flats, all of which had stalled while she was recovering in England. They were not the social housing project she had been dreaming of, but they would be a challenge nonetheless. All the flats involved creating communal spaces, developing a micro-community. None would exceed twenty units – nothing like the architect's colossal Unité – but she thinks this has its benefits.

She did not, in the end, spend much time in Kandy. Nell Cottage, with its glorious rose bushes, all planted by her late mother, was all too familiar. Her father was doing well enough without her, busy advising Party members on legal matters. A few days after her return, she travelled to Aunty Sheila and Uncle Reggie's in Mount Lavinia which is now her base for the Colombo project.

Laki visits frequently. While she was in Europe, his paintings caught the attention of the Cinnamon Garden set which meant he finally had enough money to hire a place on his own. He had written to Minnette of his slowly ascending reputation while she was still in England, but he had been characteristically self-deprecating about it. When Minnette arrived, she was surprised at just how successful he had become. He even had an apprentice, a young man of exceptional physical beauty who followed him around like a tail.

Minnette has followed her own well-worn path, back to Reggie and Sheila's. Her aunty and uncle's home has provided the gentlest of transitions back to Ceylon. Minnette wakes each morning to the sizzle and roar of the sea against the shore. Her room overlooks the beach, and from her bed she can see rising and ebbing tides. The Brohier flat is a distant and unpleasant memory. She has no need for it. Her room is large enough, her table and shelves accommodate her drawings and books comfortably. Everything about the place is reassuring, including the predictable routines, and eccentric guests drifting in and out like dust.

Amongst them are Laki and his pretty apprentice, Lal. They rarely stay for long, visiting only when the energy at the Brohier flat turns sluggish. Laki went back there after Thomas Brohier's return. He had become accustomed to the studio and with Siri gone, there was nothing to stop him from living there again. Thomas Brohier had been looking for a lodger and Laki was looking for a place to stay, and it seemed excessive to start looking for another home when he found the place perfectly reasonable.

Nevertheless, Laki stops at Mount Lavinia for a few days each month. 'It's the beach, darling,' he told Minnette one day, and she understood him immediately. The ocean, with its eternal pull and push, was life-affirming to her. She knows this isn't always the case for Kandyans, but for a coastal boy like Laki, the sea is life. She knows the architect understands this more than anyone, with his hermit's cave in Cap Martin.

Minnette has made her room in Mount Lavinia her own cave. In it, she draws precisely, unhurriedly, but with a sense of urgency. Most of her clients say they have little money, a refrain she now expects. At least one has decided to move the interior columns she had planned for his modest block of flats, then congratulated her for taking his suggestion philosophically. *I have done no such thing,* she wrote back to him. *It does not matter what you or the engineer says.* That same engineer had thwarted her earlier because he could not take the word of a woman. *Neither of you are architects so neither of you will understand or be able to visualise the way those columns would have delineated the space. That is my job. I wish you would let me do it!*

The largest block of flats, which consists of two buildings arranged around a courtyard, is situated in Gregory's Road. Minnette has been embroiled in meetings, site visits, calculations and drawing since her arrival in Ceylon a few months ago. She has imagined a central courtyard, galleried staircases and airy interiors, all nestled within tropical vegetation. The greenery will protect residents' privacy in the communal space. The interiors will have polished black floors and shuttered windows. The clients are happy with her designs and have parted with their money without too much complaint. The project has run exceptionally smoothly.

So smoothly, in fact, and so without anxiety, that Minnette allows herself the luxury of outings to the races, the clubs, even the occasional dinner dance. Laki, as always, offers himself as her chaperone, leaving Lal to clean his brushes or tidy his studio on those nights when he cannot accompany them. Lal never complains of this indignity. Like most apprentices, he moves about furtively, erasing himself even as he stands before you. Minnette has no doubt that in the privacy of the studio, his relationship with Laki is more vocal. But it is an unwritten rule that apprentices remain silent and industrious when in public.

'What's he like?' Minnette asks Laki one evening. They are eating dinner at the Colombo Cricket Club – a banquet of fried rice, devilled squid and curried crab. Lal had been left at the flat to tend to the studio.

Laki cuts into a ring of squid, forks the segment through a chunk of green pepper and chews on it. He smiles throughout, his slim face shining in the lamplight. 'He's a good apprentice. He might make an adequate artist one day.'

'Why did you choose him?'

'He chose me. People are talking about my paintings now, Minnette,' Laki sucks on a crab claw, oblivious to the affronted looks from neighbouring tables. 'I think he thinks I will open some doors for him.'

'And will you?'

'Of course,' he licks his fingers loudly, this time in defiance of snobbish onlookers. 'If he proves himself, of course I will. But so far, he has shown a great talent for cleaning. He is much more useful than I ever was to Siri. And he is my muse.'

Minnette leans back in her chair, full, unable to finish the rice on her plate. Despite the cashew nuts and raisins and the ambrosial scent of cardamom and clove, she cannot coax another bite. Laki, by contrast, starts work on the squid. Minnette thinks how lovely he still looks, so lean and handsome, and feels it her duty to interrupt his fork in the higher interests of maintaining his figure. 'Muse? I didn't know. Aren't you supposed to show muses more respect?'

'He doesn't know it yet, dear Minnette,' Laki lays down his cutlery. 'And you're not to tell him. He isn't always at the studio. When he's out, I paint him from memory. I've hidden the paintings.'

'But why?'

'He will ask for things I cannot give right now.'

Minnette is intrigued. It is unlike Laki, whose generosity has always been endearing even when he had nothing. Minnette recalls her earlier impression of him, how she had thought him a hanger-on. But he is not a leech, and this is the difference. If he has something, he will share it. He has shared his winnings from the races, shared his lodgings. On the other hand, as long as she has known him, he has not had a dependent. Perhaps this is what makes him uncomfortable now.

'What can't you give him?'

Laki is busy chewing. He is in no hurry to answer her question. He studies the hollow crab claw on his plate, shifts his gaze to the smattering of onions remaining from his devilled squid. He scoops up two more forkfuls of rice and slips them one after the other into his mouth. This he follows with two long draughts of beer. Finally, he dabs his lips with a napkin and relaxes into his chair. He looks exhausted. 'Wouldn't it be easier if we could eat with our hands?' He glances around the room. 'Oh, they all think they're highty-mighty. We all know they eat rice with their hands at home, but they think, 'damn shame to do it in public'. Then, they put that shame onto the rest of us and make us all hypocrites.'

Minnette looks down. She, too, is a hypocrite. So repressed that she uses a fork even at home while dreaming of early childhood meals and the comforting taste of rice and curry uncorrupted by metal.

'Siri would have eaten with his hands here.' Laki's expression grows wistful. 'He didn't care for convention. He made things possible.'

Minnette frowns, wondering why Laki keeps referring to Siri in the past tense. She assumes this is something that happens when relationships end. Once excised, a former friend or lover ceases to exist in the present in the other's world.

'But look what he did. Allied himself with the fanatics.' Laki looks at her, his eyes filling with worry. 'They're getting more power, Minnette. And this government doesn't know how to stop them. The talk now is of Sinhala Buddhist nationalism. Language and religion have become one. There is no room for us in that.'

Minnette knows he is right. Much as everyone tries to forget it, the language problem will not go away. Many want Sinhala to be made the official language of Ceylon. They claim that the current government favours the upper classes. That those in power are so anglicised, they are culturally out of touch with the people who put them there. That progress and financial gain have become the preserve of a privileged elite and are firmly beyond the grasp of a Sinhala-speaking majority. Right now, the government and the opposition are pushing for both Sinhala and Tamil to be made Ceylon's official languages. But the proposal is unpopular. The Knight has shown little promise as prime minister so far. He lacks the popular appeal of Dudley's father. And he has managed to upset the Tamils by dropping a highly astute and well-liked Tamil minister from the cabinet.

'We've survived so far, haven't we? There will always be room for us, Laki. We are artists. We stand above such petty arguments.' Laki looks at her, unconvinced. He thinks she might be drunk, though she has only had a modest glass of wine. And, just as she is about to defend herself, Desmond walks in.

He is unchanged, that lock of hair still curling over his brow like a comma. He is with his sister, Lakmini. The thin one is nowhere in sight. Minnette's mood drifts higher. She has been bad-tempered with Desmond in the past and wants to make amends. She thinks back to that first evening when she met Desmond and Lakmini in Kandy with Siri, how easily they had chatted, how relaxed it all had been, and she wants to return to that point, erasing the unpleasantness in between. Almost without thinking, she calls out to them. Desmond is so taken aback by her good humour and the sincerity of the invitation that he, too, smiles. Lakmini is, as ever, unaffected. Without hesitation, she embraces Minnette and offers her condolences. Desmond takes her hand and does the same.

A pang runs through Minnette – a brief sweet pain that presses the image of her dead mother to her breast before fading away. A moment later, she smiles and everyone smiles with her. Desmond and Lakmini prove charming company. Even Laki is diverted. He avoids talking politics, even when Lakmini quips that she has to brush up on her Sinhala to hold onto her job. He is too busy staring into Lakmini's green eyes to hear what she is saying.

Minnette has seen Laki like this before – with Mimi. Looking at Lakmini, she recognises something of Mimi's feline mannerisms. But there is nothing louche about her. It is Lakmini's innocence that makes her so beautiful. She deploys her intelligence nimbly, with good humour. Never in a way that is mocking or belittling, like her brother.

'Minnette,' Lakmini lays a hand on Minnette's wrist, 'we heard you were designing some flats in Gregory's Road.'

'Yes, and three others. Small jobs, those.'

'Wonderful!' says Lakmini. 'Where are the other three?'

'One in Bawa Place, one in Ward Place and the other in, let me see… Bagatelle Road.'

Desmond nods. 'Goodness, Minnette. You've been busy!'

'Yes, yes,' says Minnette. 'I also have a few houses to do. One for the Amarasinghes – they're so lovely, of course.'

'What a relief, no?' says Laki. 'After the other two.'

Minnette shakes her head. 'We're all friends again now. They love the house.'

'They should,' Laki waggles an index finger at the table. 'It was inspired. There is nothing else like it in Kandy. Nothing.'

Both Desmond and Lakmini nod in agreement. 'I'd love to live in a place like that,' says Desmond. 'Seems wasted on those two. They strike me as the types who appreciate something only after everyone else tells them how wonderful it is.'

'They didn't know what to think until Senanayake endorsed it. Then it was, "Minnette this" and "Minnette that" – all good things. So funny.' She allows herself a smirk before turning the conversation to the pair. 'How have you both been?'

Desmond tells them about a legal case he is working on for a prominent businessman. Lakmini mentions a student she saved from hooliganism charges a month ago.

'Bravo for keeping her out of jail, darling,' says Minnette. 'But what I really want to know about is your holiday.'

'Ah, Italy!' laughs Lakmini, and she embarks on a detailed description of her recent trip. Laki and Minnette sigh at the mention of Italy, Laki because he has never been, Minnette because she has. They talk about Venice and Rome and Lakmini's glittering expression (her eyes shine like two bits of jade) is all Minnette needs to deduce that she had attracted more than a little male attention during her visit.

'The men there are such flirts,' teases Minnette, and Lakmini blushes. Desmond squirms in his seat, embarrassed at the thought of his little sister pursued by Italian men. They change the subject.

'Where is Rita tonight?' Minnette can't help asking. The sight of Desmond without the thin woman hanging off his arm like a broom is unexpected and puzzling.

'Oh, that fell apart ages ago,' says Lakmini before putting her fingers to her lips. 'Sorry, Des. How rude of me.' She stares at her hands for a moment then looks around. 'Is anyone hungry? How about some bites?'

Lakmini and Laki go off in search of a waiter, leaving Minnette alone with Desmond. She waits for Desmond to speak first. She doesn't want him to think she is nosy or unduly interested in his personal affairs. The fact that she is, is not relevant. She is aware of her perverse fascination with the lives of others. She justifies it as a function of being an architect, as an unhealthy side effect of her craft. After all, an architect must understand the person, including all their particular habits and peccadilloes, before she or he can build for them. Minnette nods to herself, convinced by this logic, before she remembers that Desmond is not a client.

Desmond says nothing for a while. He pretends to be interested in where Lakmini and Laki have gone. He scans the club, searching for signs of his sister. A few minutes later, when it is clear she has left the area and that Minnette is not going to say anything to save him, he gives up.

'Rita went away to Australia with her family. I didn't want to go, so we ended it.'

His explanation of everything is matter-of-fact, as if he is ordering a glass of water from a waiter: how her brother had moved to Australia and how this had prompted her parents to follow. How they did not want to leave Rita behind and how she, herself, was intrigued by the prospect of moving abroad. He doesn't go into details of how he feels about the whole thing, only that he would not leave his family or law practice here and, if he really had to, how he would have preferred to go to Europe rather than an ex-penal colony. This is the first trace of bitterness to slip out. It is also the last. Having summarised the details for Minnette, he promptly switches tack.

'How is Siri?' he asks.

Minnette sighs, resigning herself to sounding heartless. 'Who knows. We're not in touch any more.'

The weeks carry on in much the same way: days of intense work followed by the occasional evening out. Laki and Minnette meet frequently, sometimes together with Desmond and Lakmini. From time to time, even Lal joins them. By the time December arrives, they have all become friends of a sort. Laki and Lakmini indulge their natural appreciation of one another while Desmond and Minnette strike a relaxed cordiality.

Lal remains an engima to all of them, except Laki. *He holds himself aloof mostly*, thinks Minnette, *because he feels an outsider*. She knows it is difficult for him. When the four of them get together, they forget themselves, indulging in conversation that clips rapidly along, challenging strangers to interrupt or be damned. Lal seems shy and in awe of them. Minnette suspects he is also jealous of Lakmini, whom Laki can't help fawning over.

Today, everyone is at Mount Lavinia. It is Christmas Eve, but the five are holding a picnic on the beach in honour of Laki, who has been selected from the '43 Group of artists to exhibit his work at the Venice Biennale. It is broadly assumed that Siri did not make the list. Laki will join Ivan Peries and a number of other '43 Group painters next autumn. This is a first for Laki who has never exhibited outside Ceylon. Lakmini brings champagne; Minnette brings mangoes and papayas. It is a picnic at dusk – that point when the ocean grows louder as the sun fades away.

'So you're finally off to Italy!' Lakmini toasts Laki. 'You'll love it.'

Laki grins. Lal, who holds his glass aloft with everyone else, flinches and looks miserable. Minnette clinks glasses with him.

'You must be very happy for Laki,' she whispers. 'It will add huge prestige to your apprenticeship. Who knows. He may even be able to take you with him.' Lal looks down, chewing his lip, trying not to smile.

'Do you think so?' he whispers back.

'Of course,' she says, knowing otherwise. Laki had explained to her that there was only enough money for one ticket while at the same time asking her to join him, if she could afford the time off from the Gregory's Road project. Minnette suspected not, though she told him she would try. 'And even if he can't, I'm sure he'll bring back something extraordinary for you,' she says before realising how patronising this sounds.

Lal is not impressed. He is still looking down, his beautiful eyelashes concealing the detail of his anger or disappointment. 'Anyway, it will be a good learning opportunity for me. When he comes back. He will tell me all about it... When he comes back.'

He stresses the 'when', as if trying to convince himself. 'Of course he's coming back,' says Minnette, hoping to reassure him. But she has no real idea of Laki's plans. He is rootless; he might take the opportunity to travel further, as she has suggested. Still, he is also obliged to return to give a series of talks. Those are the conditions of his participation. 'In fact, he has to come back. You know, he's tied into giving a number of talks.' Lal nods. 'And then, there is always the possibility that he might take you – remember?' Minnette pinches herself for repeating the untruth, foolishly raising the boy's hopes. But she can see that even he knows she is only trying to placate him. Lal smiles, pours himself another glass of champagne, and gazes at the deadening sun.

'Minnette,' Laki takes her hand. He seems oblivious to Lal's growing discomfort. 'Come with me. I want to show you something.'

She walks with Laki towards the water. Pink welts thicken across the sky. The sun dips further into the ocean, setting it alight at the centre. Waves roar. 'Look,' says Laki. 'It's like that night in Batticaloa, isn't it?' She follows his gaze, sees themselves from afar, two dark figures framed by a wounded sky. *It is true*, she thinks. *Everything feels possible*.

He lets go of her hand and sheds his outer clothes, then runs into the sea. He slips in and out of the water like a frond of seaweed. When he surfaces, his back reflects copper, his black skin catching the sun's dying reflection. As Minnette watches him, she realises she is still holding her champagne glass. She raises it, now empty, towards the ocean and catches Laki in its fluted clasp. Within seconds he is gone, the sun with him.

———————

My toes are here my calves are here my knees are here my thighs are here my hips are here my stomach is here my chest is here – Siri prostrates himself before the monk, his outstretched fingers brushing a dry toenail. His forehead rests against the cool of the cement floor. He does not do this lightly, but this *bhikkhu* is a man of wisdom, someone he admires despite, or perhaps because of, his relative youth.

Sri Mangala Thero places a hand on Siri's head, releasing him from his abject position. He nods at him and wafts towards the central *bodhi* tree, preparing to address the group of novice monks. Still kneeling, Siri watches him go, then closes his eyes. *My fingers are here my nails are here my shoulders are here my neck is here my head is here my hair is here my cheeks are here my chin is here my tongue is here my lips are here –*

His lips – Sri Mangala Thero's – rarely smile. Siri feels a certain kinship with him based on this coincidence. But lately, the coincidence has lost its relevance. Whenever the monk is nearby, Siri finds himself smiling, finds his heart swelling with what he can only define as awe. He does not look too long at the monk's shoulder, as brown and smooth as teak. He does not dwell on the thick lashes or the gentle flare of his nostrils. He focuses on his words, delivered calmly, each one lighting up Siri's mind like a small candle.

The monk speaks of the new leader of the country, Solomon Bandaranaike, as the only candidate capable of wresting Ceylon back into Sinhalese hands. 'A son has beaten that crony,' he says. 'With our guidance, this son will bring Ceylon back to greatness so that the Buddha lives in each and every one on this island.'

The election battle fought by 'the crony' – the Knight – had failed to capture Siri's or any other Buddhists' votes. At one point, the Knight declared that his party had done more for Buddhism 'than any government before it, including the Sinhalese kings.' Siri had been tempted to laugh at that. The monk had been shocked enough to relax his normally severe mouth, and let his jaw drop open for a moment. Siri, distracted by the whiteness of Mangala's teeth and the soft compactness of his tongue, held back his laughter.

The image of that open mouth stayed with Siri for days. When he painted, it was there, asserting itself in the pigments he chose or the textures he worked onto the canvas. Around him, the temple slowly transformed, filling with flowers, candles and incense as monks, nuns and worshippers prepared for the Buddha Jayanti – the 2500th anniversary of the Buddha's enlightenment. The election of Bandaranaike – 'the son' lauded by the Venerable Mangala – only strengthened the *sangha's* prediction that this would be the year that Sinhalese culture would find its true place in Ceylon.

Bandaranaike won on the back of a new policy calling for Sinhala to be made the official language of Ceylon. Siri had argued many times with Laki about this, tried many times to make Minnette understand. He accepts, now, that he may have been too abrupt in those arguments. But he cannot understand why Minnette failed to see the logic in what he said – how it is impossible to be independent while still favouring the language of the coloniser.

Laki, he could forgive. Laki would have more to lose in this new Ceylon. Siri had wanted to help him, too, by teaching him. He started by demonstrating his painting techniques in Sinhala. As the weeks fell away, Laki went from looking blank to increasingly hostile. *I don't need your language lessons,* he said finally.

Siri felt sorry for him. Laki had left his family behind. He had abandoned his mother tongue – Tamil – and re-invented himself in Colombo as an artist. His skill was undeniable, even to Siri. Having chosen to leave behind such an intimate part of himself, Laki should have been more receptive to Siri's experiment. Instead, he cut him down.

Siri still feels that rejection keenly. Shut out from Laki's love, he collapsed into loneliness. He could feel Minnette and Laki hardening against him, saw how easy they were in one another's company and how awkward in his. He left the Brohier flat with riots going on around him. He walked past embattled crowds and gunpoints, unmolested and unseen. He had become as invisible as he had been with Laki and then Minnette.

He had walked for days, marching steadily south along Galle Road. At night, he slept on the beach, deaf to the roar of a black and arching sea. Sometimes, he startled lovers among the boulders flanking the shore. They would recoil in alarm and embarrassment, seemingly the only people to notice him. He would start whenever he found them, remembering with a shudder that night in Batticaloa: Laki and that wretch, Mimi, lying there like seaweed washed up onto the sand; mind white with shock, he had sketched them, tangled up in each other, their mouths gaping in a silent howl. Siri never recovered from that night. Laki – his Laki – lying with a woman, *that* woman. An English woman. A woman. He didn't understand how Laki could do it. He had seen the bald mechanics of it, had been repulsed by it. She didn't know Laki, she didn't care for him, but she opened her legs for him and he had readily obliged her.

Siri remembers her neck – how cold it had felt in his hands, like the skin of a gecko. He had wanted her dead. He had wanted the lagoon to swallow her up, extinguish the fiery curls she wore like a crown. He hated her. When he put his hand around her neck, he had thought he might take her just as Laki had, even though the idea of it filled him with revulsion. In the end, he jumped into the water to escape her – to cleanse himself of her impurity.

He never spoke of the incident to Laki, but their relationship never recovered. Siri wanted absolutes. Laki preferred to experiment. He loved Siri well enough, but his mind was always whirring, always in search of a new experience. Siri wondered about Laki's friendship with Thomas Brohier. He wondered how often the two men spent time alone with each other, how much Thomas admired Laki's drawings, and – Siri could tell – Laki himself.

By the time Siri walked into the temple, he had stripped himself clean of Laki. He hardened his mind against his ready smile and quick talent. He forgot about his fine-boned face and taut back. The Venerable Mangala Thero welcomed him to the community and Siri knew that his decision to leave Laki and Minnette behind was the right one.

Sri Mangala understood him. He looked at Siri with kind eyes and smiled with full lips. His shoulder –

muscular, defined and so unlike the puddingy offerings of so many of the other monks – shone in the sunlight. He understood and needed Siri. And in return, Siri painted. He painted a new fresco in the temple's interior – scenes from the *Buddhacarita*, the life of the Buddha. He revelled in representing the moment of Siddhartha's disenchantment: the prince surveying a scene of grotesque concupiscence – women lying asleep in disarray, semi-clothed, arms flung out in abandon. The look of disgust on Siddhartha's face is palpable. The scene is repulsive and beautiful at the same time.

When he saw it, Sri Mangala nodded. Eventually, he sat quietly in a corner watching Siri paint. And one day, he put a hand on his shoulder, leaving it there while Siri's heart jumped. Siri stopped painting. Sri Mangala did not seem to notice. Siri stared at the wall, eyes fixed on the prince's expression, too afraid to move even though moving would have saved him.

They had remained this way for several minutes until a novice ran past. Siri didn't notice Sri Mangala leave. He didn't notice that his hand had gone with him until he saw him disappearing down the corridor. The next time Sri Mangala touched him he did not leave. And Siri did not move. Not at first. But the darkness made everything possible, like that night in Batticaloa when Siri had walked into the water unclothed, with Minnette, Laki, and even that woman. The darkness claimed their slow and deliberate movements as its own. It swallowed their sighs and clothed their hunger. It pulled a blanket over their intentions, so that by the morning, they would wonder whether anything had happened at all.

Siri sits, wondering just this, as he continues to place his body in space. *I am sitting my knees are bent my palms are on my thighs my stomach draws in my lungs fill with air I am breathing I am breathing I am breathing –*

He inhales the sweet air of the temple. Jasmine and *araliya* flowers festoon copper trays. The statue of the Buddha, in the temple's heart, is surrounded by dying flowers gasping out their last perfumed breaths. Siri pities them – flowers wrenched from their roots, slowly expiring like fish washed up on the shore. He thinks there should be another way – a less violent means of making offerings to the Buddha. He does not say this to Sri Mangala, who would probably tell him he would make a good Jain.

Siri almost smiles. *My soles expand with my breath I am breathing I am breathing I am rising –*

———————

Five days later he is marching alongside a platoon of monks. They advance like a saffron cloud, up the Galle Road to Colombo. Siri walks along the perimeter of the group; Sri Mangala is at the helm. The *bhikkhus* hold their umbrellas aloft, shading themselves from the midday sun. Many of the marchers are novices – youths from local villages given to the temple by their families because they couldn't afford to care for them or because they needed to gather merits in this life to ensure success in the next. A few had joined out of devotion.

They walk together in easy camaraderie, sharing an occasional joke between prayers. Siri says nothing. He can feel himself floating among the billowing robes, moving effortlessly towards their destination. As they near Bambalapitiya, he sees a throng of *satyagrahis*, led by that troublemaking Tamil minister, the one that the Knight had removed from his cabinet. The group chants slogans, beating out a rhythm with upraised fists. The mood of the monks sharpens. Siri, who up until now has been ready to do as he is told, finds the men and women he has been sent to do battle with harmless. They are no threat to him, he thinks. They are no threat to anyone. They are a small group whose voices will be drowned out by the Sinhala majority. He pities them.

He looks around him at his own group of protesters, smiling and shrugging, as if to say they are harmless. But the look on his comrades' faces surprises him. Sri Mangala's mouth is set in steel. The other monks follow in thin-lipped determination. Siri's smile dries into a parched line on his face. He falls into step with the others and is soon caught in the wake of their flowing robes and gathering fury. The feeling is infectious and overpowering. Sri Mangala is up ahead, shouting, holding his closed umbrella like a baton. The others do the same. Siri, who has neither umbrella nor baton, holds his fist up to the white-hot sky. Then they are running, Siri with them, riding a tide of elation.

A *bhikkhu* picks up a stone. Siri does, too. He and the monk throw it at the *satyagrahis*. They reach for more stones before the first ones strike their target. Siri lobs more into the air, faster and faster, harder and harder. Someone falls. Siri doesn't stop.

The two groups are in Galle Face Green, under the constant eye of the police, yet the police seem oblivious. They cast a bovine eye on the scene before returning to conversation. Siri, who has felt apart for so long, loses himself and is subsumed into the whole. There is no Siri or Sri Mangala only this multi-armed creature of which they are a clump of hair or nail. They swarm over the *satyagrahis*, felling them indiscriminately. Bodies fall like leaves and are blown away with the wind, into hedges, ditches or the lake, until there is no one left.

———————

Later, when Siri looks back at the protest, he finds he can't recall any detail. He will struggle to remember familiar faces – indeed, any faces – in the crowd they attacked. He will ask himself why he, who has stood apart for so long, lost himself at that moment. He looks inside himself for reasons, expecting to find Sri Mangala there, and finds nothing but his own fleshy heart.

———————

The house in Mount Lavinia is quiet, save for the sound of knocking at the front door. When Minnette opens it, she finds Lal standing with terrified eyes. His clothes are torn and smudged with dirt. For a moment, she thinks he has been drinking and is tempted to close the door. But there is no odour of arrack or any other alcohol on him and the taverns have been ordered closed as part of the general curfew.

Minnette invites him in and sits him down. Lal looks through her, saying nothing for a while. When the words eventually come out, they are jumbled up, like clothes tumbling from an open cupboard: 'Beira. *Poleesiya*. Laki.' He repeats the same string of words under his breath, rocking forward and backward in his chair. Aunty Sheila gives him some tea to calm him. A little while later, he begins: 'I went to meet Laki at the temple. In Bambalapitiya. Ponnambalam came – the minister. He led us to Galle Face Green. But as soon as we got close, this – these – so many monks –' Lal cowers as if the monks are in the room with him. 'They surrounded us, cracked an old man's ribs. Kicked a woman to the ground. Knocked her teeth out.' Lal starts rocking again, looks confused. Aunty Sheila puts a hand on his shoulder.

'Someone threw a rock at me,' he gasps. 'I saw it coming from the side and moved my head just in time… but Laki was standing next to me. It was too late. He was struck on the head.' Lal saw him fall, but the crowd surged and the two were separated. 'People ran over him,' he whispers. 'I couldn't go back. The police kept moving us forward.' Then he saw two monks bend down and pick up Laki. 'I thought, at least they know what it is to show compassion. I was wrong. They took Laki by the wrists and ankles and ran with a group of other monks towards Beira Lake. And they – they threw him in. I couldn't reach him. I couldn't get past the police, the crowds.' Lal hides his face in his arms.

Minnette presses her toes into the cement floor, trying to warm her feet, and finds that they feel wet. She looks at Aunty Sheila, who is sitting motionless on a chair across from Lal, and wonders whether she has accidentally dropped something on the floor. Minnette sees nothing there, yet the floor is turning to water beneath her feet. She reasons that the tide must have come in without anyone noticing, slipping closer than it has ever done before, this time under doors and into sitting rooms.

Her sari sags against her body, feels heavier and heavier. Someone calls her name, but she is under water and the words sound like feet slapping heavily against the surface. It is dark and she can't breathe. Sparks dart like fireflies in front of her eyes. Seconds later she is breathing again, staring up into Aunty Sheila's nose. There is a tiny white hair in her right nostril. Minnette realises she has never noticed it before. Sheila keeps repeating Minnette's name, holding her head in her hands. The whole scene seems timeless, until Minnette remembers Lal's words, and an image rises to the surface – Laki floating in green water, his body decaying in its sulphurous breath.

Laki wasn't the only one who died that day. Minnette and her friends rely on rumours for confirmation of numbers, rather than the newspapers or government statements. Coverage of the incident is vague, with attackers and victims apparently indistinguishable from one another. The former are inevitably described as hooligans rather than counter-protesters. References to communal tension are scrupulously avoided. No mention is made of monks taking part in the violence. If they are mentioned at all, it is as arbiters of peace. The police, too, come off well as bodyguards to the *satyagrahis*.

Beatings, murders, revenge killings and assaults rage across the island. Gangs loot shops, targeting those owned by Muslims and Tamils. Colombo has become a military zone, with armed soldiers patrolling the city. The taverns are shut down for a few days in the hope of keeping drink fuelled louts off the streets. It is like those dark days of '53 when people protested en masse against price rises. Minnette remembers how she and Laki picnicked on the balcony at the height of the protests that time, and scolds herself for not going with him this time.

'Come,' Laki had said, some days before the planned protest. 'We must show them we won't accept this Sinhala-only nonsense.' Minnette had nodded vigorously. 'You're right. They've gone mad, no? I'll see if I can come.' When the day came, she flitted about the house until it was too late. Her face burns at the memory.

_____

One week later, Minnette accompanies Lal to the Brohier flat to help him sort out Laki's belongings. Lal gives her Laki's paintings and other drawings. He packs them in boxes and rolls, tying them neatly with lengths of coir. It is a surprisingly compact portfolio. Minnette suggests Lal keep Laki's brushes, pastels and coals, and any other drawing materials he needs. He takes them gratefully – almost reverently – saying he will put a few aside as reminders of his teacher's techniques and habits. 'Perhaps I should donate them to a museum… or to the '43 Group,' he says. He picks up one of Laki's shirts. 'Do you think anyone would take these?'

Minnette reflects on how clinical it feels going through Laki's things like this: separating, claiming, discarding. Marcia and Jaya spared her the task when Amma died. She knows she would not have been able to do it anyway. Dividing her up like that – carrying out a kind of autopsy on her lifetime's archive… She would not have been able to make the distinctions, to separate one thing from the other. To Minnette, she was a whole, even at the very end of her life; nothing was expendable.

Laki's collection is, by contrast, modest, and aside from his artwork, says very little about him as a person. No one – not she, not Lal, not any of their acquaintances – knows who his family are or how to get in touch with them. Siri might have known something more, but he, too, is nowhere to be found. Given how Laki died, Minnette has no wish to see Siri. It is left to her to arrange the funeral.

It is a simple service. Laki was not religious, so the Hindu ceremony is kept as short as possible. A pandit presides over the cremation of the body and a few prayers are chanted. More to Laki's taste is the party thrown in his memory at Sheila and Reggie's. Some of his best work adorns the walls. Artists of all types turn up, having seen the obituary posted in the *Times of Ceylon*. Many of them know little, if anything, about him. They know of him, yes, or have heard of his work (or have had more intimate, if brief, dealings with him), but very few can actually say anything sensible about him.

Desmond and Lakmini are there, too. Lakmini is particularly affected. She mentions how disappointed she is that she met Laki so late. Minnette agrees. She knows the two might have made great friends, given more time. 'He had a crush on you,' she says. Lakmini looks at Minnette, confused. Minnette can see that Lakmini has made the same assumption that many others have done about Laki. She recalls Uncle Reggie's speech earlier in the day, in which he claimed that Laki had 'preferred the freedom of bachelorhood'.

Minnette understands that this is the easier and more comfortable position to hold, but it disappoints her to hear Lakmini echoing this view. 'Really,' she says. 'He thought you were fantastic. He told me himself. The only other time I've seen him so enamoured is when he met my friend from England.'

'I should be flattered?' Lakmini is smiling, but the look on her face is uncertain. It is as if she expects Minnette to slap her on the wrist and admit it is all a joke.

'Why not? He and I have been terrific friends, but he never showed me the same – ' Minnette stops. The police had dragged his corpse from the lake. She had refused to identify it, so Uncle Reggie had gone instead. Minnette didn't want to remember him that way, bloated and grey. Reggie didn't speak for several hours after he returned. A weight slips down Minnette's throat and into her chest. She pats Lakmini's hand. 'I'm just saying that he really admired you, that's all. He said you were as sharp as coral. And as delicate.'

Lakmini smiles, this time with conviction. 'He was a very special man,' she says. 'A gifted artist… So sad about Venice. He was so looking forward to it.'

'Even if he can't be there, I'm making sure his work is represented. Why shouldn't it be part of the exhibition?'

'Quite right,' says Desmond, joining the conversation. 'Death should not preclude his "participation". If anything, it makes it all the more vital.'

Minnette nods. 'I haven't raised the question – in my mind, there isn't one. The work will speak for itself.'

'I've heard they're considering a replacement… to speak, I mean.' Lal slips into the circle.

Minnette looks at him. 'Who?'

'Guess.'

The three of them exchange glances while the answer hangs between them. The choice is obvious.

'It's Siri, isn't it?' says Minnette. Lal nods. She feels sick. The differences between the two artists are well known. To replace one with the other, thinks Minnette, is callous.

'It makes sense in a way,' says Lakmini. 'I know they fell out in the end, but for a long time, Laki was Siri's apprentice. If anything, Siri must be feeling awful. To have been passed over for the biennale in the first place. And then to be offered a place only because your protégé… you know.'

Minnette's thoughts are less charitable. It was people who thought like Siri who created the conditions that led to his murder. And it is Siri's great allies – the monks – who were the instruments of that act. To Minnette, the whole thing amounted to a cruel conspiracy. Even if fate were to blame, she can see no reason why fate should prefer Siri over Laki.

'*My* God,' Lal grabs her arm, whispering. He looks through the crowd, past Minnette's father, towards the other end of the room. '*My God*,' he says again, emphasising the two words. Minnette follows his gaze and finds Siri. She thinks it appropriate that he should resurface from oblivion at a funeral, just as he did a few years back, when her mother died. She watches him examine one of Laki's paintings. He is lost in thought, his head craning upward, one arm resting on his hip. It is a familiar stance, one that he often adopted when considering his next move in front of his easel. He stands this way for several minutes, before turning around and looking at Minnette.

Minnette blinks, frightened. She returns his gaze, but finds only emptiness. It is as if she can see through him. His face is translucent; Laki's painting – an abstract, angular portrait of Mimi based on his old Batticaloa drawings – seems to poke through him. Siri is on his own. No one, not even his fellow associates from the '43 Group, approach him. He is a void at the edge of the room, slipping in and out of sight like a shadow.

Minnette walks towards him, even as she decides not to speak to him. She lifts an arm in a half-hearted greeting and he returns it. Their eyes remain fixed on one another, yet on her approach, he grows fainter and fainter, like a mirage. By the time she gets to the painting, he is gone.

If Lal hadn't been the one to notice him in the first place, Minnette would have doubted her eyes. But Lal later assures her that he saw Siri exactly where she thought he had been.

'He looked very upset,' he says.

'Did he?' Minnette is surprised. There seemed no sadness or upset to her – certainly nothing like the misery that had accompanied the death of his photographer friend so many years ago.

'Maybe he feels guilty. Like Lakmini said.' Lal himself looks guilty.

'I doubt it,' says Minnette. 'Siri has always been a righteous sort. Or a self-pitying one. I've never seen him show signs of guilt.' She tries to temper her bitterness. 'Not that he should be feeling guilty right now, anyway.' Lal nods.

Eventually, everyone drifts towards the beach, some in groups, others on their own. Sheila and Reggie keep the guests watered and entertained. Sheila has even managed to interest a few people in buying some of Laki's work. Minnette hopes that she hasn't sold any of the paintings she had chosen for herself, although the most precious ones remain hidden away. They are the paintings of Lal that Laki told her about before he died. There are only three – small canvases, all of them – but they reveal the intimate nature of their relationship, something Minnette knows Laki did not want people to know about. She had found them at the Brohier flat, hidden in a place that Lal knew nothing about. Lal still remains unaware of them, and Minnette pledged to keep them from him, too, just as Laki had wanted.

The '43 Group delegation, including Siri, are due to leave for Venice in a few weeks. There will be a posthumous exhibition of Laki's works as well. It did not take much to convince people that this would be the right thing to do. Newspaper articles continue to note the tragic loss of a fresh and vital new talent. Society ladies and gentlemen have emerged from sundry corners to declare their deep disappointment at having missed the opportunity to own a Laki original. The fact that he produced so little has substantially increased the value of his oeuvre. Minnette knows he would have found the irony amusing. Despite all the publicity, no one steps forward to claim Laki as their long-lost son or brother. Minnette wonders whether he really was an orphan or whether he is unrecognisable to them wherever they are. Whatever the reason, she is pleased that he is finally receiving the recognition he deserves. She hopes that the attention endures beyond the excitement surrounding Venice.

She wonders whether the architect will be there, and in her grief, feels compelled to write to him. *Oh, Corbu, I don't know where to start or even how to write it. The streets are back to normal now, no more troops wandering about. But our lives are in shambles.*

She outlines the weeks' agonies before suggesting the architect go to Venice. *It would be wonderful to hear what you think of our delegation and their work. Who knows? You might even have the pleasure of meeting Siri!*

She pauses, recalling the recent letter she wrote Mimi about Laki. Mimi replied almost immediately telling Minnette how sorry she was and how awful she felt about what had happened in Batticaloa, how callously she had treated him. Minnette disagrees. When she remembers the scene she can only see two adults in an equal exchange. In fact, she thinks, it was Laki who had proved thoughtless given his situation with Siri.

So, Corbu, my dear friend is now gone. What a hole it has left inside me. He was a better friend than Siri. Siri took so much. Laki was easy-going and generous, someone I could trust. He did not care for ulterior motives. He was honest. He laughed. Above all, he spoke. Talking to him was never difficult, unlike Siri and his opaque mutterings. He was my closest friend here, and now he's gone. How lonely I feel just saying it.

Minnette lays down her pen and listens for the familiar whisper of the ocean outside her window. Waves lap the shore at Mount Lavinia with a reassuring hush. She turns towards the wall. On it hang the three paintings of Lal.

In the first, Lal is glancing over his shoulder, looking surprised, as if he feels unworthy of the attention. The second painting captures him in long shot; he is looking off to the side, but is aware that he is being watched and enjoying it. In the final painting, he looks straight at the observer; his expression inviting. It is clear that something momentous and decadent will follow acceptance of his invitation. In all three canvases, Laki's touch is palpable but not manipulative. It is probing, like the ear of a very good listener.

When I look at the paintings, I do not feel like a voyeur. I only imagine Laki sitting where I am sitting; and at that moment we are both together.

Minnette clutches the pen tighter as her chest opens up to the night air. She draws jagged breaths and weeps for her friend. Grief brings an uncomfortable clarity to her memory, and she recalls how she had disparaged him at the beginning, how she had thought him beneath her and Siri. Back then, she had believed he was trying too hard to fit in. Later, she realised he had no need to fit in to anything. He took everything as it was and expected everyone to do the same with him, and it was this that she loved most in him. She sits, staring at Laki's paintings until she recovers herself, then returns to her letter.

I am sure that I have been selfish and have failed to respond adequately to your last letter, but I am sure you understand why. I know that you are well; Mimi wrote me so in her last letter. It seems your influence and accomplishments will not go unmarked. Your greatness is proclaimed in all architectural quarters. Even here, in this paradise that has forgotten itself.

Minnette drops her pen and lets it roll off the desk onto the floor. She stands up, walks over to the window and looks out to the sea. A boy in red underpants backflips into a wave. He slips in and out of the water like a black fish, his body glinting in the sun. Kicking his long legs, he swims further and further into the horizon until he is indistinguishable from the waves.

XI

December 1956 – December 1957

16 December 1956
Paris

Oiseau, mille fois pardons! Forgive me for not writing sooner.
I was worried about you, little bird. Corbu is relieved that you
have survived this drama that is unfolding in Ceylan. It is the
same in Algérie, is it not? No, perhaps not. Ceylan has her
independence already. Algérie demands it now, though the
French resist. It is a bloody mess.

And your friend, Laki. My child, it is devastating to lose
such a good friend. Corbu would have made the journey to
Venice just to meet him; though no such efforts for the other
one – the mute. It is not for Corbu to cast judgement on such
things, but these monks, they are not true monks, non? How
can this be? Why is it allowed? Why do the people not stand up
to criticise them? Has everyone gone mad over this language
quarrel? It seems madness is seizing the world. I refer you to
Algérie again, oiseau. And to Egypt and Tibet and Hungary…
invasions everywhere. The British are not happy with Nasser's
plans for the Suez. China finds fault with the Buddhists of

Tibet. Russia will not accept revolution in Hungary. What is to be done? Corbu washes his hands of it all.

But there is good news, too, for me. At least in Chandigarh. Last week, I stood on top of the Secretariat and watched as they poured the concrete for the Open Hand. So many donkeys went up and down, with sacks of sand and stone for the mixture. And now it is real, oiseau. Perhaps by erecting this symbol of friendship and openness, the spirit of its message will be sent around the world. This symbol, at once hand and bird, now stands majestic – a sacred structure. Let it remind everyone of the generosity that Chandigarh embodies so that nothing as chaotic or selfish as has happened in Ceylan should pollute its roads.

When Elizabeth saw it, she called it crooked. The hand is banking to one side, 'somewhat bashfully', she said. She is always seeing the negative in everything, that one. 'Corb, you can't really be serious. That hand is as limp as anything!' When she said this, she looked, without meaning to, at Richard. Oh-ho! Corbu was amused. A moment worthy of Freud's notebooks, n'est-ce pas? Luckily, Richard had not heard his wife. He was pointing to something far away, talking to Trivedi. Elizabeth caught my look and pretended to be horrified. It is only when she has a glass of champagne in her hand that she admits the truth. Otherwise she plays at being the dutiful wife. Elizabeth is bored. It is obvious. But she is not cruel. She prefers to be discreet. Her journeys outside Richard's bed are a mystery to Corbu. I know, oiseau, that you think differently, but this is the truth. Corbu is a naïf when it comes to Elizabeth. Picnics, bien sur, but anything else is out of the question. She is like my daughter. Or my niece. And she is so unattractive in that English way.

But she is right about the hand. It is leaning like an old man right now. These engineers did not get it right. They will have to start again – brace the post, re-pour the foundations. I am not worried. This is India. It will be done and without too much expense. It was the first thing Mimi said when I described it to her. 'Pish posh,' she said (I did not ask what is this pish posh), 'what's the problem? They'll do it in no time. There are so many people on site. They'll be glad for the extra work – and money.'

Ah! I almost forgot to tell you, ma chère. You see, Mimi was in India last month. She said she needed a break from the theatre and was in Bombay for some days. It was not planned. I heard she had come, so I invited her to Simla. She stayed with Elizabeth and Richard, who closed ranks against her. They sat in a corner, smoking and staring at the poor girl, half-smiling at Corbu. It is obvious that their opinion of the child has not changed since your trip here. I showed her the site and left her in the hands of the wise and always trustworthy Seetaram.

Mimi shocked with her white skin and fiery hair. The men competed to bring her lunch or tea. Seetaram ignored the fuss and shooed them away. 'Like crows,' he said to me later on. 'They are curious to solve this new puzzle in their midst.' Elizabeth pressed her lips and nursed her jealousy. Richard looked like he was enjoying the drama, patting his wife's back and looking appalled when needed. Oh-ho, they made me laugh. Then it was over. Mimi left before the hand went up. Elizabeth went back to her nonchalant self, and Richard looked like he had lost something ('the upper hand', I think, is what you call it in English). Cousin Pierre, like our staunch philosophes, Seetaram and Trivedi, stood apart from it all.

And here I am in Paris again. Vonn sleeps. She has not improved, oiseau. She cries and drinks and tells me that her legs ache. I can do nothing to make her feel better. Mimi says that it is depression and tells me stories of her uncle. But there is no comparison. How can she put that smelly man in the same box *as my beautiful wife! She is crude sometimes, non? I forgive her because she is young and does not think before she opens her red-lipped mouth. And because she apologises as soon as she realises. This time it was different. She has not apologised for the recent slap. Instead she tells me how sorry she is that she didn't travel to Ceylan from India to see you. 'Poor Minnette. Just think what she has gone through!' Corbu was convinced. Because of this, I have memorised the conversation so I can tell it to you.*

Mimi kept shaking her head as she spoke. We were walking through the gardens at Luxembourg, and her curls were filling with snow. 'I wrote to her, of course. But I didn't tell her of my trip to India. Why did I do that, Corbu?'

Corbu shrugs. Why should I know anything about Mimi's motives? Mimi is disappointed that I am not more knowledgeable. Then she shakes the snow from her hair and laughs.

There is no reason given and none that can be inferred. I merely describe this crisis of conscience to you. Perhaps you will understand more than I. She is your close friend, after all.

And let me repeat how sorry I am for your friend, oiseau. He was a special man, your Laki. I understand that. He would have become a great artist. He meant much to you and now he has vanished from your life. Take heart in your memory of him, dear child. What more can you do?

Toujours
Ton Corbu

The letter arrived in a plain envelope. This envelope is now in Minnette's hand. She presses it between her fingers, feeling for its density but finds paucity instead. The letter itself bears all the hallmarks of a well-written condolence. He is sorry for her loss. He is concerned for her friendships. This is what urges him to advocate on behalf of Mimi.

How selfless, she thinks, slanting her eyes over her latest sketches. She appreciates his motives, but hasn't the time to reply.

Her persistent advocacy has finally won her the contract she has always dreamed of: a social housing project. The Watapuluwa housing scheme for public servants near Kandy is sited along the banks of the great Mahaweli Ganga. With the Knuckles mountain range ascending in the distance, the site is nothing short of idyllic, and a testament to the women – all wives of public servants – who argued for the scheme to address the growing housing shortage.

Their families represent a wide range of backgrounds. There are doctors, engineers, clerks and others. They are Sinhalese, Tamil, Burgher, Malay – all with their own ways of living, their own demands. Having seen other housing schemes fail, Minnette takes a different approach. She starts with the individual. She devises questionnaires to help determine the different householder types and thus building types that she will need to design. As always, the scheme must be economically viable, and Minnette has already decided to use the site's natural slope to her advantage, minimising the need to cut into the land. She has drawn up a detailed second questionnaire for all householders, so that she has a clear idea of more specific needs, such as movable walls that allow for the expansion of rooms for entertaining, or traditional outdoor kitchens.

She designs five house types on the basis of the first survey, and organises meetings with users of each type to run through the second questionnaire and get a more detailed picture of what the house should look like. In total, there are 200 units occupying between an eighth and a quarter acre each, depending on the householder's income.

Minnette employs nine people in her studio, an expense she does not expect to recuperate. The work demands all her attention, which diverts her from the grief that has enveloped her for years, with Amma's and Laki's deaths.

Further distraction arrives in March in the form of a Hollywood director, whose pursuit of Minnette is unexpected and thrilling. Each time she receives a letter from him, she files it in a ribboned stack. He is shooting *The Bridge on the River Kwai*, and despatches the eponymous structure in an explosion witnessed by the Prime Minister of Ceylon, as well as Minnette herself. Watching that piece of engineering being blown to bits, Minnette mourns the waste while applauding the spectacle of it. She is flattered by the director's attention and allows him to take her to evening dinners and dances. He is a careful and urgent lover, and she a discreet accomplice. Minnette has no illusions about her relationship with him. His messages grow ever more ardent, and she delights in the novelty of having a partner whose company she can enjoy without the shadow of separation.

Meanwhile the housing scheme grows, the foundations for the units go up, and Minnette has finally exorcised her self-doubt. Then the rains come and everything slows down. Faced with a hiatus, she turns to her research on South and South East Asian architecture. As she clears her desk to accommodate her notes, she finds the architect's letter from December and reconciles herself to finally replying it.

Is it spring already? Spring for you, that is. Here, we are drowning. She watches the rain sheeting down, battering the jasmine. The monks have returned to the temples to meditate and pray – *a welcome break from their usual interfering ways.* The 2500th anniversary came and went; this year the celebrations are simpler. *To be honest with you, Corbu, I am fed up of the Buddhists and their moaning. No doubt there are some bhikkhus who are sincere and have had nothing to do with the troubles that have lately beset the island. These monks remain in the forest, rarely coming out to interact with lay people. But the others!*

Minnette considers these other *bhikkhus* who have now organised themselves into a political party. She wonders whether the Buddha would have endorsed such a thing, and concludes otherwise. *But then*, she continues, *the monks of Ceylon have always found it hard to resist interfering in temporal affairs. One of our island's great chronicles, the Mahavamsa, describes an army of monks marching against the Tamil Chola king, weapons in hand (it was the subject of one of Siri's 'great' triptychs years ago). The precedent is replayed over and over again here. Just look at what happened to Laki. There was no investigation. No punishment of those responsible. No truth.*

Laki's death had been mourned as a tragedy, but the circumstances surrounding it had been recast. According to official accounts, Laki died after being struck on the head by a stone, lobbed by a random hooligan. His body was not found in Beira Lake but on Galle Face Green. There is no memorial to him, but these details formed part of the official obituary published at the '43 Group exhibition in Venice. None of the artists present diverged from this account, though they were all aware it was a lie. Privately, they admitted to it being a farce but could see no value in honouring the truth. Only the obituary Minnette had printed in the newspaper was accurate, but it was small and was buried beneath other more high-profile deaths and news.

Writing of truths, Mimi did eventually tell me she had been to India. I received an uncharacteristically sheepish note from her around my birthday. I don't know why she should feel she has to apologise to me at all. She only had a few days. That is what she said. Indeed, it is what you said as well. Minnette pauses. Had Mimi come, she realises, it would have been a relief, particularly since Laki's death. Ever since she discovered that Mimi had gone to India, she wondered why she had not made the trip to Ceylon as well. Compared to the architect, however, Mimi's negligence is trifling. After all, he has never come to Ceylon, despite his many visits to India. Minnette has not replied to Mimi's letter. She thinks she might do that next month, or perhaps the month after.

Despite our recent troubles here in Ceylon, my work has carried on. The flats in Gregory's Road are done and I must say, they look marvellous! They are my most Modern build to date, yet wholly vernacular. The central courtyard brims with greenery that reaches up and seems to embrace the two buildings. I will send you some photos soon. But the big news is my latest project. Finally, Corbu, I'm working on a social housing scheme! I have been wanting this for years – and now it's here. I have 200 units to design and build. It's a huge challenge: so many different people – different religions, ethnicities.

How can one build for all those variables? You must have had similar challenges in Chandigarh – greater ones, in fact.

For me, the answer is to start with a series of questionnaires. It seems to me that rather than force a person to live a certain way, we should listen to their needs and try to serve those needs, all the while introducing small innovations that coax the individual towards a more harmonious way of living. I'm sure you agree.

It has been several months since I came to Kandy. My work in Colombo kept me in Mount Lavinia, and I suppose I was not especially keen on being back at Nell Cottage. Papa said nothing about my prolonged absence and seems happy to have me. He is still busy with Party business despite the fact that they are now in opposition to the government. As for the Prime Minister, he seems to be making some progress with the Tamils, having reached an agreement recently. Hopefully, this will leave the whole sordid debate about language behind and we can finally get on with the business of living.

So, perhaps your Open Hand, crooked or not, has already started to work its magic from Chandigarh. You can tell that to Elizabeth next time you speak to her. And yes, Corbu, I still think you are wrong about Elizabeth and those other men. Not everyone subscribes to your code of (mis)conduct.

Do say hello to Mimi for me.

Yours
Minnette

———————

The architect returns to No. 24, with a card from Mimi in his breast pocket. He smiles, thinking of her red curls against his chest. That was a long time ago, and even then, only fleeting. His encounters with Mimi have always been brief, flouncy affairs. They are friends now, nothing more. Still, for the architect, the potential is always there; the chance that he might see that elegant body again compels him to seek her out whenever they are in Paris.

But each time, they do little more than share a meal and some conversation. Somehow, they are satisfied with just this. They eat and they laugh, and then they hug. It was the same today. Tomorrow is the architect's birthday, and Mimi met him for lunch to celebrate. The architect doesn't like thinking about birthdays. They bring him one step closer to mortality. His body has already begun to betray him. He wonders whether it is this that prevents him from revisiting old territory with Mimi.

It isn't, of course. Mimi is with someone now, and although she says little about him, the architect can see that she is gone.

He opens the card once more and reads her note to him. *To Corbu*, she has written, *may you continue to set the world on its head. Allez, allez!* He chuckles to himself and is surprised by the loudness of his own voice. He looks around. Nothing moves – there is nothing that can move, for even the little dog is nowhere in sight. '*Chérie*?' he calls, but there is no reply.

The architect approaches the kitchen. Water drips like seconds into the sink. A pigeon flies past the galleried window along the long balcony. He moves towards it, stares at the dirty sky. Then he turns and hurries to his room to check on Vonn. There, he finds the little dog licking her hand. The sound of its lapping tongue makes him think of the leaky tap. He closes his eyes and listens.

An hour later, they are all at the clinic. The architect sits by Vonn's side, holding her hand. She murmurs phrases that no one understands and tosses from side to side. He holds her hand until the end. And even when she has gone for good, her fingers remain curled around his.

He weeps. He considers this gift proffered by his wife and rejects it. He can feel his heart hardening and cracking, like a plate taken from hot to cold too quickly. When he returns to No. 24, he finds silence. The little dog is quiet, its small greying eyes searching mournfully for Vonn. The architect wants to say, it's no use. He wants to hold the little dog and explain what has happened, how it should not expect to see its dear mistress again. But he cannot say anything. He cannot admit it to himself, let alone the little dog.

He looks around. *She is gone*, he thinks. The goddess of his hearth, the woman who served him for the past thirty-six years, is gone. When he looks back at those years, he finds the American, the famous Miss Baker, Minnette, Mimi, and then countless others, all of them in one way or another known to Vonn. He tells himself he is an undeserving shit, and blubbers into his tie.

Later, he reasons that it is better for her that she has passed this way – quietly, almost painlessly. Her suffering has finally ended. Finally, she is free of the bed, the swollen legs and the tearful dreams. *My dear wife will sit forever at the centre of my Poème de l'angle droit, forever an unwilling subject.* He smiles at this, remembering her stubborn dismissal of his arguments, her casual disgust at his poetic masterpiece.

She was too young, he thinks, too young to die like this. She was his beautiful partner in life, if not intellect. And she has left him behind. He resents this. Even as he thinks of her lost vigour, her early spirit, he can feel an ache in his knees, hear an incessant ringing in his ears. His belly sags. His ankles thin. *The skin I live in is the skin of an idiot.*

No wonder he is made a fool of in Chandigarh. On his last visit in April, the governor of Chandigarh sent a broken down taxi to collect him. Crumbs littered the seat and the car was filled with stale body odour. *Why couldn't they send me a real car?* The architect shakes his head, anger blistering inside him. *The bastards in the High Court refuse to hang the tapestries I have designed. How dare they! They do not maintain the building. It is an embarrassment now. More than a week before I arrived in Chandigarh, I sent some drawings – drawings so basic, even a child could understand them. But not these engineers. The pricks provided no calculations for what I had sent them. They are stupid, as thick-headed as the oxen that graze between the rubble. And Elizabeth and Richard. They have colluded with Pierre against Corbu. With one mouth they smile and tell me I am a genius; with the other, they jeer and throw criticisms at my designs. I know this. They have coopted Trivedi and even Seetaram into their evil betrayal. Well, Corbu says, pah! Build it then. Build Chandigarh, for God's sake, so we can all be free of it!*

The architect thinks of Vonn again and his fury dissolves. He feels sad, frightened and – that feeling that so rarely afflicts him – regret. He had kept Vonn hidden away, like a housewife might her silverware, displaying her on rare occasions. They socialised in different circles. She had her interests and they were philistine. He can admit this without sounding like a snob. Her interests *were* philistine. He never complained. He was rarely there. He was busy. He abandoned her. Friends have told him that she had her male companions. The architect is relieved to know this.

He cremates her at Père Lachaise cemetery, later claiming for himself the one piece of bone that doesn't turn to ash. (Soon her vertebra will sit in his breast pocket, and it will be as if her back is pressed against his chest again.) Mimi comes for the funeral; Elizabeth, Richard and Pierre fly in, too. *Traitors,* he thinks, eyeing the trio who sit and weep beside him, but he is grateful for their company. *Let Chandigarh remain in Chandigarh,* he sighs. He is moved that Mimi is there, too, although she has come uninvited. She had heard about the funeral from her uncle, who is also there. Basquin sits by himself, isolated by his odour. The architect covers his nose and silently chastises Mimi for not making him have a bath before coming to his dear wife's service. Still, it matters little. He is comforted by the presence of his friends. Even Elizabeth's condolences, dry and double-edged, are oddly mollifying. 'She was fresh, Corb,' she says, unblinking, 'fresh and honest. Such an uncomplicated soul.' Her expression is as still as a boulder. Richard looks away in embarrassment.

At the reception the trio sit together, drinking wine, listening to stories about Vonn. Elizabeth smokes a cigarette, nodding slowly. She and Richard met Vonn twice, both times at No. 24. The architect had told them about Vonn's opinion of the apartment, how she disliked the light. This did not impress Elizabeth. It did not impress the architect either at the time, but now, he thinks of it and smiles.

Mimi and her uncle do not come to the reception. This is fitting. The American is not there either. The architect wishes that Minnette could have been there, although this, too, would have been wrong.

———

Minnette cycles through her slides of Ceylon's ancient capitals. She pauses at a projection of pillars from the

Anuradhapura period, dating as far back as the fourth century BC. A slide of the *Bodhi* tree – a surviving offshoot of the sacred fig under which the Buddha achieved *nirvana* – follows, its venerable age explicit in each gnarled joint. This, too, is in Anuradhapura, brought there from India along with Buddhism by Sangamitta, Emperor Asoka's daughter.

As Minnette clicks past each image, she reflects on the Buddhist origins of architecture in Ceylon and understands the unbearable weight of that history on the political present. She notes down this observation and continues, eventually reaching the eleventh century and Polonnaruwa. The architecture here is more ornate, includes South Indian influences, and is marked by its complex irrigation system composed of vast man-made reservoirs. It is also remarkable, notes Minnette, for its colossal carvings of Buddha statues. As she studies the supine figure of the Buddha, carved in granite, the architect's last letter drifts upward in her mind.

V*onn*, she thinks, and is suffused by guilt. Minnette feels the years of Vonn's loneliness, and now the architect's despair. *Her ashes will be buried in Rocquebrune*, he had written. She understands the architect's need to hold on to a piece of his wife, a woman he loved more than any other. Minnette has always accepted her place in the hierarchy. For the architect, there was always Vonn at the pinnacle and the rest somewhere below.

Do not despair, she later writes, a command she knows no one can obey. *Her latter years were difficult, but she is in a better place, laughing and joking again. Take heart in that, Corbu.* Again, Minnette is struck by the ineffectiveness of her words. *More platitudes.* She recalls her research slides and shuffles through her collection of postcards until she finds what she is looking for. *I am sending you this little card of the Buddha at Polonnaruwa. Carved out of granite, he is shown here reclining in his final pose as he crosses from life to death. But in this moment, he also achieves his great enlightenment. This is what can come with death, Corbu, the ultimate realisation of Truth.*

Minnette wonders whether this more genuine expression of sympathy is less comforting. What truth could Vonn have experienced in that final moment? Did the reality of her husband's infidelity blind her with its magnitude? Or did she accept all and forgive him for denying her the things she desired most? Minnette dares not speculate further, for fear of trespassing where she of all people should not. Instead she continues: *Do not be burdened by the weight of your age. You are alive in this world and still very much of it. You are widely respected. Your spirit is still strong, even vigorous. We cannot fight against the deterioration of our bodies. But our souls... these can be safeguarded, uplifted and set free.*

The architect studies the sleeping Buddha for the third time that day. He is in Chandigarh where serenity is in short supply. So he turns to this image to discover the truths to come. He himself is in a constant flight towards the truth. Truth is the kernel of all his design. His buildings must be made without too much dressing. The DNA of those builds is made up of essential shapes, and those shapes reveal certain cosmological truths. It is the same with his symbols.

The architect is creating a visual poem for the Philips Pavilion. Dubbed the Electronic Poem, it is a series of projected images and sound. He has been ruminating on which images to use and has chosen hundreds, some of which, like the grasshopper's head and the female silhouette, reference his work in India. Although visually disparate, together these symbols will be a revelation: a manifestation of a truth.

This is what he strives for in Chandigarh, too. Once the capital is finished, the architect is determined to have the town designated a heritage site so that nothing is altered. Yet no one listens. Instead, these Indians want to distract the capital complex by planting hedgerows, and hanging flowers on balconies. He can't convince them that such ornamentation equates to a kind of pollution.

Take the Secretariat. To the architect, it is the embodiment of society. Industry, community spirit and cooperation are captured in its physique – all those little windows lined up in neat rows and columns. It is commanding, clearly defined and modern. He imagines the integrity of those lines disturbed by falling petals, chaotic vines, twisting leaves. *What does that show?* he asks himself but the answer is obvious: *A government gone to seed.*

The Open Hand still stands, and is still crooked. The architect has shared Minnette's view on its spiritual properties with Elizabeth, hoping to change her opinion of it, but she waved the air with a limp hand, like a queen. 'Things must be very bad indeed in Ceylon,' she said. He realised then that talk of the spirit was of no interest to her. His team no longer feels like his. He does not trust them. Not even Pierre. They have ganged together and have almost no explanations for the architect when he asks why certain jobs are still not done.

And these Indian engineers! Where have they qualified? rages the architect. *Have they bought their qualifications from a thief in the bazaar?* He finds them impossible to work with. Every answer they give is vague. *They will not calculate, only shift their heads from side to side like puppets and smile. What is there to smile at?* He is fed up of all this incompetence. At the same time, he is relieved that he isn't here all the time. He knows this is a problem, because if he were present, the work would get done without all that whispering behind his back.

Seetaram and Trivedi are better than this, but they, too, have a habit of shuffling their necks to answer questions. They couch their phrases in philosophy to make them more palatable, but he is no wiser in the end. The architect can now see why Richard is sometimes bad tempered with the locals, though he is miserable anyway.

Mimi's advice is straightforward. The architect puts this down to her only having been to India twice: she finds it easy to make judgements based on small experiences. *You expect too much,* she had written. *Why not go to the top and get things done, instead of wasting your time with the dross at the bottom.* Her words are harsh, if practical. He decides to write another letter to Nehru, describing the incompetence he is forced to put up with. *He will not be happy,* he thinks with satisfaction.

A knot tightens in his chest, burrows upward. The architect swallows back the discomfort, but a substantial burp erupts from his mouth. Disgusted, he looks around to see if anyone has heard. There is no one there.

Minnette had been right to say the body cannot be stopped from degenerating. The architect is old and fed up. He seems to be continuously flying, walking, climbing. His knees cry out like two rusty hinges. His ears do not stop ringing. He does not want to return to No. 24 without Vonn.

He stares at the Buddha again, who lies on his side, calm and still. He is nothing like his dead wife.

XII

January – December 1958

Jaya studies the new *suddha* who has come to Nell Cottage. He has yellow hair and blue eyes like so many of them do. He smiles a lot and is tall. *Quite handsome, really.* Baby Nona has given him a room at the back. He is here to work with her. Jaya knows he came by ship, but from where isn't clear. She thinks it must be England.

Jaya's Baby Nona is always busy. She travels up and down, to Watapuluwa and back, to build houses for government workers. Jaya has seen the place only once, a beautiful site with a river and mountains huddled around. Baby Nona and the *suddha* are in Watapuluwa today, leaving Jaya free to clean.

There is no end of cleaning in this place, she sighs as she begins to sweep. At times like these, when she's alone, Nona's loss throbs like a bruise. George Mahattaya is okay, but Nona was always the kind one. She thinks of that terrible day – seeing Nona in bed, her skin grey. Baby Nona's face had gone white as coconut flesh, and Mahattaya went off to a corner with his *arrak*. He sat and drank, while Baby Nona and Jaya tried to sort everything out.

When Jaya had told her mother that Nona was gone, she beat her chest and wailed. Jaya kept quiet, remembering the Christmas cakes they had baked together, the look on Nona's face when she made her another love cake. 'Jaya, *aney* bring me another piece, can you?' she would say, and Jaya would oblige with a generous slice.

Crumbs. Even in the hallway. Jaya kisses her teeth. *I don't know **who** is eating without plates in this house. Must be that suddha. Just because he smiles at me, doesn't mean he can throw his food everywhere.* She sweeps with extra force, until the act itself calms her.

Mahattaya still gives her extra money when she needs it, but this is not what she longs for. Nona would *talk* to her. She would sit under the jasmine tree and tell her all kinds of things. 'Jaya,' she once said, 'you are a clever, decent woman. If you ever end up somewhere else, always remember you must be paid fairly. This is how we pay you, because how would we get on without you?' Jaya snorts. Nona had strange ideas. *All this talk about pay.* Jaya had never thought of working anywhere else. She has no intention of going now.

In Baby Nona's office, she finds drawings all over the floor. *How can I sweep in here now?* Jaya takes her time, walking about the room, eyeing the drawings at her feet. She observes the outlines of buildings and a series of squares and rectangles stuck together. They remind her of her Amma's drawings. She used to take a pencil and sketch little boxes like the ones in Baby Nona's designs, to show Jaya the houses she worked in. Like that, Jaya could see where the kitchen was, where the living room was. Amma was good. Jaya remembers going to a house after only seeing her mother's drawing, and knowing exactly where to find the cupboard with the sheets.

Jaya can't tell which houses the designs belong to. She has only seen Baby Nona's lodge. She grins at the thought of it. *Sha! Nothing like it anywhere in Kandy.* According to Dilini, her friend who works there, the kitchen is *very convenient.* 'The countertops are a bit high, but everything is *so* easy to clean,' Dilini often says. 'And you must see in the evenings, Jaya, how the sun reaches into the living room.' Dilini's favourite job is sweeping the balcony, because she can 'see all the little birds flying into the valley'. *She is lucky, that one,* thinks Jaya, and is comforted by the thought.

Baby Nona comes and goes. One day she is in Colombo, another in Kandy. It's hard to keep track of her. *Such a strange job for a woman,* Jaya muses, but to her, Baby Nona is not a proper Ceylonese woman. Neither is the sister, Podi Nona. When Jaya goes to market, other servants come and question her: *Ah, did you see her with that man? My, this one isn't her husband, no?* Jaya keeps quiet. It is not her business what her employers do with men. It is none of these servants' business either.

Jaya thinks the best way to stop gossip is marriage. *But what use is marriage?* she asks herself. *Mine was no use. You have to find a good man, and still, what good are they?* Baby Nona must know this, decides Jaya. She remembers that friend who went with the English *suddhi* a long time ago, the white nona. Then there was another *suddha* – the film one. He kept coming to the house. Sometimes Baby Nona hid at the back. 'Just tell him to go,' she would say to Jaya. She felt a little sorry for him. He left letters for her. Sometimes Baby Nona would go with him and not return for days. *Chi! Who knows what they were up to?* But Baby Nona was busy, too – with Watapuluwa and houses in Colombo. *Maybe she was working, who knows?*

Mahattaya doesn't notice. He is in his study most of the time. Since Nona passed, Mahattaya has been quiet. He talks to the people who come to the house. He does his politics. But Jaya has seen a look in his eyes. When he speaks to her, she knows he doesn't always remember her. 'Who are you?' he once asked when she went into his office with her broom. To Jaya, it seemed he was expecting her to come with a problem, like the others that queue to meet him. 'Mahattaya?' she had said, and that did it. He laughed and said he was only joking, but she could tell it was real: the milky look of fear in his eyes.

When the thunder comes, it throws Jaya from her bed. She stands, bare from the waist down, her *reddha* at her feet. Pulling the cloth back up, she knots it tight anticipating the lightning's return. She imagines her room flashing blue-white, and her, half naked, in the middle of it. *The monkeys will be watching – dirty fellows.* Jaya isn't fooled. *Just because they have fur, doesn't mean they don't have* sense, she thinks, peering out her window. *They watch us like we watch them. And they laugh.*

The lightning pulls shadows up her walls. For a moment, everything is visible, including Jaya. Then the rain peels down, thrashing the earth like rage. She runs to the kitchen to check the windows. One of them is open. 'That *suddha*,' she mutters. 'He's been told not to come into my kitchen, but he doesn't listen.' She clenches her jaw. *Suddhas are like this. If they weren't, the Dutch wouldn't have taken us over. Neither would the Portuguese or the British. They just come and take.*

Having closed the window, she goes to the living room

to check whether anything has been left open there, too. She walks straight into a puddle – rainwater blown in through another open window. *This suddha is a bloody nuisance.* She checks the other rooms. Baby Nona's study is dry and somehow insulated from all the noise. The thunder drags its jagged heels across the sky. The house shakes with each bellow and Jaya shakes with it. When she was little, this drama was like an epic battle to her. She would stare at the sky, searching out the two armies, her face wet with rain. Her mother would tell her to get away from the windows, that she would be struck by lightning if she stayed one minute longer. But Jaya never listened and no lightning had ever pointed its finger at her.

She leaves the rooms and returns to the corridor to get back to her own bed, but something makes her stop. Jaya sees a figure in white approaching. It's Baby Nona. Jaya steps back into shadow and pastes herself to the wall. Baby Nona is saying something in English, and her face flickers in the lantern light. Her hair is swept up onto her head and she is wearing a thin cotton nightgown and nothing else. Jaya can see through the fabric. *Shameless!* Baby Nona stands in the doorway of the *suddha's* room, whispering something to him over the flame of her lamp. Eventually, Baby Nona turns away and the *suddha* follows behind. Jaya hangs back and watches them go single-file to her room. She follows.

Jaya pauses by Baby Nona's closed door. She thinks of her, now a grown woman of forty, with this *suddha* who is probably half her age. She pictures the toddy tapper – his bragging eyes and oily breath. The *suddha* is not like this. He looked almost boyish, in his white vest and sarong, and Baby Nona like a spectre. Jaya approaches her own room on slow feet. Tiredness pours into her, slackens her limbs.

The rain is still hissing down, but there is another sound, a horrible roaring that jolts Jaya and awakens her legs. She runs towards her quarters and is just in time to see red earth filling the kitchen and flattening her little room.

In the following days, everyone at Nell Cottage grows acquainted with earth. They use buckets, pots, any receptacle available to bail the mud out of the property. The monsoon tore the side of a hill off, squeezing it into Nell Cottage. Now, a crew of thirteen people parades through, hauling it out in basins and barrows. Minnette hires more workers to repair the damage to the outside of the building. The back end of the kitchen – the sink and hob – is buried beneath slabs of clay and tree roots. It takes two weeks to restore the cottage to a habitable state despite the wind and the wet. And with the rains comes sickness. Jaya, Minnette, her father and the Dane all succumb to the flu, one after the other. They sweat and shiver in their beds while the monsoon pelts the roof like bullets.

When the clouds finally clear, so does the flu, and Minnette returns to the Watapuluwa housing estate. She also has a new house in Colombo, which she visits with the Dane, her newest import, an ambitious young architect from Copenhagen. On the way, she shows him her flats in Gregory's Road. Completed in December, they have proved popular. 'Most of the units sold before I finished the work,' she says, matter-of-factly. He looks surprised as he takes in the abundance of greenery, the shaded balconies, and the stark white exterior. 'The block is at full capacity now,' she adds, and the Dane smiles and nods, collecting each detail into his straw-topped head.

The pair continue to Sulaiman Road to inspect the house Minnette has designed for a doctor. It is extensive, with a badminton court, pool and roof terrace. The sunken garden is full of shade-loving plants – anthurium, orchids, ferns. To complement it, there is also a sun garden, where the family can enjoy flowers that thrive in full light. She observes the Dane admiring the concrete staircase curving up and over a pool of water. His gaze lingers on the white underbelly of the stairs, marbled by the pool's reflection. When he spots the *meda midula*, a garden space between the sitting room, dining room and bedroom, his mouth drops open and his eyes shine. 'Extraordinary,' he says, delighted by the air current that flows without effort through the courtyard and up into the house.

Back in Kandy, Minnette takes the Dane into her studio, and shows him the designs for the housing estate. He assists her with her inspections and some of her drawings. He accompanies her to artisan villages and to explore temple ruins. She promises him a healthy wage, but despite the many contracts she has fulfilled, payment is sparse and never commensurate with the effort she and her studio put in. Apparently clients find it hard to part with their money when the lead architect is a woman.

Still, the Dane stays on, sharing her studio, her kitchen, her bed. Together they design a house in Alexandra Place for a devoted Catholic family. Her clients' diffidence about security allows Minnette to create a wall-less lower floor, surrounded by a garden and a pool, entirely open to the elements. This theme is continued upstairs, where she builds an open-air shower, with a small tree providing company and privacy as needed. It is a soaring, light-filled home, with all the hallmarks of her earlier builds: the bespoke fired clay tiles, the concrete staircase with wooden treads, ample use of columns to open out each floor, and a *meda midula* bringing the island's flora into the very heart of the building's architecture.

Minnette is relieved to have someone working regularly in her studio. Where once she toiled in solitude, she now has a hungry young architect who is willing to share the load. His technical skill is a boon, and his presence unexpectedly comforting. His youthful energy is equally welcome. When Minnette lies with the Dane, she thinks she is feeling something of what the architect must have felt with her – a confidence and determination to take the pleasure that is her due. She also understands the architect's obsession with youth: the Dane's physical beauty is enough to shut her eyes to the discomfiting stares of others. He comes to her now, puts his hands around her bare waist, and she sighs. *It is not a permanent arrangement*, she thinks, as she revels in the temporary blasphemy of her desire.

———————

My room. It is not like my old room.

Jaya had only a few things, but they're gone. *Who wants to save a poor woman's reddhas?* Mahattaya gave her extra money to buy new clothes. He was very sorry, he said. *But he doesn't know what I've lost.* All the old letters – the letters her mother sent her are gone. A photo of her little brother, also gone. It was her only one. *No use thinking about it now.*

The rains have returned. A little while after December's earthslip, the sun emerged for a few months. By May, it was back to the thunder and lightning. *Shi!* spits Jaya.

When the monsoon started, it was as if all the *apsaras* in heaven were pouring huge drums of water on everyone. Entire villages of people have been made homeless in the north. Everything, even the rail lines, are flooded. No one can travel. No one leaves the cottage for weeks. Roads have become rivers, farmers have lost their rice crops. People climb into trees to save themselves from drowning. In Colombo, houses collapse under the weight of the rain.

Jaya holds her new *reddhas* to her chest. *Ayyo! What if it happens again? An earthslip? In my room. What if I had been in bed when it came last time? What if I hadn't got up?* She comforts herself knowing her *karma* is not as bad as some. She doesn't sleep in the newly constructed room. Not when it rains. Sometimes, she takes a mat and sleeps on the living room floor. *Let Baby Nona get mad. I don't care. I don't want to die like that. Buried alive.*

Despite the floods, the people still march. May Day brings crowds of workers into the streets. *Always complaining about something,* thinks Jaya. At the end of the month, it all starts going bad. When Jaya speaks to Dilini about it, her friend says it is 'communal violence'. They are sitting in the kitchen designed by Baby Nona, at the lodge where Dilini lives and works.

'It's like in India, when they got their independence. It's going that way here, too,' says Dilini. Both friends have heard about the dynamited vehicles in Vavuniya, up north. In Polonnaruwa, a man was beaten to death and another shot dead. Sinhalese attack Tamils and Tamils attack Sinhalese.

'Baby Nona was talking to Mahattaya the other day,' whispers Jaya. 'It seems some Tamil shops were looted and burnt down in Kolambe. In the centre, and in Dehiwala, crowds of Sinhalese swarmed onto train platforms, pulled Tamils from carriages and beat them up.'

'*Ayyo!*' Dilini puts a hand to her mouth. 'Now the government has called another Emergency. Every day, another Emergency! The last one was only two years ago. What is this country coming to?'

'Baby Nona says it isn't normal,' continues Jaya. 'We are all under curfew, and the army and navy have been sent in to enforce it.'

'Yes, yes,' nods Dilini. 'The government has banned two political parties, one Tamil, one Sinhalese. So far, it seems they have only arrested the Tamil members.' She purses her lips.

'What nonsense!' quips Jaya. 'Should we start fighting now, you and me? After all, you're Tamil and I'm Sinhalese, no?'

Dilini laughs and gives Jaya a piece of homemade ginger cake. Jaya wonders how Dilini has managed to find enough butter to make it. With the rain and the curfew and no way to travel, it isn't easy to get. 'What? Did you make the butter yourself?'

Dilini laughs again, her face bright like a butterfly. Jaya catches her breath, blinking against the glow of Dilini's dark skin and soft features. The cake is still sweet and warm in her mouth, and she smiles. Dilini smiles back at her. Outside, the rain sheets down, hammering the grass and the hedges, tearing flower petals to the ground.

'Baby Nona went away for a while before it all went bad,' says Jaya, as she stares out the window, wide-eyed. 'She left in March to go to Afghanistan. That's what Mahattaya said. I don't know this Afghanistan. Apparently somewhere near India?' Dilini nods. 'She went to India, too. She said she is writing a book. Must be like Podi Nona. *She* went to China with a big group of women.'

'China! *Sha!*' says Dilini. '*My*, such bold girls, no?'

Jaya nods, proud of her two *babas* – two girls who grew into mysterious and important women. 'There was a big article about her and the book she wrote. About Lord Buddha. I saw Baby Nona reading about it in the paper and she pointed to it and said, "Here. Look at this Jaya. Podi Nona in China."' She beams as Dilini's eyes widen with excitement.

'Baby Nona came back from all her travelling a few weeks ago. Now, the house is always full, with the *suddha* and Baby Nona and Mahattaya.' She stops and looks at Dilini. 'That's why I come here. For some peace!'

'And cake,' says Dilini, grinning, cutting Jaya another slice.

Some days later, the rain slows and Jaya convinces Dilini to join her at Udawattakele. The rains are light and will be even lighter under the shelter of the trees. Jaya likes walking in the jungle, while Dilini shrinks and jumps each time a fly draws near.

The pair keep watch for leeches. Jaya takes Dilini's hand when she gets scared, and Dilini clings to her.

'You know,' says Jaya, 'I never liked to hold that toddy tapper's hand. But you're my friend, no? So, I don't mind.' Dilini leans against her and Jaya smells how clean and whole she is.

'The other day, I saw Baby Nona holding the *suddha's* hand, just like this.' Jaya and Dilini giggle. 'I have seen them together in her room, too.'

Dilini stops and stares. Jaya covers her mouth with her hand. Her stomach falls as she realises what she has done. She cannot unsay it now. Baby Nona's secrets are out in the jungle, alive among the trees.

Dilini's face cracks with laughter. She throws her head back with uncontained mirth. 'Your face!' she gasps. '*Ayyo*, Jaya! It's no secret. Everyone has seen them together. Your Baby Nona goes all over the place with him, and he is always with his hand on her – ' she reaches out and circles an arm around Jaya's waist '– like this.'

Jaya does not know what shocks her more: Baby Nona's shamelessness in public, or Dilini's arm around her. She feels floaty inside, like fireflies are in her chest. She thinks of the toddy tapper and his large hands and hard arms. They were nice arms to look at, but she never liked them on her. No one had put an arm around her since him. But somehow Dilini's arm is nothing like his. It is warm and strong and soft and safe. Now, like a ghost, it's gone again. Dilini is still next to her. Jaya can still feel fireflies inside.

'Mahattaya might be asking for me,' she says. Dilini's face opens like a butterfly's wings, then seems to fly away. 'Me, too,' she says. And as they leave, the jungle closes its arms behind them.

XIII

January 1959 – June 1963

She sits on the floor of her studio, alone. The Dane is gone. The housing scheme is finished, and Kandy's public servants have moved in. The scheme is the only one of its kind on the island and, according to the media, is a model for future developments. The variety of housing on offer, the harmonious community relations despite the troubles consuming the rest of the island, all combine to make the scheme an enviable success.

Minnette reads an article in the newspaper – a full-scale interview with her entitled 'Ceylon's first woman architect' – and feels something like satisfaction. *Her oeuvre represents a desire to synthesise traditional and modern architecture – a modern regional architecture*, writes the piece's author, also pointing out how integral the artisan is to her builds. This summary of her achievements, replete with photographs, flatters her. But a moment later she sighs, reminded of why the Dane left her practice.

Jaya walks in, sets a mug of tea next to her, and glances at the paper. '*Anh*, Baby Nona!' she exclaims. She bends forward to study the article and grins. 'Dilini!' she points to a photo of a petite woman, standing on a stool, cutting onions at the counter. Minnette cringes, recalling her mistake with the Ariyapala Lodge: the wrong calculation, the too-tall kitchen counters. She looks away. Jaya doesn't notice. She stares at the article as if she is reading it, then withdraws without another word.

Minnette folds the newspaper into neat quarters. She has more copies, so she will clip this one and send it to the architect. She hasn't written to him in a long time. He will be impressed, as always. Perhaps he will draw parallels between her housing scheme and Chandigarh. She shrugs. Perhaps not.

Why did he leave? The question is rhetorical. She knows why. The Dane left because she couldn't pay him. Wooed away to Colombo by a bigger firm run by a recluse. It is a loss she can bear. She had grown weary of the young man and his budding arrogance. Her research trip to Afghanistan and India put necessary distance between the pair. Her return rekindled something of their earlier fire, although the effect was brief. He was dependable in the studio. This is what she misses most.

The article lies on a table, taunting her. She is vaunted for her intrepid work, but her earnings are paltry. This contradiction gnaws at her. She is known for offering budget solutions, yet even then, clients are reluctant to pay. There is no excuse for their meanness. Some are friends who exploit their relationship for a discount. Others plead penury while maintaining several properties. No one, it seems, is willing to pay her her worth. *What good are words? I can't eat words. I can't build with words.* She reaches for the newspaper, ready to tear it to pieces, but stops. It would be a pointless gesture in this empty room.

The architect stands on the rocky edge of the Côte d'Azur and lets empty waves foam over his toes. The little dog watches from above, its thin legs trembling. He sympathises. His legs shook, too, as he scrambled down the rocks to the sea.

He lowers himself into the water and lets go. Floating on his back, he watches the dog's tiny face telescope away from him. Safe in the water, he surrenders to that familiar weightlessness that makes him feel young again. He can hear the laboured barks of the little dog, which stop abruptly. Its lungs can no longer sustain the effort. The architect imagines it lying with its snout in its paws, lost now to an exhausted sleep.

He smiles and floats in the sun, his body in the sea's embrace. He thinks of *her* in her watery paradise, that jewel amidst the ocean. He has not heard from her in many months, perhaps a year. Mimi, however, has told him that according to Marcia, the situation in Ceylon is tenuous. Violence between religious groups and States of Emergency rage as destructive as floods. But no one talks about Ceylon in France. Here, it is Algeria. With De Gaulle now in charge, Algeria will finally get its freedom. It is inevitable when Tunisia and Morocco are already independent. *This is the natural order of things*, decides the architect. *Why let Algeria suffer?*

The architect flips onto his belly and begins a front crawl. *Best leave the politics to the politicians.* After all, there is far too much of it in Chandigarh. He wrote to Nehru, complaining about the many delays. The High Court opened in 1954, but is still not finished. The architect supplied drawings for the whole of the capital complex years ago. *Where is the finished product? Where are the roads? The trees? The lawns? The reflective pools?*

He slices through the water with a palm, legs scissoring behind him. His instructions for the reflective pool in front of the High Court were precise. But the water was not poured until a few days before Nehru's arrival. *They do things only when they think they are in danger of having their skins flayed. It is not for the glory of the project. No! They are stupid, lazy idiots.* He has also made clear that they must not plaster over the unfinished concrete. *If they do, they will ruin the entire effect of the thing.* This, too, he has included in his letter to Nehru.

But the architect understands there is little Nehru can do from afar. Like him, he cannot be on site every day. He must trust his delegates and it is these delegates who are corrupt and useless. *They are pricks! There is no other word for it.* They did not send a car to collect him from the airport this time. Such contemptuous treatment of him, the Chief Architect, gives him little hope that his complaints will be resolved. *If I do not take these matters into my hands, if I do not tell Nehru what is happening, then I abrogate responsibility, too. I am no better than them.*

Elizabeth accused him of impatience, of failing to understand the mindset of 'the people'. 'What have I misunderstood?' he'd replied. 'They are lazy and incompetent. There is not much more to it than that. And Trivedi and Seetaram with their waddling necks. I should attach some splints to their shoulders to keep their heads in place. Then, their words would be clearer!' When he said this, Elizabeth laughed. Richard, too, was in the background, smirking. *They are all against me*, he thinks, exhaling a stream of bubbles into the water.

He heads back to the rocks, climbs up and rouses the little dog, all the while meditating on the previous months. He had escaped the headache of Chandigarh in Brussels. He went in May to oversee the building of the Philips Pavilion and work on his Electronic Poem. The monastery for the Dominican monks at La Tourette is going well, too. It is the perfect antidote to Chandigarh.

Now he is back in Cap Martin, in Roquebrune, still building his great tomb. *I do not think that I mentioned it to you before,* he writes. His swim has restored his mood and he feels compelled to share it with Minnette. *I began work on the tomb after Vonn passed. She is here, too. Each time I visit, I am overwhelmed with dread. My knees cannot manage those stairs! So many steps like little knives jabbing under my kneecaps. Once the tomb is finished and I am gone, man and wife will lie together again. In the meantime, I visit my beloved, committing harikiri each time.*

He gazes out his window. The sun shines, the sky is an artificial blue. The sea ripples, reflecting light, looks like it is on fire. *Ah! Beyond my window, the sea rises. See how it rises, rises and rolls… rises and rolls.*

The architect returns to Chandigarh in January. He imagines himself a knight fighting the same battles, using imaginary weapons to beat all too real menaces. Today, he stands in front of the Secretariat building, Prime Minister Nehru beside him.

'Magnificent,' he says, 'you have exceeded my expectations,' and he grasps the architect's hand. Earlier, he had called the Palace of Justice 'grand'.

'You have seen the symbols that lie at this building's foundation,' declaims the architect. 'Let us hope that these will have the desired effect on those ministers and civil servants who come to use it.'

'Indeed,' nods Nehru. 'The honesty of the building's structure and design should inculcate its users with a sense of integrity and pride in their work. Let us see.'

The pair walk side by side around the building, and pause by the reflective pool. They look down and into the eyes of two doppelgangers. Nehru turns to the architect, puts a hand on his shoulder. 'Please accept my apologies,' he says as he begins to address the architect's earlier letter. He concedes that the architect's treatment was shoddy, that denying him a car was poor manners. As for the tortoise's pace at which work has been progressing in the capital complex, he shakes his head and promises to speak to his delegates and try to 'get things moving'. He then congratulates the architect on the award he received last September from the King of Sweden – the *Litteris et artibus*. The architect smiles. *Nehru is not an ignorant man. He knows his Chief Architect, and appreciates who and what I am.*

'I know you have had your teething problems here in India,' Nehru continues. 'But your successes so far have been many. This is a perfect example of East and West working together to build a city of the future. It is an exercise yet in its infancy. But it is an effort to be lauded.'

The architect commends the Prime Minister on his wisdom, although he does this within the intimacy of his own mind. Nehru's skill as a statesman and diplomat fill him with admiration. *I can only be grateful that such a man has chosen to be my client.*

With the Secretariat complete, relations within the architect's team thaw. Six of them go on a picnic. Trivedi brings his children. They all eat flat Indian breads with vegetable curries, and then mangoes. There is champagne, too, from Nehru. After lunch, Elizabeth lies in a pile of blankets next to Richard with the remaining bottle of champagne. Both wear dark glasses so no one can tell whether they are awake or sleeping. Pierre plays a game of chess with Seetaram. Trivedi has borrowed Richard's newspaper and is half-reading it while watching his son and daughter play. The architect lies on a blanket and watches everyone else.

Trivedi's children compete against each other with a hula hoop, seeing who can keep it circling longest. With each breath, the architect sees his own belly rising and falling, and thinks what a useful tool a hula hoop would be in reducing it. *Imagine it: Corbu rolling a hula hoop round his waist. Quelle comédie! But if it achieves the objective, why not?* As he lies there, considering the benefits of the hula hoop, a ringing begins in his ears. He raises his head above the grass and looks about, thinking there must be a grasshopper rubbing its legs next to his head. But there is no such insect, only a horrible, incessant ringing.

Eventually, they all sleep. Even the architect finds his eyelids drooping as silence slowly resumes inside his head. Tree branches sway above them. The land is flat, the grass yellow. A wall abuts the right side of the field they are lying in. Something flashes along it, causing him to start. He grows dizzy and his chest tightens. He is grateful that he is already lying down, for the shock of it might have felled him. 'I am having a stroke,' he cries out. Only Trivedi hears him. 'The sun is too strong; it is boiling my brain.'

Trivedi smiles and wobbles his head. 'No, no, Monsieur Le Corbusier. It is only the lightning.' He gives the architect some water, which stops the dizziness and calms his nerves. Later, the architect realises it was a freak sun storm – no rain, just lightning and distant thunder. *I am glad that Elizabeth did not hear me. Or Richard,* the architect now writes to Minnette, describing the event in minute detail. *They would have had a private joke at my expense, something which has never bothered me in the past, but now... their smug expressions irritate!*

He pauses a moment to picture their faces, swollen with self-righteousness, and scoffs. Anger sweeps through him like a wind. A moment later, it's gone. *That night I slept badly. There was a burning in my gut that I could not control without letting out several wretched burps. Even that did not alleviate the symptoms. Then an appalling itch overcame me, from neck to ankle. The dry skin of an aging body. Perhaps this is what happens to snakes when they are ready to shed their old skins. But we are not so lucky. We are condemned to carry ours about with us for all our lives.*

Age! Pitiful age! Corbu must accept that he is an old man.

Still, he hopes that his friends will not abandon him. Do not forget me, little bird, decrepit dog that I have become.

I am still your friend,
Corbu

Back in Rocquebrune, the architect re-reads her letter. It arrived in Paris last week, and he has brought it here with him so that he should not feel alone. *You may be twice my age, my friend, but for women, getting old is something that comes so much earlier, knocking us out of the sphere of desire with one blow. There is nothing gradual about it. One day you are a vixen, the next, a vegetable.* He laughs out loud at the comparison. There is nothing vegetal about her. *But you – you, Corbu, the great Le Corbusier – are certainly not decrepit! I am astonished that you should even suggest it.* He knows that much of what she writes is flattery, yet his feathers fluff with pride. *And to ask that you not be forgotten. That is almost an insult. How could I forget such a constant friend? Does my loyalty, even in the face of your own wandering heart, not mean anything to you?* He reads these words again, confused by their implication. What loyalty does she expect from him? His loyalty has always been to his wife. She has always known this. The sentiment is jarring, now that their relationship has slowed to this friendly exchange. He shrugs and focuses instead on her last words: *Of course I shall not forget you. It is not possible. Never.* He nods. In this, they are agreed.

Days later, he climbs the steep steps to Vonn's grave. It is mid-afternoon and the sun is hot. The architect fears a real stroke (unlike the hoax in that field in Chandigarh). The comedy of being found face down on top of someone else's grave is something he wishes to avoid. He laughs at the thought, though it hurts his stomach to do so.

His knees throb as he mounts the final step to the headstone. 'My Vonn, lying under the earth,' he sighs. He lays white flowers in a plain white vase. He brings the little dog, too. 'He has been lonely without his *maman*,' he tells her, gesturing to the shivering, blind thing. After she died, he lay by her bed for days, standing up and sniffing the mattress to see if she had returned. The architect feels an affinity with the dog. 'We are both unsteady on our paws and bereft at the loss of our lady,' he whispers to the tombstone. 'How you function without your little companion, I do not know. But from his stiff walk and doddering neck, I do not think you will have long to wait for him.' The architect is certain that Vonn is listening, can feel her standing among them.

The little dog curls at his feet and sleeps. He seems peaceful there. Or perhaps he is dehydrated. It is hot.

Sweat gathers in the folds of the architect's neck. The little dog pants in his sleep. The architect's lungs ache from the exertion of standing. His feet cramp (a bunion has developed on his left foot).

'It is time to wear my trousers rolled, I think,' he whispers to the little dog. 'Like a pathetic Prufrock, Corbu, too, grows old. The scanty hair. The failing eye. The thinning ankles. More and more, Corbu takes on the softening properties of a woman. This is what happens to old men, my friend. They are slowly emasculated by time. Shit. Even that does not come easily!'

It is still hot when he returns to Paris. The sun shines mercilessly outside the windows at No. 24 and, *My God,* he tells himself, *maybe Vonn was right. Right now, it is like an oven in here!* He longs for Rocquebrune and the relief of the sea that awaits him there.

The elephant sways like an ocean through the crowds in Kandy's darkened streets. Draped in maroon and gold, it ambles along a silk path that renews itself every few steps. Acrobats somersault, dancers whirl, and drummers beat out a headache-inducing rhythm that animates onlookers, compelling them to stretch their necks like tortoises as they search out the dome on the elephant's back – the Buddha's tooth.

It is August. Thousands of Buddhists have come to Kandy for the *perahera,* the annual outing of the tooth, borne on the back of the lead elephant. He is accompanied by scores of other elephants, similarly adorned. Dancers strut alongside, arms outstretched, fingers fanning, the bare torsos of the men glinting in the firelight. A man tumbles through the air, then another, flames flashing behind him. Torches spin precipitously close to the elephants so that their jewel encrusted shrouds glitter like ice under moonlight.

One elephant is grazed on its flank by blue flame. It trumpets wildly and dashes into the throng, immediately crushing two dancers. The drummers continue their beat, heedless of what has just happened. Confusion is swiftly followed by realisation. People scream and scatter like coins. Fire flashes here and there as the torchbearers career down the road. The performers leap from the crowd, taking shelter in shops, some crashing through the windows of the Queen's Hotel in a desperate bid to avoid being flattened.

The elephant stamps left and right in white fury, its side throbbing. Minutes later, it is caught by its *mahut* and tied to a lamp post. Calm momentarily descends as word gets round that the elephant has been tethered. A small group of men and women surround it, and begin jeering and throwing stones at it. When it breaks free, it treads a number of its abusers underfoot, and is eventually shot dead by the police.

The Prime Minister considers this blot on what is usually a peaceful celebration while surveying the bougainvillea from the verandah of his bungalow in Colombo. Several weeks have elapsed since the incident, but his mind returns to it time and again without warning. His sympathies have always been with the elephant, although he would never have admitted this to anyone. Publicly he praised the police for their quick action, and mourned the loss of fourteen lives. He paid tribute to the majesty of Ceylon's elephants, too, calling the shooting an unavoidable tragedy.

Today, as he wonders whether to ask the gardener to

prune the bougainvillea which are tending towards the hysterical, he thinks the elephant's life could have been spared, but for the carelessness of a torchbearer and the mean-spiritedness of the people who went on to bait it. 'Poor old Raja,' he sighs, calling up the name of the departed elephant. He sighs again and takes a closer look at the purple flowers lolling over the front hedge. Some of them seem to have turned orange. He frowns. His wife likes them running riot like this. His children prefer them this way, too.

He shrugs and turns back to the rooms he uses as an office to continue his regular meetings with his constituents. He tries not to let his mind wander too far while speaking to a schoolmaster who, the Prime Minister can't help but notice, has a good deal of shrubbery about his ears. The schoolmaster tells him how pleased he is with the ascendance of Sinhala – 'our mother language'. The Prime Minister nods graciously, thinking back to his Oxford days, when he was still an Anglican and secretary of the Union.

His next visitor is the Venerable Somarama. The Prime Minister bows his head, then prostrates himself before the monk, touching the holy man's feet. He cringes slightly at his helplessness before the *sangha*. This kind of public display is not natural to him; it is a function of his political life, a public statement of his commitment to this religion that even he finds increasingly fanatical. As he rights himself, he is struck by a blow that throws him backward. He clutches his chest and stomach, wondering whether a crow has flown into him. Lying on his back, he finds he can hear nothing, but while his eyes are still open, he sees his bodyguards leaping towards Somarama. He recalls the orange flash – more like saffron – that he saw in the hedge earlier. His hands feel wet. His back feels wet. Blood flows warmly from his wounds. One of his aides asks him something, and although he cannot hear, he says: 'Some unfortunate man, dressed in the robes of a *bhikku*.' He thinks of Raja the elephant again, and damns the meanness of strangers.

The Prime Minister's funeral takes place at the beginning of October, a week after the shooting and the subsequent declaration of a state of emergency. It draws half a million mourners. A procession of 25,000 people follows the casket from the House of Representatives, where the Prime Minister's body lay in state, to his ancestral estate. A private vault has been created for him and a Roman-style mausoleum built upon it.

Several people perch in trees, beating their chests and clutching hankies to their sodden noses. Minnette and her father look on from their reserved seats, sitting among their political opponents. Lanterns glimmer in the field, lighting up tear-stained faces. A genuine feeling of camaraderie pervades the gathering, regardless of political affiliation. The Prime Minister's passing is understood by all as the passing of a great statesman, even among those who had never voted for him.

The state of emergency runs for weeks, while a month-long period of national mourning is declared concurrently. Rumours that the Prime Minister was shot by someone impersonating a monk spread up and down the country. When it is proved that the attacker was a real monk, people are shocked. The Venerable Somarama is arrested and charged with murder, along with a senior monk from a respected temple and two others – all members of the Board of Indigenous Medicine. Details in the press are fleeting and contradictory, with the shooter initially passed off as a renegade with a private grudge against the Prime Minister. With the additional arrests, this theory is put to rest, but no other emerges to replace it.

As Minnette reads the latest news on the assassination in the *Times of Ceylon*, she thinks of Siri. She finds it difficult not to find him complicit in this latest act of hatred – just as she had when Laki was killed. She dismisses the thought, knowing it is infantile and illogical. Buddhists are a majority in Ceylon – Siri is only one among millions. She realises that she still feels betrayed by him. He is an artist, yet he allied himself with forces that have thwarted progress and freedom in Ceylon. She wonders where he is now, whether he is still one of them.

Rumours about Siri continue to circulate among his fellow artists – that he has retreated to the forest (Minnette thinks this a worthier path), that he is working on a new painting to vie with the triptych depicting the killing of Elara. The triptych was never displayed publicly. Painted during a time of personal upheaval, the triptych, in Minnette's mind, documents Siri's withdrawal from her and Laki. She remembers seeing it for the first time in that flat – the violence with which it announced itself. It was repulsive because it was telling her – and Laki – that they were no longer welcome. The triptych now lies in an anonymous private collection. Unbeknownst to her, it hangs in a dark room, behind a curtain rarely drawn.

Minnette sighs, wondering why she persists in thinking about Siri. They are no longer friends. They have had no contact since her mother's death. She can no longer recall the feelings she once had for him. He is a stranger to her, yet she feels nothing – no regret, no remorse.

It is disturbing, she writes to the architect, *this ability to erase people from one's life. I am quite adept at it.*

But I hope that never happens to us, Corbu. I do not think it could. We may differ on certain points; we may even wound each other, but somehow, the glue remains fast. Do not fret so much about getting old. You cannot stop time, Corbu. But you are mistaken if you think that you have lost your spirit. Of course it is still there, as buoyant as ever. Just look at you and Mimi. I need not elaborate. Let me just say that if you were some weary septuagenarian, she would not spend quite so much time by your side, would she? She would certainly not have shared your bed.

Minnette winces at the last sentence. Her relationship with Mimi has also come to its logical end. *Dear Mimi,* she thinks and does not know where to put the thought. The architect and Mimi. Minnette always knew it was inevitable, but the reality of it only strikes her now as she pens the words: the idea of Mimi lying next to the architect, occupying that space she knows too well, both of them united by this thing that drives them apart.

She looks out the window to the sea, and wishes for the Emergency to end.

The architect gazes towards the Himalayas. He sees their white peaks and longs for snow in Paris. Fluffy camouflage that hides the dirt and blocks out noise. It may be difficult for him to walk in the snow now, but that is not enough to tarnish the dream. He thinks of the white stuff and feels freer.

September's disaster – the collapse of the dam he had been working on at Bakra – was followed by the continued insistence among certain parties that water lilies be sown into the pools in front of the High Court building. This contradicts the architect's vision of clean, reflective surfaces that mirror the geometric splendour of the buildings. It breaks the aesthetic rules the architect has laid down for Chandigarh.

He writes his frustration into a Christmas card to Minnette, hastily sketching an image of the Open Hand for her. *I hope this finds you and Ceylan safely beyond emergencies of any kind,* he scrawls. *The picture is a familiar one to you, I know. It seems Ceylan is more in need of it than Chandigarh, though we are not without our problems here.*

He does not mention Mimi, who has been nothing more than a friend to him for years now. This is not his decision, of course, although – again, something he will not tell Minnette – Mimi was never more than a distraction, a *petit four*. He knows that Minnette is searching for reassurance while pretending to offer it, but he will not be drawn. Not today.

Two months later he is at No. 24 in Paris where the world has turned grey. The rain falls outside. The windows drip. Inside, the architect stares in disbelief. His mother, who celebrated her 101st birthday not so long ago, is dead. He considers the changes she has lived through – the rise of Communism, the death of Empire – and is weary. He remembers her birthday, how she walked unassisted, how her mind was still sharp, how her fingers were still nimble enough to play the piano.

She had even played a duet with his brother. There were no wrong notes, recalls the architect, only that intimate harmony between mother and son. The architect had watched and tapped his toe as Maman Jeanneret nodded encouragingly at his brother. They were the perfect unit, each balancing the other in pitch and tempo. If the architect closed his eyes, he would have been unable to distinguish one musician from the other, although he has never excelled in this discipline – has never had an ear for music. He listened and watched like all the other guests. Mother and son, musician and musician, were oblivious of them all.

And now she is dead, he thinks and wants to weep. She will never see Chandigarh, his masterpiece. He had been sure she would live to see it completed – in photographs if not in person. He knows the journey would not have suited her. He had taken her to the cathedral at Ronchamp when it was finished. She had said little, although he thinks she secretly liked it.

'So silent inside, like a tomb' – was one of her few observations. Also: 'The coloured windows… the patterns they make are pretty.' She insisted on attending Mass there to have the full experience – to understand the building as it is meant to be. And she followed the Mass fervently. 'The acoustics are very good,' she said later.

It is too much to lose a mother, he writes to Minnette, forgetting she has lost her own. *I know I am greedy. She had a long life, she was strong, she attacked everything with enthusiasm. I must accept that it was time for her to go. All those years without my father, yet she never complained. To have been a widow for over thirty years – how did she do it? She was not the type of woman to dwell on these things. Maman was a doer. 'Whatever you do, do it!' she always said. And that is how she lived her life, and how she taught us to live ours.*

He invites Minnette to the funeral. Mimi and Basquin have already agreed to come, along with Minnette's sister Marcia, Werner and child Clara. *You must come, too,* he writes, *to complete the picture.*

For the architect, the picture is undone. *There is an emptiness, Minnette, such an emptiness inside,* he writes, and feels the wind whistle through the hollow in his heart. *No more Vonn. And now, no more Maman Jeanneret. Eventually, Corbu will be completely abandoned. Or else, deprived of his hearth stone and anchor, he will drift away into oblivion.*

He thinks the ringing in his ears has become louder. He examines his fingernails and finds them scalloped like clamshells. *My knees still swell when I walk and my back regularly aches,* he continues. *Is this the onset of oblivion?*

He leaves for Bombay in a few weeks. His mother will be under the ground while he flies above it. He has no time to let go, he thinks, at once blaming his work while being grateful for the distraction. He lays down his pen, tilts his wet face to the window, and watches the rain fall.

————————

26 March 1960
Kandy

My dear Corbu, I am sending you this little letter in the hopes that it provides you with some comfort. I know that by the time it reaches you, you will have already left for Bombay. Still, I do not think that such sentiments are bound by time; may these words act as a salve, whenever you may happen to read them.

You do not need to explain to me the grief. You know how well I know it. I am sorry I never met your mother; from what you write, she was an admirable, sturdy soul. I keep wondering how I overcame my own loss. I pray that you do not go through the same emotional judder that gripped me for more than a year. I don't think that one ever really gets over it, but it does get better. (I'm sorry Corbu, I don't mean to feed you clichés at such an exceptional time. I'm trying to be truthful but seem unable to find a more original way to articulate it.)

As I say, it will get better. Your mother lived a long and rich life, and was lucky enough to have two extremely talented sons. She must have been so proud of you, Corbu, you who almost single-handedly transformed the face of architecture in the modern world. Remember, she lived through that, too: an aesthetic revolution led by her very own son. Imagine being the mother of such genius! No wonder she was at a loss for words when you took her to Ronchamp. Great works often leave one speechless. I have no doubt that she would have been equally impressed by your efforts in Chandigarh. Who knows, she was such a strong-willed woman, that I'm sure she would have made the trip to India. I really think she might have, had she lived. It strikes me that there was little she could not do.

I am so sorry that I could not be at the funeral. Marcia wrote that it was very moving and that Maman Jeanneret could not have hoped for a more dignified farewell. She also wrote that you looked well – that you spoke of your mother with humour and deep affection. I wish I had been there. But from what Marcia said, Mimi proved a stalwart support. I am pleased that she was there for you.

And so Corbu, I hope you have returned from Bombay and Chandigarh, having had some time to say a proper goodbye to your mother. Perhaps you will have found some solace in your great symbol of Chandigarh: the Open Hand of acceptance.

Your friend
Minnette

The architect carries her letter in his pocket. He brought it with him to India, creased and smudged like an old franc note. He has read it many evenings, to remind himself of his mother. It is not her that he has forgotten, but the pain. He reads Minnette's letter like a flagellation. *I am a monk in the desert asking for forgiveness.*

His work did not allow him to grieve for long. He buried her and was gone. He is still going. *She was old. She was ready for death. I accept that now.*

Even before he received her letter, he found reassurance in the Open Hand. By the time he returned to Paris and found her little envelope waiting for him at No. 35, he was already free from the first burden of grief. But her letter made it vivid again. *Do not feel bad about this – no, no,* he writes to her later. *I must thank you. You see, until then, I was lost in a false place where memory is disinfected, not relished.*

Now, he carries this memory of his mother around with him: Maman Jeanneret squinting up into the portholes of stained glass that filter the heavens into the chapel at Ronchamp. Her body shakes, her neck is stiff, but she closes one eye and points her chin towards one of the telescopic squares. Yellow light bathes her face; a yellow flower trembles on her cheek. She is nodding and a smile uncreases her lips. The architect pretends not to notice, considers his toes. If he looks at her again, the smile will vanish, so he holds the memory of it and keeps his eyes on his shoes.

This came to him on the plane to India. Without it, he would shout at everyone, tell them they are all shits. Because they are. He can trust no one here – not a single person. Not his team – not even Trivedi or Seetaram and certainly not that hare-brained cousin of his, Pierre. *I have been completely betrayed.* He arrived to find the trees overgrown, and the facade along the side of the Secretariat and Assembly Hall obstructed. *What do they*

do when I am not here? Incompetent, lazy, treacherous wasps.
Corbu is stung!

That Elizabeth and Richard with their false smiles and
'What's wrong, Corb?' he writes. *English shits. They have*
been plotting against me from the beginning. They have no
respect for me. They are making Chandigarh a disgrace.

He wonders whether Nehru knows what is happening.
Nehru had promised to assist, but so far, he has seen no
evidence of this. *It is not his fault,* he thinks. *He is running*
a country. He has made others responsible for this project, as
a good leader would. But they do not take their role seriously.
They do not take me seriously. Why should I have to continue
to fight for something as simple as banning lily-pads from the
pool in front of the High Court?

This trip has been a difficult one. The progress he
thought he had made is being eroded. The architect throws
up his hands. Having to share a drink with Elizabeth and
her chicken-liver husband is too trying. Elizabeth cracks
her usual jokes and expects him to laugh at them and sip
champagne with her. So he sips champagne, but tells her
plainly that there is nothing to celebrate, that Chandigarh
is a mess.

'Oh Corb, try to see it from the point of view of the
people here. If they want a few lily-pads, what's the big
deal?'

He folds his arms, does not reply. *What is the point in*
answering asinine questions like that? There is nothing he
can say. Richard hides behind his newspaper.

'You are the expert, Elizabeth,' mutters the architect.
'Of all the people in our team, you must know the most
about what goes through the heads of the men here.'

'You're forgetting Trivedi and Seetaram,' replies
Elizabeth, not flinching, 'I could never pretend to know

as much as they.' She strikes a match and lights two cigarettes, one for herself, the other for her husband. Then she pours another glass of champagne. 'Have some more,' she says.

The architect declines, taking a seat instead by Agent Richard (and what a poor agent he would have made. Either he is stupid or a very slow reader, because the pages of his newspaper never turn.)

Minnette should have been on our team at Chandigarh, he thinks. *We could have used her understanding and skill.* He shakes his head. She, too, would have been flattened by the inertia that dogs this project. It is not for the untested or frail (not that she is either). Everyone has an ego and an opinion and the architect is fed up of all of them.

He leaves in a few days. He has been working on repairing the damage to the dam, too. But everything is slow. The labourers are many and eager. They are not the problem. It is the lack of direction. No one is there to take responsibility and direct.

Soon, he will be back in Europe. *And when I return to Chandigarh again, what nightmare will I find then?* He can't help but feel hopeless, while hoping for better for Minnette. She has achieved much: the housing scheme, the many apartment buildings, her continuing research. He mourns their loss in the face of the difficulties she must cope with in Ceylon. *Everywhere there is turmoil.*

Upheaval leans with the heat. She can feel it everywhere, even here at Nell Cottage. When she examines her accounts, she feels a flutter of desperation. She has had no new commissions for a while, apart from the villa on Hermitage Road.

Meanwhile, the recluse in Colombo has more than he can manage. The Dane is his right-hand man, now. She has seen their new house, built for a *batik* artist. Its *meda midula* and use of traditional craftwork are redolent of her earlier Colombo builds. It is not inconceivable that the Dane has brought some of her ideas to the recluse. She feels the betrayal keenly. Her lips curl with regret. She regrets the Dane's occupation of her studio, even her bed. He was a distraction, nothing more. And yet, this thin European has cost her a great deal. She clenches her fists in atavistic fury. Tears are irrelevant in this context, more so when the island, too, is disintegrating.

Treachery exists on every level, she thinks, *most explicitly in politics.* The general election in July brought the dead prime minister's widow, Sirimavo, to power. This is a first for Ceylon: a woman standing at the helm of the country. Although Minnette feels pride in this achievement, she finds it equally abysmal. People voted not for her, but for the memory of the old prime minister. His reputation wasn't even that impressive, but it didn't matter. Death – in his case a rather spectacular one – conferred a certain mythic status, especially valuable during an election.

Minnette did not vote for her. She could never betray the Party, or her father. One of the key points of contention was the age-old language issue: whether Tamil-speakers would be given concessions when the Sinhala Only law came into force. The old prime minister, Bandaranaike, did eventually broker a deal with the Tamil party saying there would be. Sirimavo said the same thing during the election campaign. But the fanatics in the party have been stirring the cauldron and Sirimavo, like her husband before her, is powerless against them. It was these same forces that ultimately ended her husband's life. Minnette can see no chance for Sirimavo.

Despite the bitter politics, Minnette's Watapuluwa housing scheme flourishes. Buddhists, Muslims, Hindus and Christians coexist without friction. It is an idyll rarely remarked on for fear of bursting its anomalous bubble. She feels genuine pride when thinking about it, hoping that her inclusive approach to designing the houses and site had something to do with the harmonious relations that now persist along the Mahaweli. Whenever she visits, she is overwhelmed. The development feels industrious, energetic and above all, democratic.

Yet the housing scheme – rather, her contribution to it – remains unsung in the media. The papers simply refer to 'local architects', without naming Minnette and her studio. It is a blow that, as her practice dwindles, provokes even greater indignation.

Her friends – Lakmini and Desmond – and her father are full of praise. They are all equally effusive. *It is such overcompensation,* she writes to the architect, one afternoon. *How embarrassing. As if I need a pat on the back that badly! I don't care if there is nothing at all, as long as I keep getting contracts. That is the problem, isn't it? Getting contracts if you don't make a splash with your oeuvre. Of course, this is something you will not understand, Corbu. Lack of recognition – that must be a concept quite alien to you. Even if one person denigrates your work, there will be one hundred others to elevate it to the heavens. I know you think the Indians don't respect you, but who cares about them when Nehru is such a fan.*

To Minnette, being great is no more than a dream. In Ceylon, people recognise her only as an extension of her father. (*So, I am not so different from Sirimavo, though far, far less powerful*). But when she surveys her past work, she finds an uncomfortable truth: all the recognition she has received has been through family contacts. Almost all the contracts she has received have also been through contacts. Very few have approached her on the basis of her reputation. Her reputation, in fact, is generally prefixed by the word 'woman'. That 'woman' architect. *As if that somehow sullies the work I do. And if I succeed, the prefix is even more pronounced, suggesting how marvellous – and how bloody unexpected – it is for a woman to have created something so accomplished.*

Knowing these things and battling them daily wearies her. *I want to create work that lies beyond man and woman,* she writes, *but do they let me? No! They never let me forget my sex. It is used as an excuse and an accusation.*

She did not begin her letter with the intention of sharing this bitterness, but now that it has arrived, she embraces it. The architect may feel betrayed by his team in Chandigarh, but how much worse for him if, like her, he had been abandoned by his own country? *After all, when have they ever recognised me for what I am here? – a pioneer of Modernism in Ceylon. Instead I am 'that woman architect' or worse still, that 'girl architect'. That has been the root of my difficulties, if I am honest. All the concessions I made… all because they would not take the word of a woman as sound.*

The word of a woman comes under scrutiny with the arrival of new policies. As Minnette witnesses yet another spring under Emergency rule, she thinks of the architect's last note to her. It was a Christmas card with a drawing of his infamous siren: the half-bird, half-woman he imagines as the spirit of Chandigarh. *To be a woman is to have all the energy of the world within your grasp,* he had written. *Woman is power, fertility, creativity. You are all these things and more.*

'If woman is power and creativity,' Minnette mutters,

'then Sirimavo is failing to make use of her assets.' She is on the verandah at the Galle Face Hotel in Colombo, scanning the newspaper headlines. The Sinhala Only language policy was introduced in January without any concessions to the Tamils, despite Sirimavo's earlier pledges. The decision spells havoc for Tamil and English-speakers. Everyone must now conduct their business in Sinhala. Everyone must learn Sinhala. 'Nonsense!' she exclaims, but can already hear herself being drowned out.

When the law came into force, the inevitable followed. Acts of civil disobedience racked the island, mainly in the north. The government responded by declaring a State of Emergency in those areas. 'What kind of government imposes these regulations at the drop of a hat?' she complained to her father. 'Or should I say stone? Because that is what has been happening – plenty of stone-throwing and shouting. Whatever happened to diplomacy? Why is the government always so eager to throw a blanket over everyone as if we were some fire to be stamped out?'

'At least this time, Colombo and the rest of the country have been spared,' he replied, and Minnette frowned at him. He shook himself, as if from a sleep, and continued: 'A greater darkness is coming. And none of us will be prepared for it.'

Minnette looked at her father, whose clouded eyes seemed to have momentarily cleared. His predictions had always been astute, and she felt compelled to believe him this time, too. Nevermind that he occasionally forgot who the prime minister was (an idiosyncrasy she put down to an inability to accept a woman as ruler of Ceylon), his overall reading of the political situation was painfully accurate.

'The problem is that no leader since our first PM

Senanayake has had the guts to stand up to the fascists who advocate the immediate imposition of the Sinhala language on everyone,' he said. 'Where is this going to take us all? The Tamils will not back down. They have tried talking, but no one has listened. And so darkness will come, Minnette. It is already here.'

A shadow creeps across the verandah, redacting half the front page of the newspaper. Minnette returns to the architect's card, which she uses as a bookmark, and re-reads his declarations. *Chandigarh is a unique example of modern concrete architecture. No changes must be made to it – none of this ivy or green trellises hanging down like loose hair! Chandigarh will become a wonder of the world – it should be declared a heritage site and have all the protections that will give.* She concedes his point. The site is unique as an artwork, but she questions his need to suspend it in time.

He demands that Chandigarh be preserved so that it is a worthy host for the architect's foundation. *Why not?* he asked. *Why not in Chandigarh where I discovered so many things about the true nature of what matters in life and work? My foundation should be the beating heart of this architectural masterpiece. Why not?*

And then the familiar refrain. Minnette half-smiles as she reads it:

Corbu is old! Dear child, my knees never stop aching. The ears, thankfully, have stopped ringing. Maybe I have gone deaf and do not know it yet! Mimi says that I am behaving like a – what do you call it? – phobic. She is young. She can still laugh, showing all her teeth.

Minnette laughs in spite of herself. The thought of Mimi's glittering smile as she gently pokes fun at the architect's ego prompts a moment of nostalgia for their old friendship. But as the sun reasserts itself across the card and the pages of her newspaper, she lets go.

Later that evening she strolls along Galle Face Green. The streets may be heaving with tanks, but people still gather on the Green for a walk and to take the sea air. Some fly kites with their children, others begin or end affairs. She thinks of Laki, his last hours spent right here, on this benign patch of lawn. A *thambili* vendor catches her eye, and within minutes she is on the rocks, sipping the cool coconut water, watching the seaside drama. The silence around her is comforting, conjuring the wordless companionship she found in Siri. Then, she found his silence annoying, but now she realises how much she misses it, and how vital it was to their friendship.

The sun melts into the sea, leaving darkness in its stead. Minnette is back on the hotel verandah, listening to the ocean's roar as she pens a late reply to the architect. She sees nothing but blackness. *If I close my eyes, I can pretend it is ten years ago when everything was hope and passion,* she writes. She closes her eyes and the memory flickers into life, and is gone.

————————

The architect is blinded by the glare of it, and closes his eyes. He is in Philadelphia, accepting the Gold Medal of the American Institute of Architects. *Me,* he thinks, eyes still closed, still shocked by the brilliance of the metal before him, *me – now a doddering fool who cannot control his hiccups.* He is grateful for the recognition, but the Americans can never win him over to their mediocrity, the stupidity they export around the world.

To him, its influence is an occupation of the soul that, like some fly laying its eggs in an unsuspecting creature, ultimately consumes its host. *This is what America champions,* he reflects: *the superficial. It does not want you to go beyond the endless purchasing and consuming. Because if you do, the truth of its emptiness will come screaming at you, as will the realisation that you have been duped – duped by America.*

For this reason, he avoided the Boeing in March as he flew to India, even though it was managed by Indians. As always, he flew Air India in his usual seat: number 5. The care he received was gracious, reinforcing his long-held belief that the Indians and the French understand one another. *That crass, thick-necked humour Americans indulge in – there is none of that among the Indians. With them, I am at home.*

And so to Chandigarh, where his thoughts turned to the subject of doors. India has raised unique challenges when it comes to this feature. There, the door exceeds feature and lives in the land of symbol. Only a few years ago, he wrestled with a design for a door for his client in Ahmedabad. For the architect, that solution has multiple uses in India. So, as before, he has decided to install a swinging door for the Assembly entrance. It will be enamel, emblazoned with symbols that call to mind the power of the cosmos and man's relationship with it.

As for his team, relations are just about civil. The architect buries his anger and cajoles them. He listens to Seetaram and Trivedi's philosophical musings, delivered in their peculiar, metronomic fashion. He drinks champagne with Elizabeth and nods at her brittle laugh. He ignores Richard. He pretends to trust Pierre. He avoids discussions about the rest of the city, preferring to focus on the head – the capital complex – which will determine and direct the shape of the rest of the body. It must be this way, otherwise it will lack harmony; nothing will work. This, at least, the team understands and has accepted.

From India, he flew through Cairo, back to Paris and then on to America for this ridiculous award. *No, it is not the award that is ridiculous,* he corrects himself, *but the recipient. Is everyone saying goodbye to Le Corbusier? Is this why they feel they must shower me with accolades and shove me into a museum? Of course, it is great to be reassured that your work counts for something, but why do they wait until you are almost dead to do it?*

When he asks this of Mimi on one of her perennial visits to the beach at Cap Martin, she winks and replies that he should be grateful. 'Come on, Corbu,' she says. 'You know this is a rare thing. To be recognised while you are still breathing! You are lucky – lucky that they have not waited to heap posthumous glories on you.'

The architect says nothing, offering her some wine and fruit and inviting her to swim. To see her white body disappear slowly into the water is like watching Venus herself descending. For the architect, it is a life-affirming sight. He contemplates his friendship with her – how it began through his *oiseau* – and how it has remained as unchanged as Mimi herself.

She rises from the water and is almost lost in the radiance of the sun. White light on long legs. For a moment, he feels young again.

A pale light dawns in the living room window. Minnette sits at her sister's desk, lost in the first hint of sunrise. She has just arrived in London and steals a solitary moment to watch it bloom with colour, as if for the first time. She is fed up with Ceylon – the endless states of emergency, the arguments about language, the violence, the inability to just get on with work because the whole island is mired in parochial concerns. Her contracts have dried up. The recluse's practice has rocketed.

She has not decided how long she will stay, perhaps a few weeks… maybe a few months. But with her father not quite himself, her return to Nell Cottage is inevitable. Someone will have to care for him, and as the unmarried, childless one, that responsibility falls to Minnette. She ignores the thought, searching out some notepaper. She has missed the architect's birthday and pens a hasty greeting to make up for the slight.

Let me not think of such things right now, she writes on Marcia's stationery. *I have only just arrived and have no intention of returning quite so soon. First, let me congratulate you on your gold medal – well deserved as always. No – no one wishes to bid you goodbye, Corbu. Why think the worst of everyone? The profession knows that it owes you a great deal, so why not demonstrate that appreciation while you are still alive? Mimi is right. You should be pleased that this is happening now and not later when you will have no opportunity to offer your opinion on the matter!*

Marcia takes Minnette for teas and walks. 'Stay as long as you like,' she says, putting a hand on her sister's. They are sitting across from each other, separated by tiers of sandwiches and scones at Fortnum and Mason. Sunlight slants into the salon and glints off the silverware on their table. The pair discuss Minnette's comparative architectural research, and Marcia shares insights from her expedition to China. 'You really must go,' she says. 'Your research is only as good as the observations you are able to make *in situ*.'

Minnette smiles at her sister's use of this architectural phrase. 'I know, dear. This is just the start. I am going to India and Afghanistan soon. But the money… and Papa…' Marcia's face falls. Minnette says nothing further about her money problems, which are incongruous with the cakes and silver. Instead, she focuses on their father. 'Poor Jaya! You must hear how he shouts. I don't know *how* she puts up with it all.'

Marcia bites her lip. 'Yes,' she says. 'His letters to me… I don't know. What to do, child?'

Minnette shakes her head. 'There's not much we *can* do. *You* mustn't worry, darling. You have Clara and Werner to deal with. And all your work here. I am there. And there are others I can call to help.'

This satisfies them both and they tuck into a scone each before Marcia's mouth falls open and worry hollows her cheeks. Minnette stops eating. 'What? What is it?'

Marcia wipes clotted cream from her lips and resorts to a meticulous folding of her napkin before speaking. 'Don't be angry,' she says. Minnette stares at her. 'Look, I spoke to Mimi… I told her you're here.' Minnette frowns. 'I mean, I ran into her, you see. And it just – fell out of my mouth.'

Minnette's face splits with a grin. 'Darling,' she says, 'don't worry. You told her I'm here. That's all. I mean, I don't have to *see* her, right?'

Two afternoons later, Minnette walks into Marcia's study and finds Mimi there, sipping a cup of tea and fidgeting because she can't smoke in the house. The two exchange an awkward stare. Minnette thinks back to the architect's letters, her only source of news of her old friend.

Confronted with her after years of silence, Minnette feels numb. She leaves the room several times to pinch herself or bring a new plate of biscuits. Eventually there is no more need for biscuits or pinches and Minnette remains seated opposite her, watching her red nails click against the walnut of Marcia and Werner's desk. They are alone.

'I could really murder a cigarette,' says Mimi. When Minnette shrugs back at her, she sighs and begins talking about her agent. 'The idiot has only gone and given my part away. Apparently, no one wants an aging actress.' She puts two fingers to her lips as if drawing on a cigarette. 'So, I spend more of my time in France, these days.' Minnette nods. 'Of course, you know already. I suppose Corbu told you.' They flinch at the mention of the architect's name, but the moment quickly passes. 'At least French theatre doesn't share the same aversion to the older woman. To hell with London!'

Minnette smiles, feeling sorry for her friend, while understanding only too well her predicament. Mimi catches her expression and relents, 'I suppose London isn't *so* bad.' She looks out the window. The sky is grey, and tiny raindrops strafe the windowpane in waves. She sighs. 'It was good while it lasted. Still, well... anyway.' And she is quiet.

Mimi leaves shortly afterward, mentioning a reading she is doing at a fringe theatre next week. She also invites her to Paris for Christmas, and months later, Minnette is there, sitting at a table between the architect and Mimi. They eat duck and drink champagne, and remark on Time's gentle touch.

You, of course, are untainted by it, the architect writes in her birthday card the following February. *How delightful to be in the company of my two favourite ladies. I felt younger. My knees stopped aching, my bladder was strong. I must tell my doctor that this – this is the remedy I have been looking for. It was almost like the old days – almost. Let us not fool ourselves. Things have changed, bien sûr. Nothing stays the same, non? There is no point in wishing for that. I accept this just like you. And it is much easier now that we do!*

Minnette examines the card – a drawing of two winged creatures flying around an old bull, and laughs. *You do yourself a disservice, Corbu!* she replies. *Yes, it was good to be with old friends again. You do not wear your age conspicuously, so you must stop claiming it as an excuse. It is one excuse that will not work with me. From what I saw in Paris, it does not work with Mimi either, so you might as well abandon the habit now!*

Her smile fades as she downs her pen. The Christians have attempted to overthrow the government in Ceylon. Another Emergency has been declared, a habit Ceylon's leaders seem unable to break. Her return to Kandy is imminent.

When she arrives, she goes straight to Nell Cottage to see how Papa is doing. He still spends several hours a day in his study, but no longer receives the same numbers of visitors he once did. Most of the time, he lists the day's activities in a notebook, and files papers. Often, he forgets where he has put something which leads to much hand wringing, brow beating and cursing. At these points, anyone can be snagged by his temper. He makes Jaya cry on several occasions, accusing her of stealing his files. Minnette pays Jaya extra and begs her to stay on. She arranges for Uncle Reggie to drop in from time to time to give Jaya a break. Then she takes the car and drives out in search of ruins to photograph and add to her growing collection of architectural slides.

———

Up in the air, the architect slumps in the ruin of his body. He is on his way back to Paris from Delhi and exhaustion saps his ankles, his knees. It is May. Just a month earlier he flew from Rio to Rome and then to Delhi. *It is too much for this old body*, he sighs.

He is working on three studies for the new capital of Brasilia – *after Chandigarh, what other challenge for me but entirely new cities for the New World.* He is designing works for a French Cultural Centre, the French Embassy and a Brazilian cultural centre. To do this, he must study the site, examine the terrain, consider the climate and demands of those who will use these buildings. It is not like Chandigarh – it does not possess him in the way that India has. In Rio, the people are passionate, wild, Bacchic. There, physicality is unmistakeable, but the spirit of the place eludes him. *Perhaps its proximity to America carries subconsciously?* he wonders.

In Chandigarh, he continued to work on the Assembly door. His team appears to have been stitched back together and progress on the capital is moving forward. There are still the same arguments about plants, but the architect remains adamant. *This city will be protected; my vision for it must remain the constant,* he told his team, and they agreed.

Despite all the differences we have had on this project, they still understand that this city is Corbu, he reflects as the scandal of Paris looms into view. *Its survival depends on strict adherence to principles I have laid down.* The plane flies over the city's suburbs and he sees how crowded they are, how each plot is contiguous, choking the other. *Contrast this with the Unité and its 3 to 5 hectares of land, its prime position vis-a-vis the sun, its communal open spaces and greenery on various levels. Chaos vs. Order. Which*

environment do you think the suburban resident would prefer?
When do we give him the choice?

Months elapse and the architect is sitting across from Mimi in a cafe in Paris. She is chewing nonchalantly on a croissant, staring at him with gecko eyes.

'Isn't life wonderful, Corbu?' she asks, flakes of pastry gathering at the corners of her mouth like tiny moths. 'It is everything and it is nothing.'

Her white face is as calm as a slab of marble. He asks her what has made her so happy, and she laughs. 'Everything and nothing.'

They talk about the architect's impending trip to Switzerland and about Minnette, her upcoming birthday, and her travels to India and beyond. She laughs again. 'Good! Good!' she cries. 'This is wonderful news!' She strokes her chin with two fingers and adds, 'she is unstoppable, you know. Wish her a happy birthday from me.'

The architect nods, thinking of his old friend who, as the years go by, must still be as young as he remembers her. He smiles and Mimi picks up her bag, gives him two kisses, and runs out of the cafe into the rain.

The rain is like a whisper in the evening. It hisses as it strikes the sandy ground, evaporating almost as soon as it falls.

Minnette is in Rajasthan, touring temples and palaces. She photographs balconies and arches, friezes and roofs. Her last trip here – when she had entertained the Dane – was to the south, with its wealth of temples. In Rajasthan, the emphasis is on palaces and *havelis*. The architecture is more recent, a blend of Hindu and Islamic aesthetics. She is struck by how distinctly female space is represented in these buildings, and both admires and is unsettled by it.

In Jaipur, she marvels at the Hawa *mahal*. To her, its row upon row of little windows, like the mouth-holes of flutes, are reason enough for its name: the 'wind palace'. Staring up at it from street level, she glimpses a scrap of blue fabric along the top storey of its terra cotta front. *The unexpectedness of it – the exuberance of colour,* she later writes to the architect in a letter she posts once she leaves India, *transports me to another time and place, when the women of the palace would have swooped along its galleyed balconies, hidden from the world outside by a network of jali screens.*

Amber Fort is equally breath-taking. She studies its scalloped archways, sandalwood doors inlaid with ivory and narrow waterways that criss-cross the palace to cool it down. *It is like nothing I could conceive of designing*, she writes to him, filled not with envy, but with awe.

When she has had her fill of palaces and *havelis*, she takes to the desert. Acquaintances take her on a camel trek, and as she surveys the dunes and wide expanses of yellow sand, she remembers Batticaloa.

She hasn't thought of that long-ago trip for years – that intimate holiday where so many truths were uncovered like crabs swept to the surface of the sand. What a tangle they had got themselves into. And yet, how liberating. When she thinks of how all of them, even Siri, were enthralled by Mimi, she wonders whether she, too, wasn't somehow infatuated with her.

Minnette castigates herself for not predicting how things would turn out between her, Mimi and the architect. She is not bitter. *I am here in Ceylon. She is there in London and Paris*, she tells herself. *How could anything have turned out differently?*

Minnette has no plans to visit Chandigarh. She knows the architect is there, but her research compels her onward, beyond India. As her mind turns towards her next stop, she is interrupted by the sun setting into the sand. The sky briefly smoulders, then washes from purple to blue. It is magnificent, but nothing like the sunsets in Kandy, Batticaloa or Galle. This desert sunset – and the architect's famed ones in Côte d'Azur – would disintegrate next to hers. Vivid oranges and pinks: every evening, she watches them until she can taste them on her tongue. *Such sweet, citrusy flesh*, she sighs, *yes, they are a fruit to be picked and savoured.*

XIV

May 1964 – August 1965

3 May 1964
Paris

Today I thought of Jaipur. Pierre was showing me some photographs of my cathedral. Ronchamp would not be what it is today without Rajasthan. For that I owe my Indian friends much.

By the time you read this letter you will know that Chandigarh is complete. I returned from that great capital for the last time, a few days ago. I will not pretend that I am not deflated. It is the same gloom that falls at the end of any long project. Like the first time you take a woman you have wanted for a long time – that feeling of: So? What next? and then the regret of feeling that way. I do not say that I will never return to India. Only that it will be rare that I do.

The Assembly was inaugurated on 15 April and the enamel door was presented. It is a pivoting entrance/exit that opens up onto the possibilities of the cosmos. One visitor to the building described it as 'a totality of boundless architecture'. He said he was shocked upon entering it. It was like nothing he could or would ever have expected. I could not help but agree. When you see it full of light, its proportions perfect, its materials unassailable, there is no way that it could have been imagined better. It is perfection itself – a genuine miracle.

So, they have named me a Grand Officer of the Légion d'Honneur and I have been awarded another honorary degree, this time from the University of Geneva. More accolades for a calcifying septuagenarian. There can be no higher honour left to heap upon Corbu. Me. Who left school at thirteen. Who writes only as he speaks, with more truth than all those literary types and their affected language. Corbu says what he means as simply as possible so that anyone might understand. I am a man of letters. I use the alphabet to my advantage, to communicate as clearly as I can. How many so-called geniuses can do the same? Should they? Am I therefore not a genius? Why should anyone believe the magazines or spokesmen who claim false titles for their clients. I do not deserve the Légion d'Honneur. My work has been rejected by the establishment time and again. Why should they now claim to recognise me? Why add me to this hall of the famous now and make me an icon of the establishment?

At my age, there is no energy to protest. Why should I? It is about time that I am recognised for what I have done for architecture. Even if it is by this fellowship. I am now, finally, a knight of sorts. Where is my Panza? Where my shaking horse?!

Chandigarh is a place of order. It is a city like no other in India. It sits apart; yet it is embraced. They love it there. My team was relieved that it was all over. Elizabeth and Richard returned to England. Pierre thought it was time he was back at No. 35 with me. Trivedi and Seetaram were happy to wrap things up without us. I think they all like each other much more, now that they have said goodbye.

Part of me is still in Chandigarh. And you, Minnette, once my *little oiseau, you, too, are part of the fabric of that historic place. Nehru was pleased with the results. We fulfilled the brief to the letter. There was nothing to complain about. Even Corbu could not complain in the end. The pools remained clear of lily-pads, the balconies and hedges free of rabid ornamentation. And in the distance, the Himalayas continue to stand as they have for millennia: stalwart sentries, guardians of a new chapter in architectural history.*

Sitting here at No. 35, I am struck by the fact of not returning to India. That place taught me so much about what really matters in life. It taught me the value of the sandal over the tyre, the cow over the machine. It is proof that there is a viable alternative to America – that greed and the juggernaut of the machine can and must be rejected. And all of it began with you, my friend. With those tiny toes in those simple sandals and the rich silk you wrapped around your fragile frame. Above all, your wisdom informed by a great culture, a great civilization. Without you – without that – there would be no Chandigarh.

I told Mimi this when I returned. She came to see me yesterday, to congratulate me on completing this marathon of ... how many years, now? At least a decade. She told me, too, that she is thinking of getting married. So her secret is finally out!

'You must come, of course,' she said. Bien sûr. Corbu will oblige. He is, after all, a knight of the highest order. Chivalry is his middle name. Have you received your invitation, Minnette? You must come, too. It would be a charming, amusing reunion.

For once, Corbu has some time to himself to write and think. Spring has brought its many little flowers to Paris. Soon I will be back at Cap Martin, hosting a little party for Mimi and her groom... Corbu is no longer in the running for groom of choice. I accept this.

Toujours
Ton Corbu

16 July 1964
Kandy

*Congratulations, Corbu. Chandigarh is magnificent. And as
you know, we have included it in Marg. Extraordinary. How
fortunate that it was completed before Nehru's death a few
weeks later. But Chandigarh has changed so since I was there. It
is another world altogether. I feel honoured to have been a part
of it, even if that contribution was ambiguous, unquantifiable.
We are both there in its sinews. But you flatter me. To insist
that Chandigarh sprouted from my toes! Unbelievable, Corbu.
You are a romantic. No doubt you will have changed your
mind since you wrote that. It is only that you feel you owe me
something that you project such importance upon me. I had no
such natural wisdom, only the giddiness that youth brings and
the blind faith of the star-struck.*

*I am not surprised that you feel somewhat bereft now that
Chandigarh is complete. As you say, the feeling is inevitable, a
post-partum depression that passes with acceptance. You must*

be relieved, too. No more travelling back and forth to India, no more disappointments and irritations to bluster over (in India, I mean; the others will continue to be there, I suppose). Above all, you must be very proud, Corbu. A member of the Legion of Honour. This is something I would have expected for you, but still, the reality of it must be so strange. I am not surprised you feel unworthy, though you deserve it more than most.

I am sure you will miss your team more than you let on. Elizabeth in particular. She was such a feisty foil to you. In the beginning, the two of you were quite the pair. I think her observations must have been invaluable. It is always important – vital, I should say – to have someone you can trust to tell you the truth. As for Seetaram and Trivedi, I think their philosophising was something you learnt a great deal from. They were, from my recollection, thoroughly trustworthy and serious types. Types you could leave your life's work with without fear of it being exploited or cheapened in some way. No, if it was the wisdom of civilizations that you needed when tackling Chandigarh, then it was them and not I who shared it with you.

I went to Jaipur for the last time in June, so I think I just missed you, Corbu. What a shame. It would have meant a lot to me to be there at the inauguration of your life's masterpiece, as you call it. My research continues. I've enclosed a comparative essay on the architecture of South and South East Asia. Let me know what you think.

Papa is asleep in the adjoining room. He is no longer able to put up a fuss when I insist on helping him. He flails about sometimes, or tries to push me or Jaya away. But he is weak and so addled that he mistakes me for Jaya and vice versa sometimes. At other times he surprises us all by saying something politically apt and so impressive that it is easy to think he is pretending all the other times. How I wish he were.

My old friend Lakmini has been a fantastic help, sending her servant to lend a hand or undertake some of the more intimate caring duties. I have had a few requests for designs, but like so many of these recent overtures, they have come to nothing. It is frustrating to apply your vision to something, only to have it rejected. The Colombo practices seem to be doing well. One of my old apprentices, a young man from Denmark, is working for a large practice there and they seem to gather more and more work. No one thinks of me. Perhaps I made a mistake, Corbu, by choosing to have my studio in Kandy. Perhaps my fortunes would have been different had I installed myself in the capital. But how can I leave Papa now? Bringing him to Mount Lavinia is not an option as his doctor – good old Sivathamby – is here in Kandy.

Soon, I will go to Mount Lavinia to take a break from Papa. I am fortunate to have some good friends here: Lakmini and her brother Desmond. They're still around, dropping in and helping with Papa. If not for them, I don't know what Jaya and I would do. But I don't know how much longer they will stay. The Sinhala Only language law has made things difficult for everyone. Lakmini is planning to move to Australia because her Sinhala is not good enough for her to practise law here. Desmond, too, is considering the same move. In fact, several of Papa's friends have already left the country, mainly for Australia, though a few have opted for England.

I have no desire to go anywhere. Nell Cottage is my home. And as I work for myself, I have no trouble bypassing this ridiculous law. Anyway, I can get by in Sinhala if I need to talk to the labourers or suppliers, not that I have much cause for that these days. If I find myself struggling, there are any number of people who can help me out, acting as interpreter if necessary. No, I am not going anywhere. I have been here long enough – am making my mark as an architect. It will only be a matter of time before they recognise what I have achieved here. And when they do, I should be within awarding distance, should I not?

And yet, this country has gone from bad to worse. Do I really want to live in a place where states of emergency are as common and predictable as the seasonal monsoons? I continue to ask myself the question. Perhaps a few months from now, the answer will be clearer.

Many congratulations to you, Corbu.

Your friend
Minnette

PS. So Mimi is finally marrying! In fact, I did receive an invitation but thought it a joke. I couldn't possibly leave now, given Papa's condition. What a shame. I should have liked to have been there.

30 *August 1964*
Cap Martin

The sun is strong today, bleeding us of our colour and vigour.
Mimi is here with Pietro her beau, and is her usual pallor. But
the rest of us have also been bleached by this relentless Apollo.
The couple are like two stones. Right now they are lying on
chaises longues, hiding under parasols. The women here stare
at Pietro's taut middle and well-formed limbs. He is maybe ten
years younger than her. She is still beautiful, yes, but is never
without her dark glasses now. Would he be interested if she
wasn't a famous actress? It is a question I could ask you, too,
my friend. Would you have shown any interest in this old dog
had he not also been an international star of architecture? But
such lines of questioning lead nowhere. What we are defines
who we are. It is as simple as that.

Ah, I must not forget to tell you how brilliant I found your
essay. It will be an essential reference text. Your descriptions
of Angkor Vat and temples in Java, together with your

observations on Hindu temple structures in south India, were fascinating. The cycle of life and death is embedded not just in these buildings' aesthetics, but in their function as well. Formidable!

Last week I went to see Vonn at the cemetery in Roquebrune. It was hot then, too, and despite my straw boater, the sweat rolled into my collar. The little dog is still alive – just – though its teeth are long and it cannot hold its piss. Corbu will not put it down. How can I when I, too, am almost incontinent? My knees still ache, my ears still ring. And I must watch this beautiful Pietro plunge into the sea alongside a goddess. Time is at two removes. Between the two of them, there is a decade that is bridged by good genes and innate beauty. Between them and Corbu there are at least three decades – a generation – which cannot be overcome. Corbu's usefulness as a wise teacher and lover has past. While they swim, I paint. When they close their eyes, I slip into the water unobserved. Why should they see Corbu's sagging flesh?

Their eyes are closed now. Should I take advantage of the moment? The water will be warm. It will relax my bones. Why do I hesitate?

Because everything takes longer now. How long before they wake as I crab my way to the water? To have Pietro cast his beatific gaze on my twisted frame and freckled legs. To have that gaze turn to pity on contact. It is not acceptable.

What does it mean to get old, Minnette? Is it that once they have finished heaping accolades on you, they begin to shovel on pity? Is this how they bury you with age?

The wedding is next month. It would have been nice to see you again, dear friend. It is a pity we missed each other in India. Even Elizabeth and Richard will be there, although Mimi barely knows them. I think she has invited your sister, too. It is not going to be a large wedding, despite the Italian faction. Pietro's family do not like the idea of their son marrying an older woman, even if she is famous. As for Mimi, she has kept the guests to a minimum. 'I don't want all those crowds, Corbu. I want it to be simple and quick.'

You must see how Mimi lies here sipping champagne. I would not be surprised if it gets colder on her tongue. When she opens her mouth, it is like the spreading of a frost. Still, we cannot help ourselves. Not Pietro, not me, not even you. Mimi draws us all like flies to sticky paper. If we are not careful, we will lose our limbs and be lost inside her forever.

They are still asleep. I must take my chance. The sea awaits.

Corbu

5 November 1964
Kandy

Age, age! You are obsessed, Corbu. I understand your frustration, but you must consider yourself fortunate in many ways, too. I am back at Nell Cottage looking after Papa. His condition has deteriorated since last I wrote. He has become so bad tempered and stubborn. Sometimes, he does not know where he is or who I am. Sometimes he calls me Amma and behaves like a four-year-old. It is heartbreaking. His notebooks no longer contain the careful analyses of a politician, but shakily written notes describing his day. These, too, have ceased, however, replaced by stick-figure drawings and laboriously traced swirls. There are pages where he has written the numbers 1 to 10 repeatedly, as if he is afraid of forgetting them. Most of the time, his recollection of their order is correct, other times, he forgets a digit or two. I know he knows he has lost his memory. It is the shame of it that has made him so difficult to be around.

Yesterday, I found Jaya weeping in the kitchen. She said it was too hard to watch Papa slip into madness like that. 'Nona, look what is happening to Sir,' she said. 'Like a child he is now. Ayyo.'

I cannot cry, Corbu. If I do, how will I be able to carry on feeding him, changing him, listening to his tirades. There is no room for tears in that. I continue with my research. Thank you for your enthusiastic receipt of my essay. It is far from complete, but one day, I intend to publish it. I do my writing in two locations, splitting my weeks between Mount Lavinia and Kandy. I think this is the key to my sanity. Papa does not notice when I am not there. He doesn't know how long I am gone for either. It's convenient in that sense. At least he doesn't suffer at my absence.

Lakmini has, as always, been a great help. But she has told me that her plans to emigrate to Australia are moving rapidly forward. She will be gone by next February. Then what will I do, Corbu? Desmond has not yet decided what he will do, but I can tell that he wants to leave, too.

So how was the wedding? I take it Mimi's uncle gave her away? And what about you? Did you make a speech? How did Mimi look? Her Pietro sounds intriguing. I am sure he is gorgeous. Mimi only ever surrounded herself with such men. You were (still are!) among her entourage, Corbu, so don't think I don't mean you as well. It is your depth that sets you apart from the others.

Oh dear, Papa is shouting at Jaya downstairs. I must go now and rescue her. My appearance will at least quiet him down. Papa will be flummoxed. I am sure he has already forgotten that I am here.

I must go, Corbu.

Be well. And take care of yourself. You are certainly not as infirm as the little dog. Poor creature. Take pity on it.

Bisous
Minnette

PS. I enclose a card. Please don't read it as the hands on a clock but as my good wishes to you for another year.

12 January 1965
Paris

Thank you, dear friend, for your card. Do not worry. I do not see these birthday reminders as unwelcome or cruel. They are little parcels of hope. Corbu looks forward to them without rancour or regret.

I am sorry to hear about your father. It is not easy, watching a man lose himself like this. You are right, Corbu is lucky to still have all his wits. But what is happening to Père de Silva is a fact of life, non? Age is not something that can be restored or undone. Corbu knows this well, even if his condition is not as serious as your father's. It is one of those things that plagues us all. Your father is lucky in some ways. Soon he will not know what is happening to him. He will be lost in a fog of old and new memories. And he has you, his dear daughter, to care for him.

I am glad that you continue to work. I am busy, too, though mainly in Paris. Still, projects go on. There are my buildings in Firminy – the Unité, the Maison de la culture, a private house. And there are other projects, too, and my painting. I have slowed down a little, yes. But there is nothing that can make me turn off the grey matter that buzzes in my head.

You asked me about the wedding. Yes, it was an odd collection of people. The ceremony was held at a small church near Rocquebrune – Mimi's choice. Of course, Oncle Basquin gave her away. He arrived in mismatched trousers and shirt, but – dieu merci – had bathed for the occasion. Your sister was there with Werner but no child. They were taking a break from family life. (You see! Even the most loving parents want to get away from their children. Could it be that the little pétards really are as messy and irritating as I have always said?) Elizabeth and Richard occupied a bench at the back. The bride wore white, and despite my earlier reservations, looked radiant – like a minimalist interior. No ruffles or silly bits of lace. Mimi's ringlets fell like ribbons down her back – the only thing to disturb the still whiteness of that scene. Pietro could not stop smiling. Even Pietro's family members – the few who bothered to come – were struck dumb by the apparition. Corbu was shaking in his shoes.

At the reception, all of us took turns dancing with the ghostly goddess. When it was my opportunity, Pietro was already too drunk to stand. 'So, ma chère,' I said, holding Mimi's slight waist in my hand. 'You have your dress. You had your cake. Is it a successful wedding?'

Mimi smiled, her whole body humming with happiness. 'What do you think, Corbu?' She kissed me on the cheek. 'It is so wonderful to have you here. I wish Minnette could have been here, too.' So you see, little bird, you were missed! Corbu understands why you could not come, but imagine the party if you had.

Alors, what more is there to say? The sun shone on the couple as they drove away. Werner and Elizabeth got very drunk.

Oncle Basquin wept on Mimi's departure. And Corbu? I felt such peace as I have not felt in years. Even if it does not last, my friend, this marriage has begun in the right place. What else can we ask of it?

That was so many months ago now. The snow falls thickly, blotting out the sun. The apartment is quiet. The little dog passed away at the end of last year. I woke up one morning and found its stiff little corpse still curled by the bed. What a pitiful sight he was, but finally free. Vonn has waited a long time to have him. Let us hope that they are happy in their reunion.

Corbu

14 March 1965
Kandy

My dear Corbu, Papa is not improving. His moments of lucidity, previously so frequent, have all but disappeared. He recognises me from time to time, but as a much younger version. As a result, he usually refuses to listen to me. 'What! You, slip of a girl, trying to tell your father what to do? How dare you!' etc., etc. Jaya and I take turns fielding his curses. Papa mistakes Jaya for Amma almost every other day. There is no point in telling him that Amma is dead. Why make him suffer? And anyway, he would not believe us, not with Jaya about.

Last week he told Jaya she was working too hard. 'Darling,' he said, 'you cannot keep pretending that you are fine when you are suffering such a terrible illness. Put down that dust cloth. We have a servant for these things.' I was surprised, not to mention embarrassed for Jaya. Papa had never before been prone to such expressions of candour. Particularly not when it came to Amma's illness.

I apologised to Jaya. And she, in turn, pretended she hadn't heard or understood Papa. She is not as despondent as she once was. She does not have to be with Papa every day of the week. Often she escapes to the Ariyapala Lodge to see her friend Dilini. I let her. Poor thing. We now also have Lakmini's old servant, Samuel, at least three days per week. Lakmini asked us whether we could provide a job for him since she was leaving. 'I can't just abandon him, you understand. He has worked for our family for decades.' Of course I agreed. Samuel has been such a help. For some reason, Papa thinks Samuel is his dead grandfather. This both frightens Papa and chastens his spirit. He is far more pliant in Samuel's old hands. So Jaya and I leave the more challenging tasks to him.

So, yes, Corbu. I have lost yet another friend. Lakmini, my only friend in Kandy, left for Australia at the beginning of this month. She took me out for an early birthday meal, then told me her news. I could not be anything but happy for her. Why stay here in this godforsaken place? At least, that's what she asked me. She has a point, too. Ceylon's economic boom is well and truly over – in fact, it ended decades ago, only we all refused to notice. Relations between the Tamils and Sinhalese are so fraught, there is no hope of any agreements being established between the two. Violence and unrest pepper the island. We continue to float in out little bubble, but how long before it bursts?

And yet, I could not do anything but stay here. For now, anyway. With Papa like this, I have no choice. I can't abandon him. I could have said all this to Lakmini, but there was no need. She knew why I couldn't leave. She's gone to Sydney. 'You must visit, Minnette,' she said.

I miss her very much, Corbu. I have no one else to talk to. Desmond is in Colombo and isn't half as intelligent as his sister. Anyway, he, too, will probably leave. And then what?

All these years I never really noticed how lonely Nell Cottage could be. When I returned here from London, I thought this place quiet and empty — only because you were missing from it. In fact, I had so many friends around me, not to mention both my parents. There was so much promise back then, yet I buried it in my own misery. What a foolish girl I was. Now look at me. Do I really have the career I deserve? Had I been a man, Corbu, the doors would have opened with a clap of my hands. Just look at how they all run to that man in Colombo? Even my old clients. Where once they would have come to me, now they go to him. I suppose he is more fashionable. I must skulk around, prising contracts from friends of the family or friends of friends. I still have not been formally recognised for my contribution to modern architecture in this country. I still have to contend with clients, especially male clients, referring to me not even as a woman, but a girl. Me! A woman of forty-plus. It is inconceivable. And yet, it is probably the same the world over. Where in this world do women really get their due?

And so I must sign off. The house is too silent for my liking. I must check on Papa and Jaya to make sure one has not done away with the other!

Bisous
Minnette

12 June 1965
Paris

Chère enfant, I am sorry to hear that your father is not improving. I understand. With Vonn, it was like that: a gradual disintegration. Memory steps in to fill in the cracks, yes. For a while, the patient is taped together by our memories of her or him. We are like film projectors, casting whole images onto a surface and binding it. But soon, even that is not enough. It cannot be.

Do not despair at the loss of your friend. She will be a worthy correspondent. You will travel more as your successes grow. Do not be impatient, dear child. Corbu understands your frustration. It is remarkable that they have not shown you the respect you deserve in Ceylon. But look at how France has treated Corbu! It is only recently, as I approach the end of my days, that they choose to give me awards.

Mimi and Pietro are in Paris these days. Mimi is taking a break from her acting. This is what she says. But she has not been getting as many parts as she did even a year ago. 'It's drying up, Corbu,' she said, 'just like me.'

Corbu, too, has dried up. The work is there, yes. But the body is not as willing. I am old, Minnette. All this travelling, even within France, strains the back and the knees. The bladder is still weak, the ears still ring. And I am alone. Maman is gone. Vonn is gone. Even the little dog is gone. Pierre has been a dedicated servant at No. 35. I am grateful for that. But I prefer to be in Cap Martin, painting in my little shack. I will be there in a few weeks. And then I will stand in my room where every ratio has been perfectly calculated and look out my one window onto the sea and the sun. The journey from cabin to water will be private (no youthful eyes ogling Corbu's withered scaffolding).

To walk into the sea, to plunge into its waters, is to embrace weightlessness – a state in which I am most at peace. Like those plane journeys to India, in which I was suspended in the sky, observing every nook and angle of the earth's surface below. In the sea, it is like that, too. In the sea, I will float and feel young again.

Corbu

PS. I enclose this drawing. I hope it will make you feel better, dear friend. I think it is a good likeness.

20 July 1965
Kandy

Oh, Corbu. What can I say? How can I say it? I have been here before, but that doesn't make the telling easier. Papa is gone, and I am an orphan. Samuel found him at the bottom of the garden. He had been bitten by a viper. I suppose in his addled state, he may not have seen the creature. He certainly would not have been alert enough to worry about the possibility of encountering a snake. Who knows what world Papa was striding through when the viper struck. I comfort myself with the thought that he would not have understood what was happening, nor would he have known that it was real. I don't know how he came to be on his own for such a long time, but none of us was especially fond of spending much time in his churlish company. If anyone had abdicated responsibility, it was I. And while I miss Papa dreadfully and am seized by a sense of guilt at the manner in which he passed, I also feel relieved. Papa as I knew him had disappeared a long time ago. The departure of this bitter shell that we had all been propping up had, if we were honest with ourselves, taken too long and debased the memory of Papa too much.

But I have said more than I should have. Do I even know what I am writing any more? I have walked through the last month in a daze. Desmond came up with Aunty Sheila and Uncle Reggie as soon as they heard. Marcia was here with the family within a week. The funeral was big – full of Party people and many of those whom Papa had helped over the years with land or other disputes. It felt like the whole of Kandy had turned up to pay their respects. We did not have an open reception after the funeral – we kept that within the family. But the church service was grand, moving and packed with weeping mourners. Up to that point, I had never connected the string of visitors to Papa's study – people from all backgrounds who felt they had suffered one injustice or another – with the results of his intervention. In other words, I never realised how much Papa had helped ordinary people in the community. I had always thought of him as a solitary politico, secluded in his study, occasionally doling out morsels of wisdom to the lucky few who could reach him. How wrong I was. Papa was a man of the community. It was only us, his family, whom he had secluded himself from. He always said that we were independent, that we didn't need him to watch over us. And he was right. The only person he fussed over – and that, too, much later in life – was Amma.

Aunty Sheila and Uncle Reggie left a few days ago, but Marcia and Desmond are still here. I have missed my sister, Corbu. She keeps asking me to return to London, telling me I can stay with her and finish my research. 'Stay. You will find contracts,' she said, 'maybe some teaching.' I am tempted. Now that both Papa and Amma are no longer here, there are no real family reasons for me to remain. But what about my future here? If I leave now, I risk undermining all the steps I have made towards truly establishing myself here. London will be infinitely harder. It has been so long since I lived there. If people are reluctant to give me contracts here, what hope have I in London? I know. You will say that I am discounting the experience I have gained. That I am underplaying my role as an advocate of modern architecture in the East. But does any of that make a difference in London... or Paris, for that matter?

So Marcia's imprecations continue to fall on reluctant ears. She told me about Mimi's wedding, by the way. She and Werner had a lovely time. Apparently, you were quite the host – behaving suspiciously like a proud father. How very unlike you, Corbu! And what a strange turn of roles for you. A decade or two ago, you would have been the jealous rival. But you have transplanted those feelings into the heart of a caring, if over-protective, father. That must have taken some effort. Full marks for achieving it so convincingly.

Full marks to Marcia, too, for not asking me the obvious. In the early days, she was obsessed with finding me a good fit. But after the whole Desmond thing, she hasn't asked about marriage or settling down. 'You're free now,' she said. 'Make the most of it.'

When everyone leaves, it will be I who remains at Nell Cottage. Samuel will no longer be needed. Jaya will stay, of course. Already the house feels bigger, overwhelming. But I think some solitude will be good for me right now. I imagine you at Cap Martin in your room for one and don't feel so alone, Corbu. You and I in our mutual solitude – there is comfort in that.

Your friend
Minnette

PS. Thank you for the drawing. I have pasted it on my wall to remind me of all those flights we took together so many years ago. Two birds with wings entwined. It is a fair likeness, yes.

26 August 1965
Galle

*Dear friend, did you get my last letter? I still have not heard
from you. Papa is gone, Corbu. As always, I wrote to No. 35,
knowing they would forward anything of importance to you
wherever you are. Perhaps it has gone astray? I am in Galle
for another few days, then back to Mount Lavinia to see Aunty
Sheila and Uncle Reggie. Desmond brought me here to recover
from the summer's events, and to say goodbye. He leaves at the
beginning of October.*

Write soon, Corbu. I long to hear your news.

Bisous
Minnette

                    Miss Minnette de Silva
          de Silva Studio of Architecture
                             Nell Cottage
                 c/o 4 Mission Avenue
                            Mount Lavinia

35, rue de Sèvres
Paris (6ième)
7 September 1965

Dear Miss de Silva

I am sorry that I have not written to you
until now. I know what a good friend you
have been to M. Le Corbusier. He spoke
of you with great fondness and was always
willing to help you in whatever way he
could. I am sorry, too, to hear of your
father's passing. I forwarded your letter
to M. Le Corbusier in Roquebrune, but it
seems he did not have the chance to send
his reply.
   As you know, M. Le Corbusier was in frail
health. Nevertheless, he continued to work,
even though he had given up long travels to
India and elsewhere. We all did our best to
make sure he did not overstretch himself,
sparing him the worst of the pressures that

can afflict an architect. As always, he went to Roquebrune for his August holiday. He loved his petit cabanon. There was someone to look after him there, too, to make sure he ate well. But none of us could stop him from taking his daily swim. In that, M. Le Corbusier was adamant.

It is with great sadness that I must tell you that on 27 August, M. Le Corbusier went out to take his sunset swim. While in the sea, he suffered a heart attack and despite all the doctor's efforts to resuscitate him, he died. He did not suffer.

The French Government organised a national ceremony in honour of M. Le Corbusier. Friends and disciples came from all over the world to pay their respects. His body was later cremated and his ashes now rest with his wife Yvonn's, at Rocquebrune.

I know I do not have to say what a great loss this has been for all of us and for modern architecture. But M. Le Corbusier led a distinguished and dynamic life. He remained sharp and creative to the very end. We shall all miss him greatly.

Yours sincerely

Pierre Jeanneret

6 October 1965
Mount Lavinia

My dearest Corbu, can it really be possible? Is it really true? I look out onto the ocean and know that this same water claimed you, swept you away in its embrace. This morning, I stood on the beach and felt the waves foam around my feet. Aunty Sheila was watching from the verandah at the back of the house. She must have thought I was going to follow you in. Always prone to such fantasy, our Aunty Sheila. I suppose she can't be blamed. I had been unable to speak when I first read the news in the paper. Then came Pierre's letter last week. I spent days staring at the ocean, at once cursing and praising it.

Marcia's letter arrived not long after Pierre's. She said the funeral was beautiful and moving, that the great knight had finally laid down his sword. She told me Mimi was there, too, crying behind her dark glasses. As always, she was there to fill in for me. Wasn't that what it was all about with her? She was there and I am here.

Thousands of people came to say goodbye to you, Corbu.
I could not.

Desmond left for Sydney a few days ago – in fact, the day before Pierre's letter arrived. We will write, of course, but I doubt there will be much to sustain years of correspondence. He will find himself busy with his new practice and new friends. There will be meetings and dinner parties, theatre shows and court dates. The fervour will abate, the letters will grow sporadic, life – real life – will take over.

Not so with us, no, Corbu? Our words sustained us. What was it that I wrote to you so long ago? Let us use words when words are all we have. And now, those words are all I have left of you: tied up in ribbon, arranged in boxes, so many letters to delight and annoy me in the coming years. Yet, you are everywhere. Your achievements continue to amaze the world. Who can look at a modern build and not see its roots in you? As much as my own work has taken a flavour and direction of its own, your ideas, too, are embedded within it.

You will be pleased to hear that my research gains ever more detail – my collection of slides is prodigious. I continue to write. My thoughts on comparative architecture have grown somewhat although the essence of that piece I sent you years ago remains. You called it 'brilliant'. As always, you supported me. There were times when only you believed in me and in those moments it was your confidence in my ability that convinced me to believe in myself. Today, I no longer have to dig quite so deeply to find that self-belief. And yet, what good is that belief when the landscape is so hostile?

The country I live in now is not the one I approached with so much hope all those years ago. Yet having invested this much in it, how can I leave? Since March, we have had a new government – our Party at its helm, but I don't know whether it makes any difference any more. Aren't they all the same in the end? I am only glad that they had come to power before Papa died – not that he was in a state to notice.

So, what is to become of us now? I picture you floating freely in the water and am overwhelmed by the sheer joy of it. The sun on your back as it sinks into the sea. You: weightless, serene, flying through a liquid sky. So much like the old days, when two birds lay with wings gathered about their trembling hearts. I think you were overcome by the bliss of it. I know you were.

I shall always be your oiseau, Corbu. And as I sit here on this desolate island, this squandered paradise, I can still see your eyes. I will remember them to the end of my days.

Epilogue

8 December 2005

The student delays her return to the capital once more. At the last minute, she asks the trishaw driver to take a turn that winds them down the hill right to the edge of Kandy Lake. The heat thickens as they descend, and the student thinks she would jump into the lake if it weren't for the trail of scum lining the shore.

She walks through a *torana* – a dragon-framed arch – and into what looks like a vast village hall. Staccato drumbeats intersperse with applause; another cultural show has drawn to an end. Within moments, the student is engulfed by tourists streaming from the auditorium. She stops, looks up and is lost in the geometry of the roof trusses: warm wood bracing an enormous, clay-tiled roof, all resting on elegant columns.

The arts complex is an ambitious fusion of indigenous Kandyan craftsmanship and modern architectural design. It is the architect's boldest work to date and the epitome of her experiments with indigenous building methods. Its beauty is in its subtlety, never competing with the supremacy of the Temple of the Tooth further along the lake. The architect retained the original nineteenth-century building, restoring and expanding it, while ensuring minimal disruption to the natural landscape.

The landscape is a part of the architectural space. There are hills which afford views across the lake, a natural amphitheatre formed of an excavated area to the east of the building, and plantations of trees and shrubs that evoke a Kandyan village setting.

The irony, thinks the student, is that this bucolic landscape was a fantasy at the time. The complex was built at the start of a war. By the time the architect had returned from Hong Kong, where she had been lecturing on the history of Asian architecture in the 1970s, the country had flexed and transformed. It was the early 1980s and the island was on fire. It still is.

The architect withdrew to her studio, throwing herself into an opportunity she had been denied for so many decades by the recluse. The result is this architectural wonder. The arts complex is multi-levelled and sprawling, with a gallery space, crafts centre, artisan workshops, a courtyard and what was once a semi-open-air theatre surrounded by trees.

Despite the many changes made to the architect's original vision, one thing remains: the arts centre belongs to the artisans. Their craftsmanship is displayed in every corner of the building, from the balusters to the lanterns to the chairs, and the workshops where the artisans themselves can be seen creating their wares. She has always championed them, integrating them into every build she created over her fifty-year career.

The student has heard that the roof – a great, wide thing – collapsed just before the complex was completed. She can hear the laughter of the men who so often chided the architect for her ambition. She fancies she can also hear the architect's retort: *They can go to hell!* The student nods. The architect would have drawn her tiny frame up to its full height and looked her critics in the eye. *Wisdom comes from the mistakes we make, and God knows I have made many.*

They gave her a gold medal. Finally. They gave the recluse one almost ten years earlier – even though he came ten years after her, using her ideas to make a name for himself. She was the first, but it is him they talk about: the tall recluse who lived in Colombo and designed five-star hotels. These hotels squeezed everyday people off their land and out of their homes. And it is to make room for these same sorts of hotels, this same school of privilege, that the architect's builds are razed to the ground.

The sun begins to bleed out. Shadows blur. The call of the brainfever bird shrills in the reddening light. The student slips back through the *torana*. Soon she will be in the familiar trishaw, and then on the train.

A crow caws above her. She turns her eyes towards it.

Author's note

This is a work of fiction. Minnette de Silva and Le Corbusier are, as we know, fact. But how they interacted, who they were friends with, indeed, what they wrote to one another – these were all fodder for the writer. Much like Minnette's gorgeous saris, real or imagined, fact and fiction have been woven together to create this narrative. Whether it matches the subtle weave of those saris is up to the reader.

I have taken many liberties with the facts – Marcia de Silva, for instance, who actually went by the name of Anil, never had children; the names of Le Corbusier's Chandigarh team of architects are fictionalised, as are some of Minnette's builds. I have introduced numerous anachronisms: Le Corbusier's *cabanon* in Cap Martin, for instance, was actually built in 1952 and not 1951 as I have it in the text; and many of Minnette's builds have been moved up and down the timeline. In real life, Minnette's father died before her mother, and neither passed in the manner I've imagined. There are plenty more examples of these disparities throughout the novel. An assiduous reader might have fun uncovering them.

Acknowledgements

Key resources were Minnette de Silva's *The Life and Work of an Asian Woman Architect Vol.1* (Smart Media Production, Colombo, 1998) and her chapters on South and South East Asian architecture in Sir Bannister Fletcher's *A History of Architecture* (Athlone Press, 1975); *Sketchbooks of Le Corbusier* (1950 – 1964); Minnette de Silva's letters to Le Corbusier (Fondation Le Corbusier, Paris); Charles Jencks' *Le Corbusier and the Continual Revolution in Architecture* (The Monacelli Press, New York, 2000); Flora Samuel's *Le Corbusier, Architect and Feminist* (Wiley-Academy, Chichester, 2004); Channa Daswatte's interview of C. Anjalendran: 'An overview of 50 years of architecture since independence in Sri Lanka', June 1998; David Robson's 'Two pioneers of Modernism in Ceylon' (https://thinkmatter.in/tag/david-robson); Ulrik Plesner's *In Situ* (Aristo 2012); Anooradha Iyer Siddiqui's 'Crafting the archive: Minnette De Silva,

Architecture, and History' in *The Journal of Architecture*, 22:8, 1299-1336; selected volumes of *Marg* magazine; and personal interviews with architects and those who knew Minnette de Silva, mentioned below.

Research and development of this book was made possible by grants from the Society of Authors and the Arts Council England.

The author wishes to thank Charles Beckett formerly of the Arts Council England; Lalitha Colombage of the Sri Lanka Institute of Architecture; Channa Daswatte; Arnaud Dercelles at the Fondation Le Corbusier; Ashley De Vos; Lilani de Silva; Dharshani Dias Abeysinghe; Mrs CF Fernando and her son Charith; Ashok Ferry; Illayaz; Jill Macdonald of the Galle Literary Festival; Deepali Modi; Mithila, Nirasha, Lasitha, Sabine, Anju and Manori Premaratne; Ismeth and Delini Raheem; Malkanthi Perera; Prianga and Eranga Pieris; Pradeep; Mr Ratnavira and Mr & Mrs Wijesena of Kandy; David Robson; two anonymous but intrepid trishaw drivers; a wonderfully hospitable friend of a friend in Chandigarh; the (late) British Newspaper Library; the British Library (St Pancras).

Special thanks to the late Minnette de Silva whose life inspired this book, C. Anjalendran for generously sharing his memories and materials with me, Scott Harvey for reading early drafts with a critical eye, Sanya Semakula for pulling my ms from the pile and making it better, Kit Caless for believing in this book and lending it polish, Rajeev Balasubramanyam and Courttia Newland for helping me keep the faith, Selva

Sandrapragas for his fantastical tales, my family and N. for supporting me, and my daughter, L., whose imminent arrival galvanised me into action... and eventual completion.